SUBLIFE CRISIS

SUBLIFE CRISIS

Argus

Podium

This is a work of fiction. Names, characters, places, and incidents are either products of the author's imagination or used fictitiously. Any resemblance to actual events, locales, or persons, living, dead, or undead, is entirely coincidental.

Cover design by Driss Chaoui

ISBN: 979-8-3470-0523-9

Published in 2026 by Podium Publishing
www.podiumentertainment.com

For Raven and Quetz, who I love very much.

SUBLIFE CRISIS

CHAPTER ONE

There is an interstitial moment where I am nothing. Not asleep, not awake, not *alive*.

I open my eyes again, outside of reality, and subjective time resumes.

Sometimes, I think I can feel something in that moment of death. A loved one calling my name, the feeling of light, or fire, or the depths, a sad temporary welcome. It's probably a hallucination because the only time that moment comes is when I'm dying, and most evolved brains have a mechanism to dump a large quantity of dopamine to make the last experience a little less traumatic.

I say probably because I'm not going to reject the idea of an afterlife when I've already had scores of them.

My body sinks into the blankets of my return point as it finishes becoming what passes for corporeal around here. For a while, I lay unmoving, letting the sensations of this form become familiar to me again. I haven't done much customization on this in-between body, so it's mostly what I became familiar with in my first long life, with a couple of traits from my original childhood, and one thing as a reminder.

Five feet tall, smooth copper skin, wavy hair that drops down half my back, breasts that comfortably fail to get in the way, a form that *could* have been broad shouldered and tough if I'd ever bothered to mod on muscle. My eyes are one of two reminders of my origin, a smoky and dull amethyst. The thick scaled tail with a line of bone plates running down it is the last remnant of the best life I ever lived.

The tail gets tangled in the blankets every time I wake up. My thoughts emerge from the smoke of nonexistence, quickly piling up as I fail to process anything. Nerves begin to send sensations; the blankets are cool and soft but a little rough, my back no longer hurts, my eyes do not scream at the light.

It is always a powerful relief to wake up here and be reminded of how many small pains you accumulate in a life. And then to feel a euphoria as every one of them fails to check in.

I've been staring at the ceiling for two thousand heartbeats. I know this because there is one notification that I *always* check when I get back, before anything else. I can spend a long time ignoring a lot of what this unworld has to offer, but what I always want to know is how long? How long, until . . .

Well. I checked.

Welcome back to the Between, intercessor. 3,456,000 heartbeats remain. Prepare yourself.

In every life, you're always on the clock. Twice out of all my nearly hundred lifetimes, I've managed to hit immortality in one way or another, which *should* feel like a relief but really doesn't. You're just on a different clock. It's always ticking. But the thing about being alive is the time is *obfuscated*. No one knows exactly how long they have left.

But here? Here I know. Down to the fucking *heartbeat*, I know. There is a moment when this body will be removed—not even the dignity of being really destroyed—and I will be reborn. Again. Again, and again, and again. Back into a real world, and a real life, and a messy, chaotic, loud, angry existence.

On average, this body runs at eighty beats per "minute." Arbitrary here, but it doesn't actually matter. Everyone tries making a form with a massively reduced heartbeat at least once, or one without a heart at all. The thing doesn't care. It rounds down. No heart? You're out almost instantly. One beat a "month"? Well, you get exactly one, then. No overflow. Ever. Even if you would have had *almost* two months subjective, you only get one beat.

I spend a thousand heartbeats feeling sorry for myself before I actually get up.

My room is the same as I left it because the cost to get into someone else's room is stupidly high, and the cost to mess with it even higher. The return point, the bed, is a circular bowl of mundane blankets and pillows in the center of the space. Overhead, a chandelier made of salvaged pipes hangs, a souvenir from a dead world and a kind friend. It paints the place in a soft orangish light that comforts me. The color of a summer evening when all the chores are done.

There's a door. It's not an impressive one. And then the rest of the room, all the extra space I haven't used, is blank.

Not even white. Just . . . not there. Unused. I don't have any other furniture, or any assets to add. It's partly because I don't care, and also partly because I have something better to spend my bestowed currency on.

I finally muster the energy to rise. It's annoyingly easy. My body moves to my slightest whim and without complaint. The tail, once I exfiltrate it, helps me balance and is as much a part of me as it ever was. Nothing hurts; nothing rushes me. One of the perks of not having actual biology is that I won't ever need to hurry to use the bathroom after waking up.

There are exactly two things I can check: the door or my notifications. I don't feel like I have the energy for the latter, so I touch the central glyph of the door and let it pull itself open for me. It's got one charge on it, same as every time I wake, and it only goes to one place. I had to trade two other doors, a room, and six skills for it a long time ago, but I think it was worth it.

I step through, into Bastion's.

Behind me, my room closes and won't open again until I either buy a better door or die somewhere else. I don't care. It's not like I'm storing anything there or keeping any valuable secrets. And despite the fact that I'm walking around nude, I have no expectation of inviting anyone back to my place tonight.

"Luri!" The first voice I've heard in this entire subjective continuity greets me with a well-worn enthusiasm. "Put some pants on before you put someone's eye out with that thing!"

Mark grins at me from behind the counter of Bastion's. Default human male, taller than me, buffer than me, certainly more cheerful than me. The man has boundless optimism that I find as exhausting as I do endearing. He's standing behind an oak counter wearing a loose toga patterned to look like dragon feathers, shaking something in a glowing crystal mixer.

I ignore his demand for pants and make my way through the empty room, passing a hodgepodge of different styles of chairs surrounding the three tables we have in here. A staircase made out of a steel-grate stepladder bolted to the wall leads up and around a corner to a balcony overhead, where we've got a couple more small tables, and also the comfy chairs. That's also where the library is.

We call it a library. But it's mostly board games. Getting books here is next to impossible without a souvenir or a random drop. Building the slim collection we have is already an accomplishment to be proud of.

I nod at Mark, trying to manage a smile for him as I sit on one of the stools by the counter. Saying nothing, I settle my bare ass onto the cracked black leather and slowly pitch forward. Elbows on the counter, head in my hands, eyes drooping.

I am so tired.

"Welcome back," Mark says softly, setting down whatever nightmare drink he's putting together. I think it's glowing stronger than before, but he leaves it as he circles around from behind the bar, kicking open a wood barrier to join me on this side. His arms wrap around this remade shell in a hug that feels too real.

I know it's not. I know nothing here is supposed to be real. But I don't care. I let him hold me as it all starts catching up. A lifetime of pain, fear, and exhaustion, all of it for *nothing*. All of it leading to just another pointless death, and then back *here*, and I am crying and wordlessly wailing, and I am so, so, so very tired.

After I've wasted three hundred heartbeats on self-pity, I dry my eyes on a shitty paper napkin from our infinitely refilling dispenser, throw it into nothingness, and take a deep breath. Once I'm a bit better, I offer Mark a thankful nod and return a proper hug.

"You're the first one back this time," Mark says as he maneuvers so that my lack of pants bothers him less. I don't care; I've lived too long to actually care anymore. But also, I haven't felt like spending on pants when Bastion's needs ongoing touch-ups. I'm not poor, but I'm not rich by Between standards either, and I don't want to pull out one of my outfit souvenirs today. "Well, other than me. But hey, we can't all roll sparks, right?"

I nod but still don't say anything. Mark doesn't press me on it. He knows what I'm waiting for.

"Welp! Here! First drink of the cycle!" He cracks open the crystal mixer, and it *hisses* as he pours something that looks like liquid ice into a pair of shot glasses. "Salude!"

We clink our glasses together and drink. It tastes like mangoes and moonlight. Another notification adds itself to my list, and Mark and I grimace at the same time as we're hit with both the words and the alcohol.

"Holy shit, that . . ." He wheezes. I'm struggling to try to no-sell his concoction myself and let out a distressed cough, both of us pounding our fists on the bar as cold fire lights up our guts. "For fake bodies, these things sure are lightweights!" he coughs out.

From behind us, there is the sound of a door opening. And then a voice cuts over our gasps. "Oy!" The woman even *sounds* like a blue eye. "Are you two drinking without me?! Mark, you promised!" Ellin's voice is heavy and heated, and I spin my stool to watch her stalk in. Her striking figure she custom built for war before realizing what this nowhere place really was: seven feet tall and all hard muscle, curved horns with spiral ridges ringing her bald head, and green-white nomad wraps covering her body. All she's missing is a war spear and she'd look right at home on the cover of one of the comic books we have upstairs. "Bastard!" she punctuates her complaint. "Ah, hello, Luri!"

"I did no such thing!" Mark defends himself as he pours her a shot of whatever horror cocktail we're drinking, and seconds for me and himself. "I told you we'd share a drink! Now come get it before it melts . . . I mean before we're done with this and I have to make a new one." He glances at me. "And give Luri a hug," Mark adds.

Ellin does both at once, bracing her chin on the crown of my head, the coarse fabric of her outfit pressing into my skin as she wraps an arm around me and we drink together. "Ah! Yes!" She slams the shot glass down so hard I'm worried she'll put a hole in the counter. "The perfect end to a shitty life!"

"No good?" Mark asks, and I tip my face up to give her a questioning look myself.

"Sexist." She sighs. "Again. Couldn't kill enough people to change it either. Old Hist knows I tried though!"

Mark shakes his head. He's new. Sixteen lives, I think; found us early. And still a pacifist. He doesn't say anything though.

A voice from upstairs does though. "Ellin, you utter brute." Prim and proper. Bit of a French accent, though he keeps saying it's Martian and refuses to explain anything about wherever Mart was. Jules's door went unnoticed as he slipped into Bastion's, and now his inhuman form looks down on us with amusement.

Ten coiled tentacle limbs, six of them thick like structural columns and supporting the rest of him, the other four weaving around his body like he's dancing. Jules's face is covered in the same smooth midnight-black skin, glistening in the light of this place, while a triangle of red slitted eyes looks over us. Out of everyone, I think he heard that he could reshape himself here and *really* got excited. The ex-nobleman, freed from all social and biological restrictions, finally allowed to be who and *what* he wants, whatever that might be.

"Don't lecture me on etiquette, you walking fear fantasy!" Ellin yells back. "Also get down here! You should try this stuff before it kills one of us!"

"It's not *that* bad," Mark protests. And I agree with him. It's growing on me. Like some kind of invasive parasite.

"Who're we waiting on?" Jules asks as he drops to the floor, ignoring the stairs I spent so long on, his tentacles making a wet slap on the polished wood floor. "Tee-kon, Molly, and Six?"

"Molly went on ahead," Mark says quietly, and my heart aches. Fresh pain for a new body. Not the first ache I've ever felt, but the first one of this type this time around. It's always a novelty to feel the exact mix of chemicals to pair with your emotional trauma. "And Tee . . . I dunno. We'll see if it's coming this time."

"Ah, alas, I will miss Molly. Though I have several million beats myself, perhaps we will cross paths again." Jules shakes the orb of his head in a sympathetic motion, a light humming vibration of regret filling the air around him.

Ellin snorts. Not unkindly, but her words are blunt. "You just wanted a roll in the hay with your girl," she accused.

The hum cuts off as Jules turns his eyes to look at her, all of them sliding around his head as one tentacle grabs the new shot glass Mark sets down and he clinks it with the rest of ours before slamming it down next to Ellin's. "Yes!" The word almost makes me burst into giggles. It sounds so out of place coming from the normally elegant and noble figure. "I did! Is that so wrong? To find comfort with someone who *connects* with you?"

"Course it ain't. You know that. Ellin's being an ass," Mark says. "Which is why we love her. Every group of ragtag friends needs one asshole in it."

"Of course." Ellin pulls herself up to full height. "That is known! I thought it was Luri."

I *almost* say something. Jules jumps in before I can though. "Ah! Luri! My apologies. I did not formally welcome you. Hello, hello again, good friend." Two of his tentacles wrap around me in a hug that I return warmly. "Still quiet for now?"

I nod. He bobs back at me.

Ellin snorts again. "*Romantics.*" She says it like it's a curse.

"I think it's cute," Mark protests. "Besides, it's not like we don't have the time to be a little silly."

"Ah, fair, fair." Ellin shrugs her muscled shoulders. "How long are you waiting this time?"

I check my heartbeats. I usually round to about the nearest hundred thousand. Just in case, I suppose. But sometimes that can be a little too long for my immortal patience, and my timer ends up being more about what feels right than what makes sense. So I hold out a hand to mark with five fingers extended.

"Five hours this time? Not bad. Subjective, right?" I nod at Mark's words. "Well, I'm down to play bartender this time. Anyone checked their log yet?"

We all shake our heads, with one degree of vigor or another. I usually put mine off for a while, until I'm feeling calmer. Or until the last minute. Though the rampage of whatever I've been drinking is certainly helping with the nerves. The others . . . Well, Jules likes to check right away and then purposefully ignore it until later. Ellin likes to make a party game of hers, and often drags us into it too, so she'll wait for anyone else to show up. Mark's like me. He'll wait, though not because he secretly hates it and more because he wants to maximize his time with his friends. He also enjoys the party games.

"Am I late?" A monotone voice cuts through our little gathering, and we all turn to the door. A pale slab of gray flesh roughly cut like a human stands there, mostly featureless except for a glitter in the eyes and a thin line of a smile. "I hope I am not late."

"Come on in, Six!" Mark grins, shaking his mixer. "I wanna see if *this* can get you drunk!"

"Is *that* what this poison is?" Jules curls his tentacle up over his head, all three eyes aligning on the empty shot glass like he's scanning it for chemical composition. "You made something to get a golem drunk and gave it to *us*?"

"You can't die. You'll be fine, you big baby," Mark says with a laugh.

I rise from my seat and give Six a hug as he enters; the monotone voice and lack of features on his face is utterly at odds with the compassion he puts into the simple gesture. "Hello, Luri," he says to me. "I have missed you." A smile is all I offer in return, though it's a wide one, and Six nods in understanding as he disengages and mechanically takes the shot glass Mark has poured, downing the drink without comment. "Has anyone begun checking their messages yet?"

"Damn it," Mark mutters, looking at his crystal mixer like it's a son that just embarrassed him at a family reunion.

"I'm waiting for Luri's timer!" Ellin declares. "I want to *hear* her be aggravated by me!"

The others laugh. I do too. Slowly, bit by bit, real warmth creeps back in. Not from the alcohol or the radiance stone in the floor, not some mundane heat that you can replicate with something as petty as clothing. But the kind of warmth that comes from feeling like no matter how tired I am, and how long it takes to come back, I'm not alone.

I claim a chair at a table as Mark and Six head behind the counter and start making some kind of food for us all with the bits and bobs we have stored and Jules and Ellin start sorting through their notifications to clear the low-interest ones, things where the payout is a handful of cysts or something small.

Perhaps it is foolish that I allow myself to *hope*. Things are feeling good, so I trick myself into thinking that they could get better. That this time . . . it will be okay.

Molly really doesn't show up. She must have had a *really* bad life to have already gone on ahead. And it's unlikely I'll see her within the next three million heartbeats here; we seem to die on cycles after all. I'll miss her because we're friends. Tee-kon doesn't show either, for an unspoken reason. But they're not who I'm waiting for.

The timer in the corner of my vision, heartbeats ticking down, occupies more and more of my thoughts as it gets closer to my self-imposed deadline. I stop hearing the others laughing. Stop smelling whatever apple sausages Six is cooking for us on the camp griddle. I barely notice when one of Ellin's drops is a red silk bathrobe, which she passes to me as an act of charity, despite the fact that I *know* Ellin doesn't mind if I'm nude. Despite her protests, which are hollow and joking anyway.

I think I stop breathing at one point, to try to extend it. That actually works, though never for long. Real or not, these bodies still act like bodies in many ways, and they'll start up again when you pass out. But the problem isn't the number. It's the time it represents.

Mark pulls up a seat next to me, a handmade wooden chair from an extinct tree on a high-desert frontier of a world where civilization was just getting started. He settles into it like it's a vaguely uncomfortable chair and not a priceless historical relic. Everything here is a priceless historical relic, unless you count the cost in marks and memories.

He doesn't say anything, just sets a hand on mine on the green felt surface of the table. Ellin and Jules go quiet as they watch me as well, more overt pity in their eyes, though Ellin's has a bit of contempt in hers. I don't blame her. It's a bit stupid.

I'm so many lives old, and I'm still acting like a lovesick teenager who just got dumped before prom.

I take a deep breath. "They're probably not coming," I say out loud. Then I shake my head, put on my best fake smile for my friends, and turn to Ellin. "So, got anything good for your murder spree?"

The woman beams at me, Jules rolls his eyes, Six sets a plate of sliced and salted alien vegetables and a few cut sausages into the middle of the table, and Mark pats my hand before settling back next to me in comfortable companionship. The room rushes back in, and I feel the light and warmth and smells again.

Ellin starts loudly checking off notifications, dropping metareal items into the center of the table in a growing pile, and inviting cheers and jeers as she reads off her accomplishments. Mark gets up to go back behind the bar and try to see if he can drink himself into thinking her stories are impressive.

I sit. And I enjoy this slice of real life, here in the nowhere and nothing, in between lives and outside of death.

And secretly, I do not stop waiting for them to come through a door.

CHAPTER TWO

A clarified moment occurs.

The five of us all look up as it passes through Bastion's. Mark is behind the bar, picking out bottles and one clay urn from the thin selection we have on the shelves, preparing to engage in some kind of alcoholic war crime against the rest of us. The rest of us are at the *nice* table, Six and I seated in old chairs, Jules on a pile of sand pillows, and Ellie standing over us, hands flat on the worn green felt surface.

A clarified moment is hard to not notice. They don't happen often. We swap stories, constantly, and none of us have *ever* felt one while we were alive. So they're probably a thing that only happens here, which is nowhere, which is odd.

The feeling sweeps the room, and briefly, everything makes sense. Which turns our heads because that never happens to any of us.

Then it's gone.

And I'm crying again. Stupid eyes that I saved leaking tears as the moment is replaced by a hollow void. The abstract memory that I saw the shape of it all and then had it taken away. And elsewhere, a spot in this between nowhere contains someone who has it even worse than I do. Someone who *started* it. Learned something so well they spread an infectious sense of understanding through the fake air.

"Ah, my word, I will never become used to such a strange thing." Jules shivers, a high-frequency buzz coming off the central stalk of his form as his tentacles wave in anxious patterns.

Six nods. "Odd." The golem agrees in his monotone. "Luri?" He doesn't exactly sound concerned as he looks at me, but Six only ever says people's names when he's addressing them or concerned.

"I'm fine," I lie, wiping off my face on the sleeves of the bathrobe Ellin has me in. The prude. "Ellin, keep going." I'll shake it off. Our large friend was telling a story from her last life.

She doesn't seem entirely convinced by my words, but Ellin doesn't question me. "Well!" she says. "Like I was saying, got meself started early this time! Had to ditch the family route after I took out the second brother and got caught. From there, wasn't much for me to do. Couldn't route into a trade or study, since I rolled the wrong sex. So I just survived. I was picking up bits and pieces when I learned about the orbit-fragment thing this world had going on, and how you could petition *physics* for a change in operations."

"Ugh, one of *those*." Jules sounds contemptuous as a tentacle daintily wrapped around a fork spears one of the cold sausage strips on the plate in the middle of us. "I find myself shocked it wasn't already dying."

"It likely was," Six comments, the golem's gray skin wrinkling as he turns to address Jules. "Though perhaps not faster than any other world."

"Ouch," Mark says, seating himself on my other side and sliding two mismatched glass pitchers onto the table. "Okay! I've got . . . Wait, where are the glasses?" I point behind the bar. "Okay, well, I made the achitas, so someone else get the cups."

I stand and flap a sleeve of my new robe against his face. "Lazy," I say with a smile as I head to lean over the worn wood and collect our drinking tools of choice. Mine's a goblet because I felt like it. Six has some kind of ceremonial basin, Jules just has a thick glass stein, and Ellin some kind of art deco blue frosted dinner glass. Mark's isn't here. "Mark, where's your cup?!" I interrupt whatever part of her story Ellin is on.

"Is it not there?" He leans over the boxy metal frame of his seat. "Look behind Molly's!"

I make a trip back and lay our drinking vessels out on the table. "Molly's is there. So's . . . everyone else's. But yours isn't."

"Just bring me a spare." Mark shrugs as he starts to pour from both pitchers into each of our cups, the liquid steaming as it meets its counterpart.

I stare at him. I want to say something, but I don't know what. The thought of replacing anything, especially here, makes my teeth hurt and my breath stop. My lungs itch as I struggle to articulate what is wrong with this situation. To tell him that when we start treating things as disposable, we give up our fleeting rearguard action against the impermanence of all things. And every surrender is one step closer to giving up *everything.*

Every waking moment, alive or here, is exhausting. It leaves me tired beyond limits I thought I had. But the thought of giving up is anathema to me. It is the one thing we *cannot* do.

But also . . .

It's just a cup.

And maybe Mark doesn't need my anxieties now, before we've even settled into our deaths this cycle. Also, really, what's more important is that he's the one drinking out of it. Especially if I've been given free rein to pick anything for him. So I find a half a dried coconut shell and a loopy straw and add that to our table as I sit back down.

Mark gives me a *look*, but I just offer a fluttering smile, and his gaze softens to the at-peace understanding that my friend has for me. "I love it," he says. "If it doesn't melt from the achitas I'm making this my new mug." Mark wraps an arm of corded muscle around my shoulders and gives me an awkward squeeze. "Thanks," he whispers.

"It's just a cup," I say. "Really though. It's a cup. It'll be okay. Life goes on, right?"

"Ha!" Ellin barks out a noise that fills the room with its volume as she tosses back her horned head to continue her rowdy laugh. "It does! For us at least!"

"So, what happened to you next?" I'm curious about the story; we've all had a lot of lives and a lot of quests, but that doesn't make the stories any less interesting. "Did you find a . . . shard?"

"Orbit fragment! Pay attention, you delinquent!" Ellin reprimands me.

Six looks up from the steaming drink that he's been staring into like he can scry the future in its fumes. "Will there be a test?" he asks.

"My dear boy." Jules snakes a tentacle over the table and between the two pitchers to pat Six's hand. "Ellin *is* our test."

Ellin wraps long and nimble fingers around her cup, tipping it up to down a third of its contents with one brave swallow. She lets out a long gasp of satisfaction after she drinks and then shakes her head at us. "Didn't find shit. It found *me*. Some mercenary group that had delusions of grandeur. Picked me up when they stumbled across my camp."

"As a mercenary?" Six inquires.

"As a sex slave." Ellin snarls the words. "I was subjective about twelve at the time. Took me a good two months before I could unlock enough to start killing them. Oh, the new Strike variety I got? Unlocks at adulthood. *Wrong* call to take that one. Should have stuck to the classic." She takes another drink, and I see her hand shaking. "We should . . . I mean, if you're all cool with it . . . maybe spend some marks on the Ability Compactor thing that . . . that we . . ."

Silently, I rise from my seat and circle the table. Ellin is strong. It's the image she projects and the persona she cultivates. Strength. But not invincibility. Not imperviousness. Ellin persists with us because she loves *life*. Loves being in it, loves engaging and giving it her all. She's never separate from the worlds she lives through.

Usually, I need hugs when I get back. Physical comfort makes me feel safe, lets me let out just how bleak I feel without tearing myself apart or burning away my memories. It's *bad* when I'm the first one back. I got lucky this time, and Mark was here first, and all the others hot on my heels. But Ellin?

Ellin needs hugs when she needs to be reminded that her lives aren't still happening.

I wrap myself around her, engulfing her in the bathrobe she gave me and trying to pull her off-balance as she drinks. It doesn't work because applying pseudohostile effects out here is made harder, and also because she's two feet taller than me and weighs more than our collection of furniture. But I still hug her.

"Ahhhh . . ." She breathes out as she finishes her drink and lets me cling to her side. "Ha. Yeah. Okay, that one . . ." She trails off as Jules adds a comforting layer of smooth tentacles to her shoulders, like a fleshy mantle.

"There is no shame in pain," he tells her, red eyes formed into triangular notes of sympathy. "We all know this."

"Bah," Ellin says flatly. But doesn't shake us off.

"So, you left a trail of bodies out of the camp?" Mark asks her as we disentangle. He's *technically* a pacifist and doesn't approve of us starting wars or anything, but for this? Mark isn't going to have a problem with Ellin's path of carnage. And I admit, I'm hoping for a bit of catharsis there too.

She shrugs like it's no big thing. "Something like that. I unloaded a lot of my per-life charisma shit on the ones that were left and led them on a crusade. Took out some kind of doge, conquered a bunch of small towns, tried to end slavery." Ellin shrugs again. Ending slavery is a hobby of hers. "I wasn't expecting it though. I was taking Molly's advice, yeh? Going for a quiet life this time. So. Dead."

"Was it spectacular?" Jules asks curiously.

"Was it *stupid*?" Mark adds his question.

Six and Ellin look at me. "What?" I say. "That's what I want to know, too. Wait, no, was it *both*?"

"It was both!" Ellin taps her cup down onto the table, one of her fingers running around the wet rim before she slides it gently toward Mark for a refill. "Some old guy who was collecting orbit fragments thought I was *competition*!

Like I'd *want* to break reality even more! Hit me with some kind of curse mid-skirmish that made me shit myself to death."

"Eugh." "Vile!" "Unpleasant." "*I'm drinking, you can't say that!*" Our chorus drowns out Ellin's laugh for a minute.

"That's not the best part though!" Ellin adds. "The *best* part is that I still got the guy I was dueling! Spear through the eye! While shitting to death!"

"Please. Stop. I regret this intently," Jules begs, tentacles wrapping around his eyes.

"I'm joining Team Please Stop." I add my own nod, shifting in my seat and taking a small sip of the nutty liquor Mark poured for me now that the acidity has settled. There's one question I do want to ask though. One that's still important to me, no matter how many lives and deaths I struggle through. "Did you . . . Did you make a difference?" I ask.

Ellin's shoulders droop, and she drops her eyes down to stare at nothing in particular. With a short huff, she grabs her refilled cup and drains half of it. "Not enough," she states, lifting her hand to run the base of her cup along one of her horns. "But for someone, yeah. I made a difference."

I think it could be all too easy to forget. Forget *so* many things that should be important to us. Forget why they should even be important at all. So we ask each other these questions sometimes. Just to remind ourselves of what matters. And that there are other people out there, people who never end up here, as far as we know. People who just have the one life. And they deserve their lives too. If we're going to be meddling in the worlds outside these walls, then we should make a difference. Good or bad, we should do *something*. Stagnation, isolation, noninterference, those are all just different words for dying. *Really* dying. Dying in the spirit, if not the body.

"Oy. Well. That's my life in brief." Ellin arches her back, bones popping with a satisfying sound. "A handful of things for war. No souvenirs since nothing really mattered to me. Another resistance unlock. The only good ability was Desecration in Defecation, which I *know* you can guess at. But it's *bad*, even by your low standards, and it takes three slots with high weight."

"Ability, not a perk?" Mark asks curiously.

Ellin shrugs as she sits herself back down. "Haven't gotten a new perk unlock in two lives. And I'd rather spend what I have on us. *Speaking* of, I've got about eight hundred thousand beats left. At two hundred thousand, I'll be heading for the halls, wandering until I find a shop or vendor. Anyone want anything specific?"

"That's days away. We can worry about it later," I say quietly, and Ellin gives me a rueful look. "I mean . . . No, sorry . . ."

"No, you're right." Ellin laughs. "I can run pretty fast! Maybe I'll cut it shorter. Get some games of Encounter in before we split?"

Six coughs lightly, the noise alien coming from the normally unemotional golem. "I will agree to that only if you are not allowed to sit near the card piles."

"Decks, Six." Mark laughs. "But *yeah*, Ellin you *cheat at a cooperative game*! Who *does* that?"

"You lack vision!" Ellin scoffs.

"You cheat *against us*!" Mark's words have a slight lisp to them as the alcohol catches up, even though alcohol doesn't work properly here. "Oh, whatever. Jules, how was your last life?"

"Disappointing." The noble gives a sibilant sigh and begins to regale us with a tale of youthful romance, transgressed boundaries, Jules-standard body dysphoria, and a career rising through the ranks of some kind of sacred museum to attain societal permission to create art. His story is punctuated with readings of his notifications, the list of achievements and their unlocks, some of them known to us and many not. Some understandable, many impractical to replicate.

Like, for example, Lost Heart of an Ascendant Dreamer, an aura layer that Jules has earned for a hyperspecific combination of artistic talent, civilization-wide popularity, and heartbreak. Was it always waiting for someone to find it, or was it made for him? And would the difference even matter to us, small little bugs in this cosmic machine?

I make the mistake of asking what it does and get an explanation that wastes three hundred of my precious heartbeats, only to amount to a fairly simple end result. It makes charisma and wisdom traits and skills that work through art amp by about 10 percent. It's . . . more tedious and complicated than that. Also possibly more subtly powerful. But it's an aura layer, so that's more or less normal, and it'd always be on at least. I still regret asking, and I think Jules regrets explaining it and not just saying it wasn't important.

Jules's life was almost singularly focused around his pursuit, so he has a lot of achievements, but they tend to be stackers. Piling up on each other and upgrading rewards. The only really interesting thing he brings to the table *now* is a souvenir.

"Behold!" he says, flourishing his tentacles as we all become increasingly drunk. "My prized creation!"

A glass rectangle pops onto the table, about two feet displaced from where he's gesturing. All of us lean forward to look inside at the splash of green-and-brown vegetation growing within. A tiny willow tree, roots growing out of an uneven dome of rock. Around it, grasses and reeds spring up, proportioned at the same ratio as the tree itself. They sway in the wind, the white clouds passing overhead against the pink-and-purple evening sky. A summer evening captured in moving stillness, complete with the chirping of cicadas.

"I made this . . ." Jules stops, staring at his own work. His eyes turn away, and his tentacles droop. "I made this," he says finally. "It seemed . . . important at the time." His enthusiasm has lost some of its luster.

"It's beautiful," Six monotones. "Is it alive?"

"In a sense. This . . . This *place* has stripped some of the artistic magic from it. But we can feed it heartbeats to move it in time." Jules pushes it away with a curled tentacle. "It will serve no purpose but to be a pretty bauble though."

The sadness in my friend threatens to crush my soul. Jules looks so alone in that moment, looking at anything except the most beautiful art he made in his last life. "I think it's beautiful," I murmur to him. "I think *you're* beautiful too."

"Ah, well. I suppose I must be, to make something *you* find value in, yes?" He chuckles with a bass pulse. "Perhaps we can stick it on a shelf."

Mark glances up at the library balcony. "We've got a bunch of shelves." He nods. "Who feels like climbing *stairs* right now?" None of us reply. "Cool! You know what we need in here? A bed. For napping."

"Or *other things?*" I suggest.

"I thought for sure Jules would beat you to that one." Ellin has long since stopped sounding disappointed in us. "Lewd perverts, the lot of you. Especially you, Luri! Strutting around in the nude! We could have *guests!*"

"Prude." I stick my tongue out at her. "Also Bastion's has a strict no-making-fun-of-the-proprietors rule. Haven't you read our signs? And I'm not nude. You gave me a robe!" I'm proud of the signs. It took a long time to get the resources to make them stick in this unreality.

"The signs degraded to elsewhere." Mark shakes his head sadly.

"Fuck, my signs!" I exclaim. I'm feeling better. Alcohol and friends and a little momentum. I could do this all day. All cycle. All life. Over and over and over. I could do this forever. Or at least long enough to get another plank and some paint.

In the moment, I almost believe it.

Jules glances between Mark and me. "If we are not actively generating beds for activities, perhaps some food? I could prepare us a real meal. I have some small things to share and the faith marks to activate our kitchen."

"I could eat," Mark concedes.

"I have not eaten in two hundred and four years." Six's eyes, neutral as they are, seem to peer into the beyond with the most harrowed look I've ever seen on the golem. "Oh. And these sausages. I would eat."

Ever so slowly, Jules slides his eyes sideways to where Ellin is carefully turning her own head to meet his gaze. "Yeeeeeah . . . Food sounds . . . good right about now," she says. And then perks up. "Oh! Who wants to help me plan my next build?"

"Will you be optimizing for *murder* again?" Mark asks, exasperated with our friend.

"Well it's either that or marine biology, and *some* worlds don't have oceans, but *every* world has punching," Ellin says, staring up at the slowly rotating aircraft turboprop engine that we use as an overhead fan for airflow. "*So far* anyway. And the last world I never made it to an ocean. Because of the—"

"Yep, thanks!" I cut her off. "Jules, go make food before Ellin keeps up her kill streak and takes out our appetites. I don't wanna know if she gets a notification for that."

"How 'bout you, Luri?" Mark asks, thumping one of his legs into mine under the table as Jules heads off to busy himself and Ellin starts waving her hands to open up a barrage of translucent screens and windows that contain her collected upgrades and associated nonsense. "How was your life?"

I pause. Consider lying. But Mark's would notice, and I don't really feel like it anyway. "Could have been better," I say with a little strain. "Could have been worse!"

"I know you don't like to see anything until toward the end," he says as Six bluntly stands and walks away to loom near the counter and stare at Jules while the tentacled noble cooks. "But got anything for Bastion's? Like, anything that might be a couch or something? I love that we have all the chairs, but Luri, I'll love you forever if you can give my hypothetical ass a cushion here."

"You'll love me forever anyway." I smile at him.

Mark gives me a goofy grin, the handsome man half my age not denying it. "I would," he says serenely. "I really would. But it'd be *better* with a sofa."

"You damn romantic." I flush a deep red that creeps up the copper skin of my face. This body isn't even real, and I'm still blushing. Subjective centuries alive and I'm still getting flustered. "That's supposed to be my job. Why are you suddenly this suave?"

"Eh!" Mark shrugs. "Picked up some wisdom last time around. *Real* wisdom, not the knockoff Between variety."

I laugh at his derision as the smell of something savory and hot starts to fill the air. "Well, I'd invite you back to my place, but I burned my only door."

"Which is why a *sofa* . . ." Mark waggles his eyebrows at me as Ellin comes back from clearing off the table. "Ellin, back me up here. A couch. A love seat. Anything."

I shake my head as the two start coming up with more words for cushioned seating, playfully laughing with each other as we fall into the familiar routine of friendship and shared jokes. Internally though, I'm glad I dodged answering for now.

My notifications, the scroll of unopened messages from . . . Well. The unopened-messages list out in my soul, waiting to be acknowledged. Waiting for me to receive my just rewards for accomplishments, as recognized by the strange and shifting set of parameters we find ourselves living under. They flicker with familiar indicators, colors and textures and in some cases smells, all denoting type and rarity and sometimes more specific things.

One of mine is an off-yellow, metallic, and tastes like strawberries. And I know what that one will say. That I changed the fate of a world. That I am due a reward.

I don't want to talk about it. And I doubt it will give me a couch.

"I got nothing," I tell Mark and Ellin as I notice them watching me. "Well, on the seating front. Uh. I might have a new book for us though?"

"Ah, check it later. No rush." Mark's easy words wash away my woes. "So Ellin, got any less gross war stories for us?" The woman's face lights up, and she launches into another story from her life. Something about a river, a goat, and a humiliated opponent.

I listen, but also I just exist. I try to etch this moment into my memory, though without the heartbeat counter ticking down. There's never enough *time* with them, so I want every moment to count. Even Ellin's somewhat disturbing stories of goatnapping and drownings. Not of the goat, she is quick to remind us. The goat is fine.

The joke breaks me out of my dip back into despair. *How can I be sad when the goat is fine?* I repeat the words just as Jules and Six call us over, and the others stare at me with confused looks until Jules himself perks up. "Yes!" he cries. "Yes, that's it, isn't it? How *can* we be sad when the goat is fine?" The tentacled chef raises the dual spatulas he is wielding over his head. "Ah, Luri, you bring us the finest metaphors."

"I . . . didn't, no," I try to say.

"No no." Mark pats my back. "Let him have this. He needs a good metaphor."

"The goat is fine, and dinner is served!" Jules announces to us.

"The goat is fine, and thank you," Six says.

"I'm eating in the library. You're all barbarians," Ellin grumbles. I join her, and we manage to get up the wobbling metal steps braced against the wall of Bastion's without spilling anything. Sitting at one of the small tables near the rickety fence and listening to the others continue their happy yelling below us as we eat the unreal fish and fake rice that still somehow manages to be savory and filling. "Luri." Her voice catches me out, and I look up to see her pointing a curved and possibly cursed fork from ten lifetimes ago my way. "How are you holding up?"

"Bad." I'm honest with our resident warrior. But I say it with a shrug. "But what else is new? It's fine, Ellin. I'll be fine. I'm always fine." I take a bite, and something meaty and citrusy explodes across my tongue. Jules is an excellent chef, especially here. "Really! Don't look at me that way."

"I'm worried," Ellin tells me, like she's confessing a dark secret. "And I just . . . What are those idiots doing down there?" She sighs. We look over the edge. The three of them are composing a song about the goat. "You did this," she accuses me.

I smile. "I made a difference," I say.

CHAPTER THREE

'm sitting across from Mark about twenty thousand heartbeats later, the two of us going through the seminecessary motions of reincarnation in our own ways.

The chairs in the library aren't great. They're actually uniform, unlike everything else we have in here. Bought out of one of the vendors in the halls of the Between. They're a fake wood—actually fake, not just Between fake—a kind of lacquered brown with painted-on wood grain. The dark color is pleasant from a distance but looks kind of sticky up close. The cushions on them are a fragile lie and make me glad that I actually kept Ellin's robe. Even if it is awkwardly hiked up around my tail.

The tail is poking out the back of the chair, under the last of the three horizontal slats. These chairs are just wide enough to let me poke through, which is their only selling point over the mixed stuff we have downstairs.

Mark is writing with a two-foot-long feather quill on the back of brown diner napkins he's pulling from our endless dispenser and arranging them on the table. I'm just quietly poking at low-priority notifications to clear them from my mind.

You have completed 1,000 local hours of farming: +10 marks of labor.
You have completed 1,000 local hours of farming: +9 marks of labor.
You have consumed enough food for 3,400 average locals: +1 mark of wealth, +3 perk cysts, +3 aura drops. Perk—Glutton of Norinton—has triggered.
You have completed 1,000 local hours of farming: +8 marks of labor.

You survived the song of a *Stymeria kallukala* (eradicator mountain harpy): +5 marks of battle. Perk—War Song—is unlocked.

"Another singer perk," I comment to Mark, who looks up from where he's trying to get a stack of napkins to neatly layer on each other, and failing. The turboprop engine ceiling fan is just powerful enough that, up here on the edge of its domain, all my friend's attempts are at constant risk. "I could finally try for that next life. I've never been a singer before."

"How many is that now?" he asks, dragging a finger through the air to reposition one of his display windows so that he isn't staring through some kind of translucent pane to look at me.

"Ten, twelve depending on how you count." I shrug at him, my eyes drifting over to Jules's bonsai terrarium tucked into one of the shelves, under an anemic row of paperbacks and over the shelf where we stack all the board games that have started fights. "Most of them are add-ons, not learners or uppers. So maybe not yet. I should spend a life messing with the profession and see if I get anything really defining."

He shakes his head at me. "Luriiiiii." Mark gives me a cute little pout that makes me want to offer him some kind of comfort, but in a very condescending way. "You're doing it again! You don't need *this* place to tell you what you can be!"

I freeze briefly, but for a shiver of anxiety down my tail, tugging my robe back tight on my thin shoulders. Mark's right. I don't have my mental defenses up, and I'm letting this get to me again.

There's this somewhat odd, somewhat totally reasonable impulse to try to optimize. I'd say it's a human thing, but Six and Ellin do it too. This . . . whatever this is . . . This looping cycle of life and death and tweaking our souls' power in between, it comes with a lot of perks. Perks, that is, as enforced by the Between, not the simpler kind of perks that are usually unenforced by local employment laws. Among other things.

We do things, and we get rewarded for them. If we take those rewards into lives and specialize, we can reach higher and higher, becoming better and better at the things we do. Iterations and retries letting us push our limits and stress the worlds we land in. Sometimes for the better, often not.

Except . . .

What a lonely fucking way to live.

Say you like cakes. So you spend your first life, before you know, becoming a baker. You learn to make the batter, get the perfect oven temperatures down. You're a master of the frosting thing. The bag thing that they squeeze frosting out of. Whatever that thing is. You're good at it.

Then you die. And you wake up here, in a flat form, with blinking yelling alerts in your head, prepared to offer reassurance that you *did a good job*.

You pick up a perk that lets you improve a cake three times a life. You trade your cysts for an aura layer and fill it with a thing that makes your muffins taste better. You equip a tethered item that lets you learn your favored profession from your last life 10 percent faster.

You're born again. You know what you want to do. You want to be a *baker*. You were good at it last time, and now you can be better! Your passion hasn't diminished just because you died once or twice depending on how you count.

So you do. Because it's what you want to do. You live a full life, as the best damn baker out there. You meet someone at your bakery. You cater for kings and presidents. You take your craft further than ever before.

Then you die.

And you do it all over again.

And it might be ten more lives before you realize that you can't distinguish the faces of your apprentices. That you keep slipping up and asking for flour that doesn't exist on this world, or fruit you haven't seen in a hundred years. That your perks aren't just helping you; they're *defining* you. You've turned into a cake-making machine. Like one of those bag things, but automated. And what's left of you, your hopes, your dreams, your passion, it's being squeezed out like it's fucking frosting to decorate whatever world you've landed in this go-around.

Specializing too far and too long hollows people out, and it takes you to a level of madness that is hard to adequately describe. It turns a baker into a cake.

"Right!" I flick my tail against the floor and my fingers against the small table. This is the perfect place for a romantic, if we had some candles, but instead it's just cheap napkins and me being sad. "But hey, I want to make some art this next roll, I think. Jules brought back a fucking magic tree, and look how much it brightens this place up. I should do that!"

"Luri . . ."

"I've never sung before. Not *really*," I tell Mark softly, reaching out to wrap my thin hand around his larger fingers still holding his quill. "It could be fun. And hey, I don't *have* to be a singer. I'll just take one or two of the passives, and it'll be an option. I'm not slipping again. Don't worry."

"Alright, alright. I'm in the anxiety too much I suppose." He flicks my nose with the tip of his quill, and I sputter, flailing and sending half his napkins flying into the void they return to as my robe is flung off one of my arms. "No, my Jumps!" Mark throws himself over the table. "Monster!"

"Heh. What're you working on anyway?" I ask.

"Oh, my own base-build stuff. I'm trying to sort out my aura budget now, so I can avoid duplicate abilities." Mark sighs. "I hate . . . having to do this here." He sits up and leans back, staring at the ceiling. His quill slips onto the tabletop as he takes a deep breath, his eyes glassy and far away.

One of Mark's hands layers over the other, and I see his fingers making a well-worn turning motion. Rings are common across a lot of our lives, as a symbol.

My face twists into pity, then a grimace, then a sad smile. "What was their name?" I ask in a low voice. I don't want to broadcast it to the others who are hanging around downstairs playing cards with the stakes as embarrassing stories from their last lives.

Mark doesn't look down. Just keeps staring up at the dusty wood overhead, allowed to be dirty but forever missing the classic cobwebs. "Oona," he says after a pause. "Her name was Oona. She was a florist in our city. There was . . . There was nothing special about her." Mark's face has a smile on it when he says that, and I can sense the echoes of an old inside joke.

"You must have loved her very much." The words are part prompt, part reminder.

"I did," he says, pulling his hands up behind his head, trying to look casual, infusing his voice with that classic Mark optimism. "I really did. I still do. Stupid, right? I'd been hoping . . ."

"It's never stupid," I tell him firmly. "I wait, every time, for ever-changing someones who aren't coming. You can too. There's no rules here that make sense, Mark. We're all making it up as we go." I help him start to reorganize his surviving napkins, stacking similarly named notes on his available perks in messy rows. "Do you regret it?"

"*No.*" Mark's answer comes instantly. "Never. *Never.*"

I almost shake my head. Almost tell him that people like us can't say things like never. But I don't because, not so secretly, I agree with him. Never regret loving someone.

"Did she have a good life?" I ask instead.

"Best I could give her." Mark smiles. "Well, best she could give us both, I guess. We lived in *weird* times. She took her business underground at one point, when petal runners were the only way to get anything into the country. And we ended up making the news sheets a few times, for evading the law!" He's laughing, a nostalgic and sappy smile in his eyes. "Laws change though. We weren't really part of the whole thing. It was just . . . She wanted to be a florist, you know? And I was happy to be part of it."

"I feel like there's some stories there." We both laugh at my words; Mark's still fairly new here, but it's a well-trod humor between us all.

Down below, Jules's and Ellin's voices rise up, not loud enough for us to make out but enough to indicate they're having fun. The warmth of it wraps around me and staves off the cold of loss for a bit.

"Did you have anyone?" Mark asks suddenly. "'Cause, Luri, I vaguely know you're always waiting for people. But . . ."

"I had a few someones," I say, staring past him. "Suitors, mostly, for social convenience. Nothing that went far. Just . . . I didn't . . ." The words catch, and I shift against the seat, the hard cushion suddenly more painful now that I'm trying to find anything to think about. "I didn't . . . want to. Not this time. Maybe later. I just didn't want to add to the list this time."

"I'm never going to see her again," Mark whispers to me, voicing the dark truth that we're both trying to not let in. "I'm never going to hold her. Or kiss her. Or be her getaway driver. It's all done." He meets my eyes with a grim panic dancing beneath the surface of those soft brown irises. "It's happening again, Luri. How many times? How many times before I forget her name? How many new loves before loving hurts too much? Before I . . ."

Before he ends up like me?

I cut his thoughts off before they can ram him down the same path I almost took a dozen lifetimes ago. "I don't think any of us should be saying words like never." My voice is oddly steady. "Mark, where are we? *What* are we? We don't know anything. Never? *Never?* Bullshit. We're . . . Wherever or whatever the Between is, it can't be everything. And even if it is, that means all we have to do is stick around long enough, and you'll meet them again. All of them. Everyone you've ever loved. That's just statistics; a nonzero chance is a surefire bet when you've got infinite time to roll the dice."

"But how long before it doesn't matter to me anymore?" he asks, a man begging for an easy answer and an easy out. I joke about Mark being young, but he has lifetimes of pain piling up in his soul, and it's not hard to hear it. "Luri, when do the faces blur together and the names go away?"

And there it is. The question that he's been worried to ask since he learned what my deal was. But he's asking it now. And I don't ever want to lie to my friend, not here, where friends are all we have left. "I . . . It . . . It'll happen when you don't notice it," I say, curling my fingers around my arms and tugging the bathrobe back up to cover more of my skin. I'm not cold, but I don't feel like being exposed right now. My voice is still easy, somehow, even if I can hear the hurt creeping in. "One day you'll be making a list of your top ten lovers for fun to tease Ellin, and you'll realize that there's someone missing. Jules will ask you about that time you were a royal concubine, and Six will have to fill in the king's name for you. Or maybe you just realize that you can recall the soft moments and the feeling of being loved, but not the color of their eyes, or the texture of their fingernails."

"And then they're gone," he states. "And what the fuck do we do then?"

"They're not gone," I disagree softly. "No, Mark. They're never gone. If you want, we can get you a book, or a scroll, or have Jules make you some kind of memory tree or something. But . . . You're still here. For as long as you're with us, you'll be here. Like I said, people like us shouldn't say things like never. But you know what word I like? Always. Oona . . . You'll always have part of her with you. The part of her that was interwoven with your life. Maybe it's different because you knew where you were going and she didn't, but that doesn't mean she couldn't change you." I sigh and look around for something to fidget with or drink. Failing to find anything, I settle for picking at the wood of the banister. "Did you make a difference?"

"In her life?"

"Sure."

The hum of the overhead fan takes over for a second before he speaks. "Yeah." Mark nods after a while. "I did."

"Did *she* make a difference?" I press. "Not something that shows up on a perk or your pool list. But to *you*. Did she change you?" The question doesn't catch him off guard. But he still takes time to think about it seriously. And then nods once. "Then even if you forget her, what she did, it'll be there always, won't it?"

"It's not the same," Mark complains.

And he's not wrong. Of course it's not the same. It never will be. We're separated here, by an enforced unknowable boundary, kept away from everyone we come to care for, whether they're waiting in a distant afterlife or just gone forever. There's no blissful reuniting, no joining them in oblivion, and certainly no going back.

Downstairs, Ellin bursts into a roar of laughter at something Six says. It's no pure and untainted sound; she's carrying just as much pain as the rest of us. But it's real, and happy now.

We can't live in the past. No one can, really; the past is another world. It's just a little more literal for us.

"At least we've got each other," I tell Mark. "I'm not going anywhere."

"Ha. Me neither," he says, though he says it with that cadence that tacks on an unspoken "Unless . . . ?"

The chair creaks under me as I let go of Mark's hand and curl in on myself. Old memories and old fears floating on the surface of my thoughts like buoys in the bay. I need to sleep, soon, before I start to mentally crumble and waste more of my heartbeats here.

You would think that bodies that are more like suggestions than physical forms would be resistant to things like sleep, but it turns out, while they struggle against outside influences, you can make yourself tired just fine. Emotional exhaustion is real, and dangerous. Pushing through the waking moments to come to Bastion's and meet everyone who's here this time is a ritual that's always worth it, but it can't last forever.

Oddly, I don't think of sleep as a waste of time here. This body can dream and always wakes up without physical pain or ache. So it's often a pleasant little reset, a good night's sleep that eases woes and lets me adjust to being back among the never dead. The things that have my mind running loops settle down for a while; the worries seem further away.

There's only one problem.

"We still need a bed in here," I grumble.

Mark glances up from staring at his napkin notes. "I appreciate the offer, Luri, but I'm not feeling it right now." I give him a *look*, and the deadpan straight face he's putting on slowly cracks. "Okay, okay. Well, we all *know* we need a bed. But . . . What're we supposed to do about it?"

"Maybe I'll go find a vendor and bring one back next life." I sigh. "Or just gut my return room and bring that one in?"

"You will do no such thing, young hellion!" Jules's voice doesn't startle me because I saw his tentacles creeping over the edge of the balcony we're sitting on to pull himself up. Jules seems allergic to stairs. "Bastion's is a *shared* place. We will find a way to manage a bed. Until then, Six is setting up a hammock down below, which you may avail yourself of."

I don't protest being chastised. He's not wrong; all our doors to Bastion's are one way and one use, and stumbling back by accident is unheard of. We could spend marks on better doors, but . . .

Usually we just spend them restocking the bar or getting a new lamp or something.

I've been cracking notifications open like geodes this whole time, and I'm still only sitting at about nine hundred marks of labor, which might sound impressive, but isn't enough to buy the chair I'm pretending to tolerate sitting on.

"And!" Ellin's voice is closer than it should be, and I cock an eyebrow as I watch her crawling up Jule's form like he's a mobile training course. "You can't ruin the atmosphere by doing anything uncouth in a *hammock*!"

"Oh no." Mark and Jules sigh together.

To me, the words are like a challenge. How exactly Ellin has made it this many lives while still pretending to keep up a kind of strange shell made out of ideas from her original culture and a few new taboos picked up along the way baffles me. We live eternal, running observation laps through every kind of society. The idea of hanging on to the way a first life taught etiquette to us as children, or how that opening trial run of social existence conditioned us to think about relationships, all the way from *then* to *now*? Here at the end and beginning of dozens of lives, it just doesn't seem that important what people from a thousand subjective years ago thought was uncouth.

And I can tell it seems odd to everyone else too. Which I know because we've *all* enjoyed each other at different times for different reasons. *Even Ellin*, which makes her frequent verbal jabs something of a hypocrisy. And one that I quite enjoy taking aim at and zeroing in on.

But I am tired. And we have millions of heartbeats left here for me to remind her of just how creative I can be. So I wave off Mark's and Jules's concerned looks, like they're wondering if I'm about to throw the bathrobe off and dive tackle Ellin off into open air. "You're right," I say instead. "Nothing weird about a bed made of rope."

Ellin's face shows that she has already seen the error in her judgment. "Now wait . . ."

"I'm kidding. Mostly." I smile at my friend. "I just want to sleep. Does anyone else need it? I'd sleep on the floor, but . . ."

But I can't. Because you can't sleep when you're not in a bed here. No one knows why, but it's inconvenient.

"I shall give you a tap when Six is done," Jules says politely, slowly lowering the black dome of his head back below our vision, tentacles uncurling from the wooden posts and slipping after him as he touches the floor below.

"Thanks, Six!" I yell down and get a cheerfully monotone noise of acceptance from the golem.

Mark and I sigh. We're still here, and still happy to have each other, but we do need to sleep and let our minds reset. The first heartbeats back are the hardest. Our last lives are still fresh; our return hasn't sunk in yet. For me, I know the pattern, and I know how hard it hits me. Mark . . . Well, maybe he's still new enough that it won't hurt him too bad. He could go a couple hundred thousand heartbeats and decompress on his own.

But I like waking up and feeling new. It's not a real reset, but it has a certain sense of a fresh start to it. Like novelty is just around the corner, but even if it's not, that I'm new enough that things can look a little hopeful.

"Hey, do you have a four-part outer aura layer you don't want?" Mark asks as the two of us sit. I'm just zoning out and staring into space. He's actually gone back to trying to get his setup done. "One of the ones that's a two-and-two right angle, not a line or something weird."

I flip through my own inventory and grab something to hand to him. "Do you care that it's dumb?" I ask, and he shakes his head as I pass over Hiker IV.

"This isn't dumb at all." Mark gives me a worried look. "Are you sure?"

"I have spent most of the last ten lives in cities. The closest I got to a hike this last time was . . . Well, you can win that off me after I nap." I push the meta-object into his hand and close his fingers around it. "Don't worry about it. Finish your build. I'm gonna clear some more low-priority stuff before Six is done."

He's still giving me a look that says I probably gave a gift that was a little too good, but I don't care. I don't need it. We don't *need* any of this stuff, though it does start to take on weight and meaning when it's what lets us help or heal those we come to care for. And that's what really matters; everyone else, they're just a little newer, and all still a little better at *connecting* with the real mortals we live with. They care in a way I'm terrified I'm starting to lose touch with. So maybe my gifts are better spent on them than on me.

I sit back, let my tail thump onto the floor, consider smashing this chair into a pile of debris, and go back to checking notifications.

You have completed 1,000 local hours of farming: +7 marks of labor.
You have completed 1,000 local hours of farming: +6 marks of labor.
You have participated in 10 local religious ceremonies: +5 marks of spirit.
You have spent 1 local year without speaking to a sophont: +3 aura drops.
Ability granted—Targeted Silence.
You have completed 1,000 local hours of farming: +5 marks of labor.

I sigh and stop cracking open notifications as Six mercifully comes up the stairs and signals me. It's daunting, to see a whole life reduced to a handful of after-action reports like this. At least this time, for me, it's not *messy*. The chair thunks backward and the floorboards creak as I stand and stretch, winking at Mark as he looks up at me with my hands arched over my head. "I'm going to sleep," I say. "And be better tomorrow."

"Good night, Luri." Mark grabs my hand as I pass by and gives it a squeeze. "Hey. I'm glad you're still here," he says.

I look at him, then over to the main room where Ellin and Jules are staring at a golden bottle on the counter between the two of them, then over to the patiently waiting Six. My friends, through who even knows how many years. Still here. We're all still here.

"I'm glad I'm still here too." I surprise myself when I hear my voice. "I'll be more fun to be around tomorrow. Promise," I offer.

And I'm not even lying when I say it.

CHAPTER FOUR

Waking up is a delight compared to the abrupt transference that is not dying.

When death comes for me while I'm out busy living a real life in a real world, it's often deeply unpleasant. Dying is almost never happy. Age or disease or violence—there aren't a lot of great options for it.

Age is the worst. A whole life of aches and pains, cumulative damage building up and a body that's shutting down, all of it compounding to a threshold where the mind simply opts out of the whole affair. But getting there is painful, undignified, and long. Your *teeth* hurt, almost every time around that I've lived. We try to tell anyone we meet that's new: Pick up Dental Durability or something.

Surprisingly, violence isn't the easiest. Violent deaths hurt and often come with horrible emotional trauma. Usually if you're dying that way it's *not* some dramatic last stand to save everyone you ever cared about. Usually it's them going with you, if you're not just dying alone for no reason. There's also, for me, a certain malicious anger to having a life cut short by a random mugging just as I was getting into it.

Disease is easy. Fever and delirium, disease that takes you out does it with your thoughts unable to process what's even happening to you most of the time—as long as it's not one of the cancer subtypes. I've never been angry to die to a disease. Not until afterward anyway. It still sucks though, the slow loss of control, the pain you can't fight back against.

And then, over the edge, and opening remade eyes here, and that's another death done.

It's abrupt, and while I appreciate the relief from the pains, there's a kind of spiritual severing that comes with it. I will *never go back.* That life is closed, that world off-limits, a chapter now concluded. Those people are lost to me for . . .

Not forever. I don't like the word. But a while, until statistics reunite us.

Waking up though is different. There's no sudden disconnect, no jarring sensation of suddenly opening my eyes to be back in the Between. Instead, I've been here the whole time. There's a comfortable continuity to the whole process. My mind isn't just rebuilt; it's been resting and dreaming. And when I wake, it is to a feeling of being abstractly refreshed. In a newly built replica of my favorite body, in a place that feels safe. With lifetimes of trauma safely put into mental boxes and tucked away to not bother me for the heartbeats that I have here, now, with everyone that really is permanent in my life.

I keep my eyes closed and shift in the hammock that Six put together. It's not going to be giving me any buffs, but between the sturdy rope and the blanket I'm cocooned in, I find it deeply enjoyable. Even better, hangovers don't exist in the Between, unless you *really* work at it.

A voice comes to me as I drift. ". . . Not too erratic, I guess." It's Mark, from somewhere nearby. Probably behind the bar that the hammock is partly strung up against. "Still worried though."

"Let them sleep," Six's familiar monotone replies. "They have never had a good first day back. Things will be better. You will understand."

"I've been to Bastion's a dozen times now, Six." I can practically hear Mark folding his arms. "I'm not dumb. This is different though."

Ellin chimes in from nearby. "Six has triple the lives on you, and I've got more, *and* half your stops here were low on heartbeats. We won't gainsay you, and there's nothing wrong with caring because you love them, but trust us when we tell you Luri isn't going insane." She pauses. "More insane."

There's a sound of Mark making some wordless utterance in the back of his handsome throat, but Six cuts in again before Mark can worry. "You could simply ask them. They are awake."

"It's impolite to blow my cover like that, Six!" My voice comes out muffled by the blankets that surround me. The golem offers a deadpan sincere apology as I crawl out, dropping over the hammock as the ropes flip and threaten to fling me to the floor. It's an amusingly novel sensation; not that I've never been in a hammock, but it's never been routine for me. Maybe next life I'll try to be a . . . sailor? Sailors use hammocks, I think. On some worlds anyway.

Mark looks away from me sheepishly as I windmill my arms and rise up to my feet, my tail helping to keep me standing. I'm pretty sure it's because he's worried I overheard and not because I'm not wearing anything again. For all that he makes jokes sometimes, I know Mark likes how this body looks.

I don't blame him for worrying. Each life feels like a lifetime, especially to someone who's new. When you've been through five or six lives, the next one can feel like a big commitment, a lot of time.

It's not. It doesn't take long to either go mad or cross the threshold. I'm on the other side; each life is real and can feel long when you're in it. But then I'll be back here again after. And I'll have my own time, *my* life, my real one, with my friends.

There are different philosophies, obviously. I've met enough people here to know that not everyone agrees with me, and we can have some pretty grand yelling matches about it. I don't think anyone is actually right or wrong here; there's so many questions we just can't answer. It's all guesses and shadow play anyway. Though even that is a philosophy someone could try to debate me on.

"Thanks for caring." I bump a fist on Mark's upturned jaw in a light tap. "I'm fine. Promise."

"Really?" Mark looks back down at me with a disbelieving stare. "*How?*"

I don't really have a good answer for him. How *am* I okay? I'm currently dead, technically, I think. I've lost more friends and family and lovers than most people will ever dream of. There's no end in sight, and no way to stop even if I wished there was. I'm trapped in life, whether I want to be or not. So why do I feel okay?

"I had a good nap." I give a glib grin. "But also . . . I've got a subjective month here. That's a pretty good chunk of a vacation. I can either be okay or not okay, and for as long as we're here, I'm choosing okay." I smile and reach around the bar to grab one of the generic cups and fill it with water from the overpressured spout, taking a sip as the stray droplets run down the back of my hand. "It's a bit dumb, but then again, so is being given codified magic powers for eating too much or whatever."

"I can't believe you actually ran the Glutton of Norinton perk." Ellin spins on her barstool. "Also, oy, now that Luri's up and pacing, anyone else want to use the hammock? I could go for a nap, but I'm immune to the verdant submersion of dread, so I can wait." None of us react to her claim. We're all used to turning our lies into jokes.

Finishing my water, I set the glass down on the counter with a thunk. "Where's Jules? Didn't he want to sleep?"

"Ah." Mark points across the bar, and I follow his finger. Jules is sitting in his own coiled tentacles at one of the tables, across from someone that I hadn't noticed when I woke up. "New kid came in," he says softly. "Jules is trying to keep him calm."

"Oh. Shoot." I glance around and find the bathrobe Ellin gave me, tossing it on and swishing my tail against it.

Ellin rolls her eyes at me. "*This*. This makes you get dressed."

"Okay, to be fair, I'm still barely dressed." I turn to her and spread my arms to show off my form, and she scowls at me but doesn't look away while Mark stifles a laugh. "But that's a *kid* kid," I say, pulling the robe shut and tying it off around my waist. "And I'm gonna go say hi, since I'm the most normal person here."

"That is a falsehood at best," Six informs me. "Also, I wish to speak with you first."

"Course! What's up, Six?" There's an energy to my words that makes me happy to feel again. The slow fading of the pain of death, before the upcoming responsibility of life, it leaves me able to simply exist in the now and be content with it.

The golem turns up his palm to me, showing off a metaitem. "The Between has decided I have crossed a threshold and allows me now to purchase limited doorways," the golem says. "I know many of you have this ability, but now that it is within my reach, I wish to explore the Between before returning."

Part of me suddenly hurts. But I refuse to let that show. I've lived enough lives to have a keen sense of where emotional blackmail starts and ends, and I refuse to perpetuate that particular bullshit. "Well, I can't say I like it, but I understand," I tell him instead, setting one of my hands on the durable gray skin of his arm. "I'll miss you though! But I hope you find something out there."

"Oh." Six blinks his wide and circular eyes at me. "I have eight million heartbeats here. I believe that I will have ample time once the rest of you have moved on. I simply wished to ask for help with the funding."

"Oh!" I gasp in relief. "That's so much easier! Of course! What do you need? Marks? Drops? Some other nonsense?"

"Marks of labor and skill, yes." Six nods. "I would offer that we work out the details later. Do not think I would abandon you, Luri." The compassion in the golem's words don't fit his monotone voice. "There is much to be done here, and much to enjoy. I still wish to hear stories of your time, and there is intellectual satisfaction in our games."

"Thanks, Six." I smile. "I missed playing board games with you too." I give the golem a light hug before I turn back to the room. "Gonna go say hi now."

"Good luck," Ellin comments, raising a glass of something at me in a salute. It almost sounds mocking, but I can see through her tone.

This place, this *room* in the Between, isn't perfect. We call it Bastion's, but it doesn't have an official name that the Between recognizes, and no one has saved up enough to unlock that. Technically, it's not even its own room. It's legally defined as a subhallway that happens to be connected by a series of one-way doors to a set of return rooms.

This distinction isn't especially important, but it does mean that it's possible for people to stumble in here. It also means we pay a lot of our extra marks into keeping things here from degrading.

Time in the Between is subjective, meaningless, and unconnected to the lives we live. My next life might last eighty years, while Mark gets a bad run and dies at twenty to a falling piano. But I could still show up here before him, even if we left at the same time.

Because of this constant unknowable amount of time, it's a challenge to set up meeting places like Bastion's. To the point that we didn't even set it up; I inherited it from someone. Our group just puts points into it to keep it stable, and we've been trying to update the decor and the collection of alcohol and board games. But we do have some control over the space, and we do know that unless someone is actively hunting for it, the Between won't create doors or corridors to it unless one of us is here.

But if we are? Well. People can stumble in.

We aren't the only eternal dead. There are, presumably, an infinite number of us. Though I've only met about a hundred. An infinite number of people in an infinitely large space means it's infinitely unlikely that we ever bump into each other, so I'm pretty happy with the handful of friends I do have.

Another thing that's unlikely is to meet someone young. And yet, despite the impossible odds, sitting at the table across from Jules and drinking lemonade out of a ceramic coffee mug is a child. Also despite the impossible odds, I have experience in this situation. You can tell when someone is a child, or just in a child body. It's the eyes. The way they look at everything like they're halfway between blind fear and intense curiosity.

"Hey there." I speak softly as I claim a chair between Jules and the kid. He's half my height, dark skin and an angular face that tapers to a flat line of a chin. The kid has whiskers, which makes me wonder if he also has a tail hidden beneath the blank white set of clothes the Between gives first timers. "How's the lemonade?"

He pulls the cup closer, biting down on the straw like he's worried I'll steal it away. Internally, I chalk that up to some kind of abuse. Which doesn't shock me as much as I'd like. Of the ways to die, children *generally* don't get old age. Which really leaves two very bad options.

"Has Jules been a polite tentacle monster to you?" I ask, grinning softly. The kid shrinks back a bit, but the question forces him to consider the situation.

Before he can answer, Jules huffs at me with a sonorous vibration. "Luri, I am the *picture* of polite etiquette. No one is as polite as I. I have charisma running from my every orifice."

"Ew." I scoot my chair slightly farther away from Jules, making a face at the kid, who lets out an abrupt giggle before fear takes over his face again and he silences himself. Jules and I have a strategy though, and it's working. Some people play good cop, bad cop. We play good reincarnator, *weird* reincarnator. "Don't ask him about the orifice thing," I whisper conspiratorially to the kid. "I've never asked, and I'm kind of scared to at this point."

The boy nods before realizing from my smile and the tone of my words that I'm kidding and leans in to whisper back a nervous "Okay." His voice comes out as a rasp.

"So. As long as Jules is oozing in a friendly way . . ."

"I resent this intently." Jules hams up his disgrace, folding tentacles over his body in a mimicry of crossing his arms.

". . . I'd like to ask you a couple of questions. Do you think you're up for it?" I keep my tone as kind as I can. No raising my voice, even for a joke. He nods, and I take a deep breath. "Okay. First thing. When you got here, something would have shown you words—or spoken if you can't read—to tell you how many heartbeats you have. Can you tell me how many?"

The kid nods, his whiskers drooping as he gets a worried look on his slim face. "O-one and three and zero, zero, zero," he says, his throat making the words sound pained.

"Thirteen thousand," Jules reads back. "Damnation. That's . . ."

"That's plenty," I say, flicking a finger at one of Jules's tentacles that's within range on the green felt. "Hey, go tell Ellin that I need a copy of the thing from her," I order. Jules's trio of eyes rotates into curious upward-angled slits, but he shrugs his tentacles and heads back over to the bar anyway.

"What . . . is that?" the boy asks.

"Jules?" I say. "He's French," I answer, knowing he won't know what that means. The kid looks at me with that expression that says that he's *very* smart for his age and he knows that I'm full of shit and that my jokes are *unappreciated*. A smile is all he gets in return. "Jules likes having a different body than the rest of us, and this place, the Between, lets him change it. And we don't mind because he's our friend. He's a nice person," I follow up, before abruptly changing the subject. "One other quick question for you. Do you want to try again?"

". . . Try what?" the boy asks.

"All of it," I say. "Start over from the beginning. A different life, a different family, a different world. Do you want to *do it all again?*"

He looks around at Bastion's. At the mismatched tables and wood floors that seem to generate a dusting of sand when we're not looking, at the turbo-prop engine overhead and the creaky stairs to the library. "Am I dead?" he asks, not sounding too concerned by it.

"Sort of," I say, setting a hand on the table between us. "But also sort of not. Maybe, but also very yes." He looks down at his hands, poking out of the sleeves of his white shirt as if he's only just waking up. Which happens. People who are new can sometimes wander the halls of the Between for longer than they have heartbeats before they even notice what's going on. "Not as bad as you worried, huh?"

"I have my hand," he rasps out. "But my voice?"

I nod and start to speak quickly, giving the information that I have ready for exactly this situation. "The Between restores your first body to what you think should be its normal version. You see your hand as missing, so it fixes it. You think your voice is supposed to sound that way, so . . ." I shrug. "It's not being mean to you, not on purpose. It just doesn't know. But now, I need to listen. Do you want to try again?"

". . . Will it hurt?" he asks, and no amount of years behind my heart would ever make the sentence not stab at me.

"Sometimes." I won't lie to a child. "Sometimes it won't. I can't tell you that it *will* be better. But I can tell you that it *could*. And that we can help you make sure you'll have a better chance."

He looks at me with those eyes on the verge of tears, like I'm a god offering him paradise. And I feel bad because I know I'm not, and I know that by the next time we meet, if we meet again at all, he's going to maybe think differently. But all I can do now is help the child suffering in front of me. He nods, reaching out to set his hand in my palm like he's accepting a contract.

He's not. I was just offering a hand. I think he understands as I smile at him, while Jules returns and hands me a metaobject with a layer of thinly disguised disgust. "Okay," I say. "You don't have a lot of time here. When you run out of heartbeats, you'll be removed from the Between and put in a new world. And you'll be back here when you're done, and you can try to find us again if you want to. This place is called Bastion's. Now, let's get your voice fixed, hey?"

His eyes light up as Jules and I guide him through the process of opening the translucent window from his mind that will let him adjust his body. The two of us show him where to focus and how to determine what it will cost.

Because it's technically a form of healing, the cost is vastly reduced, and I do take a minute to wonder if perhaps the Between *is* playing some cruel joke. Or maybe trying to find a way to motivate people to learn their inventory screens.

We front him the cost in marks of vigor that it takes to repair himself. The boy cries as he says words that don't hurt, with a voice that isn't scarred.

And then I ask how many heartbeats he has left and get a number that's rapidly dwindling.

"Okay," I say. "One last thing. You should have a perk slot open. You'll get more. You'll have time to fuck around with everything, to learn and to grow and to set your own grand quests, okay? But right now, I want you to do me a favor." I hold out the thing I had Jules fetch me, kneeling down to meet him eye to eye. "Take this. And think really hard about equipping it, okay?"

"What is it?" he asks, already pulling the strange nonobject from my hand and curiously looking at it.

The next words I speak are grim, but necessary. "Heart-Stopper. It will let you end your next life early, if you need to," I say. "Later, maybe, you'll be strong enough to punch through anything that hurts you. But this time? If things get bad? You can *know* that you'll end up back here. So you never have to be afraid again, okay, little brother?"

The metaitem vanishes, and the boy stares at me with eyes that have experienced too much pain for someone so young.

"Okay," he says in a painless whisper of a voice.

"Good." I lean back on my heels. "Now. You're all set to leave soon, aren'tcha? Never enough time! Want a hug before you go? One for the road? Jules, get over here and help me give him a hug!" The kid shrinks back, but when I make no move toward him except to open my arms and offer, he straightens up and slowly moves toward me.

When I wrap him up in a loose grip and feel Jules's tentacles encircle us together, I slowly feel his small body untense and start crying in my grasp. "I don't wanna go yet," he says with a pitiable sob.

"I know," I whisper back. "Never enough time. But don't worry. You're going to do great things, and you'll make a lot of friends, and if you're very lucky, you'll find happiness." I rustle his curly hair, paraphrasing and echoing the words that dozens of parents have told me when I was on my way to my first day of school. "And when you get back, we'll see you again, and you can come up with a good name that's *yours*, and you'll have plenty of time, okay?"

"I have a name." He sniffs into my bathrobe.

"Not yet," I tell him. "We don't have names here until we pick our own. And you can tell me when you make it . . ."

He's already gone, and now Jules is just holding me, and I'm hugging one of his tentacles.

"... Back," I whisper.

The others make their way over as I let myself drop to a sitting position on the floor, taking deep breaths of the fake air and shaking my head as if that will somehow help clear my thoughts.

"You okay?" Mark asks.

"Oh, yeah, what a great question," Ellin says. "I can see how your lives of experience are shining through."

"Fuck off." Mark's use of the most common human expression across every world we've all been reborn in makes me snort out a laugh.

I stand up, relying on Jules's daintily provided tentacle to brace myself. "I'm fine," I say. "I'm glad he found us, and I hope he does okay. That's always hard, but . . . but he'll be okay." He has to be. Not just because it would be unfair on a cosmic level if he wasn't, but also because *I demand it* of the universe he ends up in. And if experience has taught me anything, it's that when a universe and I disagree, it's in the universe's best interest to not fuck with me too much. "Yeah. He'll be okay. Safe journey, kid. And a better life this go-around."

Everyone echoes the last words along with me. The closest we ever get to a prayer.

"Okay." Ellin claps. "After that, forget sleeping. I want to get drunk. Mark, make that thing that kills people for me!"

"I would also welcome a distraction," Six says. "Would anyone join me for a round of Leaves and Branches?" The others groan, and I join them, but agree anyway. Six's favorite games are the ones that require a lot of staring at a board on the table trying to derive what your opponents are doing based on secret information, and I love them, and also love him, but the *only* reason I'm agreeing is because at least here the game can't drive us to try to kill each other.

Also Six has the unfair advantage of twice as many heartbeats as any of the rest of us. Though *no one* would ever use that clock as a tactical advantage. That's a cruelty, not a joke. And for all that we're a little silly a lot of the time, it's done with the attitude of spirited banter, never to actually hurt.

I start rearranging chairs around our good table and wiping chip crumbs off the felt and into nothingness. I've got a month left here, and I intend to savor every heartbeat of it.

CHAPTER FIVE

I t's easy to lose track of time when you don't have a way of measuring it. We *do* have a way; our heartbeat counters are always there, always pulling us closer and closer to our next lives. But a lot of the things you get used to when you're alive just don't worry us here.

None of us will ever really get hungry, or have to sleep, or need to find a bathroom. That last one is important because I have never once seen a bathroom in the Between. Like with sleep, it's an *option*, but nothing enforces it, and that's critical when we can't open doors out that will let us come back without paying a steep cost.

This makes things that are enjoyable a lot easier to become the focus of our hours. I don't even particularly cherish the game Six picked out, but we play for two subjective days before someone is declared the winner.

The end of the game comes with a collective sigh, a release of tension, a satisfying conclusion, and a little something extra besides. Six is excellent at this game, but it was Ellin who took over this round, and she flicks away the notification that the game itself offers upon its conclusion.

Very little in the Between is actually its mundane form. There are, obviously, several different theories about the place. I'd say thousands, but that'd be a lie. There aren't. Everyone thinks their take is unique, but they really just boil down to being from a handful of broad categories, and then reincarnators who haven't learned how to not be pedantic in five hundred years of living argue with each other endlessly about it. But personally, while I don't think the Between is alive exactly, I do think that if it were it would be sarcastic.

Leaves and Branches is an intense board game, and *technically*, it is a form of gambling. Except the buy-in is in the form of the literal heartbeats spent to play it, and the payout is something the Between conjures up for the winner. Typically, depending on how long and abstractly good the game was, somewhere between a 2 and 8 percent boost to mana production next life. Not really that fancy, especially since a lot of worlds don't have mana and it won't even convert to exa or seep or any of the other common ones, but it's still not nothing.

Ellin ignores it. Instead, she's much more interested in what she's *actually* won. "Oy, yes!" The towering woman kicks her feet up onto the table, tilting her chair back dangerously far. Not for her—we can't die here—but I'm terrified for the safety of the chair. The tree it's made of was extinct before whoever brought it here died. Replacing or repairing it is going to cost half my soul if she breaks it, if it's even possible. "Alright, Six! Pay up!"

The golem looks up from where he is tracing a line between two piles of cards with one of his gray fingers, an intense analysis in his round eyes. "Me, then? Very well." He stands and moves to the head of the table. "Where do I start?"

His monotone question has Ellin rubbing her hands together in excitement while Mark and Jules and I just settle in. "Oooh, let's see. Well, first off, species? World class? Lifespan?"

"Orc standard, preindustrial, and forty subjective years." Six rattles off his answers.

"Tell me . . ." Ellin considers, then snaps her fingers. "Tell me what was important to you," she decides. "Like, what did you *love* pursuing?"

Six gives a curt nod. "Very well." He thinks in silence, preparing his response, which buys me time to go rummage under the bar for anything to snack on. We are, unfortunately, out of bursting zee, and popcorn, and even just crackers. There's nothing here that wouldn't require cooking, and I don't want to waste the time. I make my way back empty-handed, tapping Mark's leg with my tail as I sit.

"You didn't miss anything," he whispers like we're in a theater. Which, in a way, we are.

Every world I've ever been on has something like the magic circle. The storytelling drive where we can transport each other willingly to far-off lands. And somehow, despite having lived fantastical lives and seen amazing and unbelievable things, it is still a delight to share with each other. To tell stories, to relate our lives and experiences, to make it all *real* here again.

So when Six starts to speak, paying off his story wager, we all shut up and listen. "On the third hide of the scrolls of Kasu, there is a record of the origins of the Koo Hasu. The term, in our language, is literal, and means 'good people.'" I love Six's history lessons. They come with citations and tangents for all sorts of things like this.

"When I was eight summers old, the other children and I were taken to a field to learn. Learning for the Koo Hasu is sacred, so it was natural to them that our learning take place in a sacred site. The field in question had been skipped by a wildfire six summers prior, and was considered blessed. The first of the scrolls concerned how to live good lives, and generally matched Luri's and Jules's ethos. The second scroll concerned how to find the divine. The third related to where our people came from." Six pauses and looks down at his hands before shaking his head. "I regret that I will never see them again." He speaks simply, but the words hold a weight that he typically never lets his voice contain. "Regardless," Six continues, "the origin of our people was written as a fall from the moon. Both the writing and illustrations showed a descent with wings, which our people were said to have lost. As with many pre-information era writings, it was metaphorical and I assumed inaccurate."

"Now *that's* interesting," Mark mutters next to me, eyebrows going up. And I agree with him; Six doesn't say things like *assumed* unless he's about to admit fault. I take a sip of my drink and enjoy the pleasant burn as I listen to the story.

"Yes," Six continues with a look in Mark's direction. "My assumption was flawed. As the world lacked the standard signs of active divinities, magic, thaumaturgy, or whispering, I had falsely believed that the story was a story and nothing more. A fiction that was falsely believed for comfort, as answers always are." Six almost hits a note of irritation when he says that. Our golem is a renowned atheist, which tends to get him into trouble on worlds that do have nonmetaphor gods. "The scroll was copied from the original writing. Or from a copy of the copy. But learning was sacred, and so every copy was made verbatim. Two summers later, for my knowledge, I was apprenticed to the recordkeeper and given the task of making a new copy of the first three scrolls. Recordkeepers were semireligious figures, but not leadership, and all youth were required to undergo an apprenticeship. And on close inspection, I found a detail that I had assumed—yes, Mark, falsely—to be decoration."

"Oooh, a mystery!" Ellin grins a wide and toothy smile.

"Correct. And I am not immune to curiosity." Six's voice almost makes that sound like a condemnation, but I smile because I know him too well. This one thing probably made the entire life for him. "I asked questions and learned the recordkeeper had copied it from the previous version. It took two more summers to obtain permission to seek another tribe of the Koo Hasu from which our recordkeeper had originated. Following the trail of copies, I eventually found a version that had been preserved for more than eight hundred summers. And, along with it, preserved copies of other scrolls that had related context."

"Suppressed knowledge?" Jules asks. It's not really an interruption. When a story pulls us in, asking questions is to be expected. "Some sinister plot."

Six shakes his head in a mechanical back-and-forth. "Worse. Time and information rot. The copies of the other scrolls had not been considered valuable enough to be copied alongside the others. They did not spread, and the information was not well-preserved. Because of previous information rot, they were not understood, but because of my nature, I could make sense of them. The markings on the third scroll were not decorations. They were coordinates."

"How mapped out was the world, if it was preindustrial?" I find myself asking.

"It was not mapped at all," Six says. "Our charts related to herd migrations, wind currents, and meeting places. There were no coherent maps of the world. And no use of coordinates." He holds up a hand to forestall more questions. "The truth of the matter was difficult to understand. I now have the benefit of context, but at the time, performing translations and mild archaeologies was the work of several years. I became a known figure in my people, and took several apprentices. It was not until near the end of my life that I found a record that could align to my deciphered coordinate system. At that point, I did what my curiosity compelled me to."

"You went where the scroll pointed." I'm grinning now. I can't wait to see where this ends.

"Yes. The journey took three summers and a pilgrimage with members from eighty different tribal bands of the Koo Hasu. It was a large undertaking." I love the way Six can say something like that. A large undertaking my tail. Probably the most powerful cultural event in his people's history; it's like calling a planet a sizable rock. Technically true, usually, but come on. "Arriving at the coordinate site revealed nothing except a strange formation in the ground. We set up camp and began exploration." Six tilts his head up, a tiny incline that's almost imperceptible but on him speaks a lot to the nostalgia at play. "And then we found a door."

"What, just standing around?" Ellin asks, confused. I just sip my drink and point at her in agreement. "I mean, that *happens* sometimes. I'm not saying that's off the table."

"No, Ellin, the door was buried. We had to dig for it. It was made of a titanium alloy." Six states the fact like that's a normal thing to say. "I opened it with a Rogue Aspect use, which I had no need for over the course of an otherwise peaceful life. Several of our expedition, me included, began to explore what was buried. The discovery gave context to the third scroll; the structure was a crashed starship."

"That's so fucking cool," I mutter. "So you actually did fall from the sky."

"Yes. Unfortunately, that was the end of my life," Six says. "Though Ellin did not win the knowledge of my death, I would like to share it. When we ventured too deep, the ship's systems reenabled, and the defenses targeted us at once with their remaining power. I kept my companions safe long enough for them to flee, which I am proud of. But the last piece of information I extracted was the language of the automated systems, calling us escaped prisoners." Six shakes his head. "My people, with hundreds of years as peaceful seekers of knowledge and harmony, were the descendants of a crashed prison ship."

"I wonder what happened." Mark sighs wistfully. "I know we'll never know, yeah, but I *wonder*. What changes a people like that?"

"Eight hundred years?" I comment. "Things change, man. That's forty mothers' worth of time for most orc species. All it takes is someone starting a tradition and sticking to it to snowball into civilization."

"Ah, right, that one time." He taps his foot against my tail in a comforting bit of contact. "Thanks for the story, Six." Mark addresses our tale teller.

"Yeah, that was *great!*" Ellin is beaming at him, and Jules applauds with a pulsing vibration as Six takes a perfect forty-five-degree bow. "That's so much better than my life. I got *stabbed*."

Ellin has been stabbed in every life she's lived. I think she invites it.

We don't, as a group, tend to play the game that the Between wants of us. We don't chase perks. We don't optimize for any kind of perfected soul powers that will let us set ourselves up as the salvation or destruction of worlds. We just live. And in living, we find meaning and purpose and love.

But I am *pretty sure* that Ellin is trying to get a reward for being stabbed in twenty consecutive lives.

I can't prove this. I could ask her, but I think if I did, she'd deny it and then have a story about getting stabbed again next time around anyway. Or maybe it's something else, like she wants an award for surviving a thousand total stabs or something. And she'll use that technicality to deflect my question.

Deflect it like she always seems to fail to deflect knives.

Part of me wants to offer to stab her here, just to see if she'd say yes, as a way to test my theory. But that's not really how the Between works. And these bodies aren't technically ours, or real, anyway.

"Are there any further questions?" Six asks, still standing, and I refocus on him.

"What was on the first scroll?" I ask. I'm always curious how different cultures define a good life.

Six answers with the mechanical precision of an encyclopedia. "One, act in defense of the community. Two, act in defense of the other. Three, act in defense of the self. Four, do not take from the world what cannot be replaced. Five, create that which brings freedom. Six, do not forget to love."

Ah. He was correct, then. I *would* have liked those people, very much. I find myself holding a hand over my heart as I listen, happy tears in the corners of my eyes.

"They sound very kind," I tell him with a soft smile.

"They were exceptional people," Six agrees with me. "It is my desire that I added to their culture. My notifications indicate I did, but the Between cannot be trusted."

I wince. He's not wrong. Sometimes notifications about influence or culture get muddled. Whatever is deciding on the names and value of our achievements sometimes has a weird view of what matters and doesn't seem to have a sense of scale or time frame. I once got a perk called Thousand-Year Tyrant for doing eight years of accounting work at a tech corporation. So either I honestly *did not* get the memo about what our screen lenses were doing, or else there was a miscommunication somewhere along the line in the Between.

"Were there any particular accomplishments you would like to share?" Jules asks politely, his soft accent hiding how much I know he loves learning about new potential areas to develop. Jules doesn't actually optimize or waste his time on things just for the prizes, but he likes the cataloging, I think.

"Nothing of note. We already knew about the Archaeology subset," Six states. "Due to the nature of my death, I have a new aura layer for Coherent Plasma Resistance, which I find novel."

"Ah, to live in a world with spaceships!" Jules sounds wistful. "I am ever born too early to explore the stars."

"You're also born too often with two legs," I add. "Not to needle you or anything. I just find it depressing. I wish we had a way to help with that."

"I am certain that one life I will find a favored form," Jules reassures me. "In the meantime, I reassure myself that I will ever return to this place, where I can enjoy *this*." He snakes a tentacle around behind me and taps me on the opposite shoulder, and despite hundreds of years of experience, I still look, by reflex.

"Damn it, Jules." I only barely try to keep my laughter in. Why resist it, when the whole point of being forever here is that we can express ourselves without fear or pain?

"So, what now?" Ellin asks as she too stands and stretches. Artificial or not, it still feels good to work those muscles. "Another game? Pool points and do a little shopping? Something else?"

It's good to see her relaxing. But despite the lack of aches around here, I do still have a semisocial need I require caretaking of. "Whatever it is, do it without me for a bit," I say, rising to my feet and balancing on Mark's shoulders. "I need some time alone. I'm gonna go read a book, see if we have anything I haven't read a dozen times."

"You know we absolutely don't," Mark states under me. "We should see if we can get an empty as a drop and put Six's scrolls on it."

"That would be a pleasant reminder," Six flatly states. "I have not yet finished processing my notifications. Perhaps one of them is a souvenir." He turns to me. "Enjoy your reading. Thank you for the time together."

"You say it like I'm banishing myself forever." I laugh as I head for the stairs.

I'm only here with them for a month. And yet, despite the limited time together, I cannot socialize solidly the entire time. It's not feasible, and I will go mad and find a way to kill one of them. Probably . . . Ellin? Not Six, at least.

So I take quiet time. Twenty thousand precious heartbeats spent sitting on the floor because fuck those chairs, my back against a sturdy bookshelf, everything narrowed down to the eternally worn and yellowed pages of the novel I'm reading.

I've read it before. I read it every time I'm here. It's about a spaceship captain and his alien boyfriend. It's absolute trash and I love it so much. For a couple of subjective hours, my reality is this story and nothing else. Abnegation through storytelling.

Much like sleep, it's a form of refresh for the soul. The consumption and exploration of art. Even though it's well-worn and lovingly read, it doesn't really get old. There's always more to explore, a way to get a little further into the author's thoughts, or a new angle on the themes from something I learned or experienced in the last life.

Sometimes this ruins stories for me. I've lived through traumas that have turned books I've enjoyed into nightmares as context unfurls. But often, it just lets me understand better.

Maybe that's what I'm here for. Understanding. Growing. Maybe that's what the Between is *for*, just a way to make us learn a little before our real deaths, if they ever come.

I'm not too worried. I'm busy mentally workshopping steamy erotica about these two characters, even as I'm reading about them surviving a crisis by sharing an air tank for the thirtieth time.

I'm almost at the end when I hear the door open downstairs. I don't stop though. If it's important, Jules will crawl up here and inform me. If it's not, I'll get to them when I get to them. My little decompression ritual is what I'm focused on right now, and really, I've got heartbeats to spare this time around.

Mark's voice calls a cheerful greeting to someone, and I smirk as I remember that he's playing bartender this time. Technically, Bastion's is a bar. Or a pub? I've lived so long, and I've never actually learned the difference between the two. I know we're not an inn, at least. No rooms and no beds.

The point is that it's not impossible for people to walk in and order a drink. We charge reasonable prices, and I like to think we're good company. You can literally get a drink for a song here. Well. A crystallized song. Or an actual playable song, if that exists! Or even just some sheet music.

I reach the end of my novel, completing my little ritual by reading off the publisher's information, author's biography, and advertisement for the next book in the series. I've never been to the world it was published on, the author has been dead for two thousand subjective years, and the sequel is *probably* not something I can put in an order for. It used to bother me. Just like it used to bother me that this is book three out of at least four, and I've never read books one and two.

After a long enough period of experiencing art in a weird way though, things tend to stop bothering me. It's not a frustration anymore; it's just a quirk of reality. It's a lot like my lives, really. I'm seeing a snapshot of creation, one way or another. I'm never there when it starts, and I'll be gone before it ends, unless I deeply fuck up. But that doesn't mean it isn't beautiful.

I wish that writing worked better in the Between, or that we had paper that wasn't disposable napkins. Because I would really like to commit my fan fiction to record. But I doubt the Between will let me lock that in, unless I've got points to spend and the right vendor to buy from.

With a grunt, I push myself up against the bookshelf, steadying myself on the old wood. The book slides back into its slot perfectly, the motion practiced over lifetimes. Idly, I acknowledge that there's a new notification for my having read the book this time around. I ignore it. It's at the bottom of my list, and I'm only a third of the way through my whole set of notifications.

I don't care right now. They can wait until later. For now, we have a guest. Or maybe two, judging by the voices Mark and Ellin are talking to. And meeting new people is always a fun time.

Maybe they'll have some new books. Or, failing that, some stories. If we're unlucky they'll be optimizers, but even then, we can just trade one of Mark's weirder drinks and send them on their way.

This place could use some life and vibrancy outside the five of us though. It's a little too big and too empty with just us. So I hold out hope.

That's all I ever can do, I guess. Hope and wait, and sometimes say something I think is poignant at the right time. We'll see which one of those tactics gets me a good outcome here.

CHAPTER SIX

"We seek perfection," the person on the left says. Their companion, positioned to their side and keeping a suspiciously specific set distance from them, nods.

It's not much as far as greetings go. Mark is pouring them shots from a bottle that I think gives you a bonus percentage to healing if you can take it without wincing, and I doubt they will. He rolls his eyes but doesn't comment as he flips the bottle over and slides it back onto the shelf behind him.

Jules and Six are discussing something a table away, though they're both clearly listening in. I think they're not especially interested in our newcomers but are willing to be surprised.

I size up the two potential optimizers. They're not quite identical, but they've got a shared style. Digitigrade legs, no shoes, clothing made out of a dozen banners and an equal number of belts that all dangle with charms and trinkets of varying descriptions. They've both got sashes with a pair of swords sticking out on their flanks. Fur too: mostly orange, bits of white on the cuffs and chest. I think their faces are vulpine, but I've only lived a few lives with access to things like libraries or infospheres, so I'm not sure if that's the right term or if it would be impolite.

"Hello," I say, trying to be friendly. "I'm Luri. I seek novelty, mostly."

"Ah, a hedonist." The older fox samurai nods at me knowingly. "You must yet be young."

I will not be answering that one. Instead, I just grin and signal Mark to add a third drink, moving past them to steal a barstool out from under their long snouts. "So, what kind of perfection?" I ask.

I'm not exactly expecting to be wowed by their answer, but I've been wrong before, and I still like talking.

The older one flicks his ears at me, and I don't know how to interpret that. "We wish to find the challenges of the Between and conquer them," he says. His words are stupid, which makes it kind of annoying that his voice is a rather sexy villainous rumble. "Distance, experience, violence, it does not matter. We seek to overcome this life and draw strength from the attempt."

"Sounds like fun," Mark says as he slides their drinks to either side of me, adding my own shot glass in the middle. "Find anything good yet?"

"The discovery is the first challenge," the younger fox says. I'm pretty sure they're male, but their voice is decidedly feminine. Nice combo, really. Though I'm obviously biased. "It would be no challenge if it did not require looking."

The two of them move around me, grabbing their drinks and downing them in a single motion. I do the same, the bitter flavor familiar to me. Watching both of them repress gags out of the corner of my eye is fun, though it might be mean that I take a certain amount of pleasure in denying them the bonus.

"That is *vile*," the older one growls.

"Yeah, that's . . . That's the point?" Mark shrugs. "You asked for a buff!"

"Think of it as a free challenge?" I suggest coyly.

"It's not free. I charged them." Mark flashes a pair of marks in his off hand. "No refunds, I think. I dunno. I'm not good at this one! Luri, do we do refunds?"

"You are the proprietor here?" the older fox asks, somewhat harshly. "Fascinating."

"It's more of a joint venture," I answer, keeping it friendly. "We pool resources to trade for odds and ends. Actually, speaking of, if you have any books on you, I'd be happy to help you with your seeking?"

The younger one slumps a bit, as the older fox shakes his head. "We do not carry extra weight or distractions. Our heartbeats are spent in constant pursuit of the discovery, and our lives are devoted to enlarging our time here in the Between, the source of reality."

My smile freezes on my face, though I do my best to keep the mask up. And my best is very good. I've heard this kind of rhetoric before. These are a different breed of optimizer, but I can read between the lines. "Ah. Well, so much for trade then," I say easily. "Unless you wanna buy some of our pile of Strikes off us. We have a *lot* of the things." Metaitems wouldn't weigh them down.

"Unneeded," the older fox says.

I nod. "Well, I dunno how many heartbeats you have left, but if you want, I've got a handful of books that give next-life buffs if you read them. I could rent one out to you, if you're a fast reader and have ten thousand beats to spare." I make the offer casually, making sure to downplay it. "They're not that impressive, but if you're not getting anywhere new this between, they can be handy."

His interest looks piqued; after all, he's the kind of person who bought the worst-tasting crap we have just for a chance at a single percent of advantage. It doesn't take much to haggle out a quick deal with him, and I set him up with a novel at one of the downstairs tables, making a casually false hidden show of faking a security system on the upstairs.

Specifically, at the table farthest from us at the bar.

A quick signal, flicked eyes and the click of a tongue, gets Six and Jules speaking slightly louder. When they wake Ellin and she joins them, it doesn't even require faking anything anymore. Not so loud as to be distracting to a reader, but loud enough to act as a barrier between him and my target.

"So, kid," I say, voice firm as I turn to the other fox still standing by the bar. "How many lives have you been following him?"

"Three," they say proudly, puffing out the white plume of fur on their chest. A riot of trinkets and charms rattles on their belts as they do so. Though less than their mentor. "I am lucky to have found him! He is guiding me through the nature of reality!"

"Uh-huh." I grimace, and Mark leans over the bar. We both motion for the kid to sit, and they give us a confused look before claiming one of the stools, fumbling with their tail. "You get used to that," I say, pointing to the limb. "After you've lived with one for a while. They had you change your whole body?"

"This is a more optimal form for exploration," they instantly answer. Like it's been drilled into them.

"How does this keep *happening*?" Mark asks me, sighing deeply.

"Charisma powers, mostly," I say. "The shittier kind that don't count as attacks. Attraction-based ones. I dunno. Did you hear how sexy that guy sounds?"

"Sure, I'd fuck his voice." Mark shrugs. "But he's a maniac, right? That's where this is going. I've been here long enough to see the signs, and you and Ellin talk about it."

The fox barks sharply at Mark. "Do not say that!" Their voice is shrill, but a quick glance shows their master isn't paying attention. "They have lived a thousand lives!"

"Doubtful," I say quietly. "Would you like to hear my evidence? You've lived at least three yourself. You should know the value of hearing someone out." They settle back, my calm tone easing their hackles down as they eye me suspiciously. "Alright. You're carrying artifacts from at least four different worlds, judging by art style, but half the stuff you have on you is vendor bought here in the Between. You look surprised by that, so I'll assume your master gave it to you. If you don't have an Identify or Analyze or Eye of Truth or something then you might not know, but a lot of that stuff isn't going to be doing you any favors. *That*"—I point to one in particular—"is a Friendship Charmer, which makes you slowly change your mind to like someone as long as you carry it willingly. So's that. So's that." I think they might have one on their back too but don't say it. "Your master is talking like he knows the nature of the Between, but everyone who actually learns anything about the Between *leaves*. You can feel it when they do. It's a whole event. Deeply unpleasant. Also, no one who has lived more than ten lives, who has a developed sense of interlude maturity, falls for getting separated from their apprentice so that a couple strangers can deprogram . . . them? Him? Her? Sorry, what pronouns for you? Hi, I'm Luri, by the way."

They stare at me with eyes filled with cunning and violence. Artificial, both of those things. It's not hard to feel the fear coming off them. The fear at admitting they were wrong, and at being fooled. Fear at being changed.

"You think I am being lied to. Taken advantage of." Their words are an incredulous yipping. Claws try to dig into the bar, but that's not how the Between works. You'd have to be *really* strong to make that happen, and I don't think they've got the stats. ". . . Why?"

"Why to which part?" Mark asks, setting a glass of orange juice in front of the fox, complete with a straw. I *know* I watched them both down a shot without problem, but muzzles make straws a lifestyle necessity at a certain point. "Why's he doing it?"

"Why are you telling me?"

"Oh. Because I've heard talk like his talk before," I say. I turn and stare at nothing in particular, my eyes just defocusing as I point them in the direction of the corner of the room and a spot where the wooden boards of the wall start to angle up to form the roof. "I've heard people talk about harvesting heartbeats. Especially people who walk around with swords on their hips, talking down to anyone spending quiet time with their families." My eyes meet the fox's. "He means genocide. Rack up kills, get those points, buy some more combat traits. Right? How many times have his instructions come back around to the idea that the other people on the worlds you live on aren't real? How often does he try to drill you on achievement lists that involve murder?"

"I . . . They are . . . reflections," the fox says. "That is the known philosophy of the Between." They find their spine and straighten up as their reply comes faster. "If the worlds are not reflections, then why do parts of them mirror what is found in the Between? Why are there so many of them, if they are not disposable parts of a greater machine?"

"Why do you assume the reflection is one-way?" Mark says, polishing a glass with the edge of his toga. For someone who doesn't know how to be a bartender, he sure is having fun with the image of it. "Come on, how many years on you now? You can think better than this."

"Well." I shrug and tap one of the toxic charms. "Maybe lose those."

"They help me accumulate achievement," the fox mutters, looking down at their bandolier. "They make me strong."

"Do you feel strong?" I ask them bluntly. "It took me a handful of sentences and a mild distraction to get your mentor out of the way, and your worldview has holes in it that you know will eat at you for a long time. Unless you do something about it, of course." A hand runs across the bar surface as I savor the sensation of texture in this favored form of mine. "I don't think words will turn *him* away from whatever nightmare he's making. But you? You look . . ."

I trail off, words suddenly catching in my throat. Mark picks up effortlessly where I stop, covering for my lapse as a memory collides with my rhetoric and throws me off my game. "You look too kind for this," he says for me. "You're wired to be angry, but we can tell that's running into what you're actually thinking. You could do anything. Don't do *this*."

"But . . ." The kid starts to say something, then looks sideways. It's not hard to detect the motion that newbies make on reflex when they automatically check all their notifications. "I don't understand," they whine. "Why? What does he gain from it?"

"Oh, no, kid." I wave a hand. "Don't think of this as material. We're in the Between; transactions here aren't the same as out in the worlds. He's not using you for wealth or power, even though he might get achievements for your actions if he influences you enough. He probably doesn't even think of it as *using* you, really. You've got Friendship Charmers on you because he wants you to be his friend, maybe more. And he's teaching you his philosophy because he probably legitimately believes it."

"Is his conviction not valuable?" the fox asks me, confused.

"His conviction says that he should treat people as points, as long as he can kill them fast enough," I remind them. "None of us here are unbloodied, but you tell me what that sounds like to you? Use that cunning you're told you're gifted with."

"How did you . . ."

"It's all reflections," I say with a twisted grin. "Which direction do the reflections go? Who knows. But you're wearing a reflected body and barking at the mirror."

Mark leans over the counter to me. "Luri, normally I go along with you, but that . . . That doesn't mean anything," he stage-whispers.

"Mark, please, I've only been dead for a day. Cut me some slack." I frown as I try to adjust his dragon-feather toga; his antics have it all bunched up around the shoulder. My attempt takes longer than I would have liked as I fumble with it and he just leans forward trying not to laugh, while our fox friend has an existential crisis next to me.

Eventually, the fox speaks again, staring down at the cup of juice they're trying to sink their clawed paws into. "What am I supposed to do?"

"Whatever you want," Mark and I say at the same time. I pick up the talk from there. "Ditch the charms, probably. And then just live. Be happy."

"Hedonism." The young fox snarls the word. "I was warned."

I don't smirk. That's the wrong move here. Conversations like this are like dueling someone atop a crumbling edifice. Limited time, and you need to make your strikes count. I have more experience with both than I'd like. "Yeah, sure. By whom?" I ask pointedly.

"But . . ." The word is sad. Pitiful, really. It represents a fork in their potential future; either they fall harder into the worst kind of optimizer philosophy, or they splinter off and find their own way. "I . . ."

"It's not like you have to be alone," I offer lightly. With any of my friends, I'd accompany the words with a hand on the arm or back, but I don't know this person, and I don't want to push them away. "You can always find us here in the Between. I can help you set up a door, if you want. Just stick around when he leaves and we'll sort it out. Either that or you can go your own way, and we'll help as much as we can."

"Why?" they ask as Ellin's laugh fills the rest of the room and I hear her putting Jules in a headlock of some kind behind me. "What do *you* gain?"

Mark laughs. "There's no gain, kiddo," he reminds them, glancing over at the older fox who is almost finished speed-reading the novel. "It's philosophy. Ours is that you shouldn't empty worlds of life just for a high score. And we want more people to follow it, so we talk to people like you when we get the chance." He shrugs. "You've got all the time you could ever want to get better. Why do it in the meanest way possible? Are you in a rush?"

"Yeah, take it slow. Reality isn't going anywhere," I say, spinning the shot glass in front of me under a fingertip. "I mean, as far as we know. Besides, not everything needs to be a stat buff to be *good*."

The fox stares down at the bar's counter silently, fingers clenching on the glass they still haven't moved. Heartbeats pass, and Mark and I pull back. Both of us have a lot of experience with this and know that this moment can't be forced. Only set up to tip the way we want.

After long enough that I start to worry the older one will finish and come ruin things, they start to move. Slowly, the fox leans forward and sticks the straw into their muzzle. Takes a sip of orange juice. Looks back up at us with eyes that have been redesigned to not cry. "This is delicious," they say.

"Right?" I ask, smiling.

"My name is Tenebral." They look down at the belts covering their chest and start plucking the offending charms off to set on the counter in a pile. As they remove the last one, a wave of confused relief washes over their face. "I . . . It is . . . I am glad to meet you, Luri and Mark."

Things move a little fast after that. We quickly figure out how to get Tenebral back to their return room and quietly pool marks with the others to afford a one-way one-use door for their next life to make it back to Bastion's if they choose. Some of the points come from their master renting the book he's reading, which I wish I could hose down with spiritual disinfectant after he's done with it, but that's not something I've ever discovered sadly. It's an amusing irony though.

The two of them leave together, with Tenebral having only forty thousand heartbeats left regardless. Their master never offers us a name and is already talking about achievements for things like multikills when the two of them walk out. From the master's perspective, Tenebral will simply never be seen again, and they won't know why. The odds they stumble back in here to cause trouble will be low. Bastion's isn't perfect, but nowhere in the Between invites hostility in.

"We're gonna need to get that kid a new body," Ellin says, grunting as she drops onto the barstool next to me. "Did you *see* those eyes? Oy. Fucked."

"I hope our interference was adequate," Six says, stepping to the curved end of the bar to stand and watch us. "And that the new one does not regress."

That's always the question, isn't it? Because it's possible we'll just never know. It's possible we just wasted a bunch of points for nothing, or got scammed. Or that Tenebral will just change their mind. Or be swept away by another philosophy of the Between.

In the end though, I would rather try and fail than do nothing.

There aren't really stakes here the way there are for mortals. For most people in the worlds we live in, there's always the looming shadow of death waiting as a fail state. Every idea, every policy, every philosophy, all of them can be measured against death. It's an endless eternal war; *does this*, as a tactic, kill us faster or slower? A question that can be asked over and over, often with no good answer. Or with no way to measure the results in a meaningful way.

And on the line is always the thinker's own life. You can't speak in a world and not participate; you're there too, with everyone else. Your ideas can backfire if not stated clearly, or they can attract the wrong kind of attention, or they can just suck and end up causing some kind of ecological disaster. So many things to go wrong, all of them moving the fail state closer and closer.

Here, in the Between, for *us*, it's different. We cannot die, no matter how much we might sometimes wish it. No matter how tired we are. The end is never. A word I often hate, but then just because I don't like something, that's never stopped it from being real.

So our philosophies have a different texture to them. We're playing a game, with the populations of whole worlds as the pieces, but we're not really in there with them. Death isn't real for us, and so the stakes don't quite feel the same.

Oh, if you have a heart, then it's no real change. For those of us that drink empathy like fine wine, there's very little difference. We still love and care for others; we have families and make friends and want the best for them. Just because we can't die doesn't mean we want our lovers to suffer.

And in the abstract, that extends to the broader philosophies here as well. We want people to thrive. And our enemy wants to hurt people.

We can't kill them. We don't know a way to be reborn to the same worlds and put up defenses. Although it is possible to hurt, debuff, cripple, or rob people in the Between, should you be willing to pay the cost, we have no real tools to *stop them*. Though by association, they can't do it to us either. And, while we're not exactly organized because of the way the Between works, our side works together a lot better.

Our battlefield is the minds of everyone we meet. And this is as close as I get to an act of faith. In an infinite reality, with an unending number of us being reborn, I think that our side can win. I think that we can put out more kindness than we take away.

"I think we'll see them again," I tell Six confidently, pocketing the stupid Friendship Charmers into my inventory to sell to a vendor later. "And you did great. Thanks."

"Anything you ask of us," Jules says, wrapping me in a tentacle hug. "Certainly if it means disrupting someone like that. I don't believe he was older than two or three lives himself, though how long they were is anyone's guess. He had the cadence of one of those sect elders. Perhaps that was his first life."

"Ugh. Immortals." Mark pulls a face. We all slowly turn and stare at him.

Even Six adds to our panorama of disbelief, though he does it with his usual flat expression. "What?" Mark asks. "I'm just saying. Have *you* ever met an immortal you didn't want to punch?"

Ellin spins her stool over to face me. "Luri, you're as old as I am. Can you get head trauma in the Between?"

"Apparently," I huff back. "Also *hey*, aren't you a pacifist?" I demand of Mark.

"I'm against killing," he says. "Immortals don't *die*, Luri."

"Then how do they get here?" Jules fails to realize he's making this entire situation worse by falling into Mark's mad antilogic. "Oh? Luri, are you alright? You seem unwell."

I groan out a muffled voice from where I've pulled the robe around my face and buried my head in my arms on the bar. "I'm fine. I'm just hiding until this stops," I say before throwing myself upward and taking a breath of cool air. "Okay, ignoring Mark. That went . . . okay. Yeah. I think that went okay." I look down as Mark slides my personal cup across to me. "What's this?" I ask.

"A toast," he tells me, flicking everyone else's cups to them. "To good luck, for our new mayhaps friend."

I smile, hope playing across my lips, as I raise my glass with the others and tap the rims together. We drink, and I regret it instantly, as *this* is surely the worst thing we have on offer here. But as the room goes back to feeling like just the five of us, and we return to sharing small stories of people we met last life or bizarre traits we've unlocked or setting up a game that we've been waiting decades to pick up again with each other, I relax into sipping at the wretched beverage anyway.

It tastes like kelp. I don't know why we have this.

CHAPTER SEVEN

The heartbeat counter in the Between *should* be a blur. Eighty beats a minute, assuming I'm calm, which I'm usually not, is more than a beat a second. Not so fast it's unreadable, but fast enough that any physical display would baffle the eye with how quickly it flicked through.

That's not how heartbeats work though. There is no motion to it, nothing to distract the eye or pull at the attention. It simply is the number you have remaining, and you know it.

This doesn't mean that it's easy to not hyperfixate on it. Far from it. Time is precious, free from life and among friends more so, and there is no stopping the beating of the heart. And despite knowing that every glance costs me another handful of heartbeats to the thought and the worry, I can't help but want to know how much longer I have.

I'm at least sixty lives old, and I'm still fidgeting with my clock as if looking will slow it down somehow.

Bastion's is warm, the air heavy, the lights pleasant on my skin. Jules is upstairs having a quiet moment with his art tree, some of his long tentacles draped over the edge running down the wood like black rubbery vines. At one of the tables Ellin and Mark are arguing over setup for the game of Encounter that we plan on continuing our stubborn multilifetime attempt at playing. Six and I are at the bar, listening in with a smile and Six's version of a smile.

The overdesigned, overambitious mess of a board game from a postscarcity world Mark lived on is the perfect operational example of why rustic and rural worlds all keep their games simple. In a land of steel and grit, every tavern will have one of two games: some permutation of combo-roll dice or a reinvented form of f'hai that they've renamed baccarat or king's tower or something. It's a social defense response because drunk patrons have a finite amount of mental space and a threshold for how much they are willing to gamble on games they might judge unfair.

Even in more developed worlds where free time becomes normal, the most popular games are still those that are easy to pick up, and often fit into standardized decks of cards or bags of chits. But while we have three decks of playing cards—one of them cursed!—lying around Bastion's, we don't tend toward those.

We're complex, messy, and traumatized people, and we like our shared fun to be the same way.

I still refuse to set up the table though. Currently Mark and Ellin are arguing about whether or not we should include the rules for anthropological diplomacy in the next round, and Six and I are avoiding engaging in *any* way aside from eavesdropping.

"It has been sixteen hundred and fifty heartbeats, adjusted," Six says to me as I fish around under the bar for a cutting board and a herb knife. The golem has almost finished processing his notifications from his last life and, as a reward from his Visitor to Many Cities pseudoquest perk, picked up a Chef's Herb Box, which is now sitting open on the counter as he pulls out cloth-wrapped parcels from it. "They are still talking."

"Talking is a really passive word for what they're doing," I point out as I thump the cutting board down on the bar and then stare at it, a thought nagging at the back of my head. "Do we . . . Is . . . Am I wasting time on this, Six?" I ask slowly, a suspicion clawing up my chest.

Six tilts his gray-skinned face at me. "I enjoy the experimentation of new flavors here. Oftentimes, mixing the various parts we draw from the worlds and the Between leads to unique combinations that we will only ever know here, together. I judge this worthwhile."

"No, I mean, a cutting board." I sigh.

"Proper tool use is a valuable habit and a sign of civilization," Six tells me. Then, like the slow grinding of a knowing machine, he looks down with circular eyes at the board and knife I've set next to his new herbs. With a slow curiosity, the golem reaches out, picks up the knife, and stabs it point first into the bar. "Ah," Six says as the nature of the Between prevents anything from actually happening. "I understand."

"Why do we even *have* a cutting board?" I run my hands down my back, scratching at the base of my tail. "How did this thing even get here, Six?"

"A strange reward. Perhaps it has some imbuement."

"Bah."

Six's words spark something hostile in me. I don't care about metaeffects. I just wanted to feel normal for a bit.

There are a variety of opinions on what the Between actually is. But personally, what I think is that it's a problem. Every death showers us with rewards and new toys for the next life. And how easy it is to take the words of the Between as gospel. Or, even more of a base need than that, to see the acknowledgment as endorsement.

Everyone wants to be recognized for their lives, to be told that they're worth something, to be reminded that they're seen and known. And for many people that I've met here, wandering through Bastion's in my time as one of its keepers, it's an almost welcome abnegation to replace their own search for meaning with accepting that the Between can provide it for them.

They're a benign form of optimizer. They aren't setting out to genocide populations or break worlds. But they've focused everything on filling up their notification logs when they get back. Death is a motivation, and life is just . . . a game.

I feel like it's important that I remind myself that these people aren't hollow shells just hunting for an artificial rush of joy. They're still people; no one is all one singular philosophy. We're all cracked pottery, wounds from hundreds of subjective years ago filled up with molten gold, souls made whole in ways they were never before. I've heard them tell stories of bizarre feats undertaken and truly impressive things they accomplished in record short lives.

But I very rarely hear them talk about friends. About love. Or even about rivalry, or hated foes. They have no support, and no true opponents. People might acknowledge them while they're alive, but the Between will gift them tangible powers that will last *forever*. And they've chosen what to prioritize.

This is why I don't focus on the boosts from reading my books or stomaching Mark's weird drink choices. This is why I'm annoyed that we have this possibly magic cutting board.

Six isn't quite the same as me. Six is practical, and not just because he was born a golem. The golem has an outlook that tools should be used, and that there's nothing wrong with putting our talents to work. And, in general, I *do* agree. I'm still glaring at the cutting board though.

But I already have it out, and I'm just going to not identify it and hope that it's normal. Even though I'm still suspicious of where it came from. I take a sample from the first packet of a fresh leafy herb Six holds out to me and start chopping it into thin strips. An aromatic, almost sweet tang emerges into the air. "Ooh, I like this," I say.

"Perhaps a good addition to a fruit wine," Six suggests.

"We don't have any fruit wine, since the barrel emptied and despawned." I flick my tail while I place one hand on my cocked hip and look around the back of the bar. My eyes land on one of the spouts, and I process the reading it puts into my head. "We've still got four thousand gallons of lemonade?"

"Let us attempt." Six starts setting up a row of shot glasses, reaching over to fill half of them with water and adding bits of the chopped leaf to two of them. On my side, I grab an *entirely mundane* wooden pitcher and use that to pour, not trusting myself to not screw up the pressure from the spigot. Six and I both raise our samples at the same time, clinking the glasses before drinking. I sip and savor, while he seems to suck the whole thing in at once, even though I know he takes his time processing the flavor.

"It's . . . Uh . . ." I look down at the empty glass. "You know, I kind of expected that to taste like something more than just lemonade?"

"Perhaps it needs to steep for the flavors to mix," Six suggests. "Do we have bottles?"

"No, the empties all vanished. I think the Between wants us to recycle." I frown, chewing on a bit of the leaf stuck in my mouth. "Oh, that's pretty good," I mutter. "Yeah, it's just not mixed very well. This would actually go great with a berry or something, you're right."

"Have you finalized your notification log, Luri?" Six asks me as politely as he ever is with the dull voice he keeps around as a memento. "Perhaps you could find some."

I shrug. "I've got some I don't wanna think about," I tell him. "So I'm waiting. And I don't think I have any pseudoquests."

The golem nods at me. "If you wish to speak, I am here for you," he says, and I smile at the words. Six is a good listener. Has been ever since I met him here. As we talk, he makes another pair of samples of our herb lemonade and sets them aside to wait.

I drink some water to wash my tongue as I take a sample of some kind of thin twig with spiky green bits coming off it. "I'm just being me," I tell him. "Worried that the Between will reward me for something I hate and change how I look at it."

"Luri, no one would ever properly accuse you of allowing your views to be influenced by the nature of our lives," Six points out as I sniff at the herb and cock an eyebrow at the almost *slimy* feeling of the earthy scent. "There is no fault in accepting your actions."

I set the herb down, my hand crushing it slightly into the wooden board as I lean forward heavily, staring down at the backs of my hands. "But there's fault in what I did," I whisper. "And there's guilt that I lived through it. That I'm here with you all, having a good time, while everyone else . . ." I trail off, something tingling against the skin of my palm.

"And?" Six asks.

"And what, Six? And why do I feel bad for my fuckups?" I snap. But there is no real heat to my words, just worn discomfort.

"No, I am aware of your thoughts on personal failure. I am wondering why you are upset that you continue to exist." Six slides the herb box a little farther away as he finishes parceling out wrapped cloth onto the bar. "You should not be surprised."

The words, so blunt and monotone, drag a sudden laugh out of me. I've known Six a while, but it's still too easy, with his voice and appearance, to forget that he's a fully realized person with a deep capacity to strike emotional blows when he chooses.

I collect my thoughts before I answer, pushing the crushed herb away and wiping my hand on the rear of my new bathrobe. "The thing is, there's no way to avoid thinking about things once you're aware of them. Not for me." I glance up at Six, meeting his ring eyes. "I'm no monk, Six. Even the time I was a literal monk. I've never been good at mediation or inner worlding or the . . . the thing with trying to think things hard enough that reality conforms to you."

"Magic."

"No, the other one. The one on mundane worlds."

"Faith."

"The nonreligious one."

"Manifestation."

"Yeah, that! I can't make myself believe things or overwrite my own thoughts as easily as some people can. I can't *turn off* a thought once it starts. I'm always acutely aware that I'm being influenced by propaganda."

Six drums two fingers on the bar top to punctuate his words, his motions never simply idle fidgeting. "And yet you are less affected than someone who is unaware," he says. "That is my point. It is obvious you would be affected by things within your sphere of knowledge. You are a deeply empathic person, who cares about everything you are capable of. This does not make that influence negative. You were the one who told me, two hundred and four subjective days in the Between ago, that even experiences you hate are valuable, if you can learn from them."

"Don't quote me at me," I grumble, stacking shot glasses as I lie myself across the bar and listen. "I'm clearly a terrible choice to listen to and be influenced by."

"I think you are often the only person in the Between who makes any sense," Six says bluntly. "We are set up like pieces in a game. And you are the only one I have met, aside from the others who also listen to you, who has suggested that we remove ourselves from the board and take the role of spectators."

I poke one of the shot glasses off my pyramid, the glass hitting the wood of the bar with a ringing impact that would have made me flinch if I didn't know that it wasn't going to break. "I worry when you use metaphor, Six."

"Desperate times call for desperate measures," the golem deadpans at me.

I snort. "You're not asking me to be a spectator though. You're asking me to play the game. To open the notifications and treat it like it's just a big machine to turn suffering into *fabulous prizes*. That's not sitting on the sidelines."

"This metaphor has broken down," Six admits. "And I will not be continuing it. What I am trying to convince you of is that your notifications are nothing new. You already know what you have done. They can only make you hurt by making you remember." He pauses, ever so briefly. "My own refreshed memories often hurt me. Especially those about loss."

". . . And?" I prompt, waiting for the end of that point. "You're doing a bad job comforting."

"It's not comfortable," Six says. "Pain is pain. But we are very good at enduring it. It is one of the skills we carry with us here."

I look up at him, confident round eyes looking back at me from his symmetrical gray face. It's hard not to agree; I'm *very* good at enduring. I've been doing it for a while.

But a lot of it happens in real lives, on worlds where I often feel like I am insulated from pain. Here is the place I mean to retreat to, where I can hide from it all and rejuvenate myself before stepping back into the arena. Here is not where I wish to be vulnerable.

Ah, but when do we ever get what we wish?

"Alright, I'll check the dumb notifications," I mutter. "I mean, I was going to anyway. Just not right now. Because there still won't be fruit in there."

"There is no pressure from me." Six sets his hands palms up on the bar, and I fold my fingers into them. His skin is room temperature and almost frictionless. "We have quite a bit of time here."

Never enough though. In my opinion. A subjective month this time, give or take. And with the lack of real need for things like sleep or food except for pleasure, that time stretches out. And we *will* have more time. There's always more. But the limits make it all feel so hard-fought and caged up.

I think what scares me most is that I can understand some of the optimizer mindset. I can understand wanting to do great things, to buy more heartbeats with our actions. I can easily see myself burning half my time here just to make it easier to get more of what I've spent.

It wouldn't even be that hard. But this is the mindset that our group rejects. Oh, we read our notifications, and we expand Bastion's and add our own flourishes to it, and we slot in traits and perks and aura layers and a dozen other nonsense words. And when we live, we live our best lives, knowing that we can do so without fear for ourselves.

But why rush?

The days are like water. And so long as we don't drown, none of us will *ever* be thirsty.

"Are Mark and Ellin done with setup?" I ask, derailing the conversation.

Six accepts it without comment. "No, though they *are* through arguing. What are your thoughts for this?" He sniffs at the crushed herb.

I give my own hand an experimental nose myself. "Eugh. Nothing we drink," I say. It's still tingling. "Maybe a rub for some kind of bird meat? But we don't have anything left to eat. It's been a long time since we've seen a vendor of any description come through."

We go back to our quiet task of sampling herbs, trying to decide if any of them would go well with anything we happen to have. The lemonade turns out really good after it's had time to sit for a while, though I think it would be better if it could be bottled and shaken, which makes me remember that we *do* have a mixer, and I start preparing some to share with the others. Six at some point starts an explanation of a fermentation process he wishes to try with something else from the box, but for that we're going to need a barrel, about eight different ingredients we don't have, and for time to actually pass in the Between when we're not here.

It actually might. It's never clear to me if Bastion's experiences time. Entropy is certainly on pause for many things; dust doesn't collect, books don't yellow, food doesn't go bad. Though I have a reasonable confidence that we *could* brew something given enough time. None of the clocks I've ever had worked when *I* wasn't here though, and that's really all I had to go on.

I sold the clocks for a bookshelf a long time ago. Though maybe it was only a subjective year ago, as far as the Between is concerned. Somewhere between one and five thousand years, at any rate.

I open a few more notifications as Six folds up his herb box and puts it under the counter to regenerate for later. Simple things, about training a new body up to certain skill levels, or odd world-specific things like bonding with a certain number of dogs. Every world has its own hidden things that it prioritizes. If there's a pattern, I haven't found it yet, but then, it's not *my* priority anyway.

Mostly I'm trying to psych myself up to open the big ones. The ones that hum with odd colors and grim textures. The things that I know are going to tell me that I did an *excellent job* altering the course of an entire kingdom or something. Such a good Luri, you were in the right place at the right time, and your bad decision was *impressively* terrible. So impressive it deserves its own special perk.

I don't get there before Mark and Ellin start shouting for us, and I let go of the grim feeling of personal failure to instead take hold of a pitcher of herb-dosed lemonade and join them. Jules drops off the ledge of the upstairs and hits the ground in a pile of tentacles. Mark asks if I'm okay when I sit, so there must be something written on my face as I leave the lemonade on a nearby table.

But this time, I think he's actually reading too far into it. Six is right. Pain is pain, and there's no getting around that. But I'll have all the time with these people to heal. From every wound I'll keep taking to my heart, I will have time to recover.

I settle in as Jules and Mark do a kind of board game duet, reading off the narrative and rules of this specific scenario we're playing. Fiddling with my cards, knowing I can flick them to my heart's content and cause no damage except to the emotions of Ellin who is glaring at me with a narrow-eyed stare from across the table. It's the principle of the thing to her.

As we start to play, trading small bits of conversation while we take our turns and advance a growing plot that I'm never actually sure if this game is generating on the fly or not, I relax. Not just the relaxing that I feel when I get here, when I wake up, or when I first fall into my friends' hugs. Those are all good. There's also the relaxing of the break in tension when someone I don't like leaves the room, which is less good and more just that it's an end to something bad. But this is deeper.

If the days are like water, then this is surfing.

We have friends, drinks, a board game designed by people who had a few centuries of free time, and no need to get up to use the bathroom. And it is here that I can finally stop looking at my heartbeat counter. That I can ride the waves with my companions and let myself be *lost* here.

The game lasts for hundreds of thousands of heartbeats. But I wouldn't call it subjective days. Instead, I call it what it is: a perfect fluid moment with people I love. One singular point in my life that happens to have expanded to encompass several hundred turns, three rounds of deck construction, and a story about alien first contact where I am *pretty sure* our multitude of characters are the good guys. I think.

It's hard to tell, since Ellin cheats a little bit.

On the side of the *cooperative* game. *Against us.*

But even that is simply part of the moment. It is part of the growing story of my immortality, the life that stretches on and on and on with no end in sight. But none of my lives have ever needed an ending to give them value, just like they don't need the notifications to give them meaning.

We share stories of people we met a single time in each of our last lives. The small snapshots and guesses as to who someone was, added like popcorn to our experience. We talk, we play, we laugh.

We are, together, alive.

There will always be a part of me that resents that I do not have a choice. But if I did, I do not think I would want to trade this for anything.

CHAPTER EIGHT

Mark and Jules are sitting across from each other at the main table, eyes narrowed. Mark's into soft almonds that blink on reflex, Jules's into flattened red diamonds.

I'm not actually sure about most of the details of Jules's body here. Are his eyes even *eyes*, or just convenient illumination on the flexible black skin he wears? Jules spends a huge chunk of his spare points trading for form adjustments or body modifications, and at this point, I'm not even sure if even he knows everything about what he is here in the Between.

The two of them have been thinking for two hundred heartbeats, and I'm in the process of waiting for Ellin to lean into me and whisper that we should leave them alone to their weird game when Mark raises a finger up to tap at his nose and speaks.

"Okay. Okay, here's one. It is early morning. You have ten minutes before you have to leave the house. You have eaten an oat-and-fruit bar but have nothing to wash it down with except cold water. The light through the windows is gray, you haven't put on socks yet, and you are standing alone on a hardwood floor in a house that doesn't feel like *yours* anymore."

"Hist's shit, Mark." Ellin's words are a huffed breath of surprise.

Six folds his arms and approximates a glower. "I had assumed we were friends."

I say nothing. I'm busy trying to rebuild the mental walls that were previously keeping a few lifetimes of the experience of primary school at bay. Mark's words acting like something between a scalpel and a siege cannon to open up wounds I didn't even know I was holding shut.

I can *fucking taste what he described.* Forget trying to convince people with optimism and hope to engage with their lives as things of value and joy. I'm just gonna get Mark to craft me more memetic weapons like that and go around trying to lobotomize anyone who slights me.

Jules doesn't say anything, but he does roil a pair of his moving tentacles in an undulating motion that makes me think he's doing his version of biting his tongue. Instead, he spends a hundred heartbeats studying Mark's gambling face and humming to himself. When he speaks, he draws the word out like he's suspicious of his own thoughts. "Ffffffour. Four? Four." Jules loops his tentacles over the table. "Yes. Four lives."

"*Damn it!*" Mark throws his hands up. "How do you *do that*?!" His question isn't so much a demand as it is an incredulous burst of disbelief. "We've known each other for, what, a subjective two or three years now, in all total? *Tell me your secrets, you goddamn French octopus!*"

"He's not going to tell you." Six's, Ellin's, and my own words all overlap, a triple echo of the same intent with different levels of delighted humor to each of our voices.

"It is a trade secret, my good friend." Jules polishes his rubbery skin with a curled tentacle, eyes slanted up in satisfaction that somehow doesn't seem smug. "And really, I couldn't simply tell you. That would steal away the deepest satisfaction of discovering for yourself! After all, it isn't as though you lack the time to learn."

"I'm gonna run out of heartbeats sooner or later," Mark says, and I see his eyes flick *away* from where I know his counter is; he refuses to look at it as often as he can when he catches himself.

I smirk, covering my mouth with the rim of the mug I'm sipping from. "You'll be back," I remind him. "Hone your skills out there in the worlds! Give Jules a run for his money the next time we're all here!"

"Oh, that reminds me. Do pay up, friend." Jules wobbles his central body back and forth as he unfurls a tentacle. Mark grumbles and makes a show of pursing his lips and scowling, but the man is fundamentally incapable of actually being mad at anyone. He pulls a metaitem out and drops something that looks like a weird iteration of a Brachiation into Jules's waiting limb. "Thank you, thank you, and of course, I am *always* willing to play again!"

"Luri, *how*, exactly, am I supposed to learn how to guess how many lives an experience is from when I'm alive?" Mark turns on me as he closes off his inventory. "Wait, actually, I forgot to ask since we got sidetracked for a week there! Did anyone meet another of us? Like . . . out?"

A subdued quiet comes down, and we all shake our heads. Or vibrate a no, in Jules's case.

We don't have a lot of overall goals as a group. If we did, we'd probably be a little more organized than just throwing points into the pot to restock the bar and filling our shelves with board games we liked from past lives. We might even have some kind of *group name*, if we weren't careful.

But we do have a few things we're aiming for. Gradually, bit by bit. Things we're on the lookout for, or prepared to take chances on. Beyond just the way we like to live our lives on the worlds we get tossed into.

Contact with real divinity, if it's out there. Similarly, looking for life outside the worlds we're born on; sometimes you'll get an inhabited moon, or another world around the same sun, but never anything extrasolar, so we're curious and keep our eyes peeled. Any *other* gaps in reality, like the Between, or maybe some kind of way to jump between worlds.

And most importantly, and a little bit related to that last one, we're looking for others like us.

Reincarnators, or transmigrators, or externals, eternals, immortals, endless, whatever. The five of us can't even agree on what our designation is, which I suppose is good news for the part of me that doesn't want us to give our social circle a name. We'd spend a subjective week arguing and then get distracted and forget.

The point is we look for others like us on worlds we land on.

We've never found anyone else, so we can't claim to have a working strategy. But we keep trying. Looking for people who are a little too good at things, or motivated in bizarrely specific ways. People who sometimes say things that just don't make sense. None of the leads have ever turned up an actual person like us, and it's not as if there's some force that keeps us from talking about our experience in the Between when we're alive. Usually it's just someone vaguely neurodivergent, or with a great sense of timing, or really lucky. Once it was a serial killer, for me.

Actually, that one was doubly disappointing. I'd thought I'd run across an optimizer getting started on trying to rack up Murderer or Butcher of Kin achievements, and I'd spent a while planning out how to intercept and take them down. Only to learn that I was up against a much more mundane monster and that the average human on that world lacked the capability to simply walk off an alpha strike that involved commercial-grade demolition equipment.

The main reason we're looking is because . . . because it gets lonely. Admitting it sometimes hurts because it feels like it gives a bit of power to the almost cosmic despair that we're constantly trying to fight back. But there is no shame in accepting it; it doesn't take more than five or ten lives before you start to realize that you're growing past what anyone you meet will ever really get to know. You can have friends and loves, family and foes, but there's going to be a bit of a barrier when you would need to spend years just to catch them up on things you've done and then have to *leave them* when you die.

Not even death, actually. Sometimes people just get separated. Circumstances pull you in different directions geographically, and you end up not talking to a person you knew for a while. Which does deeply suck, yes, but it's a bit worse when the more time passes, the more it feels like the people we meet in our worlds will *never* actually understand the whole of us.

Here, sitting in Bastion's, in the Between, the five of us have spent a billion heartbeats apiece just talking about our lives. *All* of them. We've shared triumphs and failures, we're there for each other after every painful ending, we're here for each other before every new beginning. We treat anecdotes like pretzels to go with a good board game, and we have no limits on learning about each other and absorbing the whole of who we all are.

I know these people better than I knew my thousand-year father during one of my technically immortal lives. I know why Six keeps his affectations in speech and appearance, and I know how many times he's been married and the name of every child he's left behind. I know about Jules's near-constant body dysphoria in a way that only sharing hundreds of softly spoken pieces of poetry can accomplish. I know the source of Ellin's comical hypocrisy, and I know how to crack it with a small touch to the right part of her body. I know what Mark's first name was and why he shuns it so utterly. I know how proficient all of them are as kissers.

When I'm with them, I am not *alone*. Because as much as I have fun pretending otherwise sometimes, I know they know just as much about me.

And in . . . I check before I can stop myself . . . In a little under nine hundred thousand heartbeats, I'll be gone, and they'll be somewhere else, and I'll be *alone again*, no matter how many mortals surround me.

So yeah. We spend some time searching for people like us. Because if it happens even once, that means it could happen again. And if it can happen again, then perhaps we can make it happen.

It doesn't really matter how many lives I go through. I've never really wanted to be isolated. Maybe that'll change in the future. I doubt it, but then, I've been wrong before.

"Well, this got fucking depressing," Ellin comments, shaking me from my thoughts. "Thanks, Mark!"

"I'm about where I was before, really," he replies. "Still reeling from being laser-targeted by Jules over there."

I smile as I stand up and stretch, enjoying the feeling of my body moving with no pain. Last life had a lot of aches buried deep in the bones, and this is a delightful reprieve before I go out and get back pain all over again. "Jules is both wise and powerful." I snicker to myself.

"You've been saying that for ten lives now," Six comments flatly. "Is there a reason?"

"I heard it a lot from a . . . friend? I think? And it stuck in my brain." An emotional ache slips in as I realize I cannot remember whom it came from, or if I could pick their face out of a crowd. "It amuses me!" I don't let it drag me down. All language is a memorial to the dead, and this is no different. Except that it's a little more personal.

"You only say it about Jules or Ellin though," Mark protests as he starts clearing away this round of cups to take back to the bar. "Am *I* not wise and terrible?"

"Wise and powerful," Six corrects automatically. "And no, you do not qualify. I regret that I am the one to inform you of this."

"What?!" He looks at me with his puppy dog eyes. "Luri! Six is bullying me!"

I nod sagely. "This is why you're not powerful," I tell him, patting Mark on the chiseled muscle of his upper arm as he grumbles with good-natured humor, playing the straight man to our jokes while we clean up.

I'm about to ask what we're up to next when the sound of a door opening and the roar of moving air interrupts us. A handful of cards from the top of one of the stacked decks we left on the table flutter away, only to be snatched out of the air by Ellin's deft fingers, while on the other side of Bastion's, a woman steps in.

She's six feet tall, rail thin, with a face that looks like it was sliced from a gemstone and then given living flesh as an afterthought. Ears like throwing knives sticking up on either side of her head. She's wearing armor and has a bow slung at her side, and every part of that is irrelevant to the look of utter exhaustion on her face.

The sad elf looks around Bastion's with a muted spark of curiosity in her eyes before landing on the five of us. Her hand goes to her bow like she's preparing for a fight, but none of us really have an interest in allowing for one, so it just won't work anyway.

"Welcome in," Mark says with an almost unreasonably perfect nod that would make him fought over to hire in a high dining establishment. "Have a seat. You're safe here. Someone will be with you shortly," he adds as he passes by and takes our assorted cups and things behind the bar.

Well, it's only fair he pawn the job off on one of us. He *did* say he'd be playing bartender this time, but that means we need someone to be a serving wench, I suppose. All good taverns need one, and I make sure my bathrobe is secured before I go to fill the role. This isn't *that* sort of tavern. Yet. Not until Ellin caves to my suggestions and we can tip the majority vote.

"Hey there," I say, sliding up to the smaller table as the elf sits herself down. All our stuff is mismatched, and this one is no exception. A pale white wood surface, but with a flourishing base of wrought metal that makes the thing a pain to move. We keep it off to the side so we don't have to think about it, and it's where she's chosen to sit. Far from everything, and a little bit obscured from the view upstairs. It's where I'd sit if I were nervous too. "What do you fancy today?"

". . . You have a tail," she says, which isn't a drink order, but okay.

I look behind me, seeing the scaled limb poking out from under my robe. "Huh. So I do." I flash her a smile. "I've got lots of appendages, really."

"What are you?"

"I'm Luri. Pleased to meet you." I sketch a bow at her. The sad elf is not amused. But that's okay. A lot of our guests aren't interested in my jokes, and so my jokes are mostly for me, not them. But I do take pity on her. "I'm a Between modified human, and I'm generally friendly."

"Is that what this place is? Between?" She looks around at the walls of Bastion's, mostly staring up at the turboprop engine slowly spinning and providing airflow.

"No. This is Bastion's. The Between is . . . this whole place. Have you been here before? Not to our little spot, but . . ." I give her a curious look. "Have you died before?"

"I think so," she says, setting her bow on the table and looking down at her own hands. "I thought it was all a long dream." Her words are a mutter.

I take pity on her. "How about I get you a lemonade and you can have the table for as long as you need," I say. "You don't need it, but, well, it looks like you need it."

"I . . . I died," she says, looking up at me with eyes like cut emeralds. "Yes. I would like a . . . lemonade?"

"Coming right up." I move away and hear her behind me as she begins to repeat back the notifications she has started to open up. Kill and survival and lifespan achievements rolling in as she either doesn't realize she's speaking or doesn't care to hide it. When I make it to the bar, Mark already has a pitcher for me. "She's not exactly new, but she's confused. Elf things." I shrug, but there's a sadness in my voice.

Elves tend to live a very long time. If someone's first life is as an elf, it can take them several lives afterward before their mind in the Between catches up to the fact that they *aren't* just having a strange nap.

"I don't wanna charge her," Mark says.

"No, no, we should," Ellin says, reclaiming a barstool near us. "I remember being that way. It's hard, but you need something to focus on. Look, she's still got her bow. She's got the marks for it. It'll help ground her."

Ellin doesn't offer personal insight like this very often, but when she does, I tend to trust her. It also matches what I sort of knew about how elves start out in the Between, so it isn't like she has to work to convince me. I take the pitcher and a thin glass cup over and get ten points back in payment from a woman who blinks at me before paying but doesn't complain. Ellin's right. It does seem to ground her; her eyes are a little more active as she takes a sip and puckers her mouth at the taste.

"She's barely awake." I sigh when I return to Mark. "I hope she'll be okay."

"All we can do is be here if she wants to talk." He returns the sigh. "Also, that's two wanders this cycle. Are we getting busier, or is it just—"

Whatever he is about to say is cut off by another door opening, this one on the other side of the room, so they have a nice view of the bar and the glass shelves behind it as they enter. The soft smell of artificial pine comes in with the new arrivals: a pair of boys who could easily be twins. But around here in the Between are almost certainly something weirder.

They take seats at the bar like they've been here a million times, order something strong, and pay up in Placement Firmament, which is an unexpected boon to our ability to keep the place going. Not that we were short on anything we actually needed for Bastion's, but there's a certain satisfaction to knowing it'll be around for ten lives and not just three if we have to abandon the place.

The twins drink and talk with one voice as they try to convince Mark and Ellin to convert to their religion of being the same person. They're a bizarre form of optimizer: looking for the ultimate *personality* as opposed to the ultimate set of Between-given rewards and upgrades. I bail out of that one to check on the elf and fail to be surprised when yet another door opens.

Usually, the five of us are enough to attract one. But they come faster when we have guests, so I think they show up to gatherings quicker when you have more people. The thing that comes through the door is a vendor, and the door isn't really the same as most Between doors. It's not for *us*; it's for something halfway between a natural force and an administrator.

There's a million and one things that you can convert your rewards into in the Between, but a sizable portion of them aren't available options just from the natural menus and selections that you have on your own. Vendors have seemingly random inventories of a variety of nonsense, both upgrades for our next lives and creature comforts to stock the Between with, and more besides. This one is shaped like a hateful nautilus mixed with a metal lamp, and has roughly a hundred thousand things on offer. Not that I'm actually counting.

At the bar, Mark pours most of his drops and marks into Ellin's hands as she rushes to join the rest of us approaching the thing and flicking open its shop window. Vendors rarely stick around for long, and we form a plan of attack as we approach.

I find myself assigned to looking through furniture, scrolling through overpriced lists of beds looking for something that we can put upstairs without bankrupting ourselves. Here's one that gives a bonus to agility perks for each heartbeat slept in it; here's one that gives a weird per-life ability to inflict crippling orgasms on a target for each sleep. Both of these sound great, and cost more than I make in five lifetimes. I'm just looking for something that will let us sleep without having to have Six reassemble a hammock every cycle.

"I've got a room here!" Ellin says excitedly. "Space addition, it's affordable, and—" She cuts herself off and swears, and I know she's found some stupid drawback. "Never mind, I saw the number two and didn't realize the cost was in true achievement."

I wince. We have precious little of that right now. I keep up my search, not knowing how long the vendor will be here. Something catches my eye as I frantically put to use all the speed-reading tricks I've learned in my lives; nestled here in the section that's sort of furniture, a two-by-two stack of barrels. It's listed as a Between decoration, and tether equipable.

Equipable items are the kinds of things you can take into a world with you. Somehow. Either they'll show up like you're destined for them, or you can summon them, or something like that. Most weapons here, like the elf's bow, are usually equipable. *Barrels* were not what I was expecting. *Tether* equipable means that the item is almost like a part of you, and a whole lot of weird things that apply to you, like your auras, overlap onto it. They're as rare as any of the weird things here can be, but I've never seen one this cheap.

But we *were* thinking of doing some home brewing. I don't know if they'll work, but it can't hurt, and it costs me basically nothing. I shove thirty marks of labor at the vendor and give an exasperated grunt as the creature raises an arc of burning wrought iron to drop a small shelf with four heavy wooden barrels on it directly onto our floor with a loud thud.

I keep searching, but the vendor isn't staying for long, and following it as it drifts toward the far side of Bastion's and then pops open one of its weird doors to slip out doesn't actually buy me the time I need to get anything else.

"Dang. No bed." I sigh. "You two get anything good?"

"I have acquired sixteen bottles of something that is labeled as Mockery Spark Wine. It is my estimation that this will advance our experimental tests to see if we can die of alcohol poisoning in the Between," Six says. Six's jokes are my favorite.

Jules doesn't have anything and seems down about it. We all reassure him that it's fine, and we'll have more chances, before Ellin gives her own answer. Ellin picked up a perk. We'll have to figure out who to pass it off to. Garden Retrieval is a pseudoquest, and it lets us generate half-alive plants here in the Between if we satisfy its requirements while we live.

It's been so long since we've had a splash of life here. She's embarrassed at the cost, but Jules and I put that to rest quickly. Jules's new bonsai tree is cute already, and I can't wait to spend some lives accruing more tiny little bits of greenery to add to our home.

Our home. That thought that I'd been kind of avoiding. I think I said it out loud, going off how Six and Ellin are looking at me. "Yeah." I add to the words I spoke without realizing. "Well. It is. Maybe we should stop pretending. Maybe it's not forever. But Bastion's is home right now."

Ellin wraps me in a hug before we head back to rescue Mark from where he's learning about a religious schism in a group of voluntary copies and begging us with his eyes to save him. Jules asks how I plan to move my own acquisition of furniture, and I suggest handing it off to Six to equip and see if whatever he brews in his next life he can bring back.

I make sure our new visitor is doing okay with her lemonade too. She's confused, and I think she was about to try to shoot the vendor. But she likes the drink and is thankful to me.

I offer her a smile and a warm hand to hold. She tells me her heartbeats are running out in a voice that says she doesn't know what that means or where she is, and I tell her she hasn't got anything to worry about in a voice I hope calms her down. I want her to be okay, and I make a wish that we'll see her again.

It's strange. You'd think that hope would be in short supply around here. But as I watch while Mark fails the most important role of bartender, which is to know how to kick people *out* of the bar when they won't stop preaching, I find my spirits high. And my supply of hope, which I admit ebbs and flows, grows to match what I need.

Still haven't found a bed though. But I suppose I've got enough hope to cover that too.

CHAPTER NINE

don't think they're optimizers. Not the way you mean it, Luri." Mark sighs as the five of us relax in the empty-again space of Bastion's. We're not anywhere in particular or doing anything special, just lounging around and talking.

Rushing to try to compact as much time together as possible into our heartbeats just makes us resent it. We've tried before. It's not worth it to us. We'll feel like drunkenly sharing songs or playing more cards later. Right now, it's a casual conversation, while Jules naps and snores with an odd whine of a vibration that is . . . more pleasant to experience than it should be.

"I do love how I keep getting surprised," I admit to Mark. "I mean, we've all met other people here in the Between. This is just the first time we've met the same person twice at the same time."

"They aren't *really* the same person," Ellin mutters into her cup of wine. I don't know where she found it under the bar, but she doesn't seem to be enjoying it at all, which makes me wonder why she's drinking it in the first place. "They're just faking it."

I shrug, pulling my tail up to hold it in my lap and scratch at an itch where one of the plates meets the scales. "Does it matter? They've got forever to get it right. Sooner or later they'll find their unity."

"Their unity is unsettling," Six monotones, sniffing his portion of the wine Ellin offered to share with him and carefully setting it back on the counter. "Why children?"

Mark perks up. "Oh, I did ask that! They said it was metaphorical of our place in the cosmic . . . thing. That we're all children taking our first steps, in the grand scheme of affairs."

"Ah, yes, a perfectly normal claim that we have an easy way to verify," Six says.

I just roll my eyes. I've heard all of this before in half the real lives I've lived. It seems like the common language of religion persists here in the Between.

Not that I'm surprised; it's certainly comfortable. Having an abstract goal that you can aim for that will give you a perfect final reward, and making that reward something intentionally unspecified and outside your understanding so you never have to think about it, is just . . . It sounds nice?

I'm not even trying to be sarcastic or dismissive. It really does just sound pleasant. If I thought that I could manage to do it myself, and not have some kind of emotional breakdown after a few lives, I might even try it. But I don't actually believe it, and I think forcing myself to change how I think would cause worse long-term damage when I start questioning it later.

I've done it before. Not for a faith, but still. It wasn't great. While I hold no belief that people are immutable, I didn't really change my core self, and it was like there were two versions of me constantly having a fight in my thoughts.

But that's not what we're here for. "No theological snark!" I chastise Six. "We should get a plaque that says that."

"We don't even have a bed in this place that is, ostensibly, some kind of rest stop," Ellin comments.

"Yeah, we only just got barrels. Which we can't sleep on," Mark comments back as he rinses out our cups and stacks them behind the bar. "Thanks for handling the vendor, by the way. Those things freak me out."

"Really? *That* freaks you out?" Ellin doesn't sound chastising so much as she's confused. Like it hadn't occurred to her that someone might be unsettled by a thing made of floating folded wrought iron and ancient streetlamps. "More than the weird twins?"

Mark shakes his head and speaks with that voice that says that he's worried about being too vulnerable before he makes a decision to do it anyway. "They make me feel *small*," he admits. "Not that, you know, it's unearned." A hand motions around Bastion's, but I know what he's really pointing at is the Between beyond the false wood of the walls, and the endless number of worlds we've lived on beyond that, and the utter vastness of all things that we can't even glimpse the outline of. "It's not even how they *look*. It's that they sell a million things."

"This one had one point eight million, rounded for convenience," Six states. I love how Six is willing to round the number but then uses some of the breath he saved doing it to explain that he rounded the number. It's just a quirk of my golem friend that makes me smile when he does it.

"Yeah, see, *that's* what gets to me. Not the kids trying to make themself the perfect person," Mark says with a glib humor that belies his unease. "Also the fact that they barely have search indexes. It makes it feel like you're supposed to get lost in there. Or that half of what we buy for ourselves is just random luck."

Ellin raises her glass in a toast to him. "Oy, yes! I'm with you there, sexy man! How many secrets are buried in the *miscellaneous* sections of the vendors?!" She slams her glass down and starts pouring more bitter wine into it. "We'll never know."

"Don't say never," I reply on reflex.

"Also stop getting drunk and calling me sexy man. I have a name," Mark gripes.

Six gives him what I think is meant to be a reassuring pat on the arm. "You do. You chose it when you chose to sculpt your body."

"Six, no, don't encourage her." Mark looks like he wants to hide under the bar.

"Okay, this is hilarious." I speak in agreement with, but also past, Ellin's lively laughter. "But, Mark, go back to the start. What do you mean you don't think they're optimizers?"

He latches on to the conversational floatation device I've thrown him. "Okay, so, you say *optimizers* and you mean . . . at least I think you mean . . . the people who turn themselves into achievement machines, right?"

"Fuckers," Ellin elocutes.

I nod like an excited dog. "What she said."

"Right. Well, they're just not doing that. They're trying to achieve their idea of perfection, but they're basically doing it . . . the same way we do?" Mark shrugs and flicks the towel he's been drying cups with over his shoulder, the perfect image of a disgruntled bartender. We all smile at the small action. "They want to live forever as the best person, so they're trying to build the best person. Calling that optimizing isn't *right* because they aren't actually doing what the Between incentivizes. They've set their own unrelated goal, and they're working for it on their terms. It would be like saying that we're optimizers because we sometimes talk about which copy of Strike we're going to run, or if we want to intentionally seek out a specific profession to try. You all just bought that one perk that can spawn plants here, as an example, and we need to figure out who should take it. That's not optimizing as a philosophy. It's just . . . You know . . ."

"Playing the game," Six says. An almost alien gentleness to his voice.

"Six?" I cock an eyebrow at him.

He makes a small hand motion, his round eyes still focused on our group.

Six doesn't fidget as much as I do. "When we sit down to share a game, we agree to engage with the game's rules. Because even though there is no meaning to them outside the game, it makes the time we spend more pleasant to do so."

"I hear ya!" Ellin slaps the bar. "It's *fun* to go into lives with upgrades, as long as we're treating the lives as mattering!"

Six nods at her. "Yes. Seeking to live good lives—or to win a board game—neither of them have stakes. Not in a way that matters to us. But that does not mean it is flawed to engage with the game."

Mark hums as he rolls the thought over in his head. It's one that I've grappled with for a while, though I rarely have people to talk it out with. "Wait, so, what are optimizers then, in this game analogy? Card counters?"

"Not cheaters, exactly. But . . . Imagine if we sat to play Leaves and Branches, and it was possible for Ellin to secure victory six turns ago, but it has been thirty thousand heartbeats and the game is still continuing because she is infuriating and wishes to drag it out for her own amusement," Six suggests. Ellin has the good grace to look a little embarrassed at the comment, and I get the distinct impression this has happened before, perhaps while I was asleep.

I don't *remember* it happening, but I'm really bad at Leaves and Branches, and so if a player could have won and didn't, I might just not notice.

"Is now a bad time to tell everyone that I've spent at least one life with Card Counting, Gambler, False Luck, Trick Card, Marked Deck, and Terror of the Rivian Dice Hall all slotted in some permutation or another?" Mark asks sheepishly.

"That is . . . No, Mark, I am using a metaphor." I don't think I've ever heard Six do a verbal double take before. This is great.

Though I do have a question. "Why did you want to be a gambler so bad?" I question Mark.

"Oh, I didn't. This was my third and/or fourth life, before we met. And I was a very good gambler in my second life because I thought I was in some kind of purgatory, so I didn't care if I lost. And then I had a bunch of gambling-related upgrades." He shrugs wide shoulders in a gesture that feels a lot less confident than I'm used to people who look like Mark being. That's part of why I love him though. It's rare to find real open vulnerability, even here in the Between where it's harder to exploit. "I traded half the perks from that for a door a long time ago though."

"Well, I don't think you're a problem," I tell him reassuringly, half throwing myself over the bar to look up at his face from a different angle. "Six is right though. Or is helping me crystallize a thought, at least. I should be more careful with words. It's not bad to plan, or to play the game of lives. It's just bad to forget that what's a game to us isn't to everyone else."

"Also to get *bored*," Ellin points out. "Your career-aversion thing, Luri. You've got that because you're afraid of getting fox holed. You don't want to feel locked into anything, right?"

I blink at Ellin as she rubs at one of her curved horns. "I wanna know where that word came from for you," I tell her. "But later. Yeah, I don't want to get funneled."

Ellin gives a shrug, rolling her neck around as she does so. "I think it's fine though. What's wrong with a life lived figuring out what you *don't* want to do? Remember that time I was a blacksmith? I didn't need upgrades to figure out I hated it!"

"But you . . . You did that for three lives. *Every time* you complained about making nails!" Mark stares at her with a baffled look on his face. "You could have stopped whenever you wanted!"

"Yes, but now I have a Box of Nails!" Ellin declares. "And I don't have to do it again if I don't want to."

I chuckle. But on a deeper level, Ellin's words make me uncomfortable.

Intellectually, I know she's right. What we do isn't who we are, and we do have lifetimes to figure ourselves out. To learn what we do and don't like. But I'm still terrified of getting wrapped up in a single path so much that I forget to actually live. I'm glad for my friend and her ability to do something she hates for subjective decades, then casually trade away the rewards for it, shrug, and move on.

But I don't actually know if I could do the same. And that scares me.

"Well, whatever." Mark snaps me out of it. "I'm still getting used to the idea of living with upgrades *anyway*. Even if I do start really planning, it'll be a long time before I can do it in a meaningful way. Most of my plans are me coming up with bold ideas, then never doing them for some reason."

"Yes." Six shakes his head sadly. "I had planned to learn to fish." The cryptic words have the rest of us looking at him with expectant stares. He barely turns his head down to meet my eyes from where I'm still lying on the bar. "Yes?" he asks.

". . . *And?*" I try to prompt him.

"And I did not," Six states. "Circumstances made it nonviable."

"Six, I love you, but sometimes you're infuriating," Mark comments, leaning on the bar over me.

Six nods. "Luri tells me I add variety. You are welcome."

"*You* made him like this?!" Ellin gasps at me. "Monster!"

"Technically I didn't make him. That's someone else's responsibility," I defend myself. "Also hey! Six is perfect! Just like you, you bully!" Ellin sputters at my words, the woman never having had an easy time accepting compliments. I'm waiting for her to come back from one of her lives with self-esteem, but I worry that she doesn't seem to be doing that. Her worlds and lives are often violent, and while she has a confidence and a decorum that I know *I* can't match, she always has this strangely durable sense that she isn't valuable herself.

So I take opportunities to remind her that she matters to us. She'll act like she hates it but secretly feel good on the inside, and I'll be satisfied for a bit while Ellin performatively blusters.

I know I'm a messed-up person, but you stick enough years under anyone's name, and they'll learn a few tricks.

The conversation drifts for a little bit as we all try to pry Six's story of failing to learn to fish out of him. I have an impression from how he described his last world that he just didn't have access to a lot of bodies of water, but no one is sure, and he's the best of us at being stoic. Jules wakes up halfway through the endeavor and joins our side.

Eventually, after multiple attempts at both rhetoric and bribery, we manage to extract the truth. Which is simply that Six got distracted, and his single-minded nature had him continually putting fishing at a lower priority than the things that caught his attention. It's deeply anticlimactic, and by the time he answers I had been expecting to hear that the entire world he'd been on had lost all its rivers in some kind of orbital impact or something dramatic.

The process is still fun though.

Time and heartbeats pass by in a warm flow. Not a *blur*, really; every moment of my time here is clear to me. I know the little conversations we're having, and the shared touches, and even the occasional time when I work up the stomach to check another notification. I remember all of them, and it's not like I'm not paying attention.

But there's a rhythm to it that I've missed. My last life was lonely. More than simply the sorrow of knowing that you'd be leaving people behind because everyone knows that, even if they aren't joining us here. Instead it was just devoid of people, for most of it. And being back here, with people I'm familiar with, and growing *more* familiar with by the day, it's not even that I'm falling into a routine.

It's that, if there is to be a routine, it's one that we're constantly building and expanding on. And the process of constructing something together, even if it's just this abstract, is emotionally satisfying.

I'm reading a book thousands of heartbeats later, one of our newer ones so it's only for the third time, and trying to force myself comfortable in the chair I've taken downstairs, when Jules says something that makes me look up.

"I think this life I am going to tell my parents." His voice stills the room, all of us looking at him, the only sound the almost imperceptible buzz of the lamps and the clicking of the overhead turboprop engine.

No one wants to tell him that never goes well. We don't really talk about it most of the time, but we've all tried it. And it's always made things worse.

"Are you sure?" Ellin, for once, doesn't sound particularly prickly with her words. "Because I don't wanna come back in a hundred years to see you all glum again." Ah, never mind. There it is.

"It would be dependent on the world, I admit." Jules rearranges his eyes like he's staring up at the ceiling in thought. "But it would be . . . Oh, what is the word to describe it? I don't wish to call it *relaxing*, as no life ever is in whole. But wouldn't it be grand to have *someone* to not hide from?"

"Well yeah, that's why I tell anyone I date for more than a year," I offer to him. "But not *parents*. Especially you, Jules. What're you going to tell them? 'Ah, yes, I have lived many lives, and my true form is a very sexy squid thing. Now, may I assist with dinner, dearest parents? Also how much do tentacles cost in this world?' You know how that ends."

Jules flushes a strange blend of orange and gray at my imitation of his accent. "My good Luri, I do *not* sound like . . . Mark, I can hear you laughing! Six, no, not you too!" Jules tries to wrap his face in his tentacles, but I can see his eyes peeking out. "Well. Humph. Regardless, I wasn't planning to reveal . . . all of myself. Simply to tell them I was an old soul in some way. Assuming there was no reason not to. I don't fancy being executed a heretic again."

I wince. We've all been there at some point. Those executions are never fun.

"It just seems like a great way to mess them up." Mark idly sits surrounded by the translucent panes of information from the Between, still trying to organize his aura, and still not actually putting that much mental energy into it. "Like, imagine if you had a kid, and as soon as they could talk, they *told you they weren't your kid*. That'd fuck anyone up, I think."

"And lying is somehow more moral?" Six asks.

"I do not know what the moral choice is," Jules cuts in. "I do not think there is one. Though we lack the choice to be born, we do *not* lack the choice in how we approach it. While there is no right answer, I would like, at least, to give my next parents the choice."

"What if they're assholes?" Ellin asks.

"Oh. Well in that case, I will assume I am some form of cosmic punishment," Jules states, eyes shaped in cheerful diamonds.

Ellin cocks an eyebrow at him. "Really?"

"No."

"Didn't think so."

I don't add anything to the short exchange. Mostly because I don't want to worry anyone by admitting that sometimes I do wonder if I, personally, am supposed to be some kind of universal answer to injustice. In some worlds, things like karma are more literal than others, but what if there *is* a method to where we're put? What if trying to live a quiet life as a farmer is actually me denying the role of righting wrongs that I was put there for?

Of course, that's about as easy to prove as saying that I was stuck on a world to cause wrongs in the first place. And just like that, those thoughts loop back into circular logic and an utter lack of understanding about our own existences.

"You know what?" I say, surprising even myself as I come to a conclusion. "If Jules is gonna do it, I think I will too." The others look at me, and I shrug, tugging on the sleeves of the bathrobe. "It's been a while since I've tried. And I kinda get where he's coming from. So maybe it'll go better this time. *I'm* smarter than last time, at least!"

"Hell, why not. I'm in," Mark adds. I give him a raised-eyebrow look, and he grins at me. "What? Why not, like you said! It's a thing to try, right? I might slot a charisma stacker ability though, just to help. Actually, does anyone have anything that confirms a truth? I feel like I saw one once, but I can't find it in my inventory."

"Oh, are we doing a group thing? Is this a bonding moment, eh?" Ellin adds a laugh, pounding once on the table with a fist. "We could make a bet on how it goes!"

"Absolutely not. You just heard Mark tell us how many ways he has to cheat," Six reminds her. "But I am not averse to the attempt. I will join you all. Now, if that is settled, how many heartbeats do you all have remaining? I do not wish to rush us, but I believe if we begin now, we can comfortably enjoy another round of Encounter."

My heart jumps, and my eyes sparkle, and I see similar reactions from the others. It *is* just a game, after all, but it's one we're all sharing. Maybe if we can't live our lives together, then experiencing a story on the same team is a close enough emulation that we can all be fairly easily convinced to try.

I help set up, while the others talk about different charisma-tied upgrades that might help us. I'm still not into the period of time here in the Between when I will almost begrudgingly read the remainder of my notifications and hastily assemble my soul for the next life. But I listen in anyway and consider what they're saying.

Part of me is still terrified of losing myself to the conditioning that the Between seems to be pushing. But . . .

It's been a lot of lives. I actually did lose count around forty, and there's only so many subjective years that can go by where you play the estimation game before someone like me just gives in and admits they don't know. And maybe Six is right. Maybe what matters more is that we play the game and throw ourselves into it. I hope my next parents won't mind too much, but I am going to try my best, whatever that entails. And if they do mind, I'll blame Jules and Six. I'm sure they'll understand.

Halfway through covering our largest table in mercifully immortal cardboard and chits and decks of cards, I remember how the setup of Encounter *always* goes and escape to see if there's something alcoholic enough to make me dizzy while Mark and Ellin restart their argument on including the module for advanced diplomacy rules.

We are building a familiarity, and a family. Right down to the increasingly stupid lines in the sand.

CHAPTER TEN

Mark goes first.

His last life was exciting, romantic, insightful, and beautiful. Which, naturally, means he has the fewest heartbeats out of all of us.

There's a few things that correlate actions to heartbeats, achievements or notifications to heartbeats, but there's so many times I've seen exceptions that I don't think it's really reasonable to try to track and plan for ways to stick around longer. Killing things seems to work, usually, except when it really doesn't. So why bother being an asshole just for the chance that you'll get a longer vacation?

The big man wraps me in a hug. "Ohhhh, stop crying, it's not like I'm *dying*," he jokes as his muscled arms do their best to crush the slim frame I wear in the Between. "We'll be back again before you know it!"

"'S not enough time." I sniff, trying not to whine.

"It never is." Ellin sighs as she rustles my hair. "What're we gonna do about it?"

"Well, *I'm* gonna do some really cool stuff, I think." Mark mostly lets go of me, leaving one arm around my waist as he turns to the others. "Next time around, I'll be out of here last, you'll see."

That's almost worse. But I don't tell him that.

Mark does a last-minute check of everything as his heartbeats tick down. He's already finished running through all the Between notifications from his last life, bought all the upgrades and unlocks he wants, arranged his build, and dumped far too many marks and drops into buying a handful of colorful glass bottles that have been added to the shelf behind the bar. There's not really anything left to check. It's just that there's an unavoidable anxiety that comes from a countdown like this.

You can make a list, verify it, have your friends double-check it, run down checking off everything on it, do a second double check of your completed tasks, and *still* have a feeling like you've forgotten something. This isn't an immortal thing, or an aspect of the Between. This is just life. A pure expression of the constant worry that you're going to return to learn all too late that you left something on that you really shouldn't have.

It's almost comforting, in its persistent discomfort. It *isn't* because that's not how emotions work, but it *could be* if my existence were art and not simply . . . life.

"I'll miss you. And I love you," I tell him, trying to put on a grin.

"Yeah, I know." Mark beams back at me. "I love you too, Luri. And all the rest of you too! Even if Ellin still won't kiss— Mmmggph—" His last word is cut off as Ellin, out of either spite or a dramatically misplaced sense of romance, does exactly that.

Mark vanishes when she is halfway through the motion, and both of us stumble forward.

"That man has excellent timing," Six comments.

"A paragon of the amorous." Jules bobs in a nod, a tentacle wrapped around Six's shoulders as he sniffs back tears. Jules takes people leaving the hardest, I think, though he disguises it as melodrama.

Ellin sighs as she rocks back on her heels, pressing palms into the table behind her as she looks at where Mark just vanished from, before angling an eye to me. "What? You too?" she asks my gleeful expression.

"I mean, maybe!" I say. "That was just really cute."

"Oy, well, thought I'd send him off with a good memory. Less crying, more confusion." Ellin smirks. "And now I have at least a few subjective years to figure out if I meant it!"

I press a trio of fingers to my forehead in a motion that I think I picked up from a cult five lives ago. I love Ellin, I really do. I love all these people, with an almost blinding feeling of roiling heat in my chest that rends away the fear and uncertainty I feel and replaces it with . . . well, mostly confusion. But a very affectionate confusion. But my problems aside, Ellin is exasperating.

And I decide to let her know it. "We *have a hammock*," I tell the taller woman, flicking a fingertip across one of her horns. "You could have spent your whole afterlife making love to Mark, and you waited until *now* to decide that you might be open to it?"

"Luri, you're the one who always tells us that we've got forever." Ellin doesn't lose her peaceful smile as she leans her head back. "Also I think I told you before, no one is having sex in the hammock."

"Correct, the ropes are not the right thickness to make it viable in a way that would be comfortable. Unless that is the intent," Six speaks up, and both Ellin and I slowly turn to eye the golem before we burst out laughing.

Goodbyes are painful. They never stop stinging. But they're also a release of emotions, a flood of sensations that push us to say and do things we never would have been brave enough to before. Each goodbye is a chance to grow. And it really does help to know that we'll all be back again.

Nothing is forever. Not hello, and not farewell.

Ellin leaves next.

She doesn't vanish like Mark does. Instead, she chooses her own departure from Bastion's. Announcing that she's taking to the halls and looking for anything neat to bring back next time around. Sometimes, if you wander far and long enough, you might find other people, other oddities, or the remains and leftovers of those who came before. And Ellin likes to try because it's a small adventure.

Six and I split some of our remaining resources with her, and everyone shares hugs before sending her on her way. There's nothing so dramatic this time as with Mark, but she does flush at my suggestive wink, and I start to think it might be worth it to invest in finding a side room or a big bed as a souvenir in my next life, just for the fun of it. Even if the fun is just getting Ellin to blush again. There's a perverse joy in flustering the occasionally stoic and always prickly warrior.

We've all had sex before. It's not an uncommon way to destress in the Between, I've found. But there's shades and nuances and layers to everything, and if nothing is forever, that means there's always value to be found in trying something—or someone—new.

And then she's out the temporary door and into the halls of the Between. I don't see where she ends up because I'm not going with her, but I hope she finds something interesting. She has a hundred thousand heartbeats left, which is both a long time and the blink of an eye.

"I don't think I have it in my old limbs to play the knight-errant this life around," Jules tells me as the three of us remaining curl up in the upstairs library. We've been reading the same book and talking about the dialogue between the characters line by line, trying to determine if whoever authored this murder mystery was exceptionally good at metaphorical foreshadowing, or exceptionally lucky to have people like us reading her novel an indeterminate amount of time down the line.

"So you'll be staying?" Six asks, closing the book around a gray finger and settling it into his lap. He and I are on the floor, with Jules's tentacles curled around us as a makeshift chair, and I hate to admit that it's more comfortable than most of our "real" furniture. The wood is hard on where my tail meets my back though. "That is good."

"Yes, well. It affords me more time with the two of you. Though time does run short, and I should determine what my intent for next life is. Or at the very least, which upgrades I wish to keep to prevent untimely deaths," Jules muses. "Luri, you die in unexpected ways often, yes? What would you say is the death you would most like resistance to?"

". . . You can't just ask me that without an explanation." I shift into Jules's rubbery tentacles to look up at his eyes. "What are your options, even? Do you have Heatstroke Resistance or something?"

"I have that," Six comments. "Do you want that?"

"Absolutely I do, yes." I jump at the chance. I know I talk a lot about not falling into the trap of thinking that the rewards are the only thing that matters, but I *do not* want to die of heatstroke again. Six passes me the metaitem without comment, and it takes almost no thought for me to replace Shovel Mastery Development in my aura with it. "Thanks, Six. Do you want anything? I can make it a trade?" He makes a downward swipe with a gray hand, and I let him get away with giving me a gift this time. Though I make a mental note to do something nice for him in the future.

Jules vibrates a chuckle at the exchange. "I was thinking that I could find an unlocked talent tree of mine and follow it to something you suggested. I *do* still have Serial Victim, but as I have never been murdered in any of the lives since acquiring it, I do not believe it is worth the perk weight that it is carrying."

I shake my head against him. "Oh, yeah, no. I had something like that too; sold it. Anything that triggers on death worries me. Perverse incentives at high velocity right there."

"I *do* wish you would give me the credit of defending my mental state from *wishing for my own murder*," Jules grumbles at me, poking my side with a manipulator tentacle. "We are not machines, Luri."

"Ahem." I love how Six just says the word. He doesn't even bother trying to make it a throat-clearing sound; he just speaks it. "I could qualify as—"

Jules pokes him too, Six taking the jab unflinchingly. "You are as much a machine as a horse." The words go in my ears, but I have to press my eyes closed to stave off a headache as I try to understand what Jules is even saying. "You enjoy your state as stoic and stone-faced, yes. But you are no more a machine than myself, Six. Your aesthetic is your own volition, of *course*, but there is a deep well of emotion when you speak of learning and teaching that no machine would ever match. Please do not degrade yourself by dismissing your own value."

". . . As you say," Six says quietly. I lean over the thick layer of tentacles between us to wrap a hug around the golem as he shifts in place. I know he's not uncomfortable, so it's something more than that. An expression of nerves that he offers very infrequently. "Thank you."

"Just 'cause you didn't get a surprise kiss from Ellin doesn't mean we don't all love you too, Six," I tell him with that confused fire in my heart. "But *also*, don't think I'm letting this sidetrack us from convincing Jules that he shouldn't *get himself murdered to build up murder resistance*."

Six nods, seemingly grateful for the return to the tangent. "Yes. Correct. Murder is logistically difficult to arrange for oneself."

Jules and I stop our bickering to turn to Six. "Okay, no, hang on." I clear my throat. "This raises a lot more questions that I didn't want to have asked."

"I'm keeping Serial Victim until I can find a better replacement," Jules states. "It is not as though it is interfering with my build, and if I *do* become murdered, I will feel a deep vindication."

Oh no. He's going to be so smug next time around if that's what happens. I actually look forward to it immensely. Seeing my friends experiencing satisfaction for their chances and choices is a source of great fun for me.

We sit and keep talking for a while, going back and forth between our impromptu book club and discussing Jules's different ability-loadout ideas. In too little time, our warm pile of bodies threatens to lighten significantly.

"Ah. Well. Almost time for me to make my exit," Jules says, eyes flickering up to look at his own heartbeat counter. "Six. Luri. It has, as always, been a pleasure to be with you."

"Love you too, Jules," I say.

"As do I," Six adds.

The two of us hold on to the ends of his manipulator tentacles while Jules tries to keep his breathing steady. More than anyone here, Jules hates being reborn. It almost always means a new body that he will feel constricted in and a new world that won't understand his desire to be *more*.

For Jules, the end of his time in the Between is far closer to the end of a life for a mortal who believes in a punishment-based afterlife than it is to feeling like a new chance.

And I can't do anything about it for him. Except to wrap my arms around his core and whisper a lewd joke and tell him that it'll be okay. That he'll be back before he knows it, that our one true superpower is the ability to over-come via attrition every suffering we face.

I don't know if he believes me. I'm sure he hears, but the words are hard to swallow when you're being taken away to something you hate.

"Well." The last words from him are a buzzing nervous vibration that tick-les my skin as he speaks, trying to leave with dignity and not the panic I can feel buried in his words. "I suppose that it cannot truly be worse than—"

I hit my head on a hard wood bookshelf as the air behind me is sud-denly empty. It doesn't hurt, but it's a little embarrassing since Six keeps almost motionless when our improvised organic-seating friend disappears.

Then it's just the two of us.

Six and I don't speak for a while. Bastion's seems too large and too cold suddenly. Which isn't exactly a new sensation for me; it happens every time, and this false life is no exception. There's an emotional vacuum being formed; where over the last subjective month we filled this room with laughter and stories, jokes and wagers, discussions of philosophy and tactics of life, now there is a void. Artificially imposed, and sucking away the ability to enjoy those things that I had found to be different facets of our ways of expressing love.

The room isn't actually colder or darker. The lights are still on—though I do hope Ellin found some better lamps; these ones could use an upgrade—and the temperature is as standard as ever. I don't know what the Between thinks room temperature is supposed to be, but I suppose Bastion's is it.

And yet, it feels more claustrophobic. It feels like something is lost. Because something *is*; the people who make this place a space I wish to be in, and not simply another oddity in the Between, they are vanishing. One by one.

Six pours me something that burns when I drink it, and I set the cup down to receive another dose of the poisonous medicine that tastes much the same as the first. "I hate this part," I mutter.

"Yes," Six agrees. "It will be quite sad without you all here. I am not sure what I shall do."

"Oh, Six." I snap my eyes up, a small mental nudge killing whatever inso-briety I was allowing the alcohol to inflict on me. "I'm sorry, I forgot you're . . . You're here for a while, huh?"

"I will have an amount of subjective time, yes," Six answers like it doesn't bother him. "Some of it I will remain here. Keep the lights on, as it were. But after that, I may wander. I am sure that I will see you again, so I do not fear."

"I hate to leave you alone."

Six wraps firm hands around my own. "None of us are alone," he says, more poetry in his voice than I'm used to from the golem. "Luri, we are all of us united by inevitability. As you say, *never does not apply to us.* Loneliness will not last. We will see each other again."

I smile, but I don't feel it. I know he's right, but so many deaths haven't ever made the process easier. It doesn't help that so many worlds I live through don't have a concept of therapy.

The next world that takes mental health seriously, I'm getting my qualifications and seeing if I can pick up a resistance to dread. A bestowable one, if I can. Maybe that's too much of a plan. I don't know.

Sometimes I think that half the reason I have an aversion to making plans is because my plans get derailed and I'm tired of whole lives being disappointing. But maybe that means I need a better attitude. Or better plans.

"Thanks, Six," is what I find myself saying instead. He still stares at me with those sunken-ring eyes of his, dark circles more astute than his uncanny appearance would let on to most people. "No, really. Thanks. You shouldn't need to be reassuring me though. I just don't want you being bored and lonely this whole time."

"I will not be bored," Six promises me. "There are books I have not read, and I can find a way to pass the time. Perhaps I will meet someone new or wander the Between. I will endure. I am more concerned with you and your final notifications, which you have been stalling."

I bite my lip and check the Between's log of my life. Three things left, yes. I've already pruned all the others. Low-priority influxes of marks and points, pseudoquests paying out, a perk or two here and there. Fifty subjective years, wrapped into a neat package and delivered to me like a poison gift.

"I'm waiting," I say.

"You do not have many heartbeats left, Luri. Do not wait forever," Six reminds me.

I take a deep breath, which turns into a long sigh, and find myself baring my teeth. Six reaches over in front of me and fills the clay cup that I'm trying to crush with my fingertips with a pour from a bottle of steaming violet liquid. He doesn't fill it that far, and I find out why as I taste from one of the things Mark left behind for us.

It doesn't just burn; it feels like it's trying to rearrange my nerves from inside my eyes and under my skin. This *cannot* have been made for a human, and I think that if I tried it anywhere but in the Between, I'd already be dead.

But I'm not real here, and neither is the drink, and even though I'm hacking out a cough, I let it get into my head just enough that I hit the mental switch on the last three mementos of a failed lifetime waiting for me to read them.

You have gone over fifty subjective years before taking a combat action: +100 motes. Ability granted—Peace Home. Talent trees expanded—Pacifist, Discipline.

You have committed regicide: +820 marks of war (modified by local authority weight, modified by Declaration of Azar Senate). Perk—Regicide (Regicide already available. 20 percent discount applied to next upgrade.)

You have died.
You lived the life of a farmer.
You lived the life of an unintended hermit.
You lived the life of one who changed the course of a people.
You lived the life of one who died doing what they believed in.
Final grade: unavailable
Final true achievement: 3 (18 total)
Final reward: King Jantu's Broken Crown
The Between calls.

That's it. That's all it comes down to.

I stare at the words with tears in my eyes. A lifetime of exile and loneliness for a crime that was committed before I was even born in that world. A tyrant that was unopposable, and a fickle decision from that hateful monarch to kill a whole town for personal amusement.

If I hadn't known better, I would have thought him another reincarnator. But he was just a mundane kind of monster.

Two years spent getting close once I knew I couldn't just let things go anymore, putting upgrades and lifetimes of skills to use to do it. All down to one moment with a knife.

Kings die like all men.

But I hate it. I hate how my hands are shaking as I remember the whole thing. I hate replaying over and over in my head the feeling of being tortured to death afterward. I hate knowing that changing the course of a people could very easily mean that I made everything worse.

I hate myself for not acting sooner. And I hate myself for acting at all. I have more power than most mortals will ever know is possible, and I despise that using it always leaves me feeling as if I have made things *worse*.

Six leaves worlds he passes through smarter and kinder. Mark leaves them a little more exciting. Jules leaves them a little more progressive. Ellin . . .

Okay, Ellin might also make things worse. But it doesn't bother her.

It bothers me.

The memories leave me shaking and crying. I didn't want to talk about this life. I didn't want to think about it all again. I *know* it's stupid, that all suffering is transitory for me, that none of it really matters. And I know that the man I killed did truly deserve it; I am no pacifist, despite what the talent tree I have claims.

But the feeling of hot blood dripping through my fingers makes me want to vomit. The sensation of a body slumping like its strings were cut fills me with revulsion. The sound of the last gasping breath of a person who no longer has an intact throat to gasp from is a personal nightmare that I cannot wake from.

This is not the first person I have killed. It will not be the last because never and forever don't come for me. This man wasn't special because he was a king, or a monster, or a tyrant, or a killer. He's nothing new just because he deserved it.

It's just one more corpse on the pile in my soul, filled with faces that I have long since forgotten and made all the worse for the fact that I find it disgustingly, painfully, *inhumanly easy* to get over what I have done.

I try to hold on to the memory of the pain, and the fear, and the blood. I try to reinforce that I can't let that become my world. That there has to be a better way to live.

But it won't last. Because nothing does. And mostly what this lesson taught me was that I should be faster with the knife when I see a thing like this would-be king.

I sigh again and look up at Six. I call up King Jantu's Broken Crown, a golden circlet set with a ruby the size of an eye, to my hand. It's cracked, presumably from where he hit the ground after I kicked his corpse out a window. But it's mine now.

"Here." I hand it off to Six. "Maybe sell this for something. I don't wanna see it again." He takes it from me wordlessly, dropping it into his inventory without checking if it has any stats to it.

The next few thousand heartbeats are me rushing to rearrange my build. As the pain fades and the mental wound heals all too quickly, I set myself up with perks and aura layers that will make me healthier and smarter while I sing, help me learn faster, and help me escape bad situations. I have a lot of stuff already slotted, but I rearrange a little bit to try something different.

"I'm almost gone," I say eventually. A few thousand heartbeats left. A subjective hour, if I weren't feeling the anxiety making my heart hammer faster and faster. The words come out cold, but that's only because I'm feeling dead and hollow.

Six's arms press around me, but I don't look up. I didn't see him cross from behind the bar to hug me.

"Everything will be okay," he lies to me.

"I know," I lie back.

"But when it isn't, you can come back and tell me that you told me so." Six lets a lilt slip into his voice.

A manic giggle slips out of my lips as I look up at his sparkling black eyes. He smiles at me, and for just a second, I *do* believe him. Believe that maybe this time I won't be so tired. Because there will always be a next time, no matter how much sometimes I wish there weren't.

I run out of heartbeats.

I go next.

CHAPTER ELEVEN

In between life and death, there is nothing.

No where, no when, no who. I don't know how long I am there because there is no me there, and no time for that lack of me to be there regardless.

I think it is a long time this go-around anyway. Which makes it slightly bitter that I do not awake rested.

One instant, I am dead. The next, my facsimile body exists, and I am on the soft blankets of the stationary bed that is my return point. My tail gets tangled again, but I don't move for some time except to pull the comforter around me loosely and to feel the fake air on false skin.

Breathing is hard. Technically I could probably get away without doing it, but struggling to breathe is uncomfortable, so I put my mind to the task. My chest begins to rise and fall slowly as I come to grips with existing here, the motion of the copper skin of my breasts out of the corners of my eyes a reminder that this body is dramatically different from the last one I was just in.

I raise a hand over my head, reaching up for the ceiling, and look at the backs of my fingers. Long, slender, no badly healed breaks or scars. Different color, yes, but that's the least of the signs that I'm back to being the form I shaped for myself.

Two things strike me instantly. The first is utter, complete *relief.* I am, finally, after so long struggling, *no longer in pain.* The second is that I have a complete lack of guilt for my relief. No life-sucking induced emotions dragging me down, no self-loathing or instinctive hatred of my own existence. Instead, I am . . .

Well, I'm as fucked up as I always am. But it's a personal and sculpted fucked up, not one imposed on me. I've still got a bad estimation of myself, and I feel more than a little like I am responsible for untold horrors enacted upon the innocent, but it's *my* trauma, and at least it's partly real.

In contrast to how my last life was, it feels like coming home to a loving embrace and a favorite meal. Contentment overwhelms me at the sharp delineation, and I feel a wide grin stretch my mouth as I consider simply lying in the blankets for the next however many heartbeats I now have.

But then I'd miss the others. And I should see how many heartbeats I have, at least, before I commit to a childish impulse.

[Welcome back to the Between, intercessor. 1,160,000 heartbeats remain. Prepare yourself.]

Less. So much less than last time. And yet, I can hardly understand how I even made that many. It wasn't a good life. Not by my flimsy semimortal standards anyway.

Moping can happen later. I stand and stretch, reveling in how easy it is and swishing my tail back and forth to shake off the blanket. Overhead, the seemingly haphazard chandelier of pipes from an old life brushes against my knuckles as I raise my arms trying to crack joints that haven't had enough time in existence to need it.

I almost get distracted just running my hands over my own skin and scales. *Every* return to the Between brings with it the relief, the sudden absence of pain that can feel like a euphoria. But there are degrees of the effect, and now I practically feel like I'm on fire.

The sigil on my door greets me, and I briefly wish that I had a way to drag my bed with me as I palm it and open the way to Bastion's. But not even the blankets will follow, and I regret for the twentieth time putting it in my room and not in the place that we all spend our days. Nothing to be done for it now; and it isn't as if metaitems give you detailed information without outside intervention. Hard to know if something will be movable once you place it. I've seen *dishware* that fixed itself in place, while whole armoires could be returned to inventory.

Bastion's greets me with warm yellow-and-orange light from the lamps illuminating the rustic wood floors. The mismatched chairs are all pushed in at the trio of equally eclectic tables. The metal stairs to the upstairs library sit cold and roped off on the side of the big room. The bar is untended, the mirrored glass shelves behind it adorned with a smattering of colored bottles that mostly serve to show off how understocked we would be if we were a real bar.

No one is here. Just me. My bare feet resist the occasional splinter from the floor as I walk across the room. The only sounds are the constant background click-whir of the turboprop engine overhead and the light burble of the endless rinse basin behind the bar.

I've been the first before. I've been the first a lot, actually. For a few lives, I was the *only*, and the arrival of Ellin and then Six was the only thing that kept me from slipping into madness. Thinking that you're truly, absolutely alone in the universe is not something that people are meant to withstand. There are artificial species out there that can cope with it, but there seems to be a kind of vulnerability to loneliness that developed alongside sophoncy, and it's been consistent in every life where it's been relevant. Maybe some kind of broader philosophical law that overrides or supplements the individual physics of any given world.

Well, it's not an issue. The others will show up eventually. My faith in that will keep me going.

I don't want to drink alone though. And not just because this body is only five feet tall and I would need to drag a chair behind the bar to reach the bottle I actually want right now from the top shelf. So instead, I . . . wait. Relax. Enjoy the quiet and the safe space.

It's hard to explain what it's like. Some lives end badly, some lives end chaotically, but all lives end, and then I'm back in the Between. And it can feel truly, utterly exhausting. Being on a roller coaster that I never consented to and can't get off. I've met people before who trap themselves in death loops just to try to stop feeling, and I can't say that I don't understand.

And while a given life can be a struggle, or be full of pain, or just be regular old traumatic, it's considered uncouth among our group to compare suffering. After all, why try? At its very best, you're only going to inflict discomfort, and at the worst your actions will minimize the feelings of your companions. So just don't. It's like trying to mathematically measure the ethics of an action; the closer you look for sharp lines to divide good and evil, the blurrier those lines become. Quantum ethics, as it were: Detailed observation ruins results.

That said, feeling trapped in an immortal cycle where I slowly refine myself into new versions of myself is practically liberating compared to feeling trapped inside my own skin. The perspective of lifetimes makes it continually easier to shrug off hypnosis or mentalist magics, but it does *nothing* against the ravages of the chemical imbalance called depression.

Of course I'm working with an unfair advantage. A safety net, of sorts. And while I'm always happy to land on a world where a competent shaman or pharmacist can alleviate the worst of the symptoms, no matter what, I know that death isn't my end. I wouldn't recommend my strategy to anyone else, is what I'm saying.

The simple fact that I don't want to die anymore is the largest pain removed from me. That, and the ache in my back.

If I hadn't known from a previous life that the self-harm urges would leave when I returned to the Between, I actually would have suicided earlier. It's not pretty, but it's our group's standard defense against permanent mental effects. The onset of dementia or the constant application of a hostile meme can, and will, change you. We aren't separate from our lives; we *are* our lived experiences. I'm not sure what the actual process is that lets me keep all that knowledge and memory stored up, but I do know that erosion to the mind when I'm alive can damage the person that I am.

One bad concussion can be enough to take out a half dozen faces of acquaintances from a hundred subjective years ago. And dementia does far worse. Ending the run and returning to the Between ahead of schedule isn't pleasant, but neither is having to rebuild a personality from first principles.

I realize that I'm trembling slightly, and my tail is hitting the leg of a barstool as I flick it back and forth. So. Perhaps being re-created here isn't as much of a refresher as I had hoped.

Okay, never mind. I'm going to start drinking alone. I grab one of the bottles of spiced wine off the bottom shelf and uncork it; technically it's been at least thirty subjective years since this was unsealed, but the Between doesn't care about time in a conventional sense. The flavor is almost too much, cinnamon and ginger exploding with the alcoholic bite on my tongue. I'm not really ready for it, and it distracts me from everything else going on briefly.

The first pour lasts twenty heartbeats as this body gets its thirst quenched for the first time. The second pour I try to savor, and find it hard to, because this actually is kind of unpleasant. I don't really like the more savory or spiced drinks; fruit is my preferred flavor set. Either way, I toy with the wooden drinking bowl I've filled with wine, swirling the half-full pool back and forth, making light waves inside as I stare at how the color of the wood and the liquid contrast.

I'm waiting for someone to show up. There's a few people who I'm waiting for who will almost certainly never arrive. I keep my first words in reserve for them, just in case. But as my thoughts drift, I eat up quite a few heartbeats and pass the invisible line in the sand of time that I tend to use as a marker. And still Bastion's contains only me.

I'm also waiting, in a more expected and real sense, for anyone from my group. It would be a delight to see Six or Jules again. Mark too. And it's been lifetimes since I've been able to talk to Molly. Also Ellin, I suppose, trying to put a joking spin on my own thoughts, even as secretly I yearn to see her just as badly as anyone else.

But I'm still here alone, and the place is still quiet. Sighing and refilling my bowl halfway, I head across the rough floor and make my way to the steps up to the library.

The bookshelves are still there, and still half filled with an assortment of scattered paperbacks and board games that we are *very careful* to put back correctly. No one wants to find out if the pieces are protected by the Between, and losing a die around here could mean subjective centuries before we can replace it.

I miss reading already. All the books here I know and love. We have a book club for a reason. But I miss the library from my last life. Low-tech, mostly academic material, but there's something about words on paper that sings to me in my blood and makes me yearn for a comfortable chair and a sunbeam to read in.

We don't have most of the ingredients for that. Some books, yes, but it's been a long time since I've seen a comfortable chair in the Between, and it definitely wasn't in Bastion's. I don't think there's ever been a sun here either.

I spend three thousand heartbeats flipping through familiar pages. It's not actually that boring. It's been years since I got to read this little space adventure, and the reminder of a nested culture I have long since left behind is pleasantly nostalgic as I let the wine do its work.

But I keep looking down at the ground floor, watching for motion. My ears perk up every time the turboprop engine fan makes a click I didn't expect. I'm tapping my toes and tail tip onto every surface they get near in nervous anticipation.

It's hard to describe how being really, deeply alone feels. Partly because I'm not there yet; I do still expect company. But company hasn't arrived, and I am left in this strange limbo state where I do not feel myself truly *alone*, but also have no one to talk to. Distractions, in this state, are hard to come by. Books I've read a hundred times just don't quite do it for me, even if it is the first time this go-around.

I spend some time carefully studying the bonsai terrarium that Jules brought back with him last life. The tree seems to be doing well, which is to say, the tree doesn't seem to have changed at all. And when I say studying, what I mean is that I'm trying to trace all the different tiny lines in the bark, and occasionally tapping the glass with one thin finger to drip a heartbeat or two into the tank. It doesn't change in a way I can see. Maybe it would take a few more to make the leaves move in the wind. Or maybe the artifact of a magical life doesn't have *wind* in it, though I actually find that less likely.

One of the downsides to being bored here in the Between is that there is an easy relief to it. It's to check your notifications. A thing that I normally shy away from, but usually, I put it off either because of a traumatic event or because I want to savor every moment with my friends and not waste it when I can fidget with my upgrades later. Now though?

My last life was awful, but in a very banal way. And my friends haven't arrived yet.

So I start poking the less interesting things. Clearing them away, at least. I have *far* fewer notifications this time, but that's okay. I'll consider this a buffer life. A . . . Not a vacation, but a lull. A prep period. The down slope before the upcoming peak. Yeah, that sounds good. I'll be sure to use that line of absurd falsity on Jules; he'll appreciate it.

[You have completed 1,000 local hours of retail labor: +3 marks of labor.]

That I know, for a fact, that the Between rewards farming more than retail is both offensive and . . . sorta checks out. There's a strange *shape* to how different awards and upgrades are . . . Balanced is the wrong word . . . Matched and compared? The Between is *not* neutral. It has opinions. Or at least, whatever puts us here and greets me as an intercessor every time I wake up does.

[You have achieved qualifications in local higher education—first stage: +15 marks of knowledge. 10 percent discount on next education perk or trait.]

Six years of my life spent doing errands for a professor. Here's another edge piece to the jigsaw puzzle of the Between; it rewards me for the *qualification*, not for the study, or the learning. This is actually something that our group knows about, but we rarely take advantage of it. It's usually just not worth it unless there's an education system that lets us test out of things, or if we actually do want to get some kind of neat new trait equipped.

[You have minorly improved the lives of more than 100 people (final count—204): +10 marks of faith, +10 aura drops, +1 Crystallized Luck.]

I . . . don't remember doing that? Is that bad to say? A lot of that last life is a blur. I know I tried to be a good person, and living in a city, even a low-tech one with a minimal total population, puts you in contact with a lot of people. But I didn't think I actually . . . Huh.

If you'd told me that while I was still alive, I think it would have made me feel worse, somehow. That I didn't notice would make me feel guilty, or that I didn't do enough would make me despair. That life *sucked*. Now though, it's one of the first notifications I've seen in a few lives that actually just . . . just makes me kind of proud.

I did that. Not killing something dangerous, or surviving something stupid, or eating enough food to bury a castle. I just made some lives better. That's nice. That feels good. And the Crystallized Luck is an excellent trade good, I've found. I don't use them myself. I've got that ongoing faith in the nature of the Between that I'll end up seeing everything eventually, no luck needed to tweak my random drops. But maybe Mark or Ellin would want it when they show up.

They still haven't shown up. I peer over the wood railing, peeking like a child looking down at holiday preparations, and see the ground level still empty.

My wine is empty, and I feel the rest of me going the same way. Not depressed or hollow, just . . . bland. I flick through notifications about tolerating jobs and classes, picking up a pittance of marks that I won't spend myself anyway. Even this distraction doesn't elicit any excitement. There are only so many ways that you can pull pride out of being given a single mark of labor for a job promotion.

I don't even remember getting a promotion. Is this from when they just added to my job duties and then hoped I wouldn't notice or quit? Did I get rewarded after my death for being shafted in life?

How utterly religious. I hate it.

But then, there's something that *does* catch my eye. Not just that, it makes me sit up and actually pay attention.

You have read and understood more than 250 local books (final count—282): +5 marks of knowledge.
This is the fifth life you have accomplished this. Aura layer—Scroll Harvester—gifted.

Having something gifted rather than unlocked is uncommon, but happens enough that it's not surprising. It saves on the various currencies that I don't spend much anyway, so that's nice. But it's as I read Scroll Harvester's typically muddled and obtuse description that I go from interested to wanting to cheer.

Unless I'm going insane, it lets me save texts from each life. Not a lot. Maybe one, until I grow it? But . . . Nothing seems to indicate I can't drop them off here.

"I'm going to build a library," I whisper into the empty air of Bastion's.

It takes me almost no time at all to pull Glutton of Norinton out of my aura and replace it with Scroll Harvester. The pseudoquest wasn't really doing anything for me anyway—it was just there to fill a weirdly shaped slot—and once I rearrange how Personal-Electronic Durability Boost is positioned, and then also make the inconsequential choice to ditch Slap Resistance, it slides in easily.

I neglect my aura a lot. I mostly just shove in whatever works or fits, never advance it, and never expand the aura itself. I only have two layers, even after all this time.

But *this*? This is something that's actually worth it. This matters. Because this isn't about me and my personal power. This isn't about optimization or accumulation. About becoming some kind of walking disaster or ultimate entity.

This is just a way to make sure that I can share my favorite books in every life with my friends.

Book club is back. I find myself laughing. My voice being used for the first time as I start to cackle. Life after life after life, all of it feeling fleeting and ever colder as I grew to realize that the only thing of any permanence was *here*. Here with a handful of equally scared and lonely idiots just like me. But now, beyond just randomly dropped souvenirs from achievements and rewards, I can *reliably* steal a little bit of each life to keep here in eternity.

I'm still laughing when I hear a door shut downstairs. Popping out of the barely padded chair and shoving it back against one of its identical siblings, I leap to grip the banister and lean over to the main room of Bastion's.

"Book club is revitalized!" I yell down at whichever friend has arrived first.

I get a shout of startled panic in response, in a voice I do not understand, as an older human man flails backward and falls on his ass, taking the chair made of extinct wood from a dying world with him. He flails on the floor, his heavy pack overbalancing him as he looks like he's trying to mix catching his breath with swearing at me.

"Oh. Uh, sorry!" I yell, pulling myself over the railing to drop to the floor, ignoring the stairs in favor of the faster way down and trusting the Between to preserve my knees. "Sorry, friend, I thought you were someone else." I offer the man a hand, which he takes and pulls himself up, his heavy and overstuffed bag towering a few feet over his gray-haired head as he does so.

I let go of his hand, and he dusts himself off. "Ahee, ahee, it is not worry, young . . . man?" He looks at me and then looks away, flushing bright red.

"Sure!" I say, glancing down at myself. "Oh, yeah, I just got back and don't have any return clothing." Which is sort of technically true. I've got a dozen statted outfits in my inventory. Including the robe Ellin gave me last time, which isn't *that* bad. But I'm comfortable, and Bastion's is *my* place, not some random stranger's, and I'd rather wear nothing than something that gives me a percentage boost.

He seems to agree with that on some level as the old man gives a light cough and a nod, though he does keep his eyes away from me. "Well, well, I'll be getting used to it, I suppose!" He chuckles.

"Are you alright?" I ask. "Your voice is . . ." The Between normally covers a lot of language barriers, but this guy is talking in an almost broken way.

"Oh, oh, yes, I learn the languages!" He perks up. "Long, long time in the Between. Not so many opportunities to refresh the magics as they pertain to my speaking. I trade, you see."

Ah, a merchant. An eclectic one at that, which is really the only kind you ever get around here. "Well, I won't waste your heartbeats." I smile at him. "What're you in the market for?"

"Ah, no, I *sell*," he says. "I am I am collecting the marks and the drops. *No, no cysts*, not at all. You are having the proper commercial-trade interface?"

I am not. I am also barely following. I rely a lot on the Between's eclectic and yet somewhat smooth translation, and this man's rejection of it is making my eye twitch. Still, I can keep up at least a little bit, though meeting this person is a novel experience even for me, with all my subjective years behind me, and I'm enjoying it.

I'm smiling when I ask, "Do you have anything to drink? We sort of run a bar here."

The merchant's smile lights up, and despite my lack of any trade skills to facilitate it, he is soon pulling random things out of his backpack. I don't know what powers the backpack itself has, but he both can't find anything easily and has a *lot* of things to find. It takes three hundred heartbeats for him to line up a couple of bottles and a clay urn on the bar, and by then I've moseyed around behind the counter to at least partially stop distracting him with my nudity.

I could get dressed. But I don't feel like it. We're dead, and if he's chosen to seem old here, then he's lived at least long enough to know that, in the Between, there's no enforced social mores to bind us down. Besides, he seems to be adapting just fine.

The bottles are some old souvenir he picked up from a person with a long and complicated story that I listen to with half an ear while I examine them. Long necked, like standard wine bottles, but sealed with some kind of wax cap. They're stamped in a pictographic language with a maker's name and a promise of how much of the delicious neurotoxin inside it would take to kill a yak.

I don't know if that's a boast, a fact, or marketing. The merchant doesn't either. We stare at the bottles for a few dozen heartbeats before he starts to reach for them to take them back and I set a hand on his wrist to stop him.

The clay urn produces a fermented-grain wine and is good for a splashing pour every hundred heartbeats you give it. It doesn't have a story attached, though he does make a point of telling me that every drink from it boosts your presence skills in the next life by a half percent each.

I care little for that effect. But I pay him in two hundred marks of war and fifteen thousand heartbeats and that piece of luck for all of it. It feels bad to spend my limited time, when I haven't even met my friends yet. But this way, at least I'll have a little gift for them when they arrive.

The merchant, satisfied with the trade and smiling at me, moves to set out again. I call after him to ask for his name, and he says something back about telling me next time he comes by to trade, which . . . I don't know. People don't typically stumble into Bastion's twice, in my experience.

But all things are cyclical. All things can happen within forever. And we have quite a bit of forever here, in the Between.

I stand behind the bar, flicking my nails on the new glass bottles and try-ing to play a loose tune with a smile on my face. And I wait for the others to show up.

The smile slowly slips. My fingers start to sting, even through the Between's protections. The heartbeats stretch on.

I've never been good at waiting.

But I stand there anyway, leaning on my arms folded on the bar, letting my eyes close even though sleep without a bed is impossible, listening for the sound of a door.

I have one last message to address.

You have died.
You lived the life of a student.
You lived the life of a broken victim.
You lived the life of one who did their best.
You lived the life of one who died without complaint.
Final grade: unavailable
Final true achievement: 1 (19 total)
Final reward: none
The Between calls.

CHAPTER TWELVE

That's where the money is, I'm telling you! I've got eight versions of Inventory Expansion and Pocket Space running, and it's never served me wrong! *Logistics.* Cross-world trade! Now, I can see the look on your face, and I'll grant you what you're thinking; no way to backtrack means some pretty poor trade routes, yes? But the goods are just for seed capital. Memorize Blueprint is where the *real* cash comes from. *Knowledge.* Take ideas and force them into reality and you can get rich *anywhere!*"

The man raps his mug down on the bar, sending a small splatter of droplets into the air. He's been talking animatedly for three thousand heartbeats, and I'm not sure why. I shouldn't have told him we were open.

It's not that I dislike company, in general. I just wish that company had come in the form of my friends, and not . . . this. There's two other people in Bastion's right now, this man with his jacket of sharp lines and thick black material and his almost glistening hair formed into a tube on his head and the quiet elf I met last time around. She sips her herbal lemonade like she's half waking up from a dream; the most communication we've had so far is sharing confused glances as we listen to the man ramble.

"It's the secret. I'm *sure* of it," he says, presenting his mug for another pour. I take it with a sympathetic nod of false understanding and refill it behind the bar as he fumbles in his half-drunken state to pay me. "It's . . . what it wants," he adds as he starts gulping from the freshly topped-off mug of alcohol.

He doesn't seem to be doing okay, and after I give him another refill, he just goes quiet. Not silent—he's still muttering about knowing the truth of all things and having figured out the pattern of reality.

"Is he well?" the elf asks me in a whisper, her compound eyes searching the man as he slumps forward onto his elbows.

It's the most she's spoken so far at once.

"Oh. Uh. No," I reply, glancing at the would-be wealthy merchant of worlds. It's rude to talk about people in front of them, but he seems to have fully checked out. "He's infected with a common memetic parasite. He'll live, though he'll be obsessed with profit margins for a while at least. How's your drink?"

". . . It tastes like a dream I was having." Her whisper as she stares down at the cup sounds like masked tears. "What is it?"

"Lemonade, with some herbs Six got last time I was here," I say. "We met back then. Do you remember?"

The elf stares at me. Long enough that I unconsciously find myself checking my heartbeats as I feel the creeping anxiety that I've been standing here being examined for a very long time. She tilts her head a half inch, achingly slowly, but says nothing as she searches my face.

Two kinds of people at my bar, it seems.

The man is starting to crack. He's objective oriented. Not a bad thing at all, when you've got an objective to hit. But it's clear he's having a hard time adapting to living forever. He hasn't said how many lives he's experienced so far, but it doesn't really matter. The Between is paradoxically both excellent at providing feedback and terrible at giving you anything to aim for. This man is almost certainly suffering, having to guess at and extrapolate what will be recognized as an accomplishment worthy of reward. So he's responding by diving further into what he already knows works; if he can *just* make enough money, maybe the Between itself will . . .

Well, I've never heard anyone adequately express what they thought would happen next. But then, I suppose that's how religions tend to work. The whole point is that whatever is next is more than we can understand now. Being able to articulate it would be a point *against* belief, really.

The woman, in contrast, is only just waking up. Natural immortals, elves in particular, have a problem with this. She's lived forever, and then died and lived another life, but that life was almost certainly as a human. Human is the most common. And thirty to sixty years . . . Well, that's a couple of cycles to an elf. That's *nothing*. But now, she's here again, lived, died, back to the Between. And elves aren't stupid. It's just . . .

I mean, dying is confusing. Especially the first time. Probably more so if you think you're just having a mild hallucination.

"I saw you in a dream," the elf says, her voice rising to a tone between a mutter and a whisper. Elf voices are hard to describe sometimes; *beautiful* isn't the word I'd use so much as *haunting*. She speaks with a kind of weight that is hard to ignore, even when she is barely speaking at all.

I shrug and try to not let the words hit me with too much force. "You saw me here," I say.

"I'm dreaming," she says. She doesn't say it with very much conviction this time. What feels like a million heartbeats later but is actually only about thirty, her eyes leave my face and look down into the glass she has a strong grip on. I watch her take another sip, watch her examine the flavor all over again, her face tasting the mixed-sour-and-sweet herbal concoction for what probably feels like the first time for her, for the tenth or twentieth time today.

I sigh and then feel bad about feeling bad. Not everyone can be emotionally available all the time.

But I wish I had someone to talk to that was.

It's selfish of me. But I am so rarely truly selfish that I think it's okay to think I've earned a few wishes. There's a sort of insurmountable challenge in trying to connect with people who aren't even acknowledging your shared reality, much less thinking clearly about it.

That challenge amuses me sometimes when I have my friends around. But when I'm alone, it goes from being a game to play between our other shared activities to an actual barrier. A wall between me and my form of existential satisfaction that I cannot climb no matter how many ales or lemonades I serve it.

It's not even that surprising, really. I've lived lives where plenty of people—me included—had hobbies that were hard-fought survival skills from other worlds. Forging a sword is sometimes the difference between life and death, and other times the difference between getting a good commission rating from someone putting together a costume.

That, actually, is something that I find over and over here in the Between; there are echoes of metaphor and event from life to life, and those echoes do not stop following us even to here, the place nested inside our deaths. It shouldn't surprise me, I suppose. The existence of the Between at all is somewhat absurd, with how it has things like beer and chairs. I shouldn't be shocked that it also has mirrored metaphors.

This type of thinking isn't my strong suit. Not here. Oh, in every life I find time for it. Especially when I'm a teenager. Human teenagers with free time, I think, produce some kind of special brain chemical that makes nervously pacing around and thinking about deep things somehow a compulsion.

But here in the Between, I much prefer to simply be comfortable, content, and occupied.

I can't *do that* though with a drunk entrepreneur and a sleepy elf. And I'm not leaving the bar unattended with someone who I suspect would willingly drink the bottle of literal poison that either Mark or Six or possibly Molly has helpfully labeled "Dangerous Poison Do Not Drink."

Why do we have this bottle? Not just why do we keep this around, but actually, *where did this come from*? I roll the green glass around in my palm, cool to the touch, the rough paper of the label stuck to it with some kind of adhesive that I won't guess at. It's not an equippable item. It doesn't have any helpful Between information on what it does presented instantly. I *could* dig through my own inventory for an Identify, but that would require rearranging the aura that I *just* got ordered the way I want it for next life.

My inventory doesn't sort itself. And I've accumulated a lot of junk in my lives. I sell a lot of it these days, but some things I want to keep for sentimental reasons, or just because I might need them. But I never ended up with a Sort or an Index like Ellin or Jules have, or the coveted Predictive Soul-Searching that Molly *never* removes from her perk rotation. This makes it a bit of a pain to rearrange things sometimes. And I could work around it, but I don't actually care that much because my upgrades aren't a big focus of my existence for me.

Also small mysteries are just fun. The nagging question of *why did we get this* asked of a bottle of poison is silly, and I find myself with a goofy grin on my face and shakes of silent laughter in my shoulders as I try to process it. I uncork the bottle and sniff it. It smells like poison. This doesn't help me understand anything.

I consider asking the merchant if he wants to try it. I know it won't kill him; that's not a thing here. Probably. But maybe it would be an interesting experience. I bet I could sell him on it if I pitched it as something marketable, but I've never actually been able to emotionally engage with business in most of my lives, and so I doubt I'd come across as convincing.

The bottle goes back under the counter, next to the mixers and the crystal pitchers that we use when we don't want to keep running back behind the bar for every drink during board game sessions. The sight gives me pause, and I find myself bending down again to move the bottle to another shelf that has Six's Chef's Herb Box along with a stack of empty snack-food bowls. No. No, that's not right either.

Do we have *anywhere* I can set the dangerous-poison-do-not-drink that isn't next to food or something that we eat food out of? I assume it can't kill me and that this fake body is resistant to whatever pain or damage it might cause anyway.

But . . . This is *not* a well-sealed bottle. And there's lifetimes of learned habit that makes me feel a deeply ingrained trepidation when I consider letting it sit next to the vessels I pour my drinks out of.

Eventually, I take a brief leave of my post at the bar to carry the bottle up the metal steps to the library so I can leave it at the top of one of the bookshelves. There are two possible outcomes here; either *someone* will ask me where it is soon and I'll get my answer, or else it will sit here for several hundred subjective years and long after I've forgotten about it someone will find it, dust off the nonexistent dust that doesn't form in the Between, and ask about it. And the poison will do its job as I die laughing.

We all have our own ways of expressing faith in what is real. Personally, I like to show my faith by casting gifts into the future for a version of myself that I might not even recognize to find. We're all in conversation with ourselves. Even within a single life we speak ideas and thoughts between different versions of who we are, who we want to be, who we could have been, and who we think we'll end up as.

It's a bit different for me, since there is no *end up*. And here in the Between, it's not always possible to leave myself notes. Journals, diaries, ways to record our own history, these things are precious treasures that the Between gives out as some of the highest awards. I think it is telling of something that it treats mementos and souvenirs as prizes to be sought. I don't know *what* it's telling of, but the end effect is that we can often change and not really know it. It's easy enough to forget where you came from with only fifty years behind you. When you're working on a scale of hundreds or thousands, it's even easier.

That's why friends are so useful. Or, well, useful is the wrong word. That makes it sound like they're here for utility and nothing else. Maybe it's better to say that there's a side effect of our shared lives, which is that we remember each other. We carry snapshots of each other's pasts around, a comparison of what we've ended up as. A way to know if we've drifted too far from who we were.

Not that drift is a bad thing, on its own. People change, even endless people like us. We are *always* changing; everyone does. The only question is if we're changing into something we like. I've lost friends here to the dawning horror that they've become something unrecognizable and monstrous, people who fall into despair, or worse, simply leave. When they realize that they don't care that they're separated from us by some chasm of an ideological divide, and they leave, and we never see them in Bastion's again.

Losing people never stops hurting. Honestly, I don't think I'd want it to. That's one of the reality checks that my friends carry with them.

This is the problem with being alone. I spend all my time dwelling on this.

On these morose thoughts and sad self-authored poetry. It's only a matter of time before I start recalling the faces of everyone I've left behind in old lives and weeping. Because no matter how long I wait for the arrival of friends at Bastion's, *they* will never be showing up.

I try to shake it off. Grounding myself on the rough wood floor and holding back a sigh as I look down at the tops of the heads of the two people sitting at the bar. It's a good reminder, in a weird way. Holding on is *hard*. Living is hard. Keeping myself from turning into a crying mess in an endless suicide loop is hard. But then I look at the kind of despondency that's my other option, and all I can think is that I don't want that. I don't want to go mad thinking that hoarding silver is the answer to life, or muddle through a series of lives like they're false dreams.

I want to live.

I just don't want to do it alone.

So after I safely store the very dangerous poison between a technical manual on a Craw-7 Air Superiority Fighter Craft and a children's book about trying to eat the sun, I grab a deck of cards from the library and head back to the bar.

At first, I just lean against the back of the counter, toss the deck box into nothingness since it will come back later anyway, and idly shuffle. A mechanical action that keeps my hands busy, but also prevents my mind from drifting. The noise of cards is sort of unmistakable though; nothing else is quite like it, no matter what the cards are for. It's a cathartic motion that also lets me check what I did actually pick up so I can know which game I'm going to try to entice the two people here with.

I'm a bit surprised when the elf looks up at me first. The merchant is still muttering into his folded arms about inventory management and cross-world logistics, which are all theoretical at best. But the elf focuses on the cards in my hands with an intensity she hasn't shown so far.

"Are you a seeker?" she asks me in a humming cadence that circles inside my ears like a lost gnat. "Is that where I am?"

"Maybe," I offer her with a quiet smile. "Tell me, what do seekers do?"

"A seeker is . . . Did I dream them?" Her voice dips again, and a look of confusion traces across her smooth face. "A seeker . . . A seeker uses cards." The elf sounds so uncertain, but she's struggling toward something she half remembers. "They tell you who you are."

I purse my lips and nod at her, my tail flicking back and forth behind me in a sort of agreement. "Well, I have cards. And they can help you know who you are, in a small way," I offer. "Would you like to play a game?"

Her eyes cloud over, and she stares at me with naked anxiety. "I don't know how. I have never met a seeker."

I smile at her, brushing nothing in particular off my bare arm. "That's alright. I haven't been one long. Would you like to learn a game?" She nods at me, slowly, like she isn't sure. About either the answer or her gesture. I shuffle the cards again, lifetimes of enjoyment of these kind of games giving me an expert touch on the small shapes. With a deft flick, I fan the deck out in a circle on the bar between us and flip over one particular card. "Alright. This is the crown. The point of the game is to claim it and then end the hand . . ."

There's another trick I've learned when it comes to games, a specific tone for explaining rules that sticks in people's minds. And, paired with that, *just* the right volume of voice to use to let the half-drunk merchant sitting two meters away listen in and have his interest piqued.

It doesn't take me long to explain the game of Regicide to the elf. It is, as all tavern games are, somewhat simple and robust. The rules also don't get exceptionally complicated for only two people; it's a game designed to be played with enough people that you can backstab half the table at once and still lose somehow. I kind of don't like it, but it's what I picked up. After I get a confused nod from the elf and deal us both of our different hands, we start playing.

It is six moves in that she wins. I let her do it, and if I do say so myself, it was masterfully done. It would take an expert at the game to realize that my loss was intentional. I give her a pleasant grin. "And you win," I say, flipping the crown face up and revealing her victory.

The elf stares at the crown card, the sharp intellect that had been creeping through as we played receding again into a foggy confusion. "And then what?" she asks.

"And then you've won," I say, trying not to laugh. "It's a game. The only meaning is what we bring in, and what we find ourselves."

"What am I supposed to find?" she whispers, staring at the bar as if she's asking the cards themselves.

I don't have a good answer for her. "That's a good question!" I say instead, refilling her lemonade that has gone empty while we fumbled through a learning game of this particular application of cards. "People find a lot of different things in games like this. Sometimes it's as simple as enjoying a small piece of time with someone else. Other times, you learn something about yourself. Some people place wagers on the whole thing. What you find is up to you."

"We should play again." It is the first thing she has said that has a little bit of life and energy in it, and I agree easily.

It is after the eighth move that I start to wonder if she has misunderstood the rules. After the fourteenth that I am *sure* of it. After the twenty-first that I reassess and realize that we are each trying to lose to each other. I concede six moves after and take the crown with a shake of my head.

And then the elf surprises me. "What did you find?" she asks without a hint of guile in her face.

"I . . ." I start to tell her that I didn't find anything, but that's not exactly true. But the thought hasn't fully crystallized, so I pause and think quietly to myself. We have the benefit of time here, and I don't think she will mind a little silence. "I find that I do not enjoy games as much when the players are not playing the same game," I eventually answer. "When you began playing for a different objective, it made the game feel invalid, until I also started competing with you under your rules." I hum to myself. "Which, really, is the point of games like this in general. Competition, but where the rules are open and understood. It's meant to be a cleaner reflection of how we compete out in the world."

"But you won," the elf says in her dreamlike voice. "You should be happy?"

"Oh?" I smile back at her. "Is happiness that simple?"

"It was, before the dream," she whispers. "Can we play again?"

"And can I get in on it?" the merchant asks, having been watching with cunning eyes ever since halfway into our second round. "I'm okay with the wagering thing too if anyone wants to stake some marks on it."

I scoff at him, even as I begin dealing a new set of hands. "Please. This is a sacred ritual, a seeking of the self. It is not *gambling*."

He stares at me with open disbelief, flicking a finger against the tube of his hair. "Oh, come on, pretty lady. I've lived at least two lives where gambling was sacred. Besides, I'm not gonna find anything about myself. I already know the secrets of the Between, even if no one believes me."

"Well, *she* needs to find herself. So no wagers, and you can help, if you want to play." I stare him down, and he sighs as he adjusts his coat and switches to a closer stool. Which I take as agreement, whether he likes it or not. "Good." I finish dealing. "Now. Let us learn about ourselves and teach about each other," I intone the words of a prayer I learned five lives back.

What I learn, after another two thousand heartbeats and five hands of Regicide, is that neither of these people knows how to play card games. They're very easy to read, and I don't think either of them realizes that part of the game is about making your opponents drain each other's resources while you lose nothing. And yet, we have fun. In our own ways.

The merchant tries to make it a matter of numbers and potential winnings, half joking about betting marks or perks on the whole thing. The elf, who barely understands that this is real, tries to make it a vision quest, looking for something that means *anything* concrete within the motions. And I just want to have something to do while I wait.

After another four hands, the merchant concedes early and stands with a groaning stretch. "Alright, ladies," he says, his voice coming out in a way that makes me think he *has* to be intentionally making himself sound slimy. No one can do it that much by accident. "My time is almost up. I'm off again to seek my fortune. But this was a better vacation than most. I'll be back again, if I'm welcome here."

"Bastion's is open to you," I tell him with a crooked grin. "If you can find it, and if you're polite enough."

"Fair top." He tips his head forward. "Next time, you'll see. I'll be drowning in marks enough to drink you dry and then some." I doubt that very much. But . . . Well, optimizing isn't something I'm in favor of, but if it's *going* to happen, at least this version of it is less horrid. This man is, if nothing else, passionate about what he's doing. "You'll see. I'll crack the secret this time," he says with one last desperate attempt to validate his theory.

I'm waving at him one instant, a cocky salute with my own glass of water that I've been comfortably sipping on, and then he is gone the next instant.

"Well. That was . . ." I turn to the elf, but she's gone too.

I check my heartbeats. Three hundred thousand left. I'm running out of time, and I don't even know if I'll be here when my friends arrive. And now I'm alone again to worry about it.

The glass of water in my hand suddenly feels wrong. Like a stupid joke. I fling it across the room, the water dispersing itself into nothing as the glass rattles on the wood and rolls under our good table.

Composing myself feels like a waste of time, but I do it anyway, taking deep fake breaths until my heart doesn't feel like it's going to try to rip itself out of my throat anytime soon. Then I find another cup and pour myself something hallucinogenic that I think is meant to be served in drops on ice. I fill three fingers of a cup instead, pause to lament that we don't have ice, and start drinking.

I hate waiting. It's making me feel like someone else.

CHAPTER THIRTEEN

Everyone has different things that they find themselves gravitating toward when they have free time in the Between. Technically, all our time is free time here; that's one of the true blessings and curses of immortality. There is no structure to it, it's devoid of real enforceable responsibility, and it's all ours. But there's a difference between the heartbeats we share with each other and the ones that pass by when we're alone.

In the past, I've spent long portions of my time here cognitively impaired in some way, but that wasn't working out for me. For one thing, if you have no regenerating metaitems to supply you, then you'll run out of drinks and powders and contained warped mana *long* before you run out of heartbeats. If you lived a life with any kind of effort, you might be here for subjective months, and with the false bodies we wear here repelling any serious efforts to *stay* drunk, you need a lot of supplies to work with if you plan on suppressing your emotions.

And since draining Bastion's dry felt like a really rude thing to do, especially after other people started showing up and contributing to it, I tried pulling myself out of my oblivion seeking in more ways than one and getting a hobby.

Six likes making things. Made things don't really *last* in the Between, but the golem is good with his hands, and part of the fun for him is that the process will always leave him with something else to do. I've spent a lot of lives as a maker, in some way. Collected a fair few perks for it too. But it's not something that I find fun, no matter how good I get or how useful it can be. I always find myself holding my breath when I'm working, like I need to finish a project before I'm allowed to let my lungs work again. I suppose it's encouragement to work faster, but that's not really the point of a *hobby*.

Mark likes . . . Well, Mark likes a lot of things. But many of the hobbies he chases in real life, like botany and ferroany, just don't translate to the Between and it's chaotic yet sterile hallways and endless old spaces. He says he sings when he's here.

Ellin practices moving. I call it dancing. She calls it haptic-adaptation training. She spends a lot of her various points subtly tweaking how her body responds, so she can mentally prepare herself for a new life, and a new form, outside of her control. It's not really a hobby, but she smiles when she's doing it, and I think she finds a kind of deep personal satisfaction in the process itself.

Jules remakes himself. Which is its own form of art, and one that I find beautiful when it lets him manifest as he wants to. When Molly is around, the two of them also indulge in a lot of sex. Not to say the rest of us don't some-times, but for them it's something with a lot more intent put into it. Intimacy turned into expertly fine-tuned performance art, rather than a private moment. Though that's not exactly something either of them can do alone.

Me, I read a lot.

And once I get my emotions under a thin layer of falsified control, I start doing a lot of it. I could be doing a variety of things, like exploring the Between, or . . . Well, that's it, I suppose. Another problem of being dead is that there isn't much to do here. That makes things like the terrarium that Jules earned as a souvenir something potentially quite useful to someone who doesn't have a library; if I had wanted to simply go on ahead, I could deposit my remaining heartbeats into it and set out early.

Books are comforting though. Partly because of how repeat readings change the nature of art, partly because of how they simply give me something easy to do that I know I can let my focus latch on to, and partly because each of them acts as a reminder of an old life.

Next time around, I'll have another one, at least. I wonder—and worry—that having too many books will make the ones we've collected less special. Maybe that worry is stupid. I have all the time in reality to learn every fold and mark of every page. Fretting that it will be too much is me letting my mind be ruled by fear. And I've been trying to do less of that here, even if it doesn't work too well.

The chairs upstairs aren't very comfortable on their own, but when I push four of them together into a long bench, they become *even less* comfortable, and so I end up once again sitting on the floor and paging through old favorites.

I could sit downstairs—no one is here to tell me otherwise—but I wrote the library's few rules, and so I feel a moral obligation to adhere to them.

Rise of the Third Extension is a historic retelling of the events that led to a world-spanning tyrannical empire and their eventual end at the hand of a terrorist organization that cracked teleportation technology first and promptly launched a series of decapitation strikes. It's from one of my own lives, where I grew up in the shadow of that empire and the birth of a new form of nation in the ashes of the old, and it was hugely important to me as a kid there. Now, reading it for the fifteenth time, I can see how the embellishments and story-telling it uses can't possibly line up with history; it's too clean, too simplified. But none of it is exactly a *lie*, and that is what makes the propaganda powerful.

It takes me nineteen thousand heartbeats to read and grants to my next life a 2 percent advantage over anyone rated below a negative eight on the axis of governance ethic. We don't have a reference for that, but I think it's safe to assume.

Old Threads is a romance epic in the Tuung style, telling the story of two lovers through the empty spaces in the narrative. At no point in the book do the characters, who are in the process of falling in love with each other, getting clan bound, and raising a family, ever speak to each other. I don't read this one often; it's also from one of my lives, but an early one. Before I had the power to fight back against a lot of things, or the mindset to do so effectively, and I felt locked into decades of an arranged marriage. The idea of a relationship without the other person gave me comfort, and the book came with me to the Between.

It takes me eight thousand heartbeats to read because I skim the conversations between the children, finding them too authentic to be enjoyable. It gives me a bonus use of a single charisma power. I find this to miss the point of the work, every time I read it.

A Functionalist's Guide to Boat Theft, Third Edition is from one of Ellin's lives, but I absolutely love it. It's part ramblings about the philosophy of piracy, part ramblings about the philosophy of functionalism, and part *actual guide to stealing boats*. There are a number of in-depth discussions of how a single person can effectively take over a ship, though most of it relies on combustion engines being a relevant technology. But all of it is written with a kind of wry humor that makes me imagine the original author was an impossibly smug old corsair who was simultaneously perpetually drunk and utterly unkillable. I've never stolen a boat, but every time I read this, I get a new desire to try to wedge it into my next life somewhere.

It takes me six thousand heartbeats to read, cover to cover, and a good chunk of that is me laughing at jokes I'd forgotten. It gives a 3 percent boost to alteration collection. Ellin says that world didn't have any magic like that as far as she knew, and none of us have ever found another that does.

Travel Times, Bina's Book is the third book in the second quartet series about a school for young wizards. It is written for someone younger than I was the first time I died, and so many lives under my belt have not made my reading level any lower, but it's still a pleasant read. This one is from a world Jules lived on that had just industrialized printing. There was almost a war fought over whether or not fiction should be allowed, and he described it once as a fight to ensure that no one had a soul, betraying how bitter he felt about the whole affair. The story itself was from an author who had found their first story suddenly mass-produced and been offered an astounding amount of money to be a figurehead for the fictionist movement by writing more. It's amateurish, doesn't understand how plot threads work, and overly foreshadows events I'll never get to read. But it's *fun* in a way that clearly shows someone working from the heart and championing the nature of storytelling itself.

It takes me fewer than four thousand heartbeats to read and gives me a 2 percent bonus to machinery resistance.

The Book of Pity is the fourth in a series of five of what I think are meant to be moral fictions called the Sins Cycle. The dust jacket informs me that the first three are regret, curiosity, and routine, with no mention of the one to come, only that it is book four of five. It tells the story of a single man and his unending slide into ruin due to his inability to look past his desire to help others. I don't actually know if it's meant to be religious in any way, but it certainly is depressing. It also comes from one of my lives, though why I got *this* as a souvenir I will never know. I read it anyway because there is an amount of novelty in it, and because I have a detached enjoyment of the feeling of ire that stirs in my chest every time part of the story mistakes compassion for pity and condemns it as a moral failing.

It takes me twelve thousand heartbeats to read, both because it is long and because I take a break to try to find something alcoholic to make the process more bearable. I don't think I've ever read the back half of this book sober, but the notification as I finish is the same familiar 1 percent boost to social conflicts regarding failure.

Flowers of North Argal is a guidebook. Informative manuals are strange to read, especially when they are meant to be purely informative. I never lived on this world; this book is from . . . I want to say it was Tee-kon, who got it from a life as a teacher. I remember very little about the world that was described so many lifetimes ago, but every picture of a flower, every description of where it can be found, what kind of soil or which sun it likes, it all brings up memories of old conversations *here*. I've never been to North Argal, I never will, and while some of these plants look similar to ones I've seen before, assuming similarities across worlds is a losing proposition. But this book is tied to real memories of shared moments anyway. It doesn't hurt that the art on display is a fascinating mix of sketches, color photographs, and chemical models.

It's a short read, only a few thousand heartbeats, but it leaves me with a feeling of melancholy more than the book that wants you to feel bad for having empathy; there's a sense of a missing friend in its pages. It reduces the time for any flower I put serious work into to bloom by one local day.

Sometimes, the rewards the books give annoy me. They feel intrusive, or perhaps a little condescending. As if I wouldn't bother to experience art without a pat on the head and a tail massage afterward. But the more I read and immerse myself in a series of twinned other worlds of fiction and memory, the less I mind.

Still, I pick my tomes at random so that I don't have to care or worry about the layer of upgrade results. It does mean that, if I'm even going to get to it this life, it will be a while before I get to read my actual go-to comfort story about the dashing space captain and his himbo alien boyfriend. But that's okay. It isn't like I won't be back later.

The thought gives me pause as I'm sliding the plant manual back onto the shelf into the perfectly suited slot for it. I will be back, of course. I've long since given up having any kind of concern for the what-if of actual death. But . . . The library will be different next time.

Not just randomly shifting slightly as we add a new board game or book or something to the shelves. But different in function. Different in structure.

One new book every life. Such a small thing. But there simply aren't that many books here. It won't be long, from my rather absurd subjective viewpoint, before the library is more new books than familiar titles. And time wears away a lot of rough edges, but it doesn't stop there with its erosion. How long, I wonder, before I am the sort of person who doesn't *want* to read about a dashing space captain and his himbo alien boyfriend?

I try to phrase it lightly, to let the humor of it insulate me from the fear. But it doesn't make the problem go away. The problem will never really go away because never and forever aren't things for me, or for any of us.

Maybe I should rearrange my aura again. Not tell anyone about this layer and let the library sit as it is. I'm sure it will still grow, but slower. More organically. Does that matter? Is there some ethical superiority to our new books being accidents, arbitrary awards from the Between for things *it* thinks are important to us, rather than the books *I* could choose simply for being what I think of as good?

I've done it before. Ditched an upgrade just to keep it from complicating things.

And then regretted it, of course.

The fun thing about living forever is that you have quite a lot of time to get past regrets though. Things to do *will* pile up, and eventually, whatever paths were left untaken simply provide texture to the person that you see yourself as, for as long as it is until you find them again at least. So I know that if I get rid of this layer *now*, it will bother me for one or two, or maybe ten, lives. But then . . . it won't. One of us will find something else to focus on, or we'll write our own books, or *something* else. Maybe we'll run into a lore master and buy a new library from whole cloth in exchange for free drinks.

There would be no consequence to simply throwing it away and letting myself remain sheltered and cozy with the small library we have, for a time.

But then . . .

But then, but then, but then. What if, what if, what if. My thoughts chase themselves in circles, looping over and over as I stand there with one slim finger resting on the corner of a book about plants from a world I'll never see. I am not so much thinking as I am along for the ride while my thoughts fail to cohere into anything useful. I am in disagreement with myself as to the nature of me, and the method by which I wish to live. Common enough for people to experience, but harder to cope with when you are dead, wearing the body of a fake replica of someone you never were, and alone.

I think I might cry or scream at some point. It is hard to tell, and quite easy to lose track of time in the Between if you aren't staring at your heartbeat counter. The truly sad part is that the protections that are in place to keep these borrowed bodies from becoming badly injured also prevent me from dissociating fully. And so I get to experience the mental cycles like a kind of roller coaster of thought, where I am strapped in and put on an endless string of loops.

A hand on my shoulder makes me jerk like I've been stabbed, the bookshelf rocking slightly as its eternally preserved unstable base tilts a little when I pull back. And I spin around, not having heard any doors opening, or anyone speaking.

Ellin's face looks down at me, the flash of a grin that she was wearing at having snuck up on me vanishing into a mask of worry as she gets a look at my face. "Oh, oy, Luri . . . You aren't looking so good," my friend says, the normal boisterous energy of her voice gone as she says hello for the first time in a lifetime.

"Oh," I say, my first word to a friend since I've gotten here a simple stumbling of speech.

If Ellin cares, she doesn't show it. Instead, the imposing woman wraps me in an engulfing hug. Her curved horns brush against the top of my head as her arms fold around me, the pale-green cloth of her nomad wraps rough against my bare skin. I don't care though; I melt into the feeling, sagging against her as if one small bit of physical contact can magically fix everything that is wrong with the rampant dissonance in my thoughts.

And yet, in some ways, it does. Our minds are impressively easy to short-circuit, and no matter how long I have lived, there has always been a kind of comfort in the illusion that someone else can take the pain away and leave you whole again.

"Bad life, eh?" Ellin asks sympathetically.

I blink away tears that are clouding my vision, leaning against her and draining warmth from my friend as she tries to maneuver away from letting me wrap my tail around one of her legs. "No, it was fine. Just . . . panicking," I tell her, looking around the library and the chairs I've left scattered away from their tables from my ill-conceived attempt to make a bench. "I got an aura layer to harvest books from worlds." I opt for honesty.

Ellin gets an indignant look on her face. "Last time you and Mark were drinking before me, *now* you're cracking notifications! I'm gonna be left out of everything if I don't die faster, huh?" She says it with humor, but also a halfway question of if she's actually being excluded.

"This time you beat Mark here," I inform her.

At the comment, Ellin looks around the upstairs before leaning slightly and shifting me in her arms so she can peer over into the downstairs. But Bastion's is still, except for the slowly rotating shadows from the hanging propeller. "Offset, yeh? Who went on ahead?"

"No one." I extricate my arms and wipe at my eyes. "I'm the first one here."

"Aw, Luri!" She renews her crushing hug with fresh force that leaves me gasping and grateful that the Between won't let my ribs snap in half quite so easily. "You've been alone here? How long?!"

"Not totally alone." I recover a bit more, talking to her helping me fake at playing it off as nothing. "The elf girl came back. And there was . . . a very dedicated merchant. Two merchants actually, but one was insane." I flick my amethyst eyes up at the overhead rafters of Bastion's. "Well, one was more insane." Had there been someone else? I don't think so.

"How long?" Ellin glares at me for dodging the question.

Something halfway between a grimace and a smile tugs at the edge of my mouth. "Nine hundred thousand, so far," I say. "Subjective, maybe . . . eight days? Ten? It's hard to tell." That's not much of a surprise.

"How long are you here for?" Ellin cuts through to the primary question. I love that she's blunt, and the insistent and uncompromising look in her eyes tells me that she won't care much for any attempts at deflection.

So I don't bother. "Fewer than two hundred thousand beats," I say. "My last life . . . wasn't bad. But it wasn't impressive. At least as far as the Between seems to think."

Ellin sucks in a breath through bared teeth. "This *place*," she grumbles. "That's not enough time."

"Never enough time in forever," I offer her wry humor. "Want a drink as an apology? Maybe the others will be here soon now."

"Bah. Bah! Fine! Ply me with liquor, will you." Her protests seem somewhat lacking in actual backing.

So I do. I take the stairs, just to feel the cool metal and the sharp texture of the holes meant to keep people from slipping on my feet. Ellin throws herself over the railing and almost breaks a chair when she lands. I know better than to ask her to stop doing that, but I also know the chairs won't really break anyway.

I pour Ellin something familiar to us that's not very good, and also not very alcoholic either, but it doesn't really matter. The point is to share a drink together.

"So, I don't want to talk about the bet," she says, and I remember that we *had* one of those, "but . . . I'm glad we're the first ones here." I don't see how the things correlate, and instead of asking, I just refill Ellin's shot glass and let her continue. We aren't using our personal cups for this; it feels weird without everyone else around. "I got some advice from . . . You know, I'm scores of lives in at this point, and it always feels weird to say *from my father?* He wasn't, not really. He didn't raise me, and wasn't really *responsible* for me, but . . . Oy . . . There was something . . ."

"I don't remember my actual father." My words come out conversationally. "I've forgotten a lot, really. Side effects of lives with pseudo-immortality, and brain damage. Sometimes . . ." Sometimes there's an impression of a face, and of a twisted fear in my gut. But that's all. "Was your not-dad good?"

"He was. Great guy, oh, *really* a great guy." Ellin nods. "Everything you'd want in a dad. I say he didn't raise me, but he taught me how to play hallball, and rode with me to community games, and . . . I guess I'm letting you know that being honest went okay for me, but it didn't make it feel less *real*."

"I'm glad." I smile at her over the edge of my fingers as I toy with my glass. "Really am. It sounds like you got lucky."

"Well, he told me something," Ellin says. We're both sitting on barstools; I didn't bother going around to pour our drinks, just leaned over and used my tail to balance myself while I grabbed stuff. And now, she leans sideways, almost awkwardly, to press against my side. "I asked him, *early* I asked him, why he was okay with everything. He said life was too short to not enjoy it."

My smile this time is more genuine. "You know, I think every good world I've landed on has had a thought like that? It's not what makes anything function, or the *reason* for things being good, but it's . . . Maybe a cultural by-product would be a good way to say it. Something that spins off as a result of the process that makes a place good to be living it."

Ellin throws her head back and lets out a laugh halfway between a delighted hyena and a failing jet engine. "Yes! This! This is why I love you! You can't just have a conversation. You have to have *analysis!*" She wraps an arm around my shoulders, tugging me against her in a motion that I admit I don't put any real effort into resisting. "It's like you want to pick apart the brain of reality itself, just to see where the thoughts come from."

"I wouldn't say no to knowing . . ." I blink, setting my shot glass on the bar and turning my eyes up to Ellin's. "Wait, you love me? You never say that. I know we all love each other, but you don't *say* it—"

I am muffled in my protests and attempt to analyze my friend by her lips against mine. The kiss is abrupt, forceful, and tastes of dull alcohol, which works as a fine metaphor for Ellin herself. And despite the fact that Ellin and I have been intimate before, I don't know that she's ever *kissed* me. Or me her.

It takes me three heartbeats to realize what is happening, and then lean into it. And then another fifty to a hundred heartbeats as I close my eyes and melt into the sensation.

Life, as she said, is too short to not enjoy it.

This time, I hear the sound of a door opening and closing. But I utterly fail to pull myself away from Ellin before a set of heavy footsteps approach the bar. I think she holds me in place largely for her own amusement, as I can feel her cocky grin against my own mouth.

"Hello, Ellin. Luri." Six's monotone is returned by a muffled utterance from the two of us. "Have I come at a bad time? I seem to be interrupting."

I try to wave a cry for help at him, but Ellin just redoubles her attempts to make things as weird as possible for all of us. I don't think she cares that it probably won't work on Six, and really, it doesn't work that much on *me* either. But we let her have her fun.

I am, sadly, lower on heartbeats than I typically am when my friends begin to arrive. Very little time left to actually share stories, trade tips and items, talk philosophy, and enjoy our freedom from mortality.

But they're starting to be here now. No more waiting. And for whatever time I have left in the Between, I know I will be okay.

CHAPTER FOURTEEN

After Six arrives and instantly starts fussing with the organization of the bar that I have apparently messed up in my time here, there's only a few more to go. Mark is next through the door, all sculpted muscles and smiles as he sees us and lets his guard slip away. Then Ellin ambushes *him* with a kiss too, getting in early this time instead of at the end of their time together.

A risky play. Mark comes back from half his lives pining for a love lost. But I'm hardly the person who would be willing to stop Ellin from wagering fire like that. Every life I live is me ticking up the counter on questionable choices I've made, and I see no reason to deny anyone else that same messy fun.

Also, while Mark has a look of shocked panic for the first few seconds of the kiss, as soon as Ellin pushes him back and sweeps him into a half-carried pose, he leans into it with either passion or good humor. I think I like this version of Ellin. Her last life was good for her; she seems more alive here after her latest death.

This is also when Jules arrives. The smooth black flesh of his core extending over the wooden railing of the library as he looks down on whatever is happening from where his door drops him off. One by one, his tentacles slide over the railing and gently lift him over and down to the floor, skipping the stairs entirely. I'm starting to feel like we should replace the stairs with another table or something, since I think I'm the only one who ever uses them.

"Good evening, good friends!" Jules cheerfully greets us in his accent that places so much deep emphasis on the first vowel of each word. "I see I am arriving late to the par— Mmmphh!" Jules is cut off as Ellin drops Mark like he's overcapacity ballast and throws herself across the room onto Jules to give him a similar treatment.

Every bone in my artificial Between-made body wants to explode with laughter. But I play it cool instead, leaning back on the bar, crossing my ankles in front of me as I lounge on the barstool and sip the cider that Six has just poured for me. And as I watch our resident tentacled Frenchman get lavished with affection, Mark drags himself up with a groan, stumbles over while brushing off his toga, and sits next to me.

"Hey, Luri," he says with the kind of voice you use when you're intentionally badly hiding your amusement. "How's death?"

"It was boring at first, but I think I'm warming up to it," I say, tipping my cup at the spectacle in front of us.

Mark gives Six a bright smile as the golem places a cup in front of him. "Thanks, Six. Also good to see you both again. And . . . *Yeah*, what happened to Ellin?"

"She appears to be less inhibited than the last time we met," Six states.

"No kidding?" Mark raises his eyebrows as Six gives him an unimpressed look. "I mean, I hadn't noticed," he continues unabated. "But then, I was distracted when I came in." He tries to cover his grin and flushed face with a sip of his drink but then pulls the cup back and cocks an eyebrow at it. "Huh. What's this? It's . . . interesting," Mark asks.

Six shifts slightly, which is more emotion than his body language normally shows. "It is one of my attempts at creating a cider. The equipable barrels do, in fact, return here with their contents intact." He points in his direct way to where he's stacked the inventory barrels at the end of the bar's shelving. It adds a nice rustic look to the already rustic-as-anything Bastion's.

"I know a merchant who'd love that," I muse. "But also thank you, Six, this is pretty good!"

"Thank you, Luri." The golem tips his head at me, only briefly flicking his eyes to watch Jules tumble past in a flail of limbs with Ellin barely holding on. Their antics topple at least two chairs, and I wince even though I know that doesn't hurt as much as it would if we were alive. "Should we stop them?"

We all ignore Jules's proclamation of "Someone help me!" as the two roil by.

"Offer them some cider," Mark suggests, trying some more of his drink and making a facial expression that says he doesn't *like* it, but he won't *stop drinking it*. "Do we have snacks? I wanna go take a table. Not to rush us or anything, but I think Ellin's about done with her romance assault, and . . . Well, I don't have as much time to share lives this round." He winces.

I set my glass down and lay a hand on his arm, which turns into a full hug as I hop off the stool and let my tail keep me upright. I might be out of time because I got here too early, but just as bad is getting bad luck on your heartbeat count. Saying any words of sympathy wouldn't mean anything though; we've all sort of agreed that we can try to keep that to a minimum. Sometimes, you just don't have the time, and the best solution is to not burn heartbeats being remiss about how little time you have.

"It's good to see you again," I tell Mark instead while Six stacks our preferred socialization cups on the counter and starts filling a pair of pitchers. "Oh, that reminds me! Did either of you put a bottle of poison under the counter here?" The two men give me looks that would be equally inscrutable for an outsider, but that I can read plainly. They have no idea. "Cool, never mind." I take the pile of cups and dance past where Jules has just thrown off Ellin so that I can claim the comfy chair before anyone else gets to it.

Six and Mark join me, with Six making a maneuver that seems like innocuous walking but actually puts him next to the chair made out of fragrant old wood from a dead world, which he loves, and always has to fight Ellin for. Ellin arrives too late as she sees we're gathering and ends up with the basket seat, while Jules just plops himself down on the heavy cushion that we keep around.

I have a little over a subjective day left by the time everyone sits. Not enough time *really*, but just enough heartbeats that I can be happy to see my friends.

"Well. I see Ellin has experienced a journey of self-discovery," Jules states as a pair of his manipulator tentacles dance across the table and begins pouring cider into the tall glass stein that he favors. "Was anyone else aware of this, that perchance could have offered this poor wayward soul some form of *warning*?"

"Honestly she moved a lot faster than I expected," Mark says with a casual shrug. He gives the dried-out coconut shell and the loopy plastic straw in front of him a grin and dumps his more mundane cup into it before taking a refill. "So hey, Ellin, what's got you in a mood?"

"It's not a mood. It's a change in perspective," Ellin says. Though she still does the Ellin thing of swiping her thumb across her chin and tilting her head away, so I don't think she's changed *that* much.

Change is a constant friend to us. You can't live a life and not change. You can't. Even if all you do is hide away from the world for seventy subjective years, you're going to end up feeling like you've mastered the art of certain daily routines. And when you come back here, you're going to wonder, when you wake up, why your legs aren't automatically moving to fetch water and your arms to begin opening shutters to greet the morning alone.

After you've lived a dozen lives, each individual one can't change you too much. For me, I take too much with me into a new world to be moved easily. In most worlds, all things have momentum, and that *typically* includes the minds and souls that dwell there. It takes decades of routine to ingrain something in me, or singularly powerful moments to give me a revelation about who I am or want to be. But when I want to change, I have the experience and will to shift myself on purpose fairly easily.

Part of being forever dying is that we can try things. And part of being friends is that we stick together, even as we make those changes. As we grow, in our own way.

Which is why I am, personally, very amused by Ellin's latest shift in persona. Because while Mark and Jules weren't around for it, *I* know that this isn't new for her. Ellin has been this person before, *felt* this way before. She knows it, just as well as I do.

A part of my make-believe heart aches with a pang. Because I know that she tried this before, tried to be more open with her love, tried to be the person she secretly wanted. And she pushed herself back. Retreated into the comfortable shell of a woman who was snarky, blunt, and dismissive, with only a few cracks showing her true nature as someone so easily flustered and eager to flirt with anyone she liked.

Ellin has lived through a tremendous quantity of pain. We all have, really, but I don't want to dismiss hers. People she has loved have been lost to us here in the Between, just fading from our eternal lives without a word. Perhaps they couldn't afford a proper door and never found Bastion's again. Perhaps they're still living an immortal life and won't be coming back for a long time. Perhaps they just . . . aren't here anymore either.

We can't know. All Ellin knows is that people she opened herself up to have left her alone, and hurt, and waiting.

But now it seems she is healed enough to try it again. Cycles of personality played out over so many lifetimes that we could easily lose count. One day, maybe we'll be so unrecognizable that we won't be friends anymore. But I somehow doubt it; I think it's more likely we'll find stable patterns. Patterns stretching across eons, but patterns where we're together.

"Oh good." Mark's voice draws a dazed blink from me. "You said something that gave Luri that look."

"Oy! I did not!" Ellin protests instantly. "'S yer own fucking fault, somehow." Her muttered defense is half-hearted at best.

Mark turns to shake his head at Six. "I'm not sure I'm fully buying into this more romantic version of Ellin," he says.

"You'll get used to it," I tell him.

Halfway around the table, Ellin reclines like some kind of large and certainly predatory cat. The noise she makes as she stretches is one of satisfaction, which I will never not find to be strange. When we are remade here, it is without pain, and that includes aches in the joints and bones and muscles. For Ellin to find stretching so satisfying, it makes me wonder if she spends some of her heartbeats after first waking in the Between doing combat drills. But even if that were the case, these bodies *don't tire*, so I know her pleased half moan is just affectation and theater anyway.

"Oy. Well!" Her clipped words draw me out of the idle shake of my head that I have going on. "Who wants to get this started?"

"Get what started?" Jules asks patiently. "And are we not still waiting for Molly? Or Tee-kon? It has been so long since I've seen either of them . . ."

I shake my head. "I haven't seen Molly since I got here. Didn't Mark see her last time?"

Mark's wistful frown hurts to see. "That was thirty years ago, subjective. I can't remember everything."

"Thirty?!" Ellin bursts out. "What happened to *you*?"

He shrugs, somehow managing to make the timid gesture look handsome. "Well, the world had a weird orbit, so more like . . . thirty-six, thirty-eight standard years? Bah, our language sucks for this. We should invent words. Anyway, car crash."

"*Again?*" The red triangles that form Jules's expression shift to one of dismay. "Mark . . ."

Even Six gets in on the chastisement. "You must be more careful. You could get hurt." The swell of our collective voices telling Mark to stop crashing cars goes still as we all turn to look at Six. The golem's utterly calm tone and cryptic gaze entirely at odds with the fact that he just told someone who can't actually die that they need to be careful.

Scrunching up his face, Mark crosses his arms like a put-out schoolchild. "I didn't come here to be bullied!" he announces.

"Nah, you came here because of a car crash." Ellin twists the knife. "But *anyway*, I hope Molls turns up, sure. But the five of us made the bet, right? So? How'd it *go*?"

We absolutely did not make it a bet. I think all of us refrained from wagering anything, despite . . . Did Ellin actually push for it? I can't remember.

The thing Mark said about it being thirty years is another issue. We are all friends, and we know we will remain consistent in our eternal lives. But there's nothing magical about the Between that lets us remember. It isn't just like yesterday that we show up here; we're all carrying new scars from new lives and faded memories of each other from last time.

I still love these people. And it does get easier the more lives you tuck away.

Still, while I don't remember if Ellin is telling the truth or not, I do remember what we agreed on. Because it was hugely influential in my life, one way or another.

"I could start," Six says, settling his etched-copper ceremonial basin on the table after taking a long pull of the cider he brought us. "As I must plead no contest. I was raised an orphan in this life. My family's village was burned shortly after my birth, and the adults put to the spear." He describes it like he's talking about going grocery shopping. While I know that Six is capable of a lot of deep compassion. Even after all this time it throws me off when his voice sounds so *placid* as he describes things like this. "I was found and partly cared for by a ranger, but he too was killed before I could speak properly. After that, I lived as a slave, with no relevant parental figures that I could make the admission to."

"Oof. I'm sorry, buddy." Ellin's shoulders slump as she loses some of her verve.

I'm in the middle of leaning over to wrap Six in a sideways hug when Jules asks, "What form of slavery? If you don't mind."

"Chattel," Six answers against my arm. He and Jules have been making an anthropological study of slavery across worlds. "No room for progression or release. The world was in decline, and I suspect will be dead soon." He does not shrug, but he does give my arm a small pat with one of his gray hands. "No one will miss it. But regardless, while I will tell stories later, for now, I have lost the gamble."

"We didn't *actually* bet anything," I remind him. "Also I'm sorry, Six. I hope your next run is better."

"Well, mine went great," Ellin says, the tall woman almost *pouting* as she tugs on one of her horns, eyes angled upward away from the table. "An' I now feel like an ass about it. Told my parents early, didn't believe me. Because of course. Pulled a few aura-layer and strength tricks. Talked to a psych. Eventually they just accepted it. Good people, both of them. And since I didn't have much to fight that life, I just spent some time helping them live their best lives." She shrugs. "Got stabbed anyway."

"You get stabbed in *every life*!" I blurt out. "I forgot to ask this last time. Are you going for an achievement for getting stabbed twenty lives in a row?!" I need to know. I can't live in the dark anymore. It's been bothering me for a whole lifetime.

Of course, now is the time Ellin chooses to learn discretion. She just gives me an almost flirtatious smile—or maybe an *actually* flirtatious smile—and then turns to Mark. "What about you, muscles? Any luck?"

Mark hums through his drink and swallows as he thumps the mostly empty coconut shell back down. "Oh! Uh, no." He shakes his head. "They called me a kin-touched, which led to a whole trial, and attempted execution, and . . . a lot of stuff happened. Not a bad life. Actually it was a big adventure, really. But my parents weren't part of it. What about you, Jules? How'd our actual resident tentacle monster do at being called a monster?"

". . . I refuse to let you shame me when I say that things went spectacularly," Jules says. "My surrogate family were accepting and understanding. I had a pleasant life, when things weren't chaotic."

"Isn't that always the case?" I give a coy laugh into my drink. "It's like road trips. Long stretches of nothing, and every now and then someone like Mark shows up."

"I wasn't even driving!" my friend tries to defend himself.

Jules's manipulator tentacles weave a circular array around him in amusement. "Ah, yes, the great condition of life. Things are either happening or they are not. And for myself, much of my life lacked the happenings. It was . . . a good break. A time to learn a little, and to understand a bit more of myself. My greatest regret is simply that the world had no active magic, and no science beyond glassblowing, so my ability to pursue the academic arts was somewhat limited." He gives a many-armed shrug. "And that is me. Which leaves . . ."

"Just me." I sigh. "Bad," I say bluntly. "I don't . . . know if I should talk about it."

"Hey, hey! We're here to talk, aren't we?" Ellin pushes, leaning forward on the table's felt surface. "Don't hold back on us now! Last time I was here, I told you all about shitting myself to death!"

Mark chokes on his drink, and Six has to pat him on the back. "Oh fuck, stop *saying* that. I thought thirty years would be enough to forget . . ."

I give him a sad smile and a shake of my head, trying to keep my tail from flicking in hidden amusement behind my chair *too* much. "I just don't want Jules to feel bad about it."

"Luri." Jules says my name like it's somewhere between an admonishment and a command. "I've been with you for so many deaths, I know you would never hold me in hostility for some attempt gone wrong. And you are poised as you so often are, as if your last life hurt you. Share with us, as you know will help you, as it always does."

It's so easy to forget that Jules has spent so many lives writing poetry that he sometimes defaults to speaking like a narrator, without even noticing. I know it's more a nervous habit of his, and that he prefers the personality of nobility that he cultivates, but I still find it soothing when he just snaps off declarations like this.

Still, I have to take a breath before speaking. And before I even get to that, I tap a finger against my goblet. "We should have had Mark mix up something alcoholic and possibly corrosive for this," I say. And then give in as the others stare me down. "Fine. Told my parents, got called a liar, tried to do the Ellin and Jules thing to prove it, and one of them doubled down on calling me a liar. Beat me half to death." I take a breath and remember that the pain is well behind me now, and that the body in the Between doesn't hurt. "This was when I was, what, eight? Tried to run, since it's not too hard to make it alone, but the world had a *weirdly* competent civil-protection force, and they kept returning me to my family, and they kept breaking my arms. Then I reached the age of majority and ended up thrown out anyway. Oh! Biological depression too!" I try to laugh, and it comes out a little bit forced. "You know what's weird though? I got a notification here when I came back for making people's lives better." My cheeks are wet, and I realize I'm crying, though I don't really remember starting.

I also don't know when Six and Mark moved closer to me, standing out of their chairs to wrap me in a double hug. I consider making an only partly joking comment about how they should kiss, but the words die in my chest.

"So . . ." Ellin says more slowly and drawn out than I've ever heard her pronounce a word before. "Does this mean me and Jules win?"

"Mark, Six, continue offering our friend comfort. I am going to strangle Ellin," Jules says conversationally, the triangles of his face shifting to a multi-pointed scowl.

And *that* is enough to make me laugh. The noise is abrupt enough that it surprises Mark, though Six keeps his arms around my shoulders. His skin feels nice on mine, which is about what I expect from the way the golem has built himself. But soon enough, my laughter stabilizes as something less broken and sudden, and more like what my ancient heart has been trying to find.

Amusement at the irony of life.

"You know what else?" I ask with a grin on my face. "I actually opened all my notifications this time, without having a breakdown."

Mark perks up, stepping back and tapping his chair in with his foot. "Progress! Soon you'll be helping me figure out how to sort perks!" he claims. He is wrong, but he claims it anyway.

I make a wave that I assume will be interpreted however he wants, no matter what I do. "There weren't that many. But I got gifted a thing for *picking up books from worlds.*"

The others brighten up, *especially* Jules and Six. "Do you mean . . ." The inky black mass of tentacles leans forward over the table, almost knocking his archaic stein over and spilling his cider into the void.

"Book club is revitalized!" I tell them with as much energy as I can dredge up. Which, it turns out, is a lot. "And this time I'm not yelling that at a random stranger."

"Wait, what?" Mark gives me an adorable look of confusion.

I settle back in my chair with a smile to explain, while the others work on making themselves comfortable again. Taking seats or grabbing different drinks. Mark goes off to mix some dire concoction. Six drags out rope from his inventory to start putting together a hammock again. Jules takes some time to check on his miniature tree from last life.

And I find that I have more strength than I thought.

Maybe it really is just the effects of waking up without a cloud of fog in my brain and a hundred pains from old wounds. This body is *mine*, built to take the bits of every body I've ever liked, and I love it. Love being in it, and love sharing it. And there's a lot of value to that, as I am reminded in a slow bloom every time I return to the Between.

And maybe it's just that my friends are here, and supportive, and the pain that it's so easy to get lost in feels further away when they're wrapped around me, or talking to each other and filling Bastion's with warmth and false life.

Or maybe it's that I'm ancient beyond what any of my lived worlds think a single person can experience. And I am starting to find that I have enough weight to shake off even the worst lives.

Behind me, there is the sound of a door opening, and behind the bar Mark calls out a greeting to a new stranger, while I settle in with some of my friends to prepare to tell deeper small stories of our lives. To listen to them open notifications and see what they achieved, to share small fragments of eternity together.

I like this.

And I'm feeling much better now.

CHAPTER FIFTEEN

S o we're at the healer, right? And I'm sitting there, being *creepy*, because hurt kids who don't cry are creepy." Ellin is telling a story from her last life and is slightly tipsy. I know this because she proclaimed it, shortly before tugging me into her lap while she talked.

Ellin talks with her arms a lot. And since we don't have any actual comfortable furniture like a sofa or a lounge or a pillowed recess, I am half held captive by gravity, while Ellin relies on her size to give me enough space to relax. She shouldn't rely on that. My body in the Between is slim, with my tail being my thickest limb, but she's not some hulking goliath that can replace an actual seat with her body.

Mark, who has recently escaped my current predicament, nods along encouragingly with her story. "I know what you mean. I'm thinking of bringing Acting-style upgrades next life just to cover for the early years. If I can find the slots."

"Oy! No interrupting!" Ellin's voice holds no real anger. "So I'm sitting there, and the healer makes the adult . . . makes my parents step out. And she asks me what *really* happened."

"I'm assuming," I guess, "that you stared at her, and said, in your very serious creepy-child voice, that you punched a horse?" Ellin scowls down at me, and I wonder if I'm about to be ejected from my makeshift living seat.

I *almost* fall when she brings her arms up to fold them over her chest, the green-white cloth wraps on her body rasping against themselves as she moves. "No," she protests.

"But you *did* punch the horse," Jules inquires. Or states.

"The horse bit me!" Ellin defends herself loudly. "I had to go to the healer for it! My hand was shattered!" She pauses, and her face briefly reflects the look that any of us might get at any time, where we remember just how old we are and how much of our histories has been erased. The tall woman massages her hand, as if pushing away a phantom pain. "Didn't really think about it, but it hurt my whole life. It just felt normal after a while. And I told the healer it wasn't the horse's fault."

"Awwww." I twist so I can try to hug Ellin, and fail, so I settle for wrapping my tail partly around her torso instead. "Defending the horse's honor!"

"Well, it wasn't the horse's fault. And I got my revenge! I didn't want it turned into stew just over a hand." Ellin sounds like she's trying to explain away basic compassion, though I can see the tinge of color on her cheeks that reveals her inner feelings. So many lives and half of us never bothered to remove the default blush from our bodies in the Between.

Six and Mark start a tangential conversation, wondering whether or not Ellin's action would count as saving someone for the purpose of the Between's often cryptic achievement scheme. This rapidly devolves into them defending different positions on whether or not a horse does, could, or *should* count as a someone.

It's so fucking nice here.

I don't join their chat. I just sink back into Ellin and let her pet my shoulders and back in an idle motion I don't even know if she knows she's making.

It doesn't take much focus to *not* check my heartbeats. I know I've got a bit more time. A few more stories, a few more drinks. And until the new beginning rushes up and overtakes me, I'm going to enjoy my time in Bastion's.

Ellin, having lost half her audience, tells me in a quieter voice about how her dad joked about feeding her to a horse for the rest of their time together. On the other side of the table, Six makes an argument that horses are a special category of life-form, and Mark makes a tautological statement about the nature of people. Jules stealthily slithers away from us, heading for the bar to pour himself something that smokes in the shot glass, apparently having decided he isn't tipsy *enough* for this conversation.

They're never going to resolve it. There are so many parts of the Between and its classifications that are seemingly willfully obscured from us. Things that might depend on the world, or the life, or a coin flip.

"Did you end up with a horse-based reward?" Mark eventually asks as he and Six agree to disagree, though I couldn't honestly tell you which side either of them are on, or if they both changed their opinions halfway through their chat.

"Ach, I didn't even *think* of that. Let me check." Ellin starts swiping at the air, brief flickers as she allows us to see notifications in the small moments before rapidly dismissing them. Ellin is a speed reader, and I think has something to recall all of them anyway if she needs to. "No, no horse powers. I feel like for something that impacted me my whole life I should have at least gotten Horse Resistance!"

"What is it with you and weird resistances?" I ask her.

"Well, if I stack enough, eventually nothing can kill me!"

The next words are out of my mouth before I can stop myself. "But then we'd never see you again."

Ellin freezes briefly over me, a shock through her body that I can feel, before she grabs the reins and goes back to her old self. "Bah! I'm sure there's always a new and innovative way to get murdered!" she declares. "You can't get rid of me that easily. Anyway, someone else's turn for an embarrassing childhood story. Mark?"

"Did you forget the part where my parents tried to have me ritually sacrificed?" Mark demands.

Jules pats him on the shoulder with a manipulator tendril. "My friend, as loath as I am to take Ellin's side"—Jules nobly ignores our friend's shout of dissent—"I think I speak for all of us when I tell you that being ritually executed is no excuse to not get up to childhood antics."

With a grunt of exasperation, Mark stands up, walks over to the bar, and ducks down under the counter. I hear the clatter of glass and decide to call over to him. "Don't drink the poison!"

"*Why do we have this?!*" Mark's muffled voice comes back, missing the more important question, which is *how did the poison get back down here.* Shortly he stands back up holding something from Six's herb box, which he adds to a mixer along with splashes of two different liquids. We all watch with curiosity as Mark shakes it vigorously, pours it into a small cup, and drinks the whole thing in one gulp. "Ugh. Horrible," he proclaims. "Okay. I'm ready for story time."

"Your life could not possibly have been that bad," Jules challenges, his triangular red expression marks shifting into something that I think is sarcastic. "Six told us a fine tale of friendship and romance, and he was *property* for much of his life."

"Being fair to Mark, I do intentionally weight my upgrades toward making my childhood easier," Six offers. "I find those years to be the most challenging for dealing with emotional overflow."

Jules ducks his central body in a gesture of acceptance. "Ah, that is fair. I apologize if I offended. Now, to give proper offense, Mark! Stop playing with your Between-given notifications and tell us of your childhood!"

I turn my head and finally decide I cannot deal with the growing discomfort of Ellin's lap, no matter how enjoyable the physical presence of someone else is. Slipping to the floor and bouncing back with my tail as a support, I grab the chair next to her and look over to see what Mark is doing.

Currently, he has about six different projections around him. Glittering gold and blue, words that I can easily read in their reversed position but decide not to. I get what Mark is doing, and I'm not especially in favor of it.

The Between gives us achievements and accolades and rewards for all manner of things. Sometimes repetition does it; different types of work are a consistent source of marks, if you're willing to put in thousands of hours. But often, it is singular events that stand out.

What Mark is doing is looking through his notifications for those events and using them as springboards for his memories. Thirty subjective years is a while to hold on to fun stories of childhood, especially if you've got twenty other childhoods in your mind. So it's understandable that a small assistance in remembering would be helpful. But there's just one problem with that.

The Between gives us achievements capriciously. What might be something that was hugely emotionally important to a life could never show up in a notification, while that time you lost your coin purse and forgot about it a week later might end up being something that gets you a new perception line. So when I say I don't like Mark using his notifications for this, it's not because I'm being purposefully stubborn, but because I worry that it pushes us to forget what's important to *us*, and to tell stories about what the Between wants us to.

"Okay," Mark says slowly as he pushes most of his notifications down and pulls one in particular up to eye level. "I was *going* to tell you about how I met a kid traveling across the southern continent. His name was Uthberi, we were *close*, and I ran into him after my . . . second or third escape? There was a lot going on. Anyway, I had this story that I remembered about the time we met an *actual* kin-touched, which are . . . The kin are sorta like spirits, but I don't understand them that well. Kin-touched were supposed to be a myth, even though they killed people accused of being them, so . . . Look, it was a fucked-up world. Anyway, I was *going* to talk about Uthberi and me meeting one of them."

"That sounds like a secret-king name," I offer. I've got a good sense for these things, and it's easy mode to acknowledge that any name starting with Uth is a secret-king name.

Mark stares at me, slowly shaking his head as he refills his coconut cup with the last of Six's outside-brewed cider. "You know what?" he asks me. "You fucking know what, Luri?"

"I can read backward, so yes."

"I can't, but I have strong pattern-recognition skills, and I have known Mark for long enough that I recognize his tone, so I also know in advance," Six provides. Ellin doesn't add anything, as she's too busy cackling at the comment.

It's almost sad watching his shoulders slump. "Okay, well, Luri, can you please teach me how to recognize secret-king names?" Mark asks. "Because *apparently* being in a romantic relationship that includes a secret king is worth an achievement."

"Wait, you were smooching the king?!" Ellin demands, suddenly invested enough to push through her laughter. Her eyes are wide as she leans forward, both hands pressed on the felt of the big table we use so often.

Mark flushes a bright red as we all stare at him, but he doesn't say anything. Which is when I decided to give him a little nudge. "So, how long, exactly, were you friends with the secret king and your not-actually-mythical kin-touched friend?" I ask him.

"I don't wanna talk about it," Mark grumbles.

"Because I just have this kind of soothing thought that, even though *you* died in a car crash, at least they'll have each other for comfort."

"*I don't wanna talk about it.*" The words sound angry, but I can see Mark starting to crack. The laughter at the ironic nature of life, mixed with the distance of death, making the whole thing an utterly hilarious experience.

Jules makes a vibrating pulse that drags attention toward him. "If you don't mind though, *I* have a personal interest in royal genealogy, and . . ."

Slowly, deliberately, Mark lowers his head down to the table and curls his arms over himself. His muffled voice comes out a second later. "I hate all of you."

Ellin tries to say something but just gasps out laughter, hammering a hand on the table as she does. When she catches her breath, she drags herself up and circles past Mark in a crushing hug. I steal her chair while her shoulders continue to shake with barely suppressed mirth.

"You know, it's strange. The majority of my lives do not involve romance," Six comments. "Perhaps I should stack upgrades for coincidences, as I am certain Mark has done."

"Fuck off." Mark's reply is so drained of any malice that it just makes Ellin start laughing all over again.

I'm not sure if he's trying to help or make things worse, but Jules politely drums two of his tentacles on the table to draw attention. "Out of genuine curiosity, and because I somehow lack Luri's ability to read your notifications backward, upside down, and across the table, might I ask what marvel was bestowed upon you for your frankly unlikely romantic life?" he asks Mark.

Admittedly, I'm curious myself. I have a lot of philosophical dislike for pursuing specific things in a way that twists how we actually live our lives, or for turning ourselves into unthinking machines by hyperfocusing on certain abilities. But some of the traits or perks we earn are so strange and wild that I cannot help but be interested in them. Especially when, as with something like this, it arose naturally from a life lived with a pure intent.

Struggling to get an arm out from underneath Ellin's affectionate pin, Mark drags his notification back down and double-checks it before opening another shimmering page and flicking his finger across it until he finds what he's looking for. "Okay. Looks like a task-style perk. Four slots, charisma base. Eight *thousand* marks of faith to buy it. And . . . Uh . . . Wait, what?"

Ellin lets him go as Mark struggles to right himself so he can read more closely. "Task is what you call quests, right?"

"Tasks are repeatable; quests aren't," Six corrects her.

"Why do we call them that?"

"Quests are more fun," I answer her gleefully, choosing to save it for later to tell her that Six uses different terms than I do.

Mark looks up from his reading to fix uncertain eyes on us. "Okay, this one does the annoying thing that Luri likes to complain about—"

"Hey!"

"Where it assigns an arbitrary value to abstract actions, and—"

"Okay fair, I do hate that."

"*And*," Mark tries to continue through my banter, "for every ten whatevers of upward social momentum, it . . . It generates a Gust Coin of Promised Nobility."

Jules, Six, and I all share a suddenly confused look. Well, I look confused. Six never looks confused. His face is as beautifully stoic as ever, and Jules is also continually himself. But *I've* raised my eyebrows.

The reason is simple. Hundreds of lives between us, and none of us have ever seen a coin of any description here in the Between. In all honesty, we'd given up on ever finding one, and I think we talked to Mark about it a long time ago. Because really, it wouldn't be the weirdest thing that is absent from the Between. There's no indoor plumbing; why should there be *currency*?

I don't know how old I am, but I am *old*. And yet I am still able to be surprised by things like this. It's a pleasant little bubble of something fascinating, and I treasure the experience. But I have a follow-up question.

"What do those do?" Ellin beats me to it. "Let you collect trophies of your conquests? Oh! I wonder what it thinks of mobility through conquest. Say I take over a city. What's that, you think? At least ten."

Ellin asks what none of us are going to know. "What *do* the coins do?"

Everything in the Between does something. But it's all . . . conceptual, in a way. We play with metaphors made physical. Even our bodies are just suggestions of what bodies are supposed to be, stripped of anything inconvenient. Books are meant to be read, despite the absolute truth that we cannot all know every language they are written in. Alcohol is meant to inebriate, despite the surety that our bodies would not process it at the same rate, or even in the same way. Beds are meant to be slept in, to the extent that *only* beds can be slept in.

All of it too provides bonuses. Additions to our next lives, in some way. Faster growth, quicker swords or sharper words, more blood or stronger bones, denser mana or deeper luck. The Between holds objects as candles that light up our souls as we leave.

The only things that stand out as frivolous, or as for their own sake, are souvenirs. Art, or perhaps memory, just for the reason of being a memory. Bastion's is littered with the things, decorated with the leftovers of dozens of lives that don't change anything except how nice our little public home is.

So what then does a coin do? Coins are meant to buy things. The lack of an economy here doesn't bother me; there are no printing presses or word workers, but the books can still be read. But what would it want us to buy? Or perhaps allow us to buy?

"Perchance it is some form of equipable," Jules muses, ignoring my own stare off into space, and also Ellin's comment about conquering a city. Sometimes I worry about Ellin. I don't think her lives sound as fun as she makes them out to be. "It is possible that it is meant to be literal currency. Perhaps taken from a lost world. At the very least, precious metals in quantity each life could offer a privileged beginning."

"Could be," Mark says with a slow nod. "Think they return each life?"

"It is your reward, Mark," Six's voice reminds him with the kind of patient steady tone that to *me*, listening in, sounds like a kind nudge toward personal learning, but I know can also sound like condescension when you're the one Six is talking to. "All the same, would you like to tell the story regardless?"

Mark sighs and drops his notifications. I think all of us are curious enough that we'll pool marks of faith later to help him afford it. "Ah, I suppose. Though I guess I have some things wrong." He sighs. "What I *thought* happened was that we had just found a good hideout when we heard about an upcoming kin-touched execution, and I prompted Uthberi to help me rescue the victim. That was when I told him what people thought I was, and he told me *his* biggest secret, which was that he was on the run from his evil uncle, which I guess is technically true but also absolutely *not the whole truth*." Mark takes a deep breath.

I choose this moment to intercede. "At least he didn't make something up completely? I'm assuming the evil uncle was someone who was trying to kill him in some convoluted bloodline ritual that would make him king, right?"

"You're way too good at this," Mark mutters.

"Luri often hides how intelligent they have grown," Six offers, which I think I'm offended by.

Both Mark and I ignore the comment. He takes a moment to grab a napkin and wipe off the bottom of his coconut before throwing the brown paper square back into nothingness. "Well, you're right again. So I *think* we're sneaking in, but now I realize that it's possible he just took the risk and ordered the guards away. Except for one guard, which is what my original story was about, because we rigged up a paint-orb trap to blind the guy and then knocked him out and put him in a supply closet, but it was such a *mess*, and we were dragging this guy around leaving a trail of red paint that looked like blood, and I couldn't stop *laughing* while we were supposed to be sneaking into a . . ." He sighs. "Okay, that part was real and fun. Anyway. We find Masubi, convince her the paint isn't blood, get out of there, and the three of us make a daring escape in a car that I now understand was far too conveniently placed for us to steal. Ugggggh. I'm such a fucking idiot." Mark buries his head in his hands again.

"There, there." Ellin pats him on the back in what I'm sure she thinks is a reassuring or romantic gesture, but that I bet Mark thinks is akin to being used as a training dummy. "It's the habit of men to make poor decisions for their friends."

"*I was a woman in that life!*" Mark's muffled yell gives Ellin brief pause.

And then she goes right back to making the same petting motion. "There, there," she repeats. "It's the habit of women to make poor decisions for their friends."

"I . . . That . . . You . . ."

"Just take the comfort, Mark," I offer him. "So, when did you end up involved with Masubi?"

"Oh, years later. We split up because, while her being actually kin-touched was fine with the two of us, she was also actually just a thief, and not a very good one at first. Kept crossing paths. Uth and I ended up tracking her down for a job when we were older and had a bad habit of playing hero. And when we saw who she was, we threw the job and started working together again. For a while. On and off. It wasn't . . . None of us were *great* people," he admits. "But we were all trying. It's what I liked about her. She was trying. And I guess it's what Uth liked about her too because . . ." He makes a sweeping gesture with his hands.

Jules slithers by, giving Mark a pat with a tendril. "It sounds like you were all quite taken with each other."

"Guess so. I'm not even actually *mad*, honestly. This is fucking hilarious. I just . . . I just wish he'd told me." Mark's shoulders slump. "I told them everything," he says, in a very small voice.

Death reveals a lot about life. For most people, it's the ripples and shock waves that spill out from getting someone's affairs in order, from last wills and estate sales, uncovering old secrets and hidden truths, or even just forcing confrontations between the survivors. And typically for the dead, all the upturned truths of their lives are . . . Well, I still don't know if worlds have their own afterlives. So it's possible that many of the dead do care.

For us though, our own deaths reveal so much we might have missed. There's quite a lot that can be dragged into the light by the simple phrasing of some of our notifications.

If it happened while we were alive, I think for everyone in our group, it would be a chance at reconciliation. Or, at the least, a strengthening of bonds. But because we're already past the worlds we came from, and have no way to ever go back, it stings all the more that we never have the chance to say one last thing.

No one likes to miss out on having the last word. And when you're separated by the boundaries of reality, and not just by the end of the night's party, it *does* sting. Mark can't even tell his friends that he's not mad at them, and that's just not *fair*.

"Ah well." Mark tilts his head back. "At least I've got you guys," he muses.

"You *do* have us!" I tell him with as much energy as I can put into a smile. "How 'bout we get someone else's childhood-antics story?"

"How about you, Luri?" Mark says.

I stare at him with an expecting gaze before turning to the others. "How about anyone else? Or a game of something? Or we can all figure out how much faith we don't have and see if we can get Mark's task unlocked."

"I forgot, I'm sorry!" Mark is having a really hard time between this go-around. I almost feel sorry for him. "Okay, how are you on heartbeats? We could play a game of something, and you can all make fun of my love life, past and present."

"I would never make fun of Ellin," Six offers as he returns to the table. "That would be foolish."

"Oy, hey!" Ellin, for some reason, protests that.

I shake my head and check my time.

I'm running out.

But not enough to worry about yet.

Which I don't tell them, exactly. "I could play something short," I say just as I hear a door closing behind me. "I learned a new weird way to play Regicide."

Jules gives a buzzing nod of agreement. "I am curious. Six, please go grab some cards. I shall go serve our new customer, and Ellin, you . . . You continue trying to seduce Mark, I suppose. Luri, I have no task for you."

"I'm fine watching." I send Jules off with a smile.

And it is sitting there, watching Ellin bluntly flirt with Mark, hearing Jules explain his form to a new passing patron, and waiting for Six, that I have a thought. It's a thought I have every few lives, but I always get distracted before I can put it into action.

If I have to live another life, I should build something like this. Out there, in a world, where it's easier. Where simple wood can become rooms and counters and tables. It's not fair that I have to wait so long for so little of Bastion's; I should carry something of it with me.

Maybe next life, I'll be able to try.

CHAPTER SIXTEEN

He hummed to me. It was so familiar, like an orchestra I heard from far away." Jules pays what he owes for needing to buy back into our game of cards. "By the time I died I'd had enough time already to no longer be missing him. But I remember how he hummed, and how it made me feel like a child again. A real child."

We play through another set. We don't really have chips or markers that are actually good for this, and until a few thousand heartbeats ago I didn't even know that coins were an *option* in the Between. So our pot looks somewhat strange, by the measure of any world I've been to. A collection of metal tabs taken from cans, sprigs of herbs, bottle caps, and small glass beads from the empty fishbowl that no one actually remembers bringing back and has never once contained a fish.

We have the values of everything written on a napkin that is carefully pinned down on the side of the table, a white ceramic urn of rice wine holding it in place. Our napkins—brown paper that is ubiquitous at diners across all logistical or industrial worlds—have a bad habit of not allowing us to clutter up Bastion's with them as litter. Which is to say, if we bump the table the wrong way and our score sheet drifts too far, it will return to nothingness and take our handwritten notes on which herb is worth how many points with it.

The bottle caps will too, but they're heavier and not at as much risk unless we toss them with excess force. Which is how Mark has lost two hundred points so far.

Ellin keeps shooting random members of the group *looks* as we play. The kind of gooey smiles that someone gets when they've just had romantic affection returned for the first time and they're riding high on the experience. Except she's managed to get it from mostly all of us at this point, everyone except Six, who *might* have leaned into her mood just to make her happy but really isn't much for romance. And I have to admit, every time one of those looks lands on me and I see her scraping her fingers nervously across her horns, even my ancient and withered heart feels an amount of stirring.

I bring this up to express that I think the only reason Ellin isn't being utterly rolled over by the rest of us in every hand is that her looks are distracting at least one person just as bad as she's distracting herself.

She still runs out of any kind of valuable and wagerable material next.

"The country I lived in had these weird flower cookies," she shares to buy herself back in. "Like, made with flowers. The fancy ones preserved the petals along the lines of the cookie; stuff *baked* weird on that world. Ech. Anyway." Ellin doesn't look up as she counts out sprigs of rosemary and tollic. "They were on the snack tray at my dad's funeral. I ate those things every summer as a kid, for years, and the only ones I can remember tasting are the ones from my dad's funeral."

We're playing a multilayered game here. Because partly, we're exposing vulnerable parts of our souls to each other, but we're also doing it while we're trying to stay focused on a game, but we're also trying to have fun. Stacking complex emotions, weaving them together, and coming out with a strange mélange of an experience.

It's a challenge, and it's not something that you casually fall into. But sometimes, when all we have is time and stories, we like to come up with overly complex games. Part of why we play Encounter when we can: It's over-engineered to the point of almost total chaos, and a session of it can take a subjective month, but we have the time.

Usually. I'm running out. But that's okay.

This has been a good cycle through the Between. My last life sucked, but I did a little good, and unrelated to that good, I also got an upgrade that actually feels *good* and not just . . .

I don't know how to describe the upgrades we often get. Not petty, exactly, or small, because many of them are quite good at turning pivotal life moments into critical parts of a whole world's history. But perhaps that's it. So many of those upgrades touch on and shape the worlds we live in. They make us kings and saints and gods and monsters. But even the most powerful Strike types don't let us touch the Between.

Ellin plays around with Strike a lot. She has over fifty variants of it, more than the lives she's lived, I think. And a lot of her lives *aren't* violent. Once she was a farmer and used it on her plow as a party trick. But she likes the simplicity. And, I think, also the power. One of them, if she lived long enough and devoted enough of her perk weight to it, she could cut something out of orbit.

But she'd never touch the Between.

I can touch the Between now. So can Mark. Small upgrades, *tiny* in the grand scheme of things. After all, what does one book matter, or one coin? We might actually be here forever; a single trinket doesn't feel like it has a lot of weight in the face of that. But maybe it does, if the trinket can be here with us for that forever.

And in addition to my new aura layer and excitement to bring back something fun for everyone next time, I've *also* gotten to spend some quality time with my friends. And Ellin, who . . . Well, I don't know what we are. Friends, lovers, something else, something more or less. We haven't taken the time to talk about it because I won't be here much longer. Our connection right now is what it always was, but with a promise running through it, that we'll *see how things go.*

We've done it before, and it was fun while it lasted, and neither of us have any hard feelings about it not lasting forever. I don't think it's healthy for a true immortal to expect relationships to last forever. But that doesn't mean that it can't come and go like a tide.

While I've been reminiscing, I've lost the round because I was thinking about aura layers and not paying attention to how Mark has been steadily baiting me into a numerical trap, and Six has collected the right combination of cards to attrition my points directly.

Clearing my throat as I stack up the right bits and pieces to buy back in with, I dredge up something appropriately melancholy.

"There was a librarian at the versity that I was going to," I start, trying to figure out how to keep the memory short and bittersweet without going on one of my usual rambles. "Young guy. Just as depressed as me, just as broke too. We didn't really know each other, but we had a kind of agreement. I'd come by in the middle of the night, and he'd help me sneak in, and I'd give him all the baked goods I'd steal from my other job." I find myself giving a sad smile as I toy with a handful of bottle caps. "It wasn't like we were into each other. But it was nice to have someone to be circularly kind to. I would have given him stolen scones even if he wasn't helping me, and I think he would have done the same."

"Oy, Luri . . ." Ellin's voice comes out with a sad twist of a smile on her face, her horns dipping down as she bends to meet my eyes.

Mark reaches over with a swift motion and plucks about thirty points worth of stuff out of her stash before shifting back to my side and depositing Ellin's score-keeping items on my part of the green felt. "Penalty to Ellin! Expressed sympathy!"

"I am not certain I approve of this metagame," Six comments. Though his comment doesn't stop him from placing a wager on two of the revealed cards, drawing, and passing to Jules.

Jules's tentacles do some kind of complex misdirection that I think is supposed to hide just how little he actually bet, which makes me think that the old noble soul is trying to trick me specifically into thinking he's bluffing. Or maybe I've just had far too much of Six's returned cider along with a few drinks from the regenerating urn of rice wine at the end of the table. "I do believe that I agree with you, my friend." Jules vibrates at Six. "Perhaps next time, we could try this reversed?"

"Reversed how?" Mark asks with sharp curiosity as he buries half his hand in a bid to hide the fact that he's going to lose the round and doesn't want anyone taking more than he can spare. "We all have to be serious and dramatic while we're playing, but then tell happy stories? Penalty points for eliciting fleeting smiles and soft moments of levity?"

"Yes," Jules agrees instantly. "Actually, yes. I believe I would enjoy that."

I flick two pieces of tollic into the center wager. "Because you enjoy drama, Jules," I point out.

"Yes," Jules agrees instantly. "Was that fact in question, Luri? I have spent lifetimes mastering my ability to be an incurable gossip."

Six gives Jules's nearest mobility tentacle a pat, uniform gray flesh in a human shape contrasting with the secretly vibrant slick black skin of whatever Jules would call his species. "And that is why we are such good friends," the golem says simply. "Also you are losing this hand and should begin preparing another dramatic moment."

"Curses." Jules's triangle eyes tilt downward. "Also I refuse to believe your lies."

I give a soft giggle at their antics as play resumes, along with all the small quips that we normally offer to each other.

Jules does lose that hand. And then after a slight recoup of his losses ends up overcommitting two hands later. Ellin uses some of her cards in the round after to steal from Jules directly, and we watch as his banter gets shorter and less thought-out as his focus narrows down to the numbers and odds of the game.

It's a shame that Jules, for all that he *is* truly good at drama, isn't much for numbers. I feel like he's told me before that he's been an accountant in at least one life, and I truly pity his clients. They may have had some pointed questions to answer to their local tax authority if they were ever investigated.

After he loses, it becomes clear that Jules has been trying to think of something. But where that thought process has led him isn't to a specific event. "I think I could have done more," Jules admits in a sibilant buzz. "This was the first life where—ah, this isn't much of a single thing, I apologize—the first life that I actually opened up. Used all my abilities, didn't try to hide, threw myself into it." He glances to Ellin.

She nods at him. "Feels kinda good, yeh?"

"Well, typically, your tales are of wars and campaigns. All the wars I've been in have been horrid affairs," Jules reminds the horned woman. "But *yes*. And yet, I cannot help but think . . . I could have done more. Not because it could have gotten me more marks and drops, but because I want to. Because it feels right."

"I can't really picture you not doing enough, Jules," I murmur into my goblet.

"Mmh." The creature that is my friend simply hums and plucks some of my points away. "Well. There's your penalty for sympathy."

"Alright, I'm coming around to this game being dumb." I sigh and check two numbers. One is my score, which is almost nothing, and the other is my heartbeats left, which is looking similarly anemic. "I . . . I think I'm done, actually." I push back my chair to stand, supporting myself on Mark's shoulder as I do so. "And almost done here too. I'm down to under ten thousand."

The words sober the group. And me as well, unfortunately. If I had planned better, I could have been caught off guard and as properly drunk as the Between lets me get before I got plucked away and back to life. But instead, I've made a mess of it.

"I'm not doing too spicy myself either." Ellin sighs. "*Peaceful lives*, bah." She folds her arms, but for all her grandstanding—and her quite real enjoyment of armed conflict—I still know her for what she truly is, a kindhearted softy. "I'll probably be going second. But . . . Ach, if I don't say it . . . It's been good to see you again, Luri." She smiles at me, sharp teeth forming a beautiful grin.

"I agree." Six nods. "All of you. It has been too long. Perhaps this time we should pledge to live bombastic lives."

"Why's that?" Mark questions as he too stands and starts to clear away the game that is being abandoned. There's something fun about the casual way he flicks napkins and bottle caps off the table and into nothing, while he takes *far* more care with the deck of cards. "Just to see who can do the best?"

Six shakes his head in an economical motion of denial. "So that when we next meet, we might all have millions of heartbeats to share."

A pair of tentacles from Jules wrap around Six's shoulders as the black form looms behind him, grappling the golem in a sudden embrace. "Ah, I *knew* there was a poetic heart under all that stoicism!" Jules exclaims, delighted. "Say something else metaphorical!"

"I choose to be stoic because it is comfortable," Six states. "And I was not being metaphorical at all. Do not question my word choice."

I try to hide my smirk behind a hand, not wanting Six to think that I'm judging him. I don't know if the others notice, but he *does* have a slight inflection to his words now. A kind of defensive tone that he rarely employs. I don't want to press him or make him feel worse though, not now, not as one of my last memories of the Between this time around. "I think I could try that," I tell him.

Mark gives me a surprised look. "Really?" he asks. "You, Luri, of all people?"

"I know I talk about not wanting to fall into an optimizer trap a lot." I shrug, flicking my tail behind me like a seminervous metronome. "We all do, for . . . reasons . . . but . . . there's nothing wrong with living, Mark. Just because I find a lot of our upgrades to generate perverse incentives doesn't mean they can't be used, and doesn't mean we can't be . . . be . . ."

I'm searching for the word. Not *heroic*, exactly. But something that makes a mark on a world. Not someone larger than life, because I want us to live, but someone who grabs life and takes it for all it's worth just for the joy of it.

"Exceptional," Six supplies.

"Magnificent," Jules offers.

"*Dangerous.*" Ellin's grin turns wolfish.

"Interesting," Mark adds. And then when we all look at him, he withers slightly. "What? Is there something wrong with being interesting? Maybe I just want to introduce some mostly safe high-chaos states to otherwise stable societies! Maybe that's what I'll do: revolutionize the package-delivery market in my next life in a way that leaves gaping and strange inefficiencies!"

I press my eyes closed. "What a . . . bizarrely specific example?"

"Is this why you were asking me about speed perks earlier?" Ellin asks. "Are you planning to do something silly?"

"Hey, social mobility has to come from somewhere." Mark shrugs. "May as well have fun with it."

I leave them to their plans for their next lives, which I am certain will be disrupted, as these plans *always* are, and wander back to the bar to replace the clay urn on its shelf. I consider one more drink from it, but a hundred heartbeats is a high cost when that minute is one of my last.

Standing there, listening with half an ear to my friends, I lean my elbows on the bar and take a good look at Bastion's. The rough wood floor and metal stairs to the oddly recessed second floor, the mismatched tables and chairs, the lamps, the hanging engine, the handful of landscape paintings on the walls from before I first found the place. All of it feels so familiar, a touchstone between lives. And yet a little empty, even with the extra mass of the equipable barrels taking up floor space by the bar and casting a new shadow on my lurking spot.

Bit by bit though, we've been filling it with our own souvenirs, our own little touches. Art and games and sometimes new chairs. The others haven't even checked their notifications for this life; they knew I was short on time, and so instead of doing it up front, they'll be waiting for me with a few surprises the next time I come back. As well as coming back with a surprise of my own, in the form of whatever new book I pull out of my next world.

I love this place. So much so that I've mostly abandoned having my own room in the Between just to pour marks into maintaining this space, keeping it stable and reachable and alive. With at least five of us, it's not even that expensive. But it's also ours. A little secret refuge where we don't have to be tired for a while. It being freshly stocked with alcohol, and a potential source for more, helps too.

I'm interrupted in my eavesdropping on that source talking about his plans to set his barrels to fermenting some kind of fruit brandy for the next fifty years of his next life, just to see if he can bring us a nice treat, by the sound of a door.

My head snaps up like a kid expecting a visit from a favorite aunt. I haven't seen Molly in three lives, and there's other friends who've been gone longer. Or perhaps someone I've met recently coming back by. Even a brief passing smile would be a small bit of buoyancy for my heart, a little something to help tide me over through however long my next life is.

Instead, what we get is someone I've never seen before. This happens around Bastion's often enough that I'm not surprised, but I do try to hide my disappointment.

The man is an orc, close to baseline, and he's tall even by the species standard. Skin so dark green that it's almost black, curved tusks that gleam like they're polished, and wiry black hair that reminds me of one of my professors in the last life. A style that just radiates career-academic energy. The look on his face is one of barely restrained ire though.

The others all watch him, and Mark gives me a look like he wants to know if I want him to take over, but I wave them off. They all keep up their conversation, but with the kind of quiet pauses that make it clear that they're all listening in as the orc stomps up to the bar.

"Are you open?" he asks directly, in a voice that I am kind of ashamed to admit catches me off guard. He has a smooth and bassy sound that comes from deep in his chest. I shouldn't actually be surprised; I've been an orc enough to know that there's no requirement to play to the stereotype. But I've also been stabbed by enough orcs to maybe have some unintended biases.

"No, I'm Luri," I say before I can stop myself and then instantly wince, look away as if breaking eye contact can restart the conversation, and look back. "Also yes, if by open you mean serving drinks."

"Thank the bloom." He claims a barstool, the fine cloth of his pants rasping against the leather. "I've been here for three million heartbeats this time, and you're the first person I've run into. And you can get me drunk. It's the pollen of fate." He raises a hand, elbow on the bar, and gives me a dramatic look as he extends two fingers. "A beer and a flame, please. Whatever you've got on tap."

I consider what he's asked for and then look around what we actually *have*. "I don't think . . . I can do either of those." I bite my lip as I let my eyes play over the various bottles, urns, casks, jugs, and growlers that we have. "How do you feel about cider and a citrusy rum cocktail?"

"I think I'm still thirsty enough that I would go to war for you to pay for it." The orc gives me a look with his eyebrows that I think is supposed to be smoldering, but I can't offer him more than a thin grin at the moment, his flirtatious voice only barely offsetting my anxiety about my upcoming departure.

Deft and practiced motions see me through the mixing and pouring of a cocktail for him. An old recipe that I can serve in four shot glasses, poured at different points in the mixing process. "Drink it in this order. Savor it as much as you want. There's no hurry." I line the shots up in front of him, feeling mildly embarrassed that we don't have better cocktail glasses. Maybe Mark or I, who tend to moonlight as bartenders for extra cash in lives where we need it, can find an upgrade that lets us harvest cups.

Now that I know it's an option, I'm excited about the prospect of harvesting cups. What has my life come to?

The orc takes a long drink from the cider, eyebrows rising as he tastes it. Personally, I thought Six's attempt was *good* but still from someone learning. The man at the bar disagrees, apparently. "Wonderful." He sighs as he sets it back down. "How do you take payment?"

"Eh." I shrug. "I'm not too bothered. Six is gonna want to empty the barrels before he leaves anyway, so he can try . . . I think brandy, but I wasn't actually paying close attention and kinda forgot. Maybe a few marks?"

The orc looks at his cup, then his eyes flick off to the side in the motion of someone checking their heartbeats. "Perhaps I could open a tab?" he asks. "Are you the proprietor of this fine establishment?"

"One of them." I nod toward the others, who all offer the kind of waves that mean they've been listening in the whole time. "Why, whatcha offering?"

He smiles. "I have recently earned a *hallway* as a reward. I don't need it, but it might be useful for someone with a property." I don't let my smile slip or at all let on that none of us actually have ownership of Bastion's. Just a very fluid relationship with the space that gives us some permissions but no controlling security. Fortunately, I'm very good at putting on a mask for customers, whether I'm alive or dead.

"It's been a while since we've expanded." I tilt my head. "Or had enough people to expand for, honestly. I'm not sure what good a hallway would do us, but I'm not saying no?"

"Well, I do admit, it would clash with your decor." The orc sighs himself as he samples the first of his cocktail shots and raises his eyebrows again in appreciation before drinking the whole thing. "Oh, marvelous. Who knew that you could get this treatment here in the Between?" He shakes his head, one large dark hand brushing at his tusks in thought. "But yes, you seem to have a rather rustic aesthetic here, and what I have is, for what I could tell you of it, somewhat *off*. All white stone and wrought iron. Midsummer techless atmosphere. It would artistically clash."

I sweep a hand across our chairs. "Matching isn't our strong suit."

"Ah, but coherent moods are the foundation for an artistic soul!" he protests, holding a hand to his chest. "And I realize I am talking down what I am offering. But I have principles!"

"Artistic ethic, I believe, we can appreciate," Jules says, sliding up to the bar next to the orc. To his credit, the man doesn't react to my friend's odd form.

Instead, he just nods eagerly. "Yes, it is a matter of . . . personal taste, but also the coherence of how we spend our time," the orc states, like he's remembering a half-written dissertation from an old life. "Still, you might find use for it in trade? I simply don't have marks on me at the moment."

"Oh, make no mistake; trading us terrain would see us use it for certain," Jules tells him, which gets a look of dismay from the orc. "Though I think you are overlooking the *deeper* artistic meaning at play . . ." He pauses and waits to see if his audience is paying attention. The orc is, a captive look on his face as he leans in. "The organic mingling of disparate styles into an emotional coherence. The art of the familiar home."

"You are a scholar of art yourself!" The orc claps a heavy hand on Jules's body, sending him wobbling, tentacles lashing around as he tries to hold himself up. "Ah, sorry, so sorry! I truly should modify this body at some point when I have the marks."

"No concern at all." Jules sounds dazed as he rights himself. "Though, Luri, were you not preparing to depart?"

"Yeah, I'm out . . . soon."

Jules flows effortlessly around the bar and wraps me in a hug, his smooth tentacles warm against my flesh. "Then I will entertain our guest. Go, say your goodbyes. And know that I will look forward to seeing you again."

"Thanks, Jules." I try not to sniff as I wrap my arms around his central body. "Hey, I don't want to come back to find you turned this place into something weird, okay?"

"Please. Trust that I have some sense of style," he says, and I smile back because I know that I absolutely do.

I nod at the orc and tell him I enjoyed meeting him and that I'll see him later. He stammers an apology because he took up some of my time, but that's just how life is. I give my time freely to others in the Between; sometimes I need some of it to myself, but it's the most valuable thing I have. And sharing it is only amplifies its worth.

The other three meet me halfway across Bastion's, between the tables where they've been waiting. "I'll miss you, again," Ellin tells me and presses me into a kiss that goes on for long enough that I'll be confused over what we are for half my next life.

"I too will miss you," Six says. "But I will not be kissing you."

"That's fine, Six. I still love you." I give him a hug, his unyielding form feeling sturdy enough to hold off the Between if he needed to, even though I know he never could. "Oh, the orc at the bar likes your cider. I think he wants all of it?"

"Hmm." Six glances over. "I will speak with him," he declares, the words as flat as ever, even as he breaks the hug and steps away. "Goodbye, Luri. I wish you well. And I will see you again."

"Thanks, Six." I turn to Mark, the last one of them. "Hey." I try to keep my smile.

He shakes his head. "Sucks," he mutters. "We just got here."

"Yeah, well, I'll live better this time," I promise. "Six said I have to."

"He absolutely did not say that." Mark snorts. "But I get what you mean. I'll do the same. We'll have half of forever next time."

I give him a hug, and his strong arms practically crush me as he returns it. Like he's trying to keep me here. "Don't worry about me. Have fun without me. I mean it! Both of you!" I look up at Ellin's smiling face. "Fall in love.

Make Jules feel awkward. Oh! The guy at the bar has a hallway he's trading us. Have fun with that! Don't wait on me."

". . . What did you do when you got here first this time?" Mark asks me, trying to peel me back so he can look me in the eye.

I don't let him. "Oh, I absolutely waited," I shamelessly admit. "I always wait. I'm waiting for so much, Mark. There are so many people who hold pieces of my heart, and I'm longing for every one of them to walk through that door. Even the ones I've forgotten. But I'm an old idiot. You're young."

"I'm over six hundred—"

"A *baby*," I overwrite what he was saying. "Maybe next time you'll catch up."

There's a moment of quiet, and I feel his chest shake with a couple of laughs while I'm pressed against it. I check my heartbeats. Not much time left. I open my mouth to say something, but I don't know what to add. So I say nothing.

Ellin's arms encircle us too. And I press my eyes closed and let myself be there in the moment. Etch the feeling onto my soul, to never be forgotten. To try to stretch it out for as long as I can. I keep my eyes shut. Maybe if I don't see it coming, it won't be so bad. This is a lie, of course. It doesn't matter. It's always bad, in some special way.

"You're gonna have a great life, Luri," Mark whispers to me. "I know—"

I don't hear the end of his reassurance. I'm too busy being alive again.

CHAPTER SEVENTEEN

Eyes that weren't real until this moment and really still *aren't* that real at all open. My heart is beating like it wasn't just created from nothing. My breath coming steadily, despite breathing being something of an affectation for the dead.

For once, this body feels *worse*. The constant projected Elben fields of that last life's world, along with doses of perfected chemical stimulants in every drink and ration bar, made feeling good a reliable part of every day. And now I'm just me again. Not happy. Not vibrant. Just myself, with the physical changes gone.

I raise a hand over my head and sigh. Bronze skin and slim fingers splayed between where I'm lying in the Between and the pipe chandelier on my room's ceiling. It feels good to move, a satisfaction as my fake muscles get a chance to stretch and breathe. It's a seminatural pleasure, as opposed to the induced joy I got used to. But despite the fact that I'm at peak health, and nothing hurts, and all the woes of life are behind me now, it still feels harder than being happy just as a default state.

But bit by bit, my psyche reasserts itself. The blankets of the bed feel electric on my naked skin, the false air of the Between fills fictional lungs with a pleasant ember, and seeing with organic eyes again, even if they're not really real, is something that has a kind of visceral excitement to it.

Words come to my attention.

[Welcome back to the Between, intercessor. 11,881,020 heartbeats remain. Prepare yourself.]

Almost twelve million. A bounty that I very rarely manage to reach, even as long as I've been doing this. A rush of relief fills my chest; I have subjective *months* here. In the moment of seeing what I have been given, the clinging remnants of my mind that wish I could just subsume myself into endless shared happiness continue slowly fading away, and real personal joy takes their place.

I don't get up right away. Instead, I let my hand drop and squirm in the recessed ring of blankets and pillows that is my return point. The wholly unmovable bed is unfortunately stuck here, but if I have time to spend like pieces of small iron, then I can stay here for as long as I want.

The nagging reminder that I am supposed to be doing something doesn't quite register to me. It's been a little while since I had to be used to thinking about things actively, and my ritual of silently waiting at Bastion's for someone who will probably never arrive is fuzzy in my thoughts. As if from a far distance, I experience a wriggling dread that I have been altered somehow, that my prioritization of euphoria is pulling me away from the person I want to return myself to.

But it is from a distance, and it is nagging, not overwhelming. And everything feels so *nice* right now, cloth recovered from two worlds mingling around me. I fumble to think that I should get a plush animal of some kind, somehow. Maybe I can become a toy maker in my next life and be rewarded for it.

I lose track of what I was thinking and just stare upward, a smile on my face despite the lingering feeling that I should be getting up for something important. But that worry is overridden when I shift slightly and the blankets brush against my body in a way that elicits a sexual rush that I haven't felt for subjective decades. The feeling triggers embedded prompts in my conscious mind, the ingrained desire to seek joy over everything else. Before I am really aware of what I am doing, I've brought myself to at least two orgasms and then promptly fallen asleep.

When I wake up, I feel refreshed in that way that only sleeping in the Between can bring. Like I might actually be able to keep going, and like the person that I know I am is the person I can *be*. Which is somewhat horrifying when I realize that the person I know I am is someone who still has a lot of very, *very* powerful conditioning in their brain.

I check my heartbeats and see that I have been asleep for subjective hours. I won't count it as time wasted, but there's an anxiety there that never goes away, telling me that I should have been doing something else. Even if I don't really know *what*.

Before I get up, I raise an arm overhead again and open a translucent screen. It's been a long time since I've made any real alterations to my body here. I like my tail because it's cool, I like my eyes because they remind me that I was once just like everyone else, and I haven't found a shape that I'm fonder of yet, so that isn't changed. I don't really change myself that often. But right now, I feel like I need to.

It costs ten marks of faith and five marks of knowledge to create a temporary condition that inhibits my false brain from experiencing overwhelming pleasure. It won't last forever, but it should last long enough for the safety net of the Between to let me overcome the emotional bonds that were placed on me in the last world.

Well, that I placed on myself. I had help, but I don't think it's right not to take my share of the responsibility.

I sigh and drop my arm back from the list of parts and conditions and mimic organs that this body has. Things feel a little more muted now, but that's not bad. With the way my thoughts are pointed, *muted* still means that everything feels a little too good. Enough that what I want to do is fall down the mountainside chasing after how good I know I *should* feel.

This, in no uncertain terms, sucks. I have recovered from addiction before, both in lives and through death. Normally death makes it simple. Your body is reset, and while your thoughts persist, the mind itself doesn't have the damage. But this time, I've set myself up with thoughts that are self-reinforcing; a cognitohazard that plays off what I feel instead of any particular trigger words.

What a terrible idea. At least with my quick brain surgery, I am capable of feeling like an idiot in full force. Which is appropriate, and deserved.

Crawling from the bed and standing up feels like an ordeal, despite the perfectly healthy form and the gently refreshed and recently napped mind. Not wanting to waste any more time, I move to open the door to Bastion's, but something give me pause. Looking down at my body, I cock my arms forward and twist to look at my tail before sighing again. Maybe it's the temporary change to my brain, but I feel an odd discomfort with my nudity at the moment.

Fortunately, as much of a mess as my inventory is, my dozens of lives worth of accumulated prizes mixed with the random things that I've picked up here in the Between makes it easy enough to find something to wear. It's an occultly armored pilot's suit, so it's not like it's *much* better than being revealed in full to everyone I meet, but having something pressed against my skin is comforting at the moment.

The door is waiting for me like it's the oldest friend I have, and if it were alive that might actually be true. I touch the glyph in the center and let it open for me and then step through the threshold to Bastion's.

Sometimes I think that the doors in the Between have something in them. Of course, this whole place does very little to conform to coherent space, but there do seem to be some rules. You can never fully cut off a room from anywhere, even if it's just a one-way door out. Someone who knows the right questions to ask could always pay enough to open a door *in* too. And the Between has a whole endless maze of hallways and rooms and strange sights outside of the stable rooms that we use.

But the doors are always just doors. You step through, and you're where you're going, even if there's no possible way for things to line up. It's honestly just not the weirdest thing I've ever lived through, so it never bothers me, but sometimes . . . Sometimes, like now, I get the impression that I'm not just stepping through a door. The feeling that there are whole worlds or stars or orreries floating in the slim threshold. Waiting, for something. Maybe for us. Maybe for something inscrutable, and thinking they're here for us is the height of hubris.

The feeling doesn't last long when it crops up. The doors are just doors, and stepping through only takes a moment.

"Luriiiiiii!" The first voice I've heard in this visit to the Between greets me with unmatched enthusiasm as I step out from the bland white walls of my mostly unfurnished room and into the rough wood and patchwork decor of Bastion's. It's a voice I haven't heard in *lifetimes*, and when I say that, I don't mean it figuratively.

Molly spots me before the door even closes behind me and launches herself off the barstool she's sitting on. The place my door drops me is on the other side of our three progressively less matching tables, but the furniture obstacles do absolutely nothing to stop her. Molly is the kind of person who revels in learning and controlling her bodies at maximum efficiency, and the three-foot-tall mixed-bloodline kobold form that she wears here is almost perfectly adapted to her brand of acrobatics.

Her aerial arc off the barstool lands her on the largest table we have. She takes advantage of the indestructible nature of a lot of things in the Between to turn what could be considered a body slam into a tumbling roll, popping out of the wheel of motion at the very end to grab the back of a chair and use the momentum to catapult herself forward faster. By the time she reaches me, she is essentially a very affectionate cruise missile.

I snatch her out of the air with a whirling open-arm catch, pushing the limits of how much stress can be put on my joints in the Between before something dislocates a shoulder and whirling around with a tearful beaming smile. It's been a very long time since I've seen this particular friend.

"You're the first one back this time!" she exclaims, jamming her snout into my neck as I try to hold her up with the thin arms I wear here, the long whiskers trailing out of her scaled maw tickling at the line of my pilot's suit. "Also, *aww*, you're dressed! I wanted to hear Mark make the same joke about you stabbing someone in the eye with your dick for the tenth time."

"Sixteenth time." I sigh. "Also that's *not* the joke he's . . . Okay, it's sort of the . . . Look, Mark has a lot of rewards and none of them start with *comedian*. And Mark isn't here?"

"Not yet. I've been here for about twenty thousand beats, and you're the first person I've seen." Molly falters. "I . . . I've been missing stuff, huh?" she says, trying to stare up at me as she resists being set down. It doesn't work because her face is longer than my upper arm and she can't actually do much more than butt into my chin. "Also you're talking already! Is this new?!"

"I slept in," I comment as I decide to just drop my friend. It doesn't work, and she just clambers up my arms and onto my back. "And I had to modify my thought processes. So I might be misprioritizing things until I'm fully back to myself."

I feel her snout pressing into the top of my head and can, without any need for my various social abilities, sense the glare that Molly is shooting into me. "You compromised yourself on purpose?" she demands.

"It was better than the alternative. I spent a lot of my last life essentially hypnotized," I explain, taking heavy steps to try to make my way to the bar, Molly's weight dragging me down but not stopping me. Just making me feel like I'm moving through mud. "It wasn't bad. I just didn't think it would persist here. So I'm a little regulated until the Between helps me strip it all out. Temporary. I know the rules."

She huffs a hot breath into my hair. "You better." Her grumble comes out as almost a squeak. "We don't replace friends fast enough to lose you."

"I'm replaceable?" I say, perking up slightly. It would be a lot of assumed social responsibility gone if I were easily replaceable. The clawed hand slapping the top of my head in response can't actually hurt me, but it does get a surprised yelp as I almost trip. "Okay, okay, I'll be good," I promise her.

"You better," Molly growls as she slides off my back and almost gets caught on the bone plates of my tail. "So, how'd you end up hypnotized? Evil wizard? Evil sorcerer? Evil fetishist? Evil . . ."

I take a barstool as Molly flips herself over the counter like doing aerial vaults is just the normal way to get around a room. "I don't think I was evil," I comment.

"Wait, *you* did it?!" The kobold's incredulous stare is almost too adorable for me to take seriously, though her being perched on a chair behind the counter means she's at eye level with me, so I don't get the added amusement of seeing her peeking over the edge. "Why would you do that?!"

"It seemed like a good idea at the time?" I ask. "And the last time I was here, we were all talking about living . . . authentically, I suppose. So I was trying to live my best life."

"Through hypnotizing yourself."

"Well . . ."

"And bringing the condition back."

I try to think of how to explain it and decide that maybe it can wait for anyone else and the kind of group sharing that we tend to do. "I'm not *contagious*, unless you want me to install an emotional conditioning in you, which I know how to do a lot better now. It might even work here, if you actually want it." I take a deep breath. "And it really did seem like a good idea," I defend myself weakly. Molly just growls softly in the back of her throat before placing a cup of something in front of me. "What's this?"

She gives me a long blink with the compassionate hound's eyes her body has. "A drink?" Molly asks rhetorically. "Do you not . . . want a drink?" She reaches out to take it. "I was going to make one for myself, but . . ."

"I meant what drink is it," I say.

"You don't usually question whatever this cycle's bartender puts in front of you. Are you *sure* you're okay?" She folds her arms, claws drumming on her thick frame in worry.

I shrug. "Part of what I changed was to make things not feel so good, so I wouldn't hyperfixate," I say. "I'll be back to being properly thirsty in a subjective hour or so." My estimate is optimistic, but the Between works fairly fast once something has been actually identified as an unwanted condition. And there's no rule that says that hostile effects have to come from someone else to be protected against; you can't hurt yourself in the Between either.

And I do wonder if what I've done is a form of hurting myself. I didn't think so at the time. But hindsight is a wondrous nightmare. And sitting here, letting the conditioning get slowly stripped off, I can't help but compare what I did to the worst kind of optimizer philosophy. Maybe I tuned it to the opposite direction from killing everyone for a high score, but I still tried to maximize my impact so I could have a slightly longer amount of time with my friends.

As if sensing that I am about to spiral into a crisis of personal morality,

Molly comes to my rescue. "So when did you all install the new side annex?" she asks.

I blink, momentarily cut off from my worries by the odd comment. "The what?" I ask like an idiot. She points a curved talon, and I follow to see that between the shelf that we use to stack empty cups on and the potted fake-dead tree that I still don't know the origin of, the supposedly solid wall underneath the library has a new hole in it. The hole is in the form of an archway, rough light white stone forming a jarring contrast with the wooden boards around it. Past the arch, I can see from my angle that there's a cobblestone pathway with wrought iron lanterns on one wall, columns making up more stone arches on the other side. Open to the elements, though *which* elements I can't see, and I have no idea what something like that would even look out on here in the Between. The lighting is different there, flickering fire in the night casting a welcoming aura, just enough to show off the hints of green from the ivy that creeps down the stone. "Oh! That hallway!"

The process of remembering something from a literal lifetime ago is a funny one. In some ways, coming back to the Between, I feel like I was gone for just a moment. Like I stepped out to get a breath of fresh air in the middle of a party that is still in full swing. But that isn't always how it feels, and right now, I'm getting the opposite effect. The feeling that someone is asking me to answer a very specific question about an event that happened subjective decades ago, and I wasn't really paying attention *then* either.

"Yeah, why's it there?"

"Six made some kind of cider in a life and then an orc showed up who liked it and paid with a hallway, and I guess they decided to apply it after I'd left?"

Molly stares at me like she's hunting for a hint as to how much of that I made up. But she finds nothing. "I love this place," she eventually settles on quietly. "That's just so weird. Also it smells nice out there." I get a hint of the smell from a light breeze drifting in: the perfume of flowers and a summer night in a world that never invented the combustion engine. It *is* nice. "What else did I miss? Catch me up!"

I think she's trying to distract me, or maybe running a mental test to make sure I'm still the Luri she knew. But that's okay; I'd do the same, and I've got a lot to tell her. "Okay. Where to start . . ." I try to think of how long it's been since she's been back to Bastion's. "We have a new tiny magic tree upstairs. Six has a bunch of equipable barrels that he's using to try to learn to brew us a stock for the bar. Ellin was in a romantic phase last time I was here and was trying to kiss everyone who wasn't Six. We've had a half dozen strays come through once or twice. Apparently we're remodeling . . . Uh . . . What else?" I try to think. "Oh, I got an aura layer that lets me bring books back! And Mark found something that makes *coins*!"

"Coins?" Molly tilts her head at me, puppy eyes shining with curiosity. "Wait, no! Don't distract me with shiny things! Was Ellin trying to seduce Jules?!"

"Yes," I answer with an honest nod, my face a serious mask. "It wasn't going well for her."

Molly clacks her claws together in an imitation of a snap. "Darn!" She huffs. "That would have been hot! You know Jules has enough tentacles to—"

I reach over and pat her on her head fur. "I know about the tentacles, yes, thank you, Molly." I try to sound put out, but I'm still smiling. Actually, despite everything, I'm feeling quite content, which means that my modifications are already starting to reset in small ways. "Oh, also, we played at least two Encounter scenarios. No one touched your character, Ellin is still cheating against us to make things harder, and we accidentally lost a planet."

She stares at me, and I look back at her, trying to keep my face impassive. Then she slowly leans forward on her chair over the lip of the counter and grabs the drink she made for me. Stealing the mug out from in front of me, she takes a drink in the only way that really works for her body type: both of her scaled hands on either side, holding it steady as she tips her whole head back to pour the liquid past her thin lips. Molly downs the entire drink in three gulps, perfect control over her body letting her miraculously not spill any of it out into the void.

The thump of the cup back on the counter and her appreciative gasp almost make it possible to miss the sound of a door closing. And then, a vibrant voice from upstairs calls down to us. "Utterly *terrible* table etiquette, darling," Jules comments as his tentacles coil around the library's railing, keeping him from simply tumbling down onto our tables and chairs as he lowers himself to the ground. "Perhaps the next vendor that comes through, we can search their wares for a proper dining straw."

Molly squeals, ignoring the friendly ribbing as her face lights up. Her eyes shine in a very literal way, red-and-orange flames dancing across under the corneas. I catch the tip of her tail on my forehead as she explodes into motion, once again launching forward over the counter and vectoring off the surface of a table to fling herself at Jules's main body, which is currently halfway down to the ground. She hits him with a noticeable thud and a wail that *shouldn't really* be surprised from Jules, his grip slipping and the two of them tumbling back through the newly opened archway, rolling into the new and somehow semioutdoor hallway in a tangle of laughing limbs and tentacles.

The sounds of laughter and affection, echoing through Bastion's in a way that turn it from just another place into something that feels like coming home, suddenly take a shift into a delighted squeal from Molly and sounds that are slightly lewder.

"Oh, hello, Jules," I say into the open air over the bar, leaning an elbow on the surface so I can sarcastically hold out an open palm. "Good to see you again too. How was your life? Me? Oh, I've been pretty good . . ." I cut off as the sounds of their reunification escalate from lewd to outright erotic. "I'm no prude, but I think the privacy hallway was a *great* investment."

"I agree," Six says from my elbow, taking a seat next to me. "Hello, Luri. It is good to see you again."

By some miracle, I contain my panicked yell and instead break into a smile. "Six! See, *that's* a good greeting!"

"Do you like it? I borrowed it from what you were saying, as I did not think that greeting you like that would be appropriate for our relationship." He angles a pointed finger toward where our two resident lovers are enjoying each other out of sight. "I thought it was clever."

"No one could *ever* accuse you of not being clever." I nod sagely, meaning every word. Then I stand and stretch, and the way the sensation feels good to me makes me think that I'm coming back to myself more fully. "I need a drink, and Molly stole mine. What're you feeling like today?"

"Rice wine please," Six states. "Is anyone else here yet?"

"Still waiting on Mark and Ellin," I say, setting two small clay cups out and pouring us two doses from an old bottle. "And maybe Tee-kon, if it's ever coming back."

"I do miss its verve." Six's studied emotionless voice makes it *really* hard to tell when he's being sarcastic, but in this case, I think I've got the golem's attitude pinned down. "It was quite excitable. It added to the mood."

"Oh, be nice," I chastise him through a laugh. Then my smile slips away, going from ear to ear down to something a little smaller. "It's good to be back," I say softly.

Six looks at me with eyes that see more than I think he ever really lets on. "It is, yes," he says. "I would—" He is cut off by a high-pitched noise from Molly that would make a hardened fertility priestess blush. "Hmm." Six blinks deliberately, in the sense that everything the golem does is deliberate. "A refill please. And I will retire to the library, where I hope the acoustics will muffle that slightly."

"Good idea. I'll bring the bottle." I smile at my friend, and the two of us cut a path across Bastion's to what is hopefully relative safety from feeling mildly awkward.

It's good to be back. It'll be nice to see everyone again.

CHAPTER EIGHTEEN

So, what did you spend your life doing?" I ask Six.

It's fun to play games with small stories as wagers, teasing out memories and moments from our lives. It's fun to sit around and make a production out of some of our proudest actions and harshest follies. The theater of it all, and the company, and the shared feeling of preserving within each other bits of lives that we'll never get back, never see again, and never remember forever; it's all a small island of comfort and sanity in the endless roil of forever that we exist within.

But sometimes it's just nice to sit with a friend and talk about things. And since I don't want to dig into my notifications from the Between yet, talking to Six is an excellent distraction. Though nothing is stopping him from going through his own list of winnings from his last life, flicking fingers through the air with precise and measured strikes as he dismisses small bonuses.

"Many things," Six says, which is a *strange* thing to hear from him. The golem is normally focused on singular ideas that catch his attention in each world; multitasking just isn't his interest. "After you left the Between last cycle, I took some time to decide how I wanted to approach your puzzle."

I cock an eyebrow at him, pulling my tail up into my lap as I try to make the chair comfortable. We need better chairs up here. Or a couch! "It wasn't a puzzle, Six. I just wanted . . ." I trail off.

What did I want? It's not even clear to me, and not just because my recovery modifications aren't fully worn off.

The last few lives have been hard. I'm not sure why, but at the same time, I know exactly what's wrong. I don't have a clear picture of what I want; all I know is that there are some things that scare me, that I never want to become, and that I cannot tolerate.

And I've been lumping those things mostly under the banner of *optimizers*. But that's a loose philosophy that has acted as a stretchy buffer against any hard questions, and that simply does not let me cope with harder questions about how I actually want to live. My last words here, last time around, were grasping at something I didn't have the picture of yet.

Am I slipping toward being what I hate, just because the Between *is* good at making that an incentive? Am I still who I want to be, or am I being shaped without noticing? And what am I supposed to do about it, when, after all, there *is* no escape?

You'd think that after a few lives, you'd have all the answers. But it turns out, when you get past the major problem of death, you just end up with a new problem. And it's kind of hard to answer the question of what you want to do with your forever. Though as soon as I dredge up the thoughts, the answer seems so easy. I wanted to live a powerful and dynamic life, and make use of my upgrades to do so, because I wanted more heartbeats here. Because what I've chosen to value is my freedom with the people who are close to me. And even when we're separated by centuries, they're still the closest thing I'll ever have to a family again.

"I just wanted to have more time." I shrug, keeping most of the thought private.

"How long have we known each other?" Six asks abruptly.

I have to think about it. Tracking actual numbers in the Between is hard when it's not something attached to a reward because you can't really write anything down. The last time Mark tried to use napkins to make a catalog of his perks, someone accidentally bumped the table and erased a thousand heartbeats worth of his work. It's not worth the anxiety to try to keep things unmoving.

But also remembering across lives gets jumbled. When I'm here, after a little while, things blur. I may as well have always been here; the lonely lives become distant, and the last day of the previous cycle feels like it runs into the first day of this one. So giving Six a real answer is tricky.

Still gonna try though. "Forty lives?" I ask. "Fifty? The math isn't too hard. Hang on . . ." I average out how many heartbeats I usually end up with, how much overlap there is, and then apply a standard pessimism filter. "Probably a bit more than a thousand days, subjective."

Six's steady and uninflected voice is at odds with the tiny smile that cracks his gray face. "If I had not learned charity across a dozen worlds, I would be offended that you are close to correct when I know every part of your thinking was a guess," the golem says.

"I love you too!" I cheerfully deflect.

"Luri, for a thousand days, I have watched you struggle to piece together who you *are*. You do it so poorly compared to our companions." I know Six isn't trying to offend me, but that stings to hear. "Some of us are making a performance of it; some of us are just building bit by bit on the self that we started with. But you? I've watched you try to jump to the perfect version of Luri three times, and after each failure, you fall into despondency."

"I don't do that," I mutter, pulling my tail against my chest, feeling the long muscle stretch almost painfully as I hug myself in this least comfortable chair that Bastion's has.

"You do exactly that," Six firmly corrects me. "Your last words were a puzzle to me, not because I believed you were trying to offer a question, but because I wish to understand my friend." His eyes meet mine, and I see the sharp and deep intelligence there that Six has always had and only ever worked to add to from life to life. "And if there is some answer that I could offer to help you avoid another period of hopelessness, I would give it freely."

It would be cowardice of me to blame the tears welling in the corners of my eyes on backlash from my modifications. Same for saying that I spent a whole lifetime in stable happiness and am now unused to this sharp stabbing in my chest. "What did you come up with?" I half choke out, a few drops of hot liquid spilling from my face into nothingness before they even hit the table.

"That a thousand days isn't enough," Six says, still watching me. "That the easiest answer then is to do what you said. Live well, live brilliantly, and then celebrate here after." A thin line of passion slips into Six's voice, an affectation I know is intentional. "And then try again and be marginally better."

"I don't want to be better at the things the Between wants to see," I counter with a bitter tongue.

Six shrugs at me. "Then don't be. Be better at being Luri." He speaks like that's easy. "I do know you will say it isn't that simple. But you've always been a good friend to all of us. I think that person is a good version of Luri. So be them."

The way Six talks always makes it catch me off guard when he hits me with things like this. Even knowing him for subjective years, it's still wild to me that someone with such a flat voice, who keeps around a lack of expression as a reminder of his origin as an unfeeling creation, can display the kind of considered compassion that he does.

"I thought I was doing that," I hear myself saying. But I already know I'm lying. "Well. Here at least. Last life I . . . might have . . . been someone else." I shake my head. "Also none of this tells me what *you* were up to! Stop making things about me, Six!"

His mouth twitches upward slightly at me as he raises his cup of rice wine and takes a perfectly measured sip. I drink as well, but with a less refined motion, just seeking a small spread of warmth through my throat as the alcohol fills me before the Between beats back the outside influence. "You are simply upset I am better at the game than you."

I glower at him, though there's no anger in it, and my face is scrunched up in a way that never stops being amusing even after hundreds of years. "Tell me what you did last liiiiiife." I draw out the word for emphasis, and to show my dedication to prying his secrets from his stoic mouth.

There is a thump from the newly instantiated hallway underneath our little library, and both Six and I look down in concern as the sound vibrates through the wood under our feet. But before he can say anything, I refocus on his eyes and insist with the most powerful look I can manage that he satisfy my curiosity. We can worry about Molly and Jules later.

Eventually, Six relents with what I think is concealed amusement. "Well, as we have some time . . ."

"It's either talk and drink or I go join them," I suggest to him luridly. Six is no prude, and I'm certainly not either, as the flat look he gives me says that he knows my threat isn't hollow. But also, we're having a nice conversation, and interruptions bother Six more than anything.

"Gnoll base-form body, finite-energy-era civilization, sixty-eight subjective years," he states rapidly, making the decision for me. "The world was almost an ecumenopolis, though I think I'll save the details of that for the others. Ellin and Molly especially will appreciate the details. What you care about is what I was doing, which was, bluntly, more things than I have kept track of."

I offer a comfortable smile as I refill our cups, even though my words are more rueful. "Oof, I know that feeling. Busy lives get messy."

"Yet satisfying. When I was in my early adulthood, before the time when I began a new fashion trend among my district that interacted with the gendered normative styles of clothing—"

"You cannot say that and then not explain that."

Six continues, doing exactly what I have ordered him not to. Despite being a golem, Six is *very* good at deliberately ignoring commands. I think he takes pride in it. Which is good! I know I would. "I had established myself as one of the early adopters of a new form of entertainment. The world did not quite have networked information sharing, but they had a form of long-distance communications that relied on doll-like spiritual receivers tuned to each other. Several other students and I found a way to make the broadcasts wider, rather than tuned."

I raise my eyebrows. "Radio."

"Just so." Six nods. "We were not the first to attempt to use the connection in a nonpersonal way. But we were the first to figure out how to let people tune to *us* instead of creating invasive emotional attacks. We were also not the first to discern how to use umbrim infusions to change the dolls, though we adopted that tactic as well to portray characters." The golem tilts his head up at the slanted ceiling of Bastion's library, giving the closest thing to a sigh he ever emotes. "I stole proudly from a score of lives to build a library of stories. And we found success and fame, which others mimicked. Half the district tuned their receivers to us to see our final performance, and the trend swept out into the broader population." He looks back at me. "I keep this body here because it is easier to manage my emotions, but, Luri, I am certain you know the elation of that kind of riotous success."

"Absolutely," I mutter. A little shrug and the thwap of my tail on the floor as I stretch out. "There's something about reaching people that's etheric, even without the Between shoving its rewards down at you. It sounds like you had fun!"

Six nods, a precise up and down like he's trained for centuries to get the most efficient nod possible. "I did," he says. "And it was just a part of that life. I have been considering . . . changing myself, here, in the Between." The words seem like an abrupt shift.

I cock an eyebrow, leaning forward, reminded briefly of the pilot's suit I'm wearing when my elbows don't feel right on the table surface. But I shake that off. "Why?" I ask him softly. "Not because of any of us?"

"No. Never." Emotionless words, still spoken so quickly I automatically know what he's putting behind them. "There is a difference," Six says more slowly, back to being measured and calm. "I go out, and I live, and every time it feels different. But it is always a struggle for me to adapt to those emotions. The rest of you slide into lives so easily and earnestly. If I practice, here, it could make it easier for me."

And at that, I cannot help but puff out my cheeks with barely contained laughter. Six gives me a stare and slowly sips his wine as he waits for me to compose myself, but I only barely manage before I start rambling. "You think we're *good at this*?!" I explode. "Six, I just came back from brainwashing a whole world 'cause I don't know what happiness is! You're the most mature person here!"

"Failing to connect with others when I am required to contend with fear and lust is not maturity, Luri," Six says, refilling his own cup and setting the bottle back down with a hollow thump that indicates we are nearing the need to return to the bar.

"We're not good at this," I restate. "But also, if you want to change . . . Just in case you're thinking it? . . . Everyone here will still be your friend."

"I'm not proposing I make myself *erratic*." Six stresses the word.

I chuckle at him over the rim of the clay cup I'm holding to my lips. "Oh, yeah, that would make you fail to fit with us for sure." My sarcasm goes unappreciated. "I'm still glad you had fun. What kind of stuff were you doing with the whole setup, anyway?"

Six relaxes ever so slightly, and I wonder if he's already started letting tiny edges of emotions creep in. Not that he doesn't feel to begin with, but more that he's *expressing* it, which is novel. But not unwelcome. I'm *good* at reading Six, but he's still a black box to a lot of people. Though I should warn him to maybe keep his expressions on a toggle so that he can keep duping Ellin in bluffing games.

"The majority of our performances were single-act monologues in the Hygorian style." Six starts and is already expanding on that before I can get a good flat stare going. "The Hygorian were an ancient people from a prior life of mine who used a form of refraction and echo technology. Copying their monologue style worked well for the format of dolling, as it was focused around anticipating and addressing statements from a potential audience without ever seeing them. Building on this style, my cadre and I wrote new monologues based off of other stories. We worked in the realm of fiction, though I am aware that others were using the style we pioneered for political and social purposes as well." I still love Six's history lessons.

"One-man plays, sort of," I muse, leaning back and letting the feel of the Between version of alcohol stir in my chest. "Except prepped for audience interaction. Educated guesses, or did you find a way to cheat?"

"Cheat, naturally. I have no compunction about fairness in art." Now I *know* Six sounds smug. "By the nature of the pseudonetwork, anyone tuned to our broadcasts was in some way sending back. We created an admittedly rough method to collect statements spoken at the performance and collate them in written form. Over time, many of our stories would shift and change as we improvised answers to questions or responses to criticisms in real time, and the game of back-and-forth became known to the audience, who took it as a form of engaging challenge."

"And then you stopped?" I ask. I know that *I* probably wouldn't have stopped, and Six is a far more focused and goal-oriented person than I am. "Out of character for you."

"Oh. No." He looks away from me before standing and moving to lean on the library's wooden railing. "When our time of youth studies ended, my cadre and I mostly broke apart. But I continued. Experimenting, iterating, trying new things. You are familiar with the feeling of security we have in knowing that death does not hold us."

I absolutely am. It's sometimes frightening, to have that power and see how fragile everyone else is when we're alive in the worlds. I rise to my feet and tip heavily onto my tail as I push the chair away and move to join Six, bumping my slim shoulder into his thicker gray flesh. "Course," I offer. "It's a weirdly shaped sword."

"That is not what that saying means." Six doesn't delve into that, instead pivoting back to his original point. "There is a similar feeling that came with anonymity. Hundreds or thousands of dolls looked like . . . not me, but the me that I crafted for them. Moved to my movements, spoke my words. But no one would ever know who *I was*. I was free to live a double life. On the one side I was a respectable academic. On the other, I spent my evenings provoking self-exploration and inciting changes in fashion and sexuality among the district's interested populace."

The words bring a bright smile to my face, and I tilt my head sideways to lean it on Six's shoulder. "Oh, so *that's* what you meant earlier! I wondered where the lust part came from."

"It is embarrassing now, in retrospect. The truth, Luri, is that I felt embarrassed by it even when I was alive there and growing older. But I never regretted it. The embarrassment was simply lack of experience and a part of the novel thrill." Six shakes his head. "Most of them would never have the chance I do. To learn from so many lives and years. And I am wasting it. It is inefficient."

The noise that comes out of my mouth is as dismissive as my many lifetimes have let me learn, and I *have* been perfecting it. "I know I need to actually focus down my philosophy about optimization." I offer a qualifier before I speak my real point. "But, Six, here's something I *know*, in whatever heart I happen to be wearing at the time. Efficiency doesn't mean anything to any of us anymore. It can't."

Six lets out a sad little breath. "On a long enough timeline . . ."

"We'll get around to everything eventually," I finish with a soft smile.

After a while of staring down at the empty floor of Bastion's, and my own personal thoughts turning to the fact that I really do want to rearrange those tables at some point, Six speaks again. "I know that you mean to offer me positive thoughts, but I am not currently ready to accept that I should live undirected lives."

"That's because we ran out of rice wine," I counter. "Somehow. I could have sworn that was one of the endless bottles. Want to go down and . . . Actually, wait, the barrels!"

"Ah, yes." Six nods. "I have low-quality beer to share."

Well that's hardly being kind to his craft. Though he did sort of imply that he spent half his life invested in something that wasn't brewing related.

I'm right behind Six, the two of us halfway down the extended metal steps that we use as a staircase, when a door opens just ahead of our path. The noise of slamming cuts over the steps as someone walks through, and between one blink and another, I find myself looking at Mark as he walks in with his arms stretched back over his head and a cocky grin on his face.

He's changed a little. A small mark on one of his arms, almost like a tattoo, poking out from just under his favorite Between fashion of his dragon-feather toga. Part of my thoughts scream that things are changing and people are changing and soon I won't recognize my friends, but the rest of me, and the part I actually listen to, says the same thing that I say out loud.

"Mark!" I throw my arms open, offering a hug that cannot happen until Six gets out of my way. "You're here!"

"Luri! You're dressed! I had a new teasing joke ready and everything!" he counters, *lying* I am sure. "Also hey, Six. Oh, it's so good to see both of you." Mark falls on us as we reach the bottom of the stairs, his thick arms wrapping the two of us in a crushing hug that I really should have expected but still catches me off guard anyway. Next to me, Six goes limp as he gives up on resisting being smooshed by our friend. "Am I late to the party?"

After making some strangled noises to indicate that I actually need to breathe to speak, even here in the Between, I return a much softer hug and give him an answer. "You're fifth. Only Ellin left now, unless we have more guests. Or depending on how into conversation with that art-critic orc Jules got last time."

"*Very*," Mark answers with an overdramatic expression on his face. "Wait, fifth. Does that mean that—"

He is cut off as a blurred form hits the side of the bar we're approaching and then kicks off in a twist that defies biological laws. Molly slams into Mark with the force of a sledgehammer, squealing in glee at his return. And to his credit, Mark recovers almost right away, spinning her around in a wide arc before returning the crushing hug right back to her small form, both of them laughing with delight at what many lesser forms might classify as assault with a deadly body but they just think of as a casual greeting.

"Oh, fuck, it's so good to see you again," Mark breathes out, pulling Molly against his chest. Then he looks around Bastion's, the expression of someone who's been away for a *long* time and is seeing an achingly familiar and nostalgic thing for the first time in a whole life. "It's good to . . ." His mask of joy slips a bit as his voice wavers. "I mean. It's . . . I . . ."

Molly comes to his rescue in the only way we really know how: providing a distraction until we can ease into our emotional breakdowns. "So I've been missing stuff," she declares. "And Luri says you found some drink recipe that kills people. And I want to try!"

"It doesn't *kill people*," I start to protest, but Mark is back to laughing, and so I drop the complaint.

"It *was* meant to get Six drunk though," he comments, trying to set Molly down and finding that the kobold simply won't allow it, instead crawling across one of his arms and wrapping herself around his back. "But sure. It's been a couple lives, but I think I remember the recipe. I'll mix a pitcher up."

"And then we can sit and drink something that I seem to remember being acidic and talk about everything and nothing," I say with a smile, already edging toward my favorite chair as Mark heads back around the counter, maneuvering so he doesn't crack Molly's skull on any of the hanging odds and ends around the bar. "And hopefully, Ellin shows up!"

"Oh yeah, where's Jules anyway?" Mark asks.

Six and I just point toward the recently created arch that leads to the "outside" environment of the new hallway. Mark glances at it and then tries to crane his neck up to look at Molly, who is starting to give a suggestive cackle.

"Ah, right." He snorts a laugh. "So I missed exactly enough then! I'm so good at dying on schedule that my timing is *perfect*."

I can't help it. This time, I do laugh. A long and giggly burst that feels more real than anything else in the Between and that gets picked up by the others as they share the moment with me, and we all settle in to wait for our last friend and turn what is otherwise a few oddly connected rooms into a home.

CHAPTER NINETEEN

You'd think that by the fifth time someone came in, Molly would have gotten tired of turning her highly tuned kobold-mutt body into a projectile weapon and testing the limits of the Between's safety measures. But no, partly because Molly is a boundless pit of enthusiasm, and partly because our bodies don't tire here.

Our minds do, certainly. Emotional exhaustion, runaway thoughts, broken focus, all of that adds up over time. There are fixes, like getting as close to drunk as we're capable of, or sleeping. But you can't get drunk without an inebriant, and you can't sleep without a bed, though at least we have *one* of those available.

Molly isn't immune. But Molly is also an extrovert, and has been for the last ten lives we've intersected after, and I both admire and envy her ability to refresh herself with company. I *love* company, I love my family here in the Between, but even when I'm watching the heartbeats slip away, I cannot do nothing but engage with them. I need to spend time silently in the library, or take a nap, or grudgingly focus on equipping talents and perks.

Maybe I'll do it a little less grudgingly this time. We'll see. I'll think about it after I finish watching Ellin frantically try to shake our kobold friend off of using her horns as a jungle gym; Ellin's towering form is no less dexterous for all her size, but Molly is both fast and *incredibly* dedicated to getting a rise out of us through what she calls physical affection.

And maybe she did tire herself out over the last few subjective hours because Ellin actually manages to catch her, and the next thing I know, there's a familiar projectile of scales and fur and whiskers zipping between Six and me.

"Now what did we learn?" Jules sounds serenely patient as three of his manipulator tendrils capture Molly out of the air and daintily settle her back on her feet. His glowing red eyes are framed in a slowly spinning open triangle as he speaks with his smooth tenor of a voice.

"Ellin is faster, and it's not fair?" Molly suggests.

Ellin takes one more heavy breath as she steadies herself, tugging the dusty white wraps around her arms and torso back into their proper place. "Hoy! Don't blame this on me!" she barks out. And then her eyes settle on the rest of us, and her face splits into a broad and toothy smile.

And I feel a bit of worry. Not anxiety—I don't have much of that about other people anymore. But I was looking forward to seeing Ellin, to seeing what we might be now, to interacting with her in a different way, to having time to *talk*. And all of a sudden, I realize that she might not have spent her whole last life pining for something the way I did. That she might not still feel the same way. That any number of things could have happened to make her change her mind away from the fleeting and ephemeral romance she wanted to try last time.

She greets Six with a bear hug and a whispered word, which the golem nods at and gently slips from his chair with his characteristic elegant precision. Then Ellin drops down next to me, and before I can say anything, I find myself being kissed.

I melt into her, letting her take the lead. It lasts long enough that my heart starts racing and then slowing from lack of breath, and I have to pull back with a gasp. Ellin's eyes seek mine, and I see a small worry there too, though she's decided to react a slightly different way. "Hoy, Luri!" she greets me.

"I had a question, but I forgot it," I hear myself stammer.

"*Perfect.*" Ellin's worry is gone, replaced with smug self-satisfaction, and I'm a little irate that she might have earned it. "Oh! Mark's here!" She pops upright, rustling a hand through my hair as she heads for the bar where Mark is carefully mixing ingredients in our crystal pitcher. I shoot him a knowing grin as I see him eyeing Ellin approaching, and he barely gets one word of protest about proper stirring before he's lost to the same treatment I got.

Whatever life Ellin lived, however long it was, it doesn't seem to have done a single thing to change her declaration from last go-around.

I let the others go through the array of greetings. Hugs, warm words, smiles, the constant familiar feeling of seeing people you've missed for *so* long.

But no matter how fragmented my own personality can get, or how hard it is to know what I actually want, I do know that I'll always love coming back to them.

A long, long time ago, death scared me. Now, it's just another front door into a place I can't wait to visit. That might be unhealthy. But it's not as if we have a clear picture of what a mentally stable deathless looks like; it turns out that sociological studies in the place between worlds are actually somewhat challenging to conduct. Who knew?

Me. I knew. I tried once. Part of me still *is* trying, sort of. It's why I like talking to everyone who comes through.

I feel like I've only just blinked when Mark is setting a familiar old goblet down in front of me and filling it with two different liquids from two different pitchers, the brew beginning to steam and bubble as the mixes meet. I eye the stuff that would assuredly be lethal to this body anywhere else, *trying* to remember if I liked it or not before tasting it, while Mark continues to circle the table as everyone sits. He's a deft hand as a bartender—he's done it across five lives, including his first—but it's still impressive how no matter how impressive his muscular frame is, he never even brushes anything he doesn't mean to as he serves our group.

Then he's settled too. Across from me, Molly, half wrapped in one of Jules's tentacles, pokes at her cup in concern. "It's *whining*," she states, snapping her eyes over to Mark. "You have a new cup! Did this actually *melt* your last one?"

"Luri gave me a new one. I like this one!" Mark defends his carved coconut shell. "Also it's not whining; it's undergoing the Yesmin reaction. Or . . . well, the pretend Between version of it. Drink it before it stops," he warns as he hoists his own drink up to his mouth and takes a pull of it, keeping his expression positive. I try the same and remember that achitas is *not* my favorite drink, that I think my entire face feels like it's on fire, and that while I'm absolutely going to drink all of this, I need to focus to stay on task and struggle to keep my mouth in a placid smile for now.

"Before it stops whining," Molly states.

"Ah, it's good! Me, I love the stuff. Makes me feel alive in a deeply metaphorical way!" Ellin's cup, even though the blue coloration makes it partly opaque, still shows the roiling insides of the drink as she slams down half of it and makes a content noise.

Molly is still suspicious. "I feel like you're all lying to me," she offers. But then she takes a deep breath and an equally deep sip through the metal straw that's sticking out of her incongruous kiln-fired mug. *Instantly* I can tell she regrets it. Her face screws up, and the smoke the drink produces starts seeping through the corners of her muzzle. "Ahhh! Ahy 'ate iss!" She tries to talk without swallowing.

"Oh, you definitely want to swallow it," Mark advises.

"Yes. Otherwise it may explode," Six comments, sipping his diligently. He nods appreciatively at Mark. "A good drink. Thank you for making it for us."

"Ahm eying!" Molly rolls out of her chair to the floor, flailing like a poked king hornet. "Jules! Help me!"

". . . How, dear?" Jules sounds split between confused and amused. "Any action I have to assist the inside of your maw, the others may take umbrage with. And really, while I value all of them, I do not think we are quite at that level of casual exhibitionism in our friendships." He pauses. "Except Luri." Another pause. "Perhaps Ellin now."

I chuckle, currently undermining his point by wearing anything. "You just have to take another sip, Molls," I say coyly. "You get used to it. It grows on you! Like plasma fog!"

Molly just lets out a low wail from under the table. The black wooden chair she was sitting in shifts slightly as her claws come up to grab the seat and she hauls herself back up. "You're all awful!"

"I do actually enjoy this," Six says with unfazed calm.

"You're all awful except Six!" Molly corrects herself, her claws scraping her muzzle and pulling on her whiskers like she's trying to wipe a spiderweb away. "You owe me for this!" she declares.

Mark shrugs, his friendly demeanor not skipping a beat. "Yeah, that's fair." He leans back and sighs, and a tension that had been with him since he entered starts to ease away. "Hi," he says softly. "I really did miss you all." At his words, Molly drops her mock aggravation in short order and settles back into her seat, scooting slightly closer to Jules as she does so.

"Hard life?" Molly asks.

"*Crazy* life," Mark answers with a wry twist on his lips.

I want to reach over to him, but Ellin is between the two of us and beats me to it anyway. "Wanna share about it?" I ask him.

"Eh." He tries to brush it off. "I'll trade you," Mark offers. And the others all groan because they know already that getting details out of me is often a feat that the Between should reward a person for.

Something about that makes me feel rebellious. "Okay," I answer simply, shrugging. Jules's eyes spike upward in surprise, and Mark's eyebrows do something similar. Ellin just gives me an excited grin, rubbing her hands together. "Want me to go first?"

"Are we doing life stories, or worlds, or just highlights?" Mark asks suspiciously.

"I was going to start rambling and see where I ended up." I give an honest appraisal and get a barking laugh from Molly. "I haven't even checked my notifications yet either, so I'll probably forget some important things."

Ellin slaps a hand against my tail as I stand and start to lightly pace around my wedge of the table. "You hate using the notifications as memories anyway!" she reminds me.

Which is totally fair. I do. I feel like they make us lose something when we do that. I *will* be checking all of mine sooner than normal this time though, if only to retrieve something that I picked up on the way through my last life.

My friends watch me with eager looks as I take a breath and try to think of how to start my story. I don't do this very often. I'm not a good storyteller when it's just the open expectation of explaining a whole lifetime. There are a lot of lives I come back from feeling outright ashamed of myself, and in truth, this one is no different. But at the same time, I'm feeling warm and a little giddy from the assuredly caustic drink Mark served, and all these people are the closest possible friends, even if they're friends from years and years ago subjective.

So I just start talking. "I was born late, and badly. That mom died when I was a year old, from complications, and I got stuck in an orphanage. Not a *bad* one, but it's where I grew up. And can I just say? It's a little freeing to just be one of the kids and not someone's special someone. Six sorta made me think of this earlier." I nod toward the golem, sipping with both hands from his ceremonial basin, before continuing. "The world was one of those human-only ones, with lots of constant border shifts instead of a single history-defining war. And it was kind of assumed a lot of the kids in my orphanage would go into a military. I beat the odds though and got a scholarship. Started studying psychology."

Jules raises one of his mobility tentacles. "Not to interrupt, but was this choice perhaps because you wished to learn how to aid anyone in particular?"

"You know, you might think that?" I bite my lip. "But surprisingly no. Mostly. I mean, if I get some kind of Ennui Resistance then I'm *not* using it. But any wisdom-backed ability that has a single-use effect would . . . I'm getting sidetracked." I shake my head rapidly to try to get off that tangent.

Six sets his basin down calmly. "Your studies," he prompts me.

"Right. So, schools weren't great. *Cities* were kind of impressive, but a lot of them had been built a while back and were just coasting. They were huge though. I think you all could have found something to love. Big towering spires with webs of paths between them, open spaces everywhere. Not much sun, though someone a long time ago had invented a bioluminescence thing that lit the streets, and it was really comfortable." I slip too easily into nostalgia for a place I'll never see again. "But I learned what I could and then got surprise recruited into a local military program."

"As a psychologist?" Mark sounds surprised. Then his face gets a sad look on it, and he glances away. "No, yeah, sorry. I just thought about it. Keep going."

"So, local physics were a little forgiving compared to what we're usually used to, but no metaeffects as far as anyone knew. No magic, no aura, none of that." I hate calling magic *magic*, but now isn't the time for Luri to go off on a much longer, much more irate tangent. "Or at least, that was commonly accepted wisdom. The thing about the program was, aside from having *really* nice accommodations, they wanted everyone to cross-train with the hardware and wetware aspects. Oh, the rooms were great though. I had so many plants. The world wasn't really that green when I got there, but I just asked and got a dozen wallvines for my room, and I understand this probably isn't what you're all looking for." I flush as I get back to the point.

The others don't look bothered. Ellin especially is just staring at me with a goofy sparkle in her eyes. "Tell us about your bed!" she demands.

"The bed was fine. It was a military installation, Ellin. The bed was only ever going to get up to fine, and you know it," Molly jumps in, rapidly chattering an answer.

Being interrupted doesn't bother me. For the same reason tangents don't bother them; we've got all the time we need now. "I *wish* Molly was wrong . . ." I leave it open to interpretation. "Also sorry, Ellin, no lurid details of how I used the bed. Mostly because I didn't. What I *did* do was remember that I have five different intellect abilities and perks slotted, and the heaviest one is actually Intuit Toward Engineering Macro-Outcome. I say remember because I didn't check anything but my aura last time, or for a few lives really, so . . ."

"You're impossible." Mark gives me a shake of the head.

"Well, that's what the engineers said too," I agree. "Regardless. The pay was good. The only problem was that we were working for part of an endless global machine that fed off a series of proxy wars and shifting borders. Which, I mean . . . Too common, really. Except this time I decided to do something about it." My chest tightens slightly, and it's not the pilot's suit constricting me. "I had that constant thought, the whole time. That I needed to do more, needed to *be* more. Needed to make sure I'd earn enough heartbeats that I wouldn't be alone. I might have panicked." Might is generous. I did, as a certainty. "So my first thought was sabotage."

Ellin butts in, loudly declaring at me as she tilts her head back to look at me upside down, "And this is why you need to always have a Strike on you!"

"Yeah, I went another direction." I stop behind her and rest my elbows amid her horns as I keep talking, pulled forward when she rights herself but staying perched on her head. "The military wanted a mental weapon. So I built one. Used all my charisma charges to get the rest of the scientists on my side, and then, we . . . built a weapon. Sort of."

"Ah." Six speaks softly. "Your modifications, as a recovery."

I give him a nod. "So it actually took half my life to get everything set up, and it was a massive conspiracy, but when we were ready, we flipped about eight thousand switches, and we . . . ended war." I shrug, like that's just a thing. "Partly I was just in the right place to make the most out of a few traits and aura layers, and also a lot of other people helped make it happen, but also partly I was there because I was trying to do something that could make a difference. So I give myself maybe a third of the credit."

"What exactly did you do?" Mark asks, leaning forward on the table, his chair squeaking under his shifting weight.

I shrug again. "Created an infectious mental command that made people repulsed by armed conflict," I say. "That was actually the *easy* part, if you can believe it."

"I don't." "Nope." "I refuse to believe that." "Yeh liar!" "Psh!" Their voices overlap and almost make me switch from dramatic regret to laughter on the spot.

"Well it was! The hard part was what came after! It took another good chunk of my life to build and tweak, but those same people I worked with . . . We made a short-term version of that. A kind of broadcast tower for emotional vibes, sort of. And then we put them up all over the place and used operant conditioning to make everyone associate positive social behavior with raw happiness."

"Oh . . . Shit . . ." Molly mutters.

"*Then* we got creative. Oh, we were absolutely in charge of things by that point. More or less. So we—"

"You took over a world." Ellin gawps at me.

"Not *alone*!" I fail to adequately defend myself. "Also I didn't take over! I was elected! Sort of. And . . . Uh . . ." I trail off, clenching and unclenching my hands trying to look at anything except the people around the table. "I wasn't trying to hurt anyone. It just got out of hand. We wanted to build a utopia." I laugh bitterly. "I think we did. That's the real fucked-up thing. I really think it worked, mostly. We mastered social conditioning. We had hypnotic trances as part of behavioral correction in clean and practiced facilities. We didn't have to *make* anyone do anything. We just told them that we'd make them happy, and the world tripped over itself to say yes."

Ellin shoves me back lightly, looking between me and Six with growing horror. "You did it to yourself too," she says. "You *idiot!*"

"Of course I did," I say, folding my arms. It's the one thing I don't regret, in a perverse way. "I'm not a *hypocrite*, Ellin! Not while I'm alive, anyway! Yeah, Six, I know that . . . *Yes, Jules*, I know I can be . . . Okay all of you stop staring at me." I flush again, ducking my head. "I was the perfect member of a perfect society. We made it safe, practical, and healthy for everyone to be happy all the time. We killed depression; we *ended fear*. The murder rate in my world was almost *nothing*, and over ninety percent of it was from people who refused to go through the process."

Six holds up a hand. "Why were those people around?"

". . . Because we didn't force anyone to do anything? Did I not explain this?" I look between them. "I mean, we didn't ask permission to wipe out the national and private militaries, but they were literally military targets. That's what that means. It means you can fight them and they don't get to complain."

"That is . . . technically correct," Jules says slowly.

Molly flicks a claw across his central stalk. "You say that's the worst kind of correct!" She sounds annoyed.

"I disagree." Six naturally sides with me. Six loves technicalities.

Ellin's face watches me sadly. "I also disagree, but only because I know Luri," she says. "I know you," she whispers. "But I don't know how you could do that."

"Ellin, I love you, but you fight someone in almost every life you—"

"Oy, no, not that." Ellin flutters a hand. "It's really hot that you're finally conquering worlds. Love that. I mean tamperin' with your mind. On purpose. That . . . You could have forgotten us, Luri." She sniffs and looks away, scrubbing the back of a hand against an eye. "You could have forgotten me."

I want to say that I doubt that very much. I want to tell her that I would be utterly unable to forget her or *anyone* seated here with us. Every part of me that cares about Ellin and Mark and Six and Jules and Molly and every other smaller friend who occasionally graces us with a visit, or whom I've only met once or twice, all those parts of my mind and whatever passes for my soul want so desperately to speak the magic words that I would *never* forget her.

But I think we'll live forever. I think the word never is a lie, and always is a cruel joke. And also, more immediately, I know that what I did, even though I was able to quickly undo it, *was* damage that followed me home.

In trying to save a world from itself, I almost threw my own mind away. What kind of person does that?

Well. Someone who didn't know what came after for them, maybe.

I think Mark sees my obvious distress because he wraps me in a hug while I stand there trying to figure out what I should say. What I even could say, except to just shrug and tell Ellin that I *know* and that I'm *sorry*, but apologies like that have a little less weight after a few hundred subjective years. So I lean into Mark's strong arms and don't look at Ellin.

And really, this was what I actually wanted. Not that I'd say it that way, but this is what I feel, in my shame, that I needed and deserved. Everyone *should* be mad at me. I broke a whole world's civilization so that I could be happy for a little while, and I almost changed myself into someone who wouldn't come back to Bastion's at all, just stare at the ceiling and occasionally masturbate and feel content enough with no thoughts or social contact or anything else. I almost destroyed my mind, chasing heartbeats. And they really should think I'm an idiot for it.

The next words I hear that aren't quiet mutters are Mark's. "Ya know," he says, letting me go and moving my unresisting form to sit, "I honestly don't know what I expected, but there's no *way* mine is going to top that. My worst fuckup was adopting a dog."

"Hey, wait, dogs are cool." Ellin instantly comes to Mark's dog's defense.

"I was a refugee! I could barely feed myself!" Mark rebuts. "Luri's decision to mind control herself is basically genius compared to me starting a dog orphanage while starving and traveling three thousand miles on foot."

He's trying to cheer me up. Mark wants me to be okay, and while I think he knows it's never that simple and it's never a moment-to-moment decision to just be fine, he's trying. He cares. No matter how stupid I've been, he cares. It's pretty open emotional manipulation. But, all the same, as I see Ellin relax and then ask me if I'm okay, as Molly and Jules relax and ask me a few world or body questions, as Six just treats me like he always does . . .

I do feel okay.

So I adjust myself in the chair, and pull my tail up, and take a deep breath. Feel my heart count down my time here in the Between. And I ask a very important question.

"So, do you have any pictures of the dogs?"

CHAPTER TWENTY

O h!" Mark exclaims in the middle of Ellin daintily trying to balance a notched piece of resin in the stylized shape of a leaf onto a similarly stylized branch. "I got to ride a motorcycle for the first time!"

It has taken him six loops around the table of us playing Vyrd's Arbor to think of a positive element from his last life. Molly made it a requirement, something about how my own sorrowful infliction of memory had to be balanced out. Which really, I thought was pretty unfair. My life wasn't *sad*. It just sort of . . . got out of hand in a few places.

By contrast, Mark's life was pretty sad. And since he already told us about his dogs, he had to think for a bit to come up with something positive to start with.

Vyrd's Arbor is a dexterity game though, and it was made by a variant of orcs that I would bet half my soul evolved from raccoons. This is the polite way of me saying that none of us are very good at it, even if it is a lot of fun to fail. Having someone yell and slap the table when you're perched on your toes and placing on a third-tier branch is *undesirable*. It's also one of I think four separate games we have that are tree themed, but that's less important.

Ellin doesn't even flinch. But she does stop moving, locking every one of her newly created imaginary muscles in place as she freezes, nothing so much as twitching except her eyes as she flicks an iron glare in Mark's direction.

Molly and Jules are catching up in the library, actually talking and taking a look at the living piece of art that Jules brought back a couple of lives ago, so it's just me and Six who get to witness this drama. Slowly, ever so slowly, Ellin tries to lower her hand back to delicately balance the game piece, moving with the kind of apprehension like she knows someone is going to interrupt her in a few seconds.

"Did you not previously reside on a world with combustion engines?" Six asks. "You have a quarter of the lives of Luri or me, but you have had opportunities."

I add to the problem, trying not to grin as Ellin grits her teeth in concentration. "Also, *also*, Mark was a smuggler! *In one of those lives!* I remember this!" It was well over a hundred subjective years ago or so, but it stands out to me. He was talking about his wife, and being a florist, and how afraid he was of forgetting. I choose to set that aside, to remember the important part for the sake of this conversation. "You had to have gotten on a bike at some point."

"First off, they didn't do motorcycles in that world," Mark starts. "Something about how gravity worked. It made balancing weird. But also, I was a *classy* smuggler. I wasn't getting into chases with the law, tearing up the byways. I was—"

"Hang on, that's *exactly* how you framed it!" I squawk out in protest.

"I seem to remember you also saying that you were part of a roving band of misfits in your last life as well. Did that one also have cars but lack velocipedes?" Six inquires flatly. I point a finger at Six, nodding in agreement.

Unamused, Mark just folds his arms. "I had other stuff going on," he grumbles. "Do you wanna hear this story or not?"

"I think Ellin wants to finish her move first." My voice carries a sly lilt to it.

The multitiered spindly tree, constructed out of dozens of pieces that we've all been adding one by one, breaks in four places and clatters to the table with a noise like a house being demolished. Ellin, still standing with her arm out-stretched, takes a deep breath and then lets her hand open, the single leaf piece adding one last plink to the noise of the loss.

"I'm going to throw you into one of Six's barrels." Ellin vows an oath in a voice somewhere between ominous and deeply sexy.

"I'm both aroused and terrified," Mark says what we're both thinking. Though he's probably a little more on the terrified side. "Wait, into as in against the side of, or into as in you're going to turn me into beer?"

"That is not how fermentation works," Six states, sipping the lemonade I brought him earlier and tipping the refurbished bottle toward Mark in punctuation. "Usually," he adds.

Ellin stares at Mark for a while before making a grumbling sigh and sitting back down to start sweeping up the resin pieces and splitting them back into piles for us. "Just tell me about tha fucking motorcycle, yeh?" she says as she shakes her head, frustration slowly being replaced by a little smile.

Looking a little sheepish, Mark leans over the arm of his rough-hewn wood chair to reach out to her, and Ellin's smile comes back in full force as he does so. "Sorry," he mutters softly before actually going into his story. "So, the . . . Wait, do we want to grab Molly and Jules? This was her idea anyway."

I point upward. "They've been lurking and watching us for a while," I tell him without looking.

Mark's head tilting upward and the somewhat surprised expression on his face tell me I was right. Our friends are probably directly over my head, staring down from the library. "Okay, that's . . . No, that's about what I expect from them, sure." He chuckles and leans back in his seat. "Okay. So."

"So motorcycles?" Ellin prompts.

"Yeah! Well, probably not what any of you are . . . Six did you call it a velocipede? . . . No, no, don't answer." Mark shakes his head. "More like a stripped-down car than a built-up bike. Huge, thick wheels, and a *lot* of shock absorbers and suspension. Really made for off-roading. I didn't build mine, but I'll bet anything that when I check my notifications later I'll have something for all the maintenance I had to learn."

"Did you live on the prairie or something?" Ellin asks.

"I didn't live anywhere. Refugee, remember? Mass climate crisis. Everyone was running from something." Mark shakes his head. "It wasn't . . . I don't know how to describe this. Have you ever lived on a world that's ending? I know Ellin has. But it doesn't seem that common."

I shrug, the pilot's suit putting up the barest hint of resistance to my shoulders, reminding me that it's there. "A few." My answer is noncommittal. Six just nods.

"Well, I don't know what's normal, but the one time I did, everything happened *fast*. Like, one day, the cloudseeds fell, and people started dying, and it was like a *wave*. Like the world got swallowed up." I remember this. Mark was hesitant to share anything about that life. Absolutely one of his worse memories. We give him somber nods, trying not to get lost in our own bad memories. "This though? This wasn't like that at all. This was . . . Everything fell apart, but it did it slowly. Social collapse on a time frame of decades." He sighs and tries to shrug, only to find Ellin's hands on his shoulders, comforting. "Farm yields went down, so food got more expensive, but there wasn't mass starvation. Places got too hot, but not enough to wipe everyone out, so cooler places got more expensive. Fights started, but not wars. And more and more, people just . . . left. Why live somewhere that was going to kill you slowly? If you didn't own anything of value, it was easy to just pack up and get on the road."

"To one of the better places?" Molly asks, her scaly and furry head poking out between the wood rails overhead. "Like a road trip, but with your life on the line? That almost sounds fun . . ."

Mark gives a bitter chuckle. "What better places? Things were getting worse everywhere. That's the point. You ended up with more people traveling, fewer and fewer havens, less food, less power, less . . . everything. It was like the whole world was quietly dying. But there wasn't anything to *fight*. A few people turned warlord, and there were some mild bandit gangs, but . . . Eh? They were in the same situation as everyone else, and there were fewer than I expected."

"So . . . What did you do?" I'm curious because he was talking about a motorcycle, and I'm not sure how we got to here from there. "I don't usually ask this, but nothing from here would help?"

It's not that I like to pretend the Between doesn't exist or that I actively avoid using the upgrades. I just try not to think of the powers as integral parts of our lives. Or at least I have been. Trying to treat them more as . . . as small intercessions from a moment of luck instead of things to plan around or ask after. Normally it's Ellin or Jules asking about things people did with their powers or Six and Mark discussing build ideas.

I've been staying out of it. But maybe I'm changing a bit.

And clearly Mark notices it, but all he gives me is raised eyebrows and a little reassuring smile and a nod that slowly turned into a shake of his head. "It wasn't any one thing. Besides, I used up half my perk slots on Cycles of Romance and Caste. And then all my ability weight on . . . uh . . . Acting . . ." He rubs the back of his head, looking incredibly embarrassed.

"Oh right, we talked about this! Because Ellin was being a creepy child, right?" I perk up. "Did it work out? I actually might try that since I sort of . . . I don't know how to be a kid anymore either."

Jules lets a very long mobility tentacle drape down from upstairs to pat me on the head. "Oh, dear Luri, I think you make an excellent child," he says, the smooth comfort of his vibrating voice making it take me a second to be insulted.

But I do get there. "Hey!"

"Honestly it didn't make much of a difference." Mark intercepts the squabble before it can start. "A lot of the early stuff related to it is . . . short-term? One-off charisma abilities that can get you through a single conversation or one good lie or something. Being a kid is a long-term responsibility." Something about how he phrases that makes me start giggling. Or maybe that's because I've cut my herbal lemonade with wine, the bottle is almost empty, and it's helping me relax. "Anyway, Luri, no. I don't think anything really tipped the life one way or another. I just kind of wandered around looking for work."

"And eventually adopted dogs. And a motorcycle?" Ellin asks. "Which sounds *very* manly of you, truth."

"I was a woman in that life," Mark comments, and Ellin throws her arms up in exasperation, getting an "Oof!" from him in reply as she practically launches off his shoulders. Mark might be the newest of us, but Ellin is the one who seems to have kept the most concrete idea of gender norms between lives. Which I find kinda bizarre because Ellin seems to take delight in stabbing people on worlds that she defines as too sexist. "And yeah, dogs. One, at first, then a few more. Then some puppies. I tried to find them good homes, but there weren't a lot of homes to go around, so I took care of them as best I could. Hunted a little, did mechanic work for food; there were a *lot* of people traveling, like I said, and once I got good at repairs, there was always someone new on the road who was willing to pay." Mark sighs.

I don't ask him how it ended. None of us do. He's got the *mood*, the look that says that he doesn't know if he wants to talk about it, the slump to his body that tells everyone that he didn't really enjoy a lot of his time, but he pushed through it anyway, and sharing probably wouldn't make him feel better, but that he might anyway in a bit.

"Hey!" Molly's voice exclaims shortly before she lands on Ellin's back. "What's the thing Mark said? The cycle perk? I've been gone. You have to tell me stuff!"

Ellin gleefully explains, even as she tries to shake the energetic kobold off of using her horns as a handhold. "Mark had a threesome with a king and ended up with a perk that generates coins when he gets promoted," she says.

"That's . . . None of that is true!" Mark protests.

"Some of that is true," Six counters, and because he is Six, everyone believes him. "Ellin is being comical, but not entirely incorrect."

I shake my head at them as they banter back and forth and stand up to collect some empty cups and bottles and go get more drinks for people. I miss having food here; it's been a long time since we've had snacks to go with board games. As I head to the bar, Mark and Ellin argue behind me about checking his notifications to see if he got a coin. Mark says he's saving them for later, Ellin says she's saving *hers* for later so Mark has to do it now, and it all turns into a circle of silly banter.

It's a bit lovely, and a bit exhausting, and a bit like having a family. A real one, a permanent one that will keep on not dying with me.

Molly follows me over to the bar after a while, taking a hopping path across some of the multitude of styles of chairs to reach a barstool. I think she's playing at not touching the floor, and I find her antics adorable. Molly is good at making games out of everything. "Whatcha drinking?" I inquire as she lands and spins once before leaning on the counter.

"Do we still have the stuff for a tropical storm?" she asks with sparkles in her eyes.

I glance at the glass shelves behind me, bottles and Molly's face reflected in the backing mirror of the bar. "No," I state with a sigh. "Also we're missing fruit. And, uh . . . the tiny jade spears? Though I guess I could just use toothpicks, but that seems lame, and doesn't work without the fruit, and also we don't have toothpicks."

Molly sprawls her upper body across the counter, arms outstretched to me. "Then I'll take a . . ." She draws the word out, her long forked tongue lolling out of the front of her muzzle. "Mmmmhh . . ."

I try to look like someone who is badly trying to look like a professional bartender, staring over her head with a mock stoic expression as she ponders the limited selection that we have here in Bastion's. I can't even offer her bar snacks we're so tapped out of a lot of things; it's not often that *I'm* the one wishing for a vendor to come through, but I think that today I'd tolerate one of the twisted semiferal presences if I could buy some popping zel.

Eventually, Molly and I crack and start laughing with each other. The little kobold reaches out a claw for me to take, and I do, and she looks up at me with serious eyes that are still watering slightly. "It's good to have you back like this," she says softly. And then, as is her way, gets immediately distracted from the emotional moment. "Oh! That reminds me! I got a souvenir for this place!"

She raises her hands like she's grabbing something and plucks an item out of her inventory before setting it on the counter between us. It's a glass jar, and a pretty big one. Maybe four gallons, a copper-banded screw-on lid, and made of thick and slightly clouded glass, not that the durability matters as much here. It's what's inside that I peer closely at though.

Dozens of tiny little spots of light. Not will-o'-the-wisps or sprites though; no, each of them is a buzzing little insect body, putting off a bioluminescent glow. A shimmering yellow or shocking orange, afterimages trailing after them as they flit around in the inside of the jar, sometimes landing on the outside. Or some of the sticks and leaves that fill the space.

"Aren't they adorable?" Molly asks, a fanged grin on her face as she presses her snout up to the jar on the other side of where I'm practically doing the same. "You can feed them heartbeats to make more, though they fade over time. Not alive, really, but . . . It's a cute little lamp. And a fun reminder for me." Her voice has a bittersweet tinge to it, and I look up like I want to ask her a question. She waves a claw in the air between us. "Someone I met when I was young. We loved each other, and we caught lightbugs together every summer. They're gone now. But now I won't ever forget them." She states the last with iron certainty.

"I love it," I whisper. "How about . . ." I look around. Bastion's needs more shelves. Or shelves in general. "How about in the middle of one of the tables? Not the felt one, but maybe the round slate table? A centerpiece and ambiance lighting all at once."

"Perfect!" Molly beams at me. "You're a good decorator, Luri."

I look around at Bastion's, with its rough wood, black-glass and mirrored bar, tables of three different makes, metal utility stairs up to a library filled with books from twenty worlds, and wall hangings in just as many styles. "You fucking liar." I don't manage to keep my voice from breaking as I say the words.

Our laughter cuts off suddenly when I see a line cut through the wall just to Molly's side and hear the familiar sound of a door opening. Molly is still wiping at her eyes as she turns to see who's come in, but I've already frozen, mirth suddenly gone, as a figure I haven't seen in a hundred subjective years walks in.

He's still just a kid.

The body is exactly as he left. Blank white default clothing, ebon skin, whiskers sprouting from sharp cheeks over a flat line of a chin. The young boy who I last saw two . . . three? . . . some lives ago. He stares up at the hanging turboprop engine, eyes filled with wondrous tears as he takes in Bastion's decor.

Then he sees me. The kid takes a halting step, head tilting to the side like he's trying to remember something long forgotten. One footfall at a time, he approaches the bar, pausing only briefly to look at Molly and her kobold-mutt body before he finally struggles up onto a barstool. Moving like he doesn't know how to be small anymore.

"Wh—" he starts to say, then claps his hands over his mouth at the sound of his own voice.

"Hello!" Molly exuberantly says, eager to welcome someone new. "First time around?" She spins on her barstool, a tail that looks a lot like my own wagging in a way mine definitely can't.

The kid looks at her briefly, then fixes his eyes back on me. Slowly lowering his hands, he's trembling slightly when he speaks. "It wasn't a dream, was it?" he asks.

"No." I shake my head, the smallest motion as I gently set down the empty glass bottle I've been cleaning out in the hopes that this one sticks around and doesn't return to the void. We have a surprising lack of bottles around here. "It wasn't."

"I died before," he states.

"Yup! And again, just now," Molly unhelpfully tries to answer with a dipping nod of her scaled-and-furred head. "It gets easier, if it's any consolation."

The kid is still staring at me. "Your name was . . . Luri? You . . . You . . . helped me. You told me it was going to be better."

I have a question that I'm a little terrified to know the answer to. "Was it?" my voice asks without my permission.

The haze of confusion drops away from the kid's eyes, and he straightens up on the barstool. His face, clearly unfamiliar to him but still subject to some instincts no matter how much the Between makes things disconnected, cracks into a smile. The coiled knot in my chest feels like it melts in relief as I get my answer. "It was. It . . . It was better, I think. Was *that* a dream?" He gives a strange look around the back of the bar, like he's suddenly noticing that Bastion's is a tavern. "Just something nice before I pass on?"

"No, that was real," I clarify before Molly can say something abrupt again. "All our lives are. As for passing on . . . Well, we don't really do that either. But I'm glad you enjoyed it."

"My family though . . ." He looks around, looking for the doors that aren't there. "Will they be here? Will I get to see them? And . . . No, no, I know I can change this body. You showed me how. I can . . . It's been so long since this was me. They wouldn't recognize me if . . ."

Molly looks at me, her gleaming yellow eyes dilating into wide slits before she nervously looks back at the others. The kobold inches away before suddenly exploding into motion, flinging herself off her stool and out of the conversation at high speed to impact Jules halfway across the wide-open room.

The kid and I watch her go before he turns back to me, voice steadying as he gets more familiar with it. "Is she okay?"

"No, she feels guilty," I say. "And even though it's not our fault, I do too."

"I don't . . . follow."

I sigh, a mask of sympathy on my face. I've been here before, been in his place before. When I was new, and then over and over and over again. Every time I've tried to love someone, I've been here before. "There's no easy way to tell you. They aren't coming." He looks at me, a haze of confusion coming back. "Your family. Anyone you knew. Your old world. They won't follow you. I don't like the word never, and the Between is a big place, but . . . But it doesn't happen. We haven't once seen it happen. They . . . They aren't . . ." I wave my hands helplessly, for some reason thinking that all my experience would have let me make this conversation easier. But no, of course not. It just drives home to me how it can all feel so hopeless.

He stares into me, face covered in betrayal. "I . . . No, no. That doesn't make sense. What happens to them when *they* die, then?"

"We don't know," I whisper. "We've never known."

"That . . . But I . . . I did better this time! I got to live! And you're telling me it didn't mean anything?!" Halfway between anger and fear is where his tone lands, an adult's words with a child's voice. Not the strangest thing I've ever heard, but it still hurts.

The words aren't a surprise. They're ones I've screamed before, at the walls, at myself, at the Between. At my friends. But at least right now, this time, I know what I would have wanted to hear after my first second life.

I reach out a hand and set it on the bar between us, palm up, an offer of reassurance. "Of course it mattered," I say with utter conviction. Because it has to, I don't add. Because it would be so utterly cruel if it didn't. "You lived it, and you did your best, and everything you did was *real*. Just because there's a gap doesn't mean it didn't happen."

The kid—well, the person in a kid's body—flinches as Mark drops onto the stool next to him. "Took me some getting used to too," he adds, making a motion like he expects me to serve him something. I roll my eyes but still flip a cup over in my palm and start filling it from what we have on tap while Mark talks. "Luri's right though. No one's really gone if they changed you. Even a little bit."

"And, of course, our worlds tend to follow us home. The trappings and decor of old lives and old memories are not so easily shaken off here in the Between," Jules's rich voice and equally varied vocabulary adds to the conversation as he settles in at the end of the bar, his mobility tentacles moving with a little restraint as he has brought Molly along with him, whether she wants to be here or not. "Hello again, little one," Jules adds. "I hope you found joy out among the world."

"Either that or something exciting!" Ellin throws in her thoughts. She doesn't sit with the others, instead circling behind the counter to wrap her arms around me. I try to tap away her attempts at kissing my neck with a twitch of my head, but her horns make that hard. "Or something very stupid. Tha very stupid things are usually funny," the towering woman adds sagely.

Six sits on the other side of the kid. "And if you didn't"—he keeps his voice quiet, the soft sound a counter to the lack of emotion in his words—"then you will always have another chance." He looks over at Mark, taking long gulps of the beer that Six himself brewed and brought back, and then makes an identical gesture to me. He gets an identical eye roll, but I serve him too.

"But I . . ." The new kid's voice cracks, his mouth moving silently as he stares at the polished black oak of the bar. "I just . . . I . . . They . . ." His hands clench and open loosely as his vision loses focus.

I reach out and take one of his hands. "Yeah," I say, everyone around me quietly nodding or sighing. Or just being Six and silently drinking his beer with a look like he's disappointed in himself. "I know. We all know."

He looks up at me, with eyes that beg me to give him all the answers and fix everything, and I just know that I *can't*. But he's not actually a child, and he seems to realize that I'm not actually a goddess or a blessed dream or anything else with real power pretty quickly. He gives a sigh and slumps his shoulders before glancing at Six, the golem holding his glass up to eye level and getting as close as he ever does to scowling at something. "Can I have one of those?" he asks.

"We can't serve a kid beer!" Ellin's voice catches me so off guard that I bark a feral laugh out before I can stop myself.

The not-really kid gives a tiny wisp of a grin, taking his hand back and brushing at his shoulders before feeling the shape of his face. Fingers twirl whiskers he probably hasn't had for subjective years as he nods. "Oh, yeah, that would be cruel." He can barely get the words out without a choke of something that's part laugh, part sob. "How do I . . ."

The rest of us pile marks and drops and crystallized abstracts onto the bar in front of him, a series of hands and one tentacle depositing the currencies of the Between—familiar to us by now but certainly bizarre to a newcomer—onto the wood. Jules gives him some advice. Ellin and Mark give more grounded advice that will end with fewer tentacles. Molly offers enthusiastic encouragement.

He changes rapidly, as is the way of the Between's modification choices. First taller, falling off his stool as he shoots upward. His face changes, more effeminate, different eyes, a different shape to the nose. But keeping the whiskers. Longer hair, smaller ears, skin color lightening to something that looks like it's secretly a very dark crimson. The first set of white clothing from the Between shifts with him, so it's hard to tell much else, but as he finishes up, his hands come up to touch his face again.

"No wrinkles," I hear him mutter.

"You can add those in, if you want," Six says simply. "There are several options."

"No! No, I . . . I'll get used to it. I guess I don't need to be old if I'm dead," the kid . . . the man . . . says. He looks like he's later in his life now, past the point when most people are ready to take on the world. A little tired, a little worn down, but still healthy and hale. Most people's first new bodies are like this. It'll be later, one or two lives from now, when he'll want his form to be younger, sharper. "What . . . What do I call myself?" he asks us.

"Up to you!" I cheerfully smile as I fill a cup for him and slide it across the bar before I start pouring a round for everyone else as well. "I stole mine from a piece of fiction in my third life that no one will *ever* get the reference for, but I assure you, it was very clever."

"I just liked how mine sounded." Ellin leans on me again. "Oy, you can't just be normal about anything can you?" her voice mutters into my hair. Of course I can. But I don't want to, and I'm dead, so I don't have to.

The newly remade person looks down at his—I think his; I'll ask later—beer, hand around the glass like if he lets go he'll lose his grip on every-thing. The foamy head of the lightly golden drink stares back, and the rest of us wait patiently. It's not like we lack for time to wait for a dramatic moment. Eventually, he raises his cup to his lips, speaking before he takes a sip. "I think I'd like to be called Shavoy for now."

The rest of us drink with him before slamming our cups down on the bar with varying levels of vigor. "Welcome, Shavoy!" Ellin declares. "To the rest of your lives!"

Our voices echo the cheer. Bittersweet, sorrowful, hopeful, angry, excited, and probably a thousand things besides.

I'm glad he had a good second chance.

CHAPTER TWENTY-ONE

Mark and I have dragged one of the small tables and a pair of the thin black chairs from the library out to the hallway that goes nowhere, and for once, we're both going through our notifications from the Between together.

Through the archway, there's something halfway between a party and a funeral going on. I've walked more than a few people through their first second death, but it doesn't really get easier. There's an emotional tension to it; you've just learned that there's no end for you, that everything you'll ever do will fade into a running sentence without enough commas. But also, you have everything, *everything* ahead of you.

Shavoy is telling his life story and trying to get drunk enough to not have a panic attack. This is helped by the Between making true panic attacks more rare but stymied by the fact that it does something similar to getting uproariously drunk. Also he's new to telling life stories, and mixed with the quarter of a barrel of Six's beer he's consumed so far, that means there's a lot of mundane tangents and confused backtracking.

It's not that I'm annoyed by it or anything. It's kind of charming, really. Someone stumbling through the first steps of eternity. I do really think he could be a good friend, or at least a regular of Bastion's. But right now, I've been socializing with other people for a solid subjective day, and I want a quiet break.

I suppose it says something about me that sitting in near silence with

Mark, each of us muttering profanity every few seconds, is what I consider a break. I don't know *what* it says, but it can't be too flattering.

Still, I'm trying to be better since my conversation with Six. And that means not running from or ignoring my notifications, not pretending that I'm just a normal person. I still don't think I'll be optimizing for a specific career or skill because I don't fully trust myself not to experience a runaway cycle with it, but . . . I'm going to try to care a little more. Care about what I can do for a world. And for myself.

So Mark and I sit and flip through hundreds of notifications. Each of us is looking for one in particular, but it's not like these things make it easy to guess at their contents.

You have achieved qualifications in local higher education—first stage: +15 marks of knowledge. 10% discount on next education perk or trait.
You have achieved qualifications in local higher education—second stage: +35 marks of knowledge. 10% discount on next education perk or trait.
You have completed 1,000 local hours of practical engineering: +10 marks of labor, +10 marks of knowledge.
You have recruited 10 people to your cause: +10 marks of passion.
You have recruited 10 people (scientist/engineer rating 4+) to your cause: +1 Crystallized Luck. Ability granted—Fluent Jargon.

"This is all actually kind of fascinating," I mutter. Admittedly, I spend a lot of my lives as a loner, and almost none of them were as a proactive leader. I've *been* a leader, but it's always in the form of someone hired for a job, or slotting into an existing structure in some way. The fact that there's a separate reward track for being the one forming the organization is . . . unsurprising, I guess. Not exactly unexpected. The Between seems to care about a *lot* of things. It's to be expected that it cares about this. But it's novel to me, and that's saying something after all this time.

Mark takes a sip of his ornate goblet of water and sighs. "Yeah, I'm learning I don't understand this thing at *all.*" He shakes his head, turning to look out over the small courtyard garden.

I really should have looked at this hallway earlier. It's so much nicer out here than I expected.

The chairs wobble a little on the cobblestones, and the table is uneven enough that Mark's attempt to note down stuff on spawned napkins has been disrupted already by a slight tip to the surface sending his hard work into nothingness. And the wall to my left is . . . Well, it's odd. It's clearly supposed to have some doors set in it. There are places where the crawling ivy and wrought iron lamps frame empty spaces in the rough pink-white stone. But there's nothing there. It's waiting, waiting for us to have more rooms to add.

To my right though is a beautiful sight. The stone columns and arches that frame the boundary of the hall look out over a little square of a garden. Roses and other hardy flowers blooming under the twilight. And it does feel like twilight, despite there being no sky. The dome over the garden is painted with what looks like an abstract starscape, constellations traced together with white paint against the black backdrop. But the endless flickering lamplight around us and the breeze coming from somewhere carrying pollen perfume on the air makes it feel like being outside again.

Seeing ourselves mirrored on the other side of the garden is a *little* weird, but after waving to myself and reaffirming that I find my own body as attractive as I designed it, Mark and I quickly settled into our quiet time together.

I blink, taking my view away from the half-blooming rose I was staring at, and reply to Mark. Neither of us are talking especially quickly, taking our time with the conversation. A few million heartbeats make all the difference in how we spend our time. "Probably not smart to assume we ever know how the Between works."

"I mean . . ." He waves a hand in the air, staring at one of the glowing notifications he has open near his head with an irate twitch of the corner of his mouth. "I must have done some of this before."

"I think some things just don't repeat." I say, thinking back; memories of my time in the Between tiny islands in the cloud of centuries. "Maybe some of them have conditions they don't exactly share with us. Keep us from . . . Well . . ."

"Optimizing?" Mark gives me a tiny grin over the field of empty cups on our table. Some of them are holding down napkins, but he gave up writing on them. Mark's a tactile person, but there's only so many times you can lose all your notes before you just surrender. "That *would* be it, if anything, wouldn't it?"

"Six already talked to me." I throw an arm over the back of my chair and try to lean back in a way that's more comfortable than the black faux-leather cushion wants me to be. "I'm working on the life philosophy a little."

Mark shrugs. "I'm not . . . Luri, I'm not like Six," he says. "Or Jules, really. I *see* where you're coming from because I want to live one life at a time. We see people come through who are mapping out skill training over . . . over . . . literal civilizational epochs." He goes to take a drink and finds everything but his water empty. Frowning, he reaches over to my side of the table only for me to playfully swat at his hand. "I think those people are crazy, but only some of them are actually evil."

I give him a low hum and a shake of my head. "I don't like that word."

"Yeah, well, I do." He snorts. "How many lives ago was it that we met that fox samurai that was preaching genocide? Or the xet cultivator who was going all in on setting xeself up as a deity and farming marks of faith?" Mark leans back and flicks off a couple of his notifications. "It's really hard to tell how to do good," he says softly. "But . . ."

"Not so hard to recognize monsters." I sigh. He's right, which annoys me. He's also right that it isn't fair to call the pattern of optimization evil in itself. I just worry that there's too few steps between trying to form a perfect trait build and trying to figure out if there's an achievement for blowing up more than a hundred people at a time.

There is, incidentally. It's one I'm not particularly proud to have gotten but don't regret the circumstances of. Though I never told anyone else here because of exactly the reason Mark and I are talking about. If we know how to get achievements and rewards, that's going to influence how we act. How we live.

But because we haven't been talking about it, that means it's strangely and surprisingly comforting now to wonder if the Between *agrees with me.*

Because Mark is right. About a lot of things, annoyingly, but also that the Between doesn't seem to want us telling each other how to get certain of its prizes. We *do* sometimes talk about the weirder ones, the funnier ones, the ones we're proud of. But I don't think any of us ever set out into new lives planning to replicate those feats. Maybe if we did, we'd find that we don't get the same thing, or don't get anything at all.

It's odd, and maybe worth experimenting with. It also still isn't specifically *true* either. So much of the Between is just looped lies, or truths in such nested patterns that none of us can understand them on our timescale anyway.

The man across the table from me drags me up from my morose mental poetic musings with a surprised grunt. "Oh hey," Mark comments with raised eyebrows. "New perk. Kennel Guard. That's . . . That's a good memory." He's wearing a sad smile, the corners of his eyes glistening.

"You made a difference." I reach out and take his hand, nudging glasses and mugs aside with my arm.

"Isn't this supposed to be the other way around?" Mark laughs. "I thought I was the steady one, and I reassured *you.*"

A laugh spills from my lips. "Mark that's not how it's gone the last five times we've met," I remind him. "I have splashy emotional trauma; you get the subtle stuff that needs quiet words and philosophical thinking."

"It's not fair if you just say it out loud." He pouts. It's adorable on his sculpted face.

We go back to looking through our notifications, feeling a little lighter and a little more tired. The paradox of being alive, sitting at a table covered in empty cups and damp napkins.

[You have learned 1 step in basic lock picking: +20 marks of knowledge. Perk—Crack—has unlocked.]

I make a note of that one for when we share small stories later. I didn't so much *learn* how to pick locks as it was a frantic lucky break when I got it right at the last second and my partner and I made our daring escape. It's just . . . a little undercut in the dramatic tension by the fact that the lock I was picking was a flimsy latch on a storage closet for cleaning supplies, and my partner was a stray cat I was trying to rescue from the school's janitorial staff.

My last life left me feeling morose and uncertain and grim, like I wasn't sure if I'd killed a world or saved it, ruined my own mind or found a new clarity. A dichotomy written in big bold letters that read "I am confused!" But . . . But it's not possible to live a life that's just one story. You can't *only* be a single big thing. Half the time when we talk here, we start with the big stuff, the central theme, the narrative that's really easy to see when we're dead and through it.

But people, even people like us, don't live that way. Maybe we could if we were actively achievement hunting and optimizing for specific jobs or skills or powers. But on the stage of life, Bastion's is full of method actors. And lives just *pile up* with small stories. A lot of them so small they might seem boring compared to the big ones, but all of them mattered to us at the time. And they're fun to share.

Breaking into a janitor's closet to save a cat seems so petty compared to anything that we might start our life stories with. Ellin tends to open hers with a body count, and it's easy to think that a small adventure like this just wouldn't measure up.

But it matters to me, and if nothing else, I can trust that Molly will ask me a lot of questions about the cat. Molly *loves* cats. We all like cats, except Jules, who has inexplicably been allergic to them in half his lives. But Molly is one step away from abandoning her kobold body and just being a house cat, and there are some days when I can't blame her; it seems like it would be relaxing.

"I just realized," Mark mumbles partly to himself, "I've got this new thing, and also a pair of animal-friend traits. Plus we've got that book that buffs charisma upgrades on targets under a certain intelligence, right?"

I tilt my head back, looking up at the roughly carved arch of stone overhead where we're sitting. "I don't know? I don't know the book perks."

"You read all the time!"

"Yeah because I love reading, *Mark*." I train my old eyes on him, amethyst reminders trying to stare threateningly into his soul. Assuming that we aren't all just free-floating souls here already. "I don't like reading for the perks."

Mark nods at me as his fingers open and maneuver a glowing pane of lit-up words to his side. "I know, I know. And that's a very Luri thing of you to love," he says with utter confidence that I'll understand that he's not being an ass. "My point is, I liked my dogs. And maybe I can do that again. Not next life, not right away. I . . . I'm . . ." He lowers his hand and stares blankly for a moment. "I need a little time, at least," he whispers.

And I'm reminded that being here, de facto, means we have experienced loss. Maybe Mark's dogs are still alive and woofing, doing great out on the plains of a struggling world. Maybe they were dead before he was. Maybe time is weird and it's already been thousands of years and their descendant puppies are evolving into a new dominant species in the vacuum left by the collapse. That last one probably isn't happening, but I like to dream big.

But no matter how *they're* doing, Mark is here. And there's an insurmountable gulf between them. He will never see them again.

That sentence is one we have to grapple with and grieve over every single time we sit down in Bastion's. We'll never see them again. Whoever we were, whoever they were.

I don't like the word never. It seems petty and meaningless to immortals like us. So maybe I'm wrong; if I had faith at all I'd pray that I was. Because I *want* to be wrong. I want to see them all again: everyone I'm waiting for, every forgotten face and missing voice.

Mark not wanting to dive back into being some kind of dog whisperer makes sense. He's got too many emotional memories right now, not enough time to mourn and heal. Diving back into it, but seeing different fur on the other end, would be too painful. We've all been there.

"When you're ready for it, I bet you'll be the best dog dad on that world." I offer him a distraction.

He huffs out a small laugh. "Big assumption. Remember that time Ellin set her whole build around pistols when she wanted to be a gunslinger, then landed on a world that thought the trebuchet was the pinnacle of projectile weaponry?"

I brighten up rapidly, leaning forward on my elbow over our cluttered table. "I *do*. That was amazing. She was pouting for a hundred thousand heartbeats."

Mark's laugh this time is more genuine. "Well, I don't wanna land on a world with only darba or something when I'm looking for dogs!" He folds his arms over his chest, tugging at the feathers of his toga. We lapse back into silence for a bit, Mark looking over my shoulder and back through the archway to the main room as someone lets out an uproarious laugh. Then he sighs. "I'm mostly done with my notifications, and I don't think I got the thing. How're you doing?"

I blink and look at the list of things the Between wants to tell me. I've got a few more to get through myself. "Well, it's in here somewhere." At least the one I'm hunting for I know is there. Mark's just been hoping. "Also I believe in you!" I tell my friend with as much bravado as I can muster up. "I'm sure you climbed the social ranks of your doggos. That's gotta count, right?"

"It absolutely does not." He flicks his fingers over another projected notification and sighs. "Nope. Okay, gonna finish this up."

We both go back to filing our way through our notifications, silently enjoying each other's company and the soothing pool of heartbeats waiting for us. It's so much easier to take your time when you have so much time to take.

You have recruited 10 people to your cause: +9 marks of passion.
You have recruited 10 people to your cause: +8 marks of passion.
You have recruited 10 people to your cause: +7 marks of passion.
Your connection is recognized: Souvenir granted—Brass Key.

The key thunks onto the table between us, making a racket as it clinks against two glass rims on the way down. Mark jumps slightly, but I knew it was coming, and both of us just stare at it.

He makes an inquisitive sound. "I don't know," I offer. "I don't . . . remember this at all? The Between sure thinks it mattered to me." I pick it up gingerly with two slim fingers, dangling it in the air between us. It has three thick teeth and an equal number of metal loops at the back. It doesn't look like anything from my last world. Which is confusing, but not actually that weird; these things happen sometimes. Souvenirs that don't line up to lives, little trinkets from nowhere at all. "Molly runs Identify, right? I'll bother her about it later."

"No, you're thinking of Tee-kon." Mark grimaces. "Or . . . Maybe? I don't actually know now. We should keep a list or something."

"On napkins again?" I arch eyebrows at him, trying not to smirk.

Mark glowers at me and slumps as he turns his attention away from the key, going back to looking at his notifications. "You're a cruel person, Luri," he says without any heat. Mark's attempts to document *anything* have never ended well.

"Maybe in your next life you should build around being a documenteer and come back with a box of paper as a souvenir!" I needle him joyfully. He's already gone back to clearing notifications though, and I'm nearly done myself, so I join him.

A couple more work thresholds for some extra marks, one kill from a particularly aggressive stray dog that I do not mention to Mark, and then I only have one left, which *must* be what I'm looking for. But I'm preempted from taking my most important prize by a sound from the table.

It's a tiny metallic clink. And I think, briefly, that one of us just nudged the key into a glass, but no. The sound is sharper than that, cleaner. And my eyes look up to meet Mark's and see the beaming proud grin on his face.

"Guess the dogs *did* count!" he says, holding up the small disk of some polished yellow metal between us. He has to fish it out of the bottom of one of the empty cups that it landed in.

It's thin, stamped with an icon of a three-leaved plant, and ridged around the edge. He turns it over, and I see the face of an aged gnoll on the other side, metal eyes blankly staring out at me. Mark turns the coin in his fingers again, staring at it, and both of us feel a shift in the false air of the Between. The thing is practically *thrumming*.

"That . . . seems . . . nice?" I desperately try to think of something clever to say and come up empty at first. "Well, you're now officially the richest person in Bastion's, at least."

"Oh, that's not true at all. Jules has that Augmented Finance trait that makes him ten percent richer, right?"

My trap springs. "Ten percent of zero is still zero, kid."

"I'm two thousand years old," Mark grumbles. "At a certain point you have to stop calling me that." He sets the coin back on the table, though his eyes don't leave it. "I wonder what it does," he muses. "I hope we get a server soon. I'm more than happy to pay the marks to know."

"I swear we can just ask Molls. I know it's her."

"You're confusing the two of them because they say the exact same thing when you ask them to identify something." Mark sounds suddenly tired as he corrects me. Then he pitches his voice higher, doing an impersonation of our friends. "What do you think I am . . ."

". . . A public access librarian?" I finish the comment, shaking my head. Neither Molly nor Tee-kon has ever told us *why* they giggle uncontrollably when that comes up. But this just reinforces my belief that Molly is someone to ask. "Well, I'm sure it's impressive. It feels impressive."

Mark nods distantly, staring at his new coin.

I decide I also want to show off something. So I open up my final notification and realize an instant too late that the table is covered in obstacles I don't particularly want to scatter to the ground.

[You have memorized 5,000 words of local literature: +2 perk cysts, +2 aura drops. Aura Layer—Scroll Harvester—is unlocked. Souvenir granted—*A Savior of Barkblossoms*.]

I grab the book out of the air as it appears, my hand flashing out to snatch it before it can make cleaning up from our quiet time together harder than it has to be. Mark looks away from his coin long enough to give me a respectfully impressed nod.

The tome has a black-and-white image on the cover of a man standing by a tree. It's clearly from a library, with a thin clear coating over it and a pair of tags indicating where it is from and how to find it in the stacks. Despite its blocky size, it's both lighter and softer than it looks. The Between does something to make the text understandable to all of us, as it always does, but I don't think anyone else will get the context of how the title is written vertically down the right side. This is *from* somewhere, and the parts of the composition tell me where from my last world that might be.

It's a true story about how a single man's obsession with a particular flowering tree led to the plant being saved from extinction. Twice. Written by his grandson, the words meander through describing an old noble estate, a fascination with arboreal arts, and the geopolitics of cultural flower sharing.

I have read this book twice because I was bored one day and the library was closed. It's not what I would have chosen to bring with me, but I didn't have a choice. And yet, despite that . . .

"How do you feel about *trees*?" I ask Mark.

"I'm fifty-fifty on them," he answers carelessly and without hesitation.

I pass the book across the table, and he takes it with eager hands as I push myself off my chair, let the Between's magic take the soreness out of my perfect ass, and start collecting our cups to take back to the bar. "Give this a try," I tell him. "I bet you'll tip at least a couple percentage points toward trees by the end."

CHAPTER TWENTY-TWO

A little to the left!" I call up at Molly.

The little kobold is hanging in the air near the wall of Bastion's that extends from where the bar ends, tail frantically wagging, wobbling in place as Jules holds her up from his own perch on the edge of the library's railing. We all know that she can't *die* if she falls, but that doesn't mean it wouldn't hurt.

Right now she's holding a loop of shaped wood, a ritual symbol from her last life that she gained as a souvenir, and trying to affix it to our wall. One of the mounting points that Six had in his inventory clutched in one hand while the other strains to keep the wooden loop aloft properly, all while Jules does his best to hold her steady.

Jules is my friend, and I love him very much, but this just looks like *such* a bad idea to me. You don't ask someone who has tentacles for all his limbs to be your ladder. In most places, physics just doesn't work that way. Get someone with rigid arms. Or, better yet, a ladder. We don't have a ladder because, even if we did, where are we supposed to keep it? Propped up in the magical fey evening in our new hallway to nowhere? That seems *rude* somehow. And while we're a lot of things here, tasteless isn't one of them.

What I *am*, sometimes, though is overly cheerful in how unhelpful I am. Which is why I'm standing below Molly, risking impact from her falling form, to heckle her. "No, your other left!" I yell.

"I thought we were friends, Luri!" she barks, the canine part of her mixed form coming through in her voice. "You're supposed to help meeeee!" she squeals as Jules almost fumbles her out of the air, catching her in a tangle of limbs as he tries to carefully move her to not be upside down.

"I am helping! I'm giving interior design advice!"

"Have you ever been an interior designer? At all?" Ellin asks me curiously. Her feet are up on one of our smaller tables, and she's reading the dust jacket of the book I brought back, an aura of casual contentedness coming off her like an almost physical force as she sips at her lemonade. "I don't have a list of things you've been. And *don't*," she preempts me. "Don't tell me we should make a list. If you can't remember it, it absolutely doesn't count for decorating here."

I think about it. I worked for a construction firm a few lives back, which sort of intersects. And I sort of remember a few years conscripted into a consecration brigade that *kind of* involved the process of setting up the ritual sites for a state church.

Neither of those are going to count, and I already know it. So I answer tactically. "In my last life, actually, there was a small island nation with a tradition of building spaces with single looping hallways. So there was kind of . . . an almost spiritual connection to how things like furniture and storage and decor were placed, with regard to that core architectural through line? It was really interesting. Also had a lot to do with *rain*, since that was kind of the default weather in the place it came from, so it never really took off in some places."

Ellin blinks at me, cocking her horned head ever so slightly. "That . . . Oy, didn't you . . . spend your last life engineering world domination?" She purses her lips at me. "When did you have time to learn how to decorate?"

"I still had a home, Ellin!" I place a hand on my breast in indignation, which I can already see I have overdone as she snorts at me. "Okay, fine, I didn't really. I'm just sort of aware the style existed. I thought if I talked fast enough, you'd believe me."

"That doesn't work on me. That *never* works on me!"

I shrug, palms facing the ceiling as I grin at her. "It might have worked on Molly!"

It probably wouldn't have. And Ellin's distraction of my unhelpful nonsense has been apparently just what Molly and Jules needed to shove her into position and affix her ritual loop to the wall. It sits proudly now, slightly offset from and over a tapestry of some kind of cat creature, but otherwise all on its own on that part of Bastion's wall. The dark-golden wood of the main room's walls contrasting with the white and living green of Molly's reminder.

I steal the good chair at our main table while Jules struggles to pull Molls back to safety, and everyone else moves about on their own little missions.

My eyes trace the hoop of wood, the small carvings in it, the places where offshoots were left to grow and shaped back in instead of being pruned, the indication of life. I let my thoughts dwell on the thing and how it might actually be, if not alive, then at least not simply dead wood here in the Between.

Near me, there are sounds. A page turns as Ellin reads. The bar's endless spout hisses as water is poured. Words and giggles and hums are exchanged upstairs. A door opens and closes, and Mark calls a greeting.

But my eyes are tracing the wooden circle and trying to understand it. Or maybe not understand. Maybe simply to explore it. Every detail leads to another; every little piece is part of something that trails to a new spot that I haven't put my eyes on before. It's not *fascinating*, but it seems ever shifting and endless in a way that a simple object should not be.

A voice addresses me, and I blink a green-and-brown world out of my eyes as I turn. The Between intrudes, tacking a new notification onto the end of what's left of my list. I tilt my head back down, the near-arcane level of neck support from the pilot's suit mixed with the way the Between keeps my body whole meaning that I don't have any soreness from staring up at a high angle for . . . almost three thousand heartbeats.

The noise I make as I look down and see Shevoy is one of almost stuttering confusion, even as I am already making the rapid mental connections that Molly's sacrosanct wall decor might be a little more than simply a neat piece of art. I follow it up with something more coherent. "Hey, kiddo." I smile at him. "Adjusting to death again?"

He looks uncomfortable in his skin. Which makes sense; he's got two different bodies mixed in there, and no matter what you do in the Between, it takes an extensive amount of time and effort and precision to get yourself to a perfect copy of a body you once had. What he looks like now, a change fueled by our influx of marks and abstracts, is far closer than he could have gotten to something he would find familiar in this life. But I know from experience that it's not "him." And it won't be. Not for a long time.

After a few lives, he'll make some more changes. Keep a few things he likes, maybe, but start to become a body that's his *here* and nowhere else. Or at least, if he does what I did. What a lot of us do. There's always the chance that he finds a different path. Maybe Shevoy will fall in with that group of perfection seekers and adopt their ideal body, or just randomize a few features and treat that as natural, or he'll decide he wants to be a three-meter-tall cross between a dog and a jet fighter and move toward that. Though that last one would cost a lot of marks. A *lot*. I wanted to be a jet fighter once, until I learned how expensive mechanical physics were to import to the Between.

But all of that will have to wait.

"I'm leaving soon." His voice wavers as he addresses me. "I . . . I wanted to thank you."

I know my face has a sad look on it, eyes looking up at him with pity that I don't mean to broadcast quite so strongly. "I didn't do this to you," I tell him bluntly.

Shevoy gives me the kind of smile that someone uses when they're feeling old and wise because they think that fifty subjective years has been enough for them to figure things out and they don't realize that there will *never* be enough time to know it all. "Not for the extra chance at life," he tells me. "I know; everyone filled me in. I mean for last time."

"Oh." I start to shrug. "I just . . ."

"Because of you, I wasn't afraid," Shevoy states with solid confidence. "I owe you my life. That whole life, if I make my guess. Not for putting me there, but for the *living* of it." He smiles, whiskers twitching on his oddly shaped cheeks. "It was worth it. You were right. And . . . I get to do it again."

Now he sounds nervous. And no matter that he looks like an adult, or that he had a whole second shot at life, I find myself standing from my ancient wood chair and giving a hug one more time to a scared child who isn't sure what's about to happen. He leans into it easily as my arms wrap around him. "You remember what I said last time?" I whisper.

"Of course." He gives a chuckle into my shoulder. "You lied to me and said I was gonna do great things."

"Ha!" I bark out the laugh as I try my best to crush him into the hug with my lithe arms. "Did I lie? Sounds like you had a family that loved you, and a place in the world. That seems pretty great to me." He starts to make a noise like he's gonna protest, and I cut him off. "And you're gonna do great things this time too. Trust me. I've got an eye for this kind of thing. You'll do—"

He's gone, and my hug slips through empty air. Kept his goodbye until the last minute and made the rookie mistake of not timing it to get the last word. He'll have to learn to do better on that next time, or he's never going to keep up with Ellin's score on sassy parting shots.

Jules slides up to me, a pair of tentacles hesitating to wrap around my arm and shoulder in comfort as I stand there in the middle of Bastion's. "Are you well?" he asks me in a low hum. The old ball of tentacles knows me well enough, and has a similar enough attitude, to know that partings are hard.

"Yeah." I surprise myself by meaning it, even as I sniff back tears slightly. "Yeah, I kinda am," I say, wrapping my arm farther in Jules's tendrils and placing my other hand on his flank. "He's gonna do fine." The words are as much a prayer to the universe as they are self-reassurance.

"I'm sure he will. He seems like a decent enough youngling," Jules agrees. His eyes slide into a pattern of amusement. "Did he tell you about his upgrades?"

I laugh because that was the last thing on either of our minds. "What could he even afford this early?" I try to think of what my first few lives were like, back when I bothered to pay attention. "Speed-Reading? Or . . . Uh . . . Jules it's been thousands subjective. I don't remember a single thing I got in my first life. They're all just in the inventory pile somewhere."

Jules vibrates out a joyful sound. "That *would* have been your first, Luri!" He coils around me in a hug. "No, the youngling borrowed some marks of passion from me, though I'll never call in the marker, to put himself on the path of charisma and buy himself the Paramour aura layer."

". . . I am . . . a little surprised that I don't have that," I mutter, dipping deep into thought. "Why don't I have that? I'm romantic with half the people in this room!"

"Fewer than half. We have a guest." Jules jabs one of his manipulator tendrils toward the bar, where a new figure is sitting with their back to me as Mark shakes something in our cold steel mixer. "And I'm *confident* you have it available. You just leave half the things you unlock but aren't gifted untouched. How many talent trees are you sitting on with the root waiting for purchase and nothing else lensed? How many aura cysts are sitting in your pocket?"

I cross my arms, letting Jules spill over me in a kind of friendly shared hostility as I try to break away and head toward the bar. "I don't answer to you!" I declare, like some kind of ancient child throwing a tantrum. "You're not my fiduciary!"

"Which is perhaps for the best," Jules agrees cheerfully as I drag him along, his mobility tentacles splaying out behind us on the sandy wood. "I would be rendered catatonic by the wealth you seem to collect and then ignore, and you would be made deeply pouty by my insistence that you do something with it." He hums in consideration. "I suspect we would find a way to kill each other within a hundred thousand heartbeats."

"We're in the Between," I remind him.

Falling neatly into his joking trap. "Yes!" Jules agrees. "This makes it all the more impressive, though perhaps your vast and dusty hoard would allow you to simply purchase a murder."

I laugh, mostly because I know how much killing someone in the Between costs and I know I *cannot* afford it, and finally shrug him off. Jules gives a similarly amused hum and lets me go while he moves to speak with Six about something. And that leaves me free to make my way to the bar and greet our new guest.

I'm not exactly antisocial, but I often find myself in a comfortable position of loneliness. Either in my lives or here. Being *alone* is bad, but being by myself when my friends are around is a warm comfort. All that said, I love meeting new people. The sound of the front door when no guests were expected is my favored noise when I can experience it as a child, and here at Bastion's is no different.

"Hey, Luri," Mark greets me as I walk up and claim a barstool near the stranger. "You were staring at our new accursed ornament for a long time. See something good in it?"

"Against all odds, yes. We still need some beds, but you should try it some-time," I say, and then clarify before he can ask. "Staring at Molly's new wall decoration, I mean. It's relaxing." He gives a small noise of understanding and goes back to grinding up something from Six's Chef's Herb Box on the other side of the counter while I turn to our newcomer.

They're wearing a gusi-style set of robes, fabric intricately folded to create lines and shapes. It's not actually gusi style—that world is far behind me, and I'll probably not see it again—but while the woodrunner fiefs were not the only society to come up with the pattern of clothing, they were *my* first. So that's what I call it.

The robes are the most interesting thing about the person too. They have a human face that I can only describe as average, and even Six would beat them in a competition of who put more effort into their body here. But they smile at me as I sit and raise the glass to me in a friendly gesture. "Good morning." Their voice, in contrast to the rest of their form, is vibrant and alive, a warm sound dripping with casual invitation to nothing in particular.

I smile back. "How do you figure?" I love learning the weird quirks visitors have for processing the Between.

"Well *I* just woke up." They try to arch a single eyebrow and end up just making a face as they move both at once. Not a *weird* face, just . . . a face. I'm getting distracted by how boring they are to look at, which is interesting all on its own. "But more importantly, it's near the start of a cycle. I call that morn-ing. I don't have a measure for it, but we're not quite to alignment or setting yet. So good morning!"

"How often do you get worlds with two suns?" I ask as Mark sets a mug in front of me and I drink without checking. This is a mistake. He's tricked me, and I have tried something that is his attempt to make an herbal wine by add-ing herbs to wine, and Mark is banned from being on that side of the counter. "Oh no . . ." I croak out, holding the mug out away from me like it's a live bomb. "No, Mark. No. What did you do?"

He glances up from where he's sniffing things out of the herb box, an innocent expression in his eyes. "Is it not good?"

"You're no longer a bartender," I tell him, tilting the mug and pouring the foul concoction out, the stream of liquid fading to the void halfway to the floor. "Swap places."

We do, Mark looking somewhat dejected but also hiding a laugh as we pass by each other and I take my place on the other side of the bar. The newcomer watches me curiously, answering my question only after I'm halfway into a palate-cleansing swig of water. "Does anyone here not work here?" they ask. "And to answer *your* question, it does seem to come up a lot for me. Makes for excellent sunrises."

"Not sunsets?" Mark asks.

"I'm a morning person."

I nod sadly. "No one's perfect." I've found that repeatedly over my lives. Some people get close, some people never stop trying, but everyone has little things that keep them from the ultimate aspiration. "And we've all got a little shared stake in Bastion's. So, cycles?"

"Oh! Yes! We're always meeting each other here as if we've arrived roughly around the same period. Subjective, perhaps a span or two?"

". . . Span being ten subjective days, or thirty?" I ask, trying to not sigh as we run into the most inconvenient problem that the Between refuses to correct for.

They look back at me with a similar exhausted expression, even if their voice is as honeyed as ever. "Is a day one sleep loop, or three?"

"When is it *ever* three?" Mark demands to know.

I don't blame him; he's still young. The stranger and I answer at the same time, saying, "Two suns," with a unified wave toward Mark. I answer their own question that my subjective days are one loop. Eventually we sort out their definition for a span landing around a subjective week, and I refuse to do the math to smooth it out. "So you have friends here too?" I ask.

They light up, their plain face showing a slim modicum of joy. "Oh, yes! Already moved on at this point. They're both new. But I . . . I like them. We've met a few times now. And we have shared Friendship traits now too, so we're drawn to each other here."

"You can do that?" Mark looks surprised.

I don't look surprised, but while I sort of knew that was possible, I haven't encountered it here. You don't get traits in the Between. You get rewards and upgrades from worlds and lives, and this is neither. We always come home to here, but we're not alive.

"We all just have doors to Bastion's, so we meet up. Cycles though, yeah. I've seen the pattern. Sometimes people arrive way too early though. Or late. Depending." I distract myself from remembering subjective months almost completely alone, not knowing what I was waiting for, not wanting to stray into the halls and valleys of the Between without being able to leave a note or see Ellin or Molly or Jules or Six or Mark one more time. My distraction takes the form of refilling an empty cup for our visitor. "You owe us three marks for this, or a fun anecdote about your last life," I tell them.

"*Fun?*" They give a bland smile. "I don't have fun. I have *adventure*."

"Three marks then." Mark chuckles. "Six, with the other one?"

"Yes?" Six says as he approaches the bar and catches Mark's comment.

Mark rolls his eyes. "No, I was talking about the marks."

"You are the Mark here." Six feigns confusion. Or maybe it's not feigned at all.

I certainly don't have to feign being irate. "No, *no*, this comedy routine exists in *every single* civilization that makes it to the invention of broadcast communication. You're two steps away from asking me who when was."

The stranger comes to my rescue. "Well," they eloquate. "I could tell you about the time I was riding a mutaform wren about three miles up at almost exactly the time that a band of plucky misfits failed to stop a mad wizard from unleashing his world-spanning spell that turned all birds into flowering plants. It was honestly a *very* impressive spell! It didn't even kill the birds, technically. Or at least, not mine. The mind was intact, and somewhat content with being a colorful piece of flora."

"Were you . . ." Mark asks slowly, "perhaps one of those plucky adventurers?"

"Oh, quite so." The stranger nods. "We'd . . . Ahem. We were distracted. For some time. Stalled, you might say."

I've heard a variation on this story a dozen times before. It's really kind of fascinating how many of us, when presented with a pressing problem, simply don't feel the pressures of time and urgency the same way. Knowing that death isn't an ultimate failure makes it easier to get distracted. This also combos in a truly horrifying way with certain mental health conditions that our living bodies can have. If you would have had problems with paying attention *before*, knowing that your focus is never *really* required certainly doesn't make it any easier to avoid flights of fancy.

"I would say that almost constitutes fair payment." Six nods at the small story. "I have two questions though." The stranger makes a sweeping go-on hand gesture, and the golem obliges. "First, is there a Between reward for falling from three miles up in the sky?"

The stranger flushes red, and I am again amazed at how their utterly boring face makes the blush look like almost nothing. "There . . . Ahem . . . There may be, yes. A pawful of marks of faith for every . . . Well, not mile, but every long measure of distance fallen all at once. And then Polina's Erring Skydiver for hitting the three-measure mark all at once without intention. Now, believe me when I tell you, I'll be finding space in my aura layer for it!" They raise their glass to me as they drain the last of it. "What was the other question?" they ask Six as they make to stand.

"Was there also a reward for surviving the fall?" Six asks simply.

"I wouldn't know. That was also my *last* memory from that life." The stranger offers a bland grin to go with their cheerful and charismatic words. "And now, friends, my companions are waiting for me out there somewhere. Thank you kindly for the drinks, and the company. Perhaps we'll cross paths again one day." They head to an open wall, waving to us as they do so, and then vanish into the Between without stalling.

"Well that was fun," I mutter. Then I turn my gaze to Six and slide a mug across the bar to him. "Also try this."

He takes a tentative sip and grimaces. "This is . . . unpleasant." This is actually the most expression I've *ever* heard in his tone.

"Yeah, Mark left some back here, and I needed to get rid of it." I offer an apologetic smile. "Hey, it looks like the others are setting up a game. Do you wanna go join them?"

"*I* do, if only to escape my own mistakes." Mark sighs.

That's a feeling that I know all too well. But at least we can feel it together. It takes me until after a comforting hug and getting everyone seated and making it halfway through the traditional argument about which rule set we're using before I realize that Mark wasn't talking in the broad and metaphorical sense, but more immediately and specifically about whatever he'd made behind the bar.

I let the shared laughter chase away the darkness for a little while though. I'm sure we can make new mistakes to regret later.

CHAPTER TWENTY-THREE

O h, that's odd." The words from Jules pull me up and out of the thick spark wine I am staring into, my wandering thoughts coalescing into something closer to an actual thinking person than I've been for a while.

I've spent the last subjective day, since I got knocked out of the game we were all playing early, alternating between trying to invent a new mixed drink and staring at the druidic meditation loop. This isn't going well because the loop of deceptively enthralling-shaped wood that Molly nailed to the wall requires me to sit near other people who are being enthusiastic, and that somewhat keeps the trance from happening, and also because I've been trying to mix things with the bottom half of a bottle of spark wine that Six bought a lifetime or two back.

The stuff is labeled by the Between as wine, and this, more than anything else, is a hint to me that this afterlife doesn't understand alcohol. It is closer to a brandy, and not a very good one, but that's not the important part. The stuff we acquire as souvenirs, or that Six brings back, that's fine. The stuff from here? It's . . . not *wrong*, exactly. It's still okay. This particular wine actually has quite the impressive kick to it, for when you want to waste an afternoon in style; it also tastes like seeing a meteorite on a clear night, so that's cool too. But it just doesn't interact the way wine is supposed to.

Jules is staring at me with his trio of red projection eyes shaped into narrow bands. "Luri?" he asks, concern dripping out of his slightly vibrating voice. "Are you alright? You have been staring at me for a hundred beats."

"Hmm?" I say. "No. Jules. Please. Of course I'm not alright." My hand waves a simple pattern that means, on a forgotten world, a complex thought about the willing sublimation of the self into a conversation for the purpose of expediently skipping over the obvious and painful details. Jules has never been to that world, but he's seen me do the floppy-hand thing often enough to get the context. Jules is smart. "What's odd?"

His eyes narrow further until they are thin red strips of light against his midnight skin. When the mass of tentacles talks next, he sounds like the most suspicious kindwoman investigator I've ever heard. And that means something because I've done a lot of crimes in some lives. "Yes. Well. Having come into an abundance of cysts since my last dance with mortality, I have opted to spend some marginal effort to *improve*," Jules tells me, a slightly sarcastic twist to his voice.

"Noble," I remark.

His eyes shift to curious long triangles. "Is it?" he asks me with a voice to match his smooth oval face.

The nod I give him is overly enthusiastic. "Absolutely. Six and Mark have been talking to me a lot lately—by the way, when you get a chance, ask Six what *he* did last life; you'll love it—and it's making me think."

"Dangerous."

"Fear not." I give him my most charming smile, and then quickly use my tongue to check if I ever removed the razor-sharp fangs that I added to this body for a false masquerade we held five or ten lives ago. Not that Jules would be one to be intimidated by *that*. He's a paramour to Molly, and her teeth outpace anything I've ever made. "We tried it, didn't we? Optimizing. For a change."

"Well." Jules is reluctant to admit to anything, especially not with that word. To everyone else, it might be just a Luri thing, something I complain about and maybe can't clearly articulate. To Jules, Six, and me, it is . . . worse. It is a chasm with no bottom, and we've seen people fall in. "In a certain way . . ."

My voice is soft as I cut his words off. "We did, Jules. I said, 'We should try to live impressive lives and spend more time here with each other.' And then we did that. Maybe we aren't hyperfocusing on career paths, farming marks, or making specialized builds. But we optimized."

"We optimized for something different though," Jules protests. "And—Ah. That is the thrust of your argument, is it?" He hums deeply.

"Please don't say *thrust* to me like that. I'm not Molly."

Jules arranges his eyes in mirth. "Would you be surprised if I told you that I can combine the tone with—"

My laugh is what stops him this time. Then the words. "Jules, I love you, and I'm as ravenous for intimacy as anyone else here, but let's at least pretend we can confront the truth first." He gives me a slight bob, then settles back, two of his manipulator tentacles cuddling his mug and pulling it closer to him. "But yes, that's my point. We meet optimizers all the time, and they're all . . ."

"Quite mad?" Jules suggests, taking over from me.

I sigh and lean on my elbow, propping up my chin so I can look at the jar of lightbugs providing mood lighting for the center of this little table. "Alien, maybe. Unrecognizable. Remember the kids? The religion that's trying to turn themselves into the perfect person, and they already decided what that person looks like?"

"Ah. Yes. The fear performance made manifest." Jules gives a buzzing snort of derision. "A fate I would prefer to avoid, you understand."

"Yes. *Yes,*" I agree wholeheartedly. "But . . . what I'm trying to say, what I'm trying to *feel,* is that I think we can be different." I don't actually feel it. But, like I tell Jules, I am actually trying. "They're all optimizing for more power, or more upgrades for their lives, or they're aiming for divinity or enlightenment or *something.* But us? We're just aiming to be better at being us." I make the argument, both to him and to myself.

Optimizing for being Luri. For being an ad hoc citizen of Bastion's.

Jules stares at me and my wide-eyed smile, my projected optimism, before he lets his tentacles droop. "No," he says simply, no vibrancy to his word at all.

"No?'

"No," he reiterates. "I can't. Not now, Luri. Not so soon. I'll . . . I will endeavor to live well, and I will always want to spend more time with the circle here. But I cannot change how I think. Not yet."

My smile is no less genuine as I reach over and run my fingers across one of his inky-black tentacles. "And that's fine too," I say. "Because we're not on a time limit, and if we optimize for anything at all, it's for *being us,* and that means listening to your feelings. Now, tell me what's odd about your aura, and we can pretend we're both okay."

". . . I do love you so." Jules's words come out as a breezy whisper that I don't know he even meant to say. "Well, having now gotten around to expanding the foundation and adding the third layer, I find call to actually *fill* it with something. And, in honor of Mark's moving story, I decided to upgrade Animal Companionship, perhaps to give as a gift when he is himself ready for it."

Jules is such a massive sap. I love how no matter how condescending he sounds or how many new limbs he adds, he's still at his core an old-souled gush that won't stop giving to others. He sees my look and starts to fractal his eyes. "Oh, you know you're cute," I snipe before he can say anything.

"*Regardless*. The part of the aura that reaches into the third layer is . . . odd," Jules says, showing off how his body processes embarrassment with a splash of color. "First layer is, of course, a boost to befriending an animal. Second layer reinforces the first and adds resistance to damage when attempting. Third layer though is . . . esoteric."

"My favorite."

"Mine as well, but genuinely, and not however you meant it." Jules misinterprets my words. I actually do love the weird upgrades, as they feel harder to exploit and easier to engage with earnestly. "The third layer says that it . . . It carries over traits of the chosen companion."

I go silent. For a moment, the noises of Bastion's take over: the turboprop engine overhead, the light wind from our new hallway, the sound of Mark tapping a barrel of Six's mediocre beer, the noise of a doorway closing behind someone new, the rustle of the pages of a book from the library, and the thump of feet as conversations hit a coincidental pause.

I hear little of it, really. I am ensnared by Jules's words. Because for the first time, someone has found an upgrade that says the magical phrase. *Carries over.*

"What . . ." I rasp out, "does it . . ."

"It's not the whole companion. No mention of a soul, or the Between, or anything like us. It simply says that traits will persist when a new companion is trained." Jules crushes my hope. "But, Luri . . ."

"Jules," I say as I push the chair back and stand. Even standing, I'm still shorter than Jules's seated form, so I'm hardly intimidating. But he listens to me anyway because intimidation isn't the point. "I understand. Why you might think . . . Why you could see us overdoing it," I admit. "But I want you to know, I think that's cool. And I'd love to see what it's like when you upgrade it again. Because if we could . . . If . . . If we could bring someone along?" I am almost sobbing, and I didn't realize it. "No one would have to feel it again," I mutter. "We wouldn't leave anyone . . ."

"Luri." Jules settles his tentacles on my shoulders as a third lifts my chin up. I was staring at the floor, eyes burning holes in the sandy wood of Bastion's unique ground. "I don't think it's going that way."

"But it might," I reply. "And I've got a pseudoquest that generates cysts. And there's no harm in finding out."

His eyes flash into angled diamonds. "Your aura layer that requires you to consume unhealthy amounts of raw food? Absolutely not. Throw that away. Listen to me, Luri. *This is how it starts! This is what you hate!*"

And he says *you*, but he means *I*. He means *we*. And he's right to say it. And what he doesn't say is "This is how we lose each other," but I hear him shouting it anyway. The words hit me like a shock of water and light. Of course, Jules is right. All it took was one good life to make me think that I could avoid every pitfall I've seen smarter people walk into before.

"Ah." I smile weakly. Then I straighten my back and bring my hands up to pat his tentacles. "I . . . Oops. Sorry, Jules. I worried you there for a second, huh?"

"Yes," he says with studied trepidation.

"I'm fine," I reassure him, grabbing onto his limbs as he looks down into my face. "No, you're right. It's . . . Hey, maybe it'll work in the future, right? And then we'll have forever to enjoy it. No need to rush."

Jules relaxes and then wraps me in a trembling hug, and I didn't realize until that moment exactly how badly I scared him. "Yes. Exactly. No sense in mutilating yourself just to go faster when we'll be here always, my dear."

I make a small noise of agreement as he smothers me. And then another small voice, sharper and sultrier, speaks up from below us. "Luri, are you stealing my mate?" Molly demands as she climbs up onto the chair next to us.

The laugh I give her is one of my two options, between either that or crying. "No, no. Jules is just reminding me of something. What's up, Molls?"

"Oh, your elf friend is here." Molly juts a claw toward the bar. "Also, I wanted to escape Mark and Six arguing about beer. Also, what's up with this tiny fern? Also I'm gonna steal Jules."

"In order," I say, wriggling out of Jules's grasp so I can count on my fingers. "Thank you, I'll go give her a proper greeting. I understand, and how is Six's new beer? The fern came back with Ellin from her harvest quest, and we've been moving it around to semihidden places to see who notices. And also have fun!"

"Do I get a say in—" Jules stops talking as Molly finishes clawing her way up onto the table and then from there makes a leap into Jules's tentacles where he catches her like he was expecting the maneuver the whole time. "Hello, darling." His eyes shine with happiness, no matter how Molly might seem exhausting sometimes.

"The beer is not great," Molly answers me as she rolls in Jules's grip and steers him toward the faux-exterior hallway attached to Bastion's. Or perhaps it would be better to say it is now part of Bastion's, a new and strange addition to our old and strange place. "Have fun yourself!" She waves to me as they leave, and Jules gives me a goodbye motion as well. He looks back at one point, like he feels as if there is more to say, but I wave them on to go have their fun.

As they round the corner, I open my inventory and look for a certain aura layer. I find it, look at it for thirty heartbeats, and then yank it out as a meta-object. There is a temptation there, to ignore Jules and his fears, to ignore my *own* fears. To simply say that I know better and that nothing will go wrong. As if that isn't exactly how it always starts with us, and exactly *why* it is such a problem.

I leave it on the table for someone else to find, in the spot where the tiny pot with the tinier fern had been sitting before Molly stole it. I'm glad she's in on the game. This will be entertaining for at least three lives' worth of time in the Between.

"Hoy! Luri!" Ellin greets me as I claim a barstool, watching Mark practicing juggling glasses behind the bar. He's not great at it, but the things are essentially as immortal as us, so here is the place to learn. "I 'ave a complaint!" She punctuates her preamble by snapping shut the book I loaned her with a muffled thump and then slamming it onto the bar like she is owed something dire and in a hurry to collect.

I look at the book, then at the stack of several empty glasses near her. I've said it before, that getting drunk in the Between is difficult. I never said it was *impossible*, and Ellin appears to be going for the attempt. "Is it about Six's beer?"

"Six's beer's the greats!" Ellin declares with only a tiny slur to her words, which I think she might be doing on purpose to try to get into character. Method acting inebriation. She leans forward and wraps me in a hug, her tall form letting her grab me from the adjacent barstool, even if her horns do scratch a bit on my stomach. The sensation sends a pleasant shock through my form, and I smile at her as I run my hands across her back. "No, 's about book club!"

"It's back," I inform her, signaling to Mark that I'll also have a drink. The man gives me a smirk that can best be described as delightfully professional as he slides the cups he's tossing around one by one into their spot on the other side of the counter, keeping one back in hand to fill with a sample from the equipable barrels Six brought back.

Ellin slowly drags her head up to look me in the eye, her horns digging against my stomach and chest ever so slightly as she raises her face. "You gave me a book about trees, Lur," she says.

". . . Yes?"

"Yes."

"Yes. I did," I give a more solid agreement to her. "Did you like it?"

Ellin pushes back and straightens on her stool. "Trees. Not even trees! *One tree!*"

"I thought it was a beautiful reminder of how community identity can come from anywhere, and how a single person's act of preservation can lead to the future rediscovery of something wonderful," I prompt.

"Nah, that's crap." Ellin slashes her hand through the air. "It's got the tone of an empire perspective to it. They never say it, but the guy, the guy with the *tree*, he stole that tree. He just stole it when no one cared, then acted like the hero because he kept his stolen tree alive. It's a story about stealing trees."

"Well, it's a history, for one thing." I clear my throat.

Ellin jumps on that. "That's *worse!*" she announces. "Because that means this world was just letting shit go extinct! You know you can get achievements for living through extinction events, right? And I barely ever get them. If this place was letting *trees* die out, that's pretty bad."

"Ah, but Ellin!" I counter. "Don't you see? The trees *didn't* die because someone *cared*! It's honestly pretty cool, especially because on a lot of worlds, it feels like one person doesn't have the . . . leverage, maybe . . . to make big changes. But Ser Evwin sure did."

"I hate that name," Ellin grumbles.

"Well, ser is a title."

"Then I hate it less," Ellin relents. "It just feels so gross to me. Paying people to make parks for your special tree project? No one *cared* until a bunch of foreigners started to care. And it's like the guy writing it was trying to . . . No, not cover it up. Tha's unfair. But gloss it?"

I nod at her as I rub a hand across my cheek. "Perspective matters. Did you read the dust flap?"

"The part where this is a library book and so you *also* stole a thing?" Ellin asks.

"I choose to believe the Between duplicates things. No, the part where it was written by his son."

"Oh. Huh." She pauses. "That . . . Well, shit, Luri. That makes me feel bad." Ellin takes a breath. "Because then it's not about the trees at all, really. Or, it is, but it's someone trying to push back the loss of a loved one by focusing on the permanent change made or staved off by them and enshrining their deeds as history. And that's different than pure impo behavior."

"Exactly what I was thinking." I take the drink from Mark as he adds one in front of Ellin too. She grimaces at it, but we still clink our glasses as we sip together. Six's new brew is sour, and bitter, and also tart. It is all these things, and somehow seems to lack deeper flavor. I don't like it. I sip again. "It's less a real history and more a memorial. But also, it's asking for their world to see the beauty in the actions of a lost father."

Ellin doesn't sip; she chugs. Her drink is half gone by the time she lowers her glass and sets it on the bar for later. "I suppose that's why there's a whole chapter about the castle grounds. Oh, I get it, hoy? It's written like a kid exploring secret places 'cause it probably was how he grew up, yeah?" She sighs. "Okay. That's something."

"So, what did you think of the book?" I ask with a smile.

Ellin opens her mouth, then closes it again, and then gives me a sharkish grin. "You could have just said book club was back," she tells me.

"I did!" I start to protest, but I don't keep up too much energy as Ellin leans across and kisses me suddenly. Lips pressed together, teeth that can't draw blood but absolutely would if they connected with my skin, an eager heat, and the taste of what we've been drinking. Ellin surprises me, but I lean forward into it with my own goofy smile I can't shake.

We break apart as Mark leans on the bar between us. "So, I've been thinking about this tree thing," he says.

"Mark, I swear by Old Hist's breath I will find a way to harm you," Ellin snips, the thing she's saying somewhat at odds with the adoring look she's pouring into my eyes.

"Stop undermining book club," I command him, face flushed.

The look Mark gives me is of a man who is eternally put-upon and underestimated. "Luri, please. I love book club. I am a *devotee* of book club. I didn't catch on that book club involved getting handsy with Ellin in front of our guest, but I'm honestly kind of okay with that too."

"Really? You must have had to get used to some new stuff in your last life, huh?" I ask with genuine curiosity and care.

His mouth thins into a line. "A few things. Heh. Maybe it's just nice to be back somewhere that people are affectionate."

"So why are you ruining it? Or did you want in on the action?" Ellin's demanding question leads into a more suggestive one. "Give me a good chat about the ephemeral nature of personal influence on long-term cultural community building, and I'll give you a grin like Luri's," she suggests.

"I'm only three chapters in because you stole it back from me." Mark reaches out slowly and pulls the soft tome over to his side of the bar. "But I am actually interested in picking Luri's brain for some historical context later?"

"I can do that." I nod. "Now's a good time for it, before I have another life and mix it all up and get sad again."

"No!" Ellin gasps theatrically. "Stop getting sad!"

"I'll be fine. I've actually been less sad the last couple hundred years. Though I've been spending more time here, so that really helps." Unbidden, tiny tears form in the corners of my eyes. "You do all really help."

Ellin reaches over to roughly rub my shoulders. "You need to take a life to relax. Just goof around and don't take things too seriously. Live a little, Luri."

"All I ever do is live a little."

"Well then you don't have a choice, so you might as well lean into it." Ellin grins wickedly at me. "Oh! That reminds me! Mark, what did Molls say about your fancy new coin?"

I turn from their conversation, leaving the two to talk and for Mark to explain once again that Ellin is thinking of someone else. I'm pretty sure he's wrong, but Molly is busy again, and we haven't asked her because the luxury of millions of heartbeats is that you can take your time and forget things. And I'll have time to listen to them bicker like an ancient pair of lovers later; right now, I want to say hello to our visitor.

Our new guest is actually a very old guest. An elf, identical to the last several times I've seen her. She sits at the bar with a faraway look in her eyes, having moved here like the process of claiming a barstool was more a matter of endless reflex and not an active choice.

"Hey there," I say softly as I circle around the outside of the bar's curve, picking a stool near her own. She looks at me slowly, blinking like her eyes won't adjust to the golden-white light of Bastion's various different illuminations. "Welcome back. Want a lemonade? We've still got some left."

". . . I had a dream about lemonade," she says quietly.

"I know," I say as I set one of my hands on the bar between us. She doesn't move, except to tilt her head and stare at the back of my hand curiously. "I was in it."

"You were." The elf's eyes drift slightly around Bastion's. Across shelves of old pieces of old lives, lines of bottles and urns, and rough wood walls and floors that are eternally familiar to me. "It was here. I dreamed of here." She pauses as she fixes her eyes on the meditation loop hanging on the high wall. "Dreams don't change like this," she whispers with a horrified hush in her throat.

"No," I say, standing to circle the bar so I can hip check Mark out of my way and find one of the mixed-herb-and-lemonade bottles sitting under the counter. I left them in the food section because we haven't had food here in lifetimes. When I come back up, careful not to jostle the suspicious poison too much, I place the lemonade in front of her and pour some into a short cup. "They don't."

She watches the drink pour and fill, long angular ears splayed out through the back of her hair twitching ever so slightly. "This is an odd dream," the elf says as she slowly reaches for the cup, watching her own hand as if she's starting to wonder if it's even hers.

"Yes," I answer with a smile. "But I kind of like it."

CHAPTER TWENTY-FOUR

Tense heartbeats pass as I face down my foe. Across the table from me, a creature that looks like some kind of aphotic castoff stares into my anima with a trio of red eyes. Though that's maybe not especially impressive because I think we just sort of *are* oddly shaped anima in the Between. Or something soul adjacent. Motivation with temporary bodies. Something like that.

I'm trying to keep my thoughts away from what I'm about to say to Jules. I think he's cheating at this game by reading minds. I don't know how he's doing it because none of our upgrades or perks work here, except for the ones that visitors have implied *do*, but none of us are using those. *Unless . . .* Unless Jules has been lying to us this whole time.

The evidence mounts against him. Of everyone here, Jules is exactly the person who would mount a lifetimes-long campaign of deceit just to pull a party trick. Six wouldn't do that to me; we've been through too much together for that. Mark I don't think could keep a straight face. Molly . . . Molls would love the idea. She would absolutely want to do it, and then she'd talk about how funny it would be and then realize she'd blown the joke early. But *Jules?* The man has patience beyond anything even I have, and I lean hard into being immortal.

My eye twitches as we gaze at each other across the wire-mesh table that comes from the coastal pavilion of some long-gone boardwalk that one of us used to visit with our lover. One of Jules's own eyes fragments in tiny particles at the edge of a corner. Heartbeats pass as I look for any sign of weakness, all while I studiously push my thoughts away from my goal.

"I'm not reading your mind, Luri," Jules says smugly, balancing back on his thicker tentacles.

Part of me wants to bark out that I *knew it*, but I rein it in. Centuries of life don't really prepare you for how you feel in the Between, how your impulse control feels peeled back and exposed again like you're back to being a hundred years old. But I have a pretty good grip on most of my flinch responses, and now I'm *actually* pretty sure that Jules is messing with me.

The information isn't that relevant. Whether he can read minds or not, I think I've already got my answer. I take a long drink of the beer Six brought us, the drink that has become familiar enough to be close to enjoyable by now helping me with an old social trick to change my voice patterns, and speak.

"It's just after dark, but still warm. The breeze moves trees around in the night, but not enough to spook you as you plod back to your apartment. Your eyes burn, and you know you are awake far too late, but you don't feel tired so much as you are simply aching and screaming inside at yourself for your own stupid lack of self-control. The stairs don't take long to climb but eat up ten times that many seconds as you stand at the bottom and stare at them, not wanting to actually make the ascent. When you finally make it back to your front door, just before you walk inside and can finally relax, you walk into a spiderweb. It gets in your nose."

I set my drink down and lean forward, one arm across the table in front of me in a way that would be leaving a grid of lines pressed into my skin if I weren't wearing the occulted pilot's suit. My eyes focus on Jules as he twists a tentacle across his face in consideration, his body wavering back and forth.

And then with a vibrating hum, he speaks. "*Three*," he says with utter confidence.

"No way," Mark softly protests from where the others are sitting. They were setting up a game of Encounter but went silent as I challenged Jules and the two of us entered our battle of wits. "Luri is, what, *seventy* lives? I feel like I've had that . . ."

"No helping!" Ellin shushes him by wrapping a heavy hand around Mark's head and pulling him backward with a muffled wail of despair. "Let him screw this up on his own!"

A small kobold chimes in without looking up from where she's sorting through her character grid. "He'll get it," Molly says with unwavering confidence. "Can't trick my love."

"No *helping!*" Ellin leans over the table and sends at least one stack of cards into a messy pile as she wraps her other hand around Molly's muzzle, adding a muffled howl to Mark's own protest.

Part of me wants to get sidetracked and say that I don't really think Molly was helping. Mark wasn't *either*, since Jules already made his guess, but Mark called me old so he can suffer. "Three? You're sure, Jules?" I ask the smooth jet-black creature across from me.

"Positive." His voice plucks the strings of the air as he settles back, his eyes turning to placid ovals. "Three. So, Luri? Have you anything to say?"

I settle myself back, trying to tug nervously at the sleeve of the pilot's suit and finding for not the first time that the material is flush with my skin and does not like being *plucked*. "You absolute monster," I grumble as I lose my challenge. "How do you *do* that? How do you even get *close*?"

"This time?" Jules says as he sighs in contentment, rising up on his mobility tendrils to stalk his way over to the larger green-felt surface that we'll be playing a game on once Ellin releases her victims. "The stairs."

Mark breaks away with an unneeded gasp of air. "Of course, the stairs!"

"The stairs?" Ellin asks, caught up in the furor. "I've got not— What about the stairs?"

"Well, I know, of course, but Jules can explain it better." Mark's words earn Molly an early release from her own capture, as Ellin pulls back and looks prepared to grapple him to the floor for his antics.

Jules gives a laugh, a cheery vibration that can be felt in the heart of every one of us. "Have none of you noticed in all our time together? Luri *despises* stairs."

"Well hang on . . ." I start to say.

But I am given no quarter, nor chance to defend myself. "Half the terrible memories Luri shares? Over the ground floor. Luri's favored dwellings? Street level. The one thing Luri intentionally keeps slotted despite the use of precious ability weight? Fall Mitigation."

"You *count* that?" I'm a little impressed, and a little worried about what Jules does with his free time. "Also I could just be afraid of heights."

"I would count that, if this form allowed for more perfect memory storage," Six muses aloud as he dutifully repairs the part of the board game setup that Ellin demolished. Placing the last few cards back where they belong with a crisp snap, he looks up at Jules. "I would like a journal, should anyone come across one. But also I do not believe for a heartbeat that Jules *counts that.*"

Jules makes an awkward buzzing sound. "Well. Yes. I can hardly be expected to track data. But I am certain Luri dislikes stairs. Which rules out the majority of lives where there was a choice in dwelling. Oh, I have a dozen small moments of insight that I could tell you add up to an answer. But the truth is, simply, that I am *just so good at this*." Jules polishes a tentacle against his central body stalk.

I love Jules so much sometimes. Not *now*, obviously, because he's being utterly smug and insufferable, but also actually kind of now because that smug insufferable jerk of a man is still just so impressive. And it's really hard to stay mad at someone who keeps their casually noble composure even when they're showing off.

As I find my place at the table, I tell him as much, and he hums a laugh at me. The others join in as we all turn our focus to our shared time here. Mark closes the book he's been trying to read, Molly fans her claws as she shuffles her personal deck of cards, Ellin checks in on the elf still sitting at the bar and staring with flinty eyes at the back wall, and Jules takes a little more time to be smug.

"Okay," Molly declares as Ellin swoops back by the table and steals kisses from me and Mark in turn. She tries to get one from Six, but is politely rebuffed, and one from Jules, but is *dramatically* rebuffed. Molly just keeps talking, ignoring Ellin towering over the back of her seat as she does so. "I *know* how long these rounds go, so I've got time for one play, okay? And then . . . And then I have to get going." Her muzzle splits into a toothy grin, even as she delivers sad news. "So someone catch me up on what I missed in the story? Luri said you all lost a planet or something?"

We did. It was Ellin's fault. Everything in this game is Ellin's fault, a lot of the time. But I still love it, and I think the others might actually earnestly share that feeling.

Ellin gets her final kiss and takes her seat next to me—and *away* from the threat deck—while Mark and Jules fill Molly in. And then the lot of us look over the organized chaos of our biggest table: piles of cards, hundreds of small tokens, dozens of map pieces, and at least one drink for each of us. Our individual cups are as special to us as the characters we're playing. Well, mine is, at least. Mark's character dies more often than the rest of us. I think it's a coincidence that we had to replace Mark's personal drinking vessel though.

The orderly but complex arrangement doesn't last. It takes two turns into the game before we have things stacked on each other, discard piles taking up too much space, and we fall into the familiar and amusing pattern of someone pointing to a few face down cards and asking where *those* came from.

We share an adventure this way. The only way we really can, here in the Between. A game between friends who can't ever have a real adventure together. But that's okay. It has to be okay, and so I make it okay in my heart. And after a few turns, the flow of gameplay and the passing of heartbeats carry the imagination deep into immersion. Ellin and Mark arguing about how to handle someone who might betray us feels so vividly possible. Jules getting caught up in the minutiae of our local star system's orbital laws is just who Jules would be in any life we lived together. Six and I having to herd the group like a bunch of feral bel to actually hit an objective before the hidden timer runs out is *worryingly* plausible. Molly asking about changing her character so she can try a new form is exactly Molly, and her accepting the in-game rules for biomodification is equally Molly.

We can't go out into our lives together. Not really. But we can face imaginary challenges like this. We can share our time as the plucky crew of a rogue starskimmer, pushing back the line of the dark and being champions for people who will never either meet us or be real.

Mark says it's poetic. Jules says the metaphor doesn't map. I think they're talking past each other. We flip an event that starts a crisis about belief in an afterlife among a planet's population, and everyone gives Ellin a *look* before the game adds another complication to the ongoing tableau of complexity. She shrugs and says something about coincidence and how she couldn't have actually had the time to read *that much* ahead just to set this up, and for once, I believe her.

I don't believe her argument at all when the next turn our ship takes a turbulence strike while our defenses are down for maintenance. I think that's entirely her fault. I think Ellin has convinced herself that Molly's lifeline is arbitrary. That if the game goes on forever, Molly won't leave.

But no one has infinite heartbeats, and our time with the energetic kobold, as well as this particular scenario of Encounter, both have to end sometime. It's not a *short* time, not at all; a little over a subjective day goes by as we play and banter and argue and laugh together. Our group builds our strength, shores up our weaknesses, and gets into messes that we are woefully unequipped for. We lose another planet, though this one is on purpose. Ellin tones down the cheating, and the challenges turn from backbreaking to simply spicy enough to keep us on our toes.

The only thing missing is snacks.

"Okay," I announce to everyone as the final piece goes back into the box, many thousands of heartbeats later. We *could* clean up by sweeping it all off the table and letting the laws of the Between banish it to the void and remake it anew. But the ritual is important. Or at least, Six says so, and I trust Six. "Next life? I'm gonna find a way to bring back some snacks."

"It *has* been some time since anyone received a souvenir snack, hasn't it?" Jules ponders as he casually hoists a giggling Molly on top of his form with several of his tentacles. "I miss the restorative Box of Bark Chips."

Mark flicks the edge of his thumb across the bridge of his nose as he shakes his head. "Those weren't *snacks*, and you know it," he accuses Jules in good humor. "Just because you can eat something doesn't mean the rest of us can. Also wait, what happened to the box?"

"Oh." I sigh deeply. "I had to sell it to pay the upkeep cost," I admit. Even in the Between, poverty can come too easily. "Bastion's . . . Well, you know. It costs to keep it here. Or maybe just to keep it accessible. You've wandered the Between at least once; you've seen the weird stuff out there. A lot of that is . . . leftovers. Places people made, or started to make, where they couldn't or wouldn't keep paying for them. So they're just out there, around."

"You can find loot in them!" Ellin proclaims, missing the point of the morose and hostile nature of entropy—and also rent. "Not most of them. But sometimes! I got a base strength once!"

Mark ignores Ellin and focuses on me. "Hey, you have what you need to keep Bastion's going, right? I know we chip in a little, but if you need more . . ." He looks around at the others, some of whom nod in agreement. Six doesn't, but Six knows already.

"Mark, you're fantastic, and I love you. But it's fine for a long time." I glance at the rough wooden floorboards, with their omnipresent layer of sand, before looking back up. "I can cover the maintenance costs with a single prize, and the way the Between hands them to me like festival candy, we don't need to worry. Save your stuff; have fun with it."

The look he gives me is utterly suspicious but says he's willing to play along for now. "Alright. Well, how do we get snacks then?"

"First things first." Six stops the conversation with a flat voice. "Molly?"

Ah. Of course. A parting. The worst part of living forever is that you have to say infinite goodbyes. And this one, as Molly darts around, flipping up onto chairs and over the table to give each of us a hug in turn before being enveloped in Jules's comforting tentacles like he's terrified to let her go, is no different. A little painful, a little scary, a little sickening. No one *wants* to let go of the people they love.

Except this one is a little different. There's an undercurrent to it of unstable hope. Molly was gone. Gone for whole cycles through the Between, lifetime after lifetime of not seeing her face or hearing her voice. She was a missing component that we were worried would do worse than leave a wound in our hearts. We were worried that wound would scab over, scar, and fade.

But no. Because she came back. Not through force of will or strength of character or devious cunning. But just because it turned out that way.

And that is weirdly reassuring. It's almost like an affirmation of my unlife motto. We live *forever*, and nothing is never, and on a long enough timeline, surely we will all see each other again. It's just that this time it didn't take long at all, and my friend is back with us, and I have a confident hope that we'll see her next time around.

"Oh, I missed you guys." Her muffled voice comes out from a muzzle poking through the rows of Jules's rubbery limbs. "And I'll do it again! I'll miss you all over! But it was so good to see you."

"Any plans for your last beats, my darling?" Jules asks her, his voice caring even while it's subdued.

Molly's arms drag her up through his grasp like she's swimming against a particularly clingy ocean. Cresting the top of his enfolding tentacles, she leans her elbows on Jules's head and gives a cocky nod. "Take me to the tree you made," she says. "I wanna see what it's like when it changes. And also I wanna hear more about who you made it for! And . . . And . . . And I want more *time* . . ." Her voice strains and threatens to crack, but she sniffs in a heavy breath and holds her composure.

Jules hesitates for only a second before he hums a nod. "Of course. Any of that I can provide, I will." His longer mobility tentacles slither up the tall wall to wrap around the library railing and begin tugging him upward, Molly still half wrapped in his grip.

She waves to us as she is carried off. "No being sad!" Molly commands us like a towering sorcerer queen, borne aloft by her loyal summon. "I'll be back, and if you're sad about this, I'll be *very upset!*"

I can't hold back a laugh that comes close to being wet with tears. It is, word for word, what she told us the last time she vanished. Well, *us*, though it was only Six and I at the time. Everyone else was gone already. So Ellin and Mark get to hear it for the first time, maybe, and be impressed by her bravado.

Some of the stuff we bring back, the souvenirs and relics and equipables, they fall into a rough category of sinks. Things that we can pour currency into and get a consistent output. Marks or cysts, sometimes, and I'm sure there's others. But the most common ones, the ones that we don't tend to play with, are the ones that eat heartbeats.

Molly left a jar of glowing bugs on a table that turns them into brighter bugs for a little while. Someone, probably me, bought a bottle of rice wine that turns them into more rice wine. We used to have a resin orb that turned them into a pheromone burst, but Ellin apologized for that a long time ago, and I haven't seen the orb in a while.

Or, maybe, they take the form of an arcane terrarium. A semisculpture of a fluffy tree on a grassy hill, the scene of it set sometime in an indeterminate spring day. Jules made it. His magnum opus from an old life as a city's designated artist. And it's beautiful. It occupies the space of one of our coveted end tables in the library upstairs.

It takes heartbeats and turns them into time. Time taken away from us and made into time for the tree. For the whole piece. In theory, the season would progress eventually, but no one wants to feed it a million heartbeats to find out. Maybe after another few lifetimes, in ones and fours, it will get there. But not for a long time.

Molly though? Molly doesn't want to flick a few heartbeats at it so her reminder from the Between is a round number. She doesn't want to make a leaf or two blow in the hint of a breeze. Molly is a lot of things, but accepting of the way of things is not one of them. When Molly leaves the Between, she makes sure she always leaves on *her* terms.

Being perfectly honest, a lot of the time those terms involve enthusiastic sex with her lover, which is a *little bit* why I've chosen to stay downstairs and check the little tree later. I've said before that I'm no prude; you can't go into lives expecting to change and grow and learn and then stay as a stuffy boor forever. Even Ellin barely lasted twenty lives before giving in at least a little bit. But my mood right now is somewhere between sobbing and weeping, and really, I don't feel like exploring how that mixes with unabashed lust this time. Maybe later. But *also*, the moment isn't mine. It's sex, yes, but it's also an unfiltered intimacy between two people who have loved each other like shining beacons across whole lifetimes. And neither sad nor horny feels like a good reason to interfere with that kind of longing.

"It was good to see Molly again," Mark says as we return to the bar, a flip of his shiny new coin making it my turn to serve him. I circle behind the smoothly polished surface as he sits down, Six and Ellin joining on either side of him. "It's always a . . ." He pauses as a delighted squeal sounds from upstairs. "Well it's never *boring*, is it?"

"I could accuse Molly of being many things, but unengaged is not one of them," Six says in his placid monotone, agreeing in a roundabout but technically correct way. "She adds something to us while she is here."

Ellin snorts. "What she *adds* is a constant sense of primal fear that she's planning a kobold-shaped projectile ambush."

"That's not really something you should worry about," Six politely informs Ellin as I pour out tall glasses of what's on tap right now and slide them one by one down the bar to be caught by my friends. Six catches his with a flat *pap* on his gray palm and mechanically takes a drink before shaking his head at his own creation.

Mark catches his with a light twirl of fingers, lifetimes of doing pub tricks for free drinks coming up as distant reflexes. "Oh, yeah. Don't be afraid of that at all. Or, well . . ."

When the last drink gets to Ellin, she just clamps her hand on top of it and stares at them without raising the cup. "Why *not?*" she demands.

"I can answer that!" I cheerfully interject. "It's because it's not an uncertainty!" And it really isn't. At no point is Molly *not* planning to rocket into someone's torso. Or, rather, it would be more accurate to say that while Molly doesn't have a plan, what she does have is a constant prepared nature, always ready to move, always ready to push into physical contact. Molly is body oriented in a way most of us aren't anymore, but I think we all can still appreciate a good hug from her. Even when they come in the form of a meter-tall mixed-blood kobold slamming into our guts at high velocity.

The Between mostly stops damage, but often not the *sting*.

I pour myself a drink, and the four of us quietly clink glasses together. "To Molly," I say. "Good luck in her next life." They echo me, a series of *good lucks* pouring out as Jules joins us, his tentacles seeming to drag sadly across the floor. I send him a drink, which he lethargically catches. "Hey. She'll be back."

"Of course she will." His tone, even saddened, is still so vibrantly filled with something bordering on arrogance but not quite tipping over the line. "She's perfect. How could she stay away?"

"Exactly," I say like I'm proving a point somehow. "You know, Jules, we were talking about optimizers earlier. But you know what? I don't think we need it for a totally different reason."

"Oh?" His eyes turn to suspicious diamonds.

Ellin flicks the rim of her glass with a long finger. "Yeah, I wanna hear this latest Luri wisdom."

"Yeah," I say. "You're all already perfect."

The sappy moment lasts for twenty heartbeats, soft smiles and emotional swelling in the breast making everyone on the other side of the counter feel like they're not just alive, but *alive.* Alive and loved.

Then Six ruins it by speaking. "Well. Subjectively perfect. Mark still requires basic education in math."

"It was *one mistake!*" Mark's protest, feeble as it is, is buried under laughter and cheers and the requests for more drinks and talk of how we plan to find a way to fetch some new snacks and Ellin retelling her semiadventure in the Between where she once found something that was almost worth it.

And at the far end of the bar, a near-silent elf who has been staring at her lemonade for a subjective day, quietly raises the half-empty cup up to eye level, and I barely catch her whisper: "To Molly." She breathes out, taking a tiny sip of the herbal citrus drink. "May your trail wind."

I offer her what I can in comfort. A small smile, a kind word, and a refill.

CHAPTER TWENTY-FIVE

We have had more guests.

The elf is gone, vanished between one moment and the next, off to her next life. Her lemonade left sitting on the counter, not a drop spilled when she moved on. But she'll be back. I don't know how, but I *know* she'll find her way back to us.

A pair came through afterward, mostly human, shorter even than me, lithe and fluid in their movements like they were partly made of liquid. Whether they were friends, lovers, or enemies I'm still not sure. Mark and I had bet on it as the two of us worked together to organize the clutter we'd been building up behind the bar, but we never got an answer before they left.

They paid for their drinks though, so they got a gold star from me. The dragon that came through more or less robbed us of some of the better bottles we had left. Partly our fault for serving without payment up front, I guess. I should have cut him off when Mark realized that the stupid lizard was talking around us, treating us like automatons and not people.

Now, there's two people actually here. One is some kind of fire-elemental snake that's having a heated discussion with Six about how it feels to grow up as an artificial life-form. They're sitting up in the library, having their conversation over a game of Lull Tricks, rapidly declaring their moves along with their conversational points. I think they're having fun? It can be hard to tell with Six sometimes. But I know him better than I know everyone else, and I *think* he's having fun.

The other person is sitting over at the little stone and wrought iron table that Molly's jar of lightbugs sits in the middle of, staring at it like he can siphon out some kind of bonus. The fox-faced golden-furred samurai is doing that because I lied to him and told him that it would work.

"He's really focused, huh?" Mark whispers into my ear.

The two of us are crouched below the bar counter, ostensibly sorting through empty bottles that we've managed to save from being returned to nothing by the Between. I think half of these actually just eat heartbeats or marks or something in order to refill themselves, which is why they're still here. I don't know about the others.

That's less important right now. Both of us have our eyes peeking out over the edge of the counter's black polished surface, peeking at the fox as he narrows his eyes even farther at the decoration. I hold in a snicker, delighting at wasting his time. "*Very* focused," I mutter, and then, unsure if he can hear me or not, I set a small trap. "I'm sure he'll get there. Maybe he'll figure out the trick with overfeeding it heartbeats."

One of the samurai's ears twitches in our direction. He has really good hearing for someone sitting under a slowly spinning turboprop engine. He's also single-minded, and oblivious.

The lightbugs in the jar start to glow brighter, then multiply. A sound like distant violins picks up as the artificial little liltopods start to sing to each other in a re-creation of their mating season. The jar never outshines the lights of Bastion's, even the low-luminescence lamps and hanging bulbs and floatflames we use. But it does become easier to see as the fox focuses too long on trying to find the trick and vanishes.

"Dumbass." Mark snorts.

"Honestly cannot believe that worked." The two of us rise up from behind the counter in unison, arms folded, heads cocked, and eyebrows raised in mirrors of the same pose. "What a . . . a . . ."

Mark elbows me lightly. "Dumbass," he reiterates. I give him a nod of agreement. Sometimes, the simple terms fit best.

We've met this particular guest before. Their companion, hopefully ex-companion, hasn't returned to us yet. But this one, the "teacher," the optimizer who so casually waved a paw at the idea of annihilating cities just to earn more achievements, did.

It's a harsh reminder. And maybe one that I need right now. It's so, so easy when it's just us. When it's just people I love and trust. So easy to let my guard down and say, "Well, just this once, right?" But it isn't. It never is. It leads to *this*. To genocide and a focus on the statistical so singular that it overrides reason.

At least it makes this dumbass easy enough to deal with. Combat doesn't work right in the Between; usually the most you can hope for is to waste someone's time, without certain perks or titles or ways to pay a cost. But we've got a lot of random stuff that wastes time, and spinning a simple trap for a simple optimizer feels like a *very* satisfying use of my own heartbeats.

"Hoy! So!" Ellin jolts upright from where she was pretending to sleep on the bar, three seats down from us. One of her horns glistens in Bastion's warm lighting from where she dunked it in a water bowl. Or at least, I hope it's water; Bastion's hasn't had a place to bathe properly for what feels like lifetimes, and while we don't pick up body odors at the same rate, no one enjoys the sticky sensation of horns coated in beer. "That was hilarious, by the way, Luri. Good one. So, who do we think is gonna wander in next?"

"Can't be anyone worse," Mark complains as he passes her a stack of napkins.

Ellin stares at the coarse and barely absorbent paper with a curious frown for a couple dozen heartbeats before a drop of something falls from her horn with a *plip* onto her nose. "Oh." She starts trying to clean up whatever her drama has gotten all over her head. "Also don't say that! It could always be a screamer. We haven't had one of those in a *while* though."

A chill cuts into my limbs at her words. I wasn't really listening, instead half watching Jules help Six clear the small library table, the two of them dropping down to the ground floor of Bastion's and utterly ignoring our carefully placed steps. The elemental is gone too, though Six seems to be in a pleasant mood, so I suppose their conversation went well. It's almost enough to help me ignore Ellin's grim omen.

Screamers don't actually come to Bastion's that often, and there are two types of them that get dealt with differently. But when they do show up, it sort of ties back into that thing about how you can't just *stab* someone in the Between. No, all you can do, if you want to hurt people, is *waste their time.* And screamers are very, very, very devoted to wasting your time.

I don't want to think about it. "Make a new friend?" I ask Six as he and Jules approach the bar.

"Yes." He nods rigidly, but there's a small smile on the golem's gray-fleshed face. "We spoke of many things."

"Meanwhile, here I sit, *neglected*," Jules bemoans, two of his tentacles coming up to the closest thing he has to a forehead as he swoons. "Secret plots and new companions and poor me, oh my, just all by my lonesome and—"

"Hey, Jules, you want to talk about Luri's new book before I have to go?" Mark *earns* the title of intercessor that the Between ascribes to us every time we wake up here. "'Cause, and I hate to do this to all of you, I'm out of here in a couple of subjective hours. Don't wanna make a big deal of it, but . . ." He shrugs. "It's been a long one, huh?"

We smile at each other. It *has*. We've been here for some time together, enough that we're reaching the point where we're gorged on each other's company. But it's been a delight to have them all here with me. And because of how long we've had, how many drinks and words and games and moments we've shared, there is less of a sting to Mark's leaving.

He'll be back. We'll be back. We know it in our hearts.

"You know what I like?" Mark says as Jules roils away to fetch the possibly stolen library book that I returned with this last life. "I like how this feels like I'm on a sortie and not an exile."

"Ooh, look at you, with your big words." Ellin reaches over to ruffle his hair, and Mark surprises her by snagging her hand and leaning down to give her a grinning kiss. "*Ambusher!*" she accuses him with a giddy laugh.

I join her in laughter. It's just that kind of mood right now. Laughter and swelling happiness and no grim tidings can stick for too long before sliding off. Mark rolls his eyes at the both of us. "I mean, I'm not being kicked out. I'm leaving to find something new to bring back. It's *nice*." He fidgets with his new coin, flicking the small disc of gleaming metal into the air with a spin before catching it, flipping it between his fingers, and making it vanish to his other hand. Sleight of hand from who knows how many lives letting him turn a trick into something he can do without thinking. "Hey. Thanks for being here," he tells us all.

"Oh, don't think that you can leave just yet, my dear man." Jules plants the book on the counter with a hollow thunk. "Say your goodbyes in an hour! Let us speak of the method on which nobility impacts the ties of family!"

"I . . . I thought we could talk about . . . trees?" Mark looks like he wants to go back to hiding behind the bar, and I jut a hip into him to start pushing him out to the main room, happily throwing him into Jules's waiting art-critic maw.

It's too late for Mark. I should know; as the one responsible for bringing book club back, I have already been the vanguard of the experience of discussing interpersonal social-strata secondary effects with Jules. Which, really, I shouldn't say like it's a bad thing. There's a certain built-up complexity to how we start to view things after a score of lifetimes, the way any of us look at the different ways the threads of a world connect, the way we see more and more the invisible influences. We all have our own lenses, and talking about them is fascinating at least, and at best is a good way to pass the heartbeats with companions.

"Hey, Luri," Ellin gets my attention. "You know Jules is gonna leave along with Mark, right?" she asks.

"Oh. Uh." Ah, yes. Good job, Luri. A mastery of languages forged over millennia, hard at work there. "I didn't. But that's fine! I'll say a real goodbye after they finish their chat."

Ellin nods and then glances at Six. "And . . . we're running low, too." She coughs into a closed fist. A holdover gesture from being alive that we all have a dozen of and never actually bother to shake. "Six and I were going to go wander?"

I smile at her. Strangely, maybe, her half question doesn't bother me this time. A million heartbeats is a long time, and we've spent almost *seven million* together. Subjective months this time around. And it has been beautiful and lovely, and we've managed to somehow refrain from utterly exhausting every consumable supply that we have in Bastion's, but also, *now* I am properly armored to survive some time alone.

"I'd offer to come along, but someone has to clean this place up," I say easily. And also because I don't really like wandering the Between. It's . . . Well, I've been out there before. I've spent a long, long time in those endless halls and paths and nowhere places. Bastion's hasn't always been my home in this place, and it's easy to get lost in the endless architectural noise. "But I hope you two have fun!"

"You will be alright, on your own?" Six asks.

"Six, I've got fifty things I can spend my heartbeats on if I really don't want to stick around on my lonesome." I start ticking things off on my fingers. "There's the tree, there's the wine, there's the *other* wine, there's the mirror . . . Heck, I could just read some books again as a way to pass quiet hours."

"There's the neon sign that we never have on," Ellin chimes in, pointing to one of the souvenirs hanging over the bar.

I always forget about the sign. It being dark makes it easy. My brain is also trying to protect me from the multistage image rendered in neon of a semi-accurate medical replication of a drake lung. I try not to be squeamish, but I have limits, and as long as the neon is dark, I can pretend that it's not there.

"What sign?" Six says placidly. Six agrees with me, and comes to my defense every time this comes up. And by defense, I mean that we act like the neon sign isn't real and hope the others forget too. I call this noble gaslighting.

"Okay, what about . . . I dunno, hope a vendor or server comes through or something." Ellin wisely drops the fight over the neon. "Ah, you already know, you don't need me giving you a list." She spins on her barstool. "It's been so good to see you happy, Luri. Everyone else too, but you . . . You've been good."

"I have, haven't I?" I smile. It almost doesn't feel like a betrayal, to feel this good when there's so many people I've left behind. Who still haven't joined us and may never set foot or tail or hoof in Bastion's. I shove that pang of remorse away, and it leaves me with a shameful ease this time. "Maybe it's some residual from my last great fuckup."

Six makes a motion to pat one of the arms I have folded on the counter. "I'm sure your next one will be safer," he reassures me.

We linger quietly together. Just seizing control of our own heartbeat supplies for a moment that stretches on into the horizon so we might be *together*. Worry and fear are for later; loss and grief are for tomorrow. Right now is for us. Just to be here.

To be in Bastion's, a place that is for all of us. A place of sand and grit on the wooden floor, of walls adorned in art from styles that don't even come from the same world let alone the same kind of color palettes. A place where we are free to take our time, to ignore the perverse rush the Between wants us to be in, to passively toy with abilities and feats and auras instead of actually grimly thirsting for them. A place where the only thing we grimly thirst for is a good drink with good friends.

Mark leaves us with a wave and a shouted "I'll miss you all! Until next time!" I hop out from behind the bar to press in on him with a crushing hug before he goes, and Ellin struts over to do the same, though she adds a passionate kiss to the mix. Mark has to struggle against her as there's a brief chime from his pocket and something flickers in his vision. "The stupid coin lets you buy social sta—" is all he gets out before he isn't there anymore.

We all falter a little, those of us hugging, when there's a sudden gap.

"Hmm." Jules vibrates, smoothing down his slightly wrinkled white frilly dress shirt that I have no idea why he is wearing. The tentacles he had encircled us with winding back to him like dejected serpents. "Well. One more thing to worry about, these coins, isn't it?"

"Worry not, friend," Six blandly offers. "I am certain we can, together, fail to care."

"A fine point," Jules acquiesces with a wave of his limbs and a laughing flutter of his triangular eyes. "Well. I have one last thing to worry about now, my lovely dears. It has been . . . an excellent time. In the next afterlife, I should say I would do it all again with you. But for now . . ." His voice starts to warble. Modulating in time with Jules's rising discomfort and panic.

I lean into him, and Ellin does the same with me, while Six just settles a cool gray hand on Jules's flank. "Hey," I say softly. "You know, you've had some really shitty luck so far. I bet you're due for getting a body you actually like."

"You *would* think so, but I can already feel Six clenching his internal organs as he struggles to not tell you that statistics simply do not work that way, Luri." Jules, even panicking about his upcoming rebirth, cannot help but effortlessly slip into poking fun. "Though perhaps I will find myself in a world where math works differently."

"Has that happened before?" Ellin asks bluntly.

Jules pats her on the horns, pulling his friend close with a muffled grunt. "Oh Ellin. It could have—"

And then he too is gone. Ellin and I stumble to the dusty floor, and all I can think is that it is horrid that the best I can do for someone who is being thrown ever forward into situations they hate is to distract them until the moment happens.

I should be able to do more. I'm so old, but I never feel like it. Hundreds of subjective years feeling like I'm a kid who hasn't grown up yet because once you're old you can fix all the problems. You can do something. Or at least do more. But now here I am, dead again, after life number I don't remember, and I can't actually change anything.

Everything just keeps happening. And even if we have spent what feels like *enough* time together, for now, it grates against every part of me to think that the choice to say good night was never my own.

My goodbyes with Ellin and Six are quiet, after that. There's an oppression that settles into our hearts when it's time to go that makes it hard to say the words that matter. But that's okay because we cut it off early this time and told each other what mattered hours ago. That we love each other, that we understand, that we'll be back.

I'm invited to come along, but I've had my fill of the endless and meaningless spaces out there. Yes, there's things to find, or things that we might see as having value. But there's also just so much pointless dross. And when you're as old as I am, and comfortable familiarity that matters to you is what you value, you do what I do, and you stay in Bastion's.

The two of them head out into the Between. Six says he's looking to learn things, Ellin says she's looking for hidden treasures, both of them are probably actually looking for the same thing, which is to simply try to pick up some glimmer of what the Between *wants* with us. I understand; I want to know too, but I can't bring myself to search for it right now. I wave to them as they leave, walking through a door that shuts in the wall behind them and leaves no trace it was ever there.

And then I'm alone. But it isn't so bad, this time.

I sit by myself and just let the heartbeats pass. The whir of the engine fan, the occasional leftover drip of water in the sink behind the bar, the odd flicker of the wrought iron lamps through the archway that leads to our disconnected hallway, I let all of it wash over me. Take me away, to a place where I don't need to think or feel or do anything but just sit and breathe and be at peace.

Soon enough I get bored of that. I've tried being everything from a monk to a spotter to a cultivator in my lives, and patience with the quiet has never really been something that was *for me*. So I find myself standing, stretching my limbs out against the resistance of the pilot's suit as I survey my now-personal domain.

It takes me about eight thousand heartbeats to clean up the bits and bobs that we've left out of place around Bastion's. The wooden board game Six was playing with his fire-elemental compatriot gets packed away and replaced on the shelf. The napkins and single wrapper of a candy bar that the elemental must have brought in get swept aside, vanishing into the air with a satisfying vibration of the void, while the ceremonial clay drinking bowls that I actually want to keep get taken downstairs so I can wash them. I collect all our cups and bottles, actually, all the ones Mark and I didn't get to by now. And spend our infinite supply of water cleansing them, diluted alcohol or fruit juice meeting the same fate as all other discarded things.

I find a cluster of marks on a table, a tip someone left, perhaps. I add them to my collection and try to remember that in however many decades when I see them next I will need to split them with the others. I pay out of that same collection to reinforce Bastion's until we next arrive, marking it as a stable space with furniture that won't degrade to the void.

I waste time undoing the sorting that Mark and I did, rearranging the bottles and clay urns one more time. I also hide that tiny fern Ellin brought back amid the glass shelves, waiting for someone to ask if they could drink it.

I read a book again. My favorite perfectly preserved, creased, and worn copy of a space adventure. I do my best to not skim, and I enjoy it even my hundredth time through. It adds a notification to my incoming messages from the Between, which I vaguely and perhaps incorrectly remember will be about a bonus to spaceship crafting or something like that. I don't bother reading it. I don't care.

But it does remind me that I have one final message left to unpack from my last life. One I have . . . well, not been dreading. Simply not doing because there were more important things going on.

I decide in a moment of confidence to prove that I am not lying to myself, and clear my incoming message log. The first one *is* a spaceship-crafting bonus, which seems *wrong* to me. Two whole percent to my work speed, a thing that

I am sure will be of use in my next life. The next one isn't nearly so good at making me smile.

You have died.
You lived the life of a planner and a plotter.
You lived the life of a conqueror.
You lived the life of one who did what they thought was best.
You lived the life of one who died happy.
Final grade: unavailable
Final true achievement: 4 (23 total)
Final reward: +2 ability burden, +1 perk slot. Ability Unlocked (charisma)—Mind Blank.
The Between calls.

Yeah, I suppose I can't argue with that. I did, in truth, die happy. So happy it followed me home and wouldn't leave until I rewired my own false brain.

I laugh to myself at the thought. "Home." I don't even know if I can have a home; all of us who die over and over again seem to be eternal itinerants. But I suppose if there is a home to be had, it's with my friends. That's always how it ends up being when I'm living on a world too. The building is just an accoutrement, and what matters is the people you fill it with.

Not that I'm good at following that advice. I tend to fill my buildings with books, cats or cat analogues, and self-imposed isolation. After all, I can't feel bad about losing people if I don't get close to too many of them.

I look down at the bar that I'm leaning on, where a row of emptied short crystal glasses sit. I barely remember pouring and emptying them, which means I've already let the quiet hours get to me. I think I lost some time to being morose and some more to staring at the meditation loop and probably a little more to trying to work up the courage to test whatever is in the bottle labeled "Dangerous Poison Do Not Drink."

I think it's poison. But I'm not actually sure. And I really want to know, but I also don't want to drink poison. The Between's protections aren't enough for me to be sure here. At least puzzling over that one is a distraction from moping.

Maybe I should have gone with Ellin and Six. Being alone didn't take more than fifty thousand heartbeats to really start messing with me. Too late now, I suppose.

I whittle away a little more of my heartbeat supply by trying to see if there's anything close to Ellin's tiny fern in our book on plants, and then a little more by remembering to fully stock my perks. There isn't anything close to the fern, with its odd little double-diamond leaves. And I slot a speed-reading perk back in, now that it could mean the difference between bringing a book home or not.

Ah, I did it again. Home.

I've still got plenty of heartbeats, and I use a few staring around Bastion's. Perched up in the library with my elbows on the railing, watching the silent and still scene below of our mismatched tables, our collected mementos, our *home*.

It's not a home without them. And I don't want to stick around just to keep the lights on.

Jules's little ecologium with the miniature tree on an even more miniature hill looks almost regal, blowing in false wind, a few leaves drifting to the ground as it starts to change with the season as I feed heartbeats into it. I have a lot left to give. But without anyone here to share it with, what's the point in hoarding? So I share it with the tree, instead. Watching the leaves continue to fall, the shade of the light changing to something lower in the sky even without a sky or sun to be seen in the glass tank. I'm maybe halfway through what I think is a version of autumn when I really start to run low on heartbeats.

Sometimes, I'm not the last one out, and I relish every last second with my friends. But right now, I think, all I want to do is speed up getting back. In a lot of my lives, I've heard that you can't go home again. But I *can*, and I am, as ever, impatient to get on with it.

My last thought from my falsely assembled Between form, watching that wonderfully crafted little tree sway in the breeze, is that I think I understand why Molly does this. It's nice, to feel like *I'm* choosing.

And then my heartbeats run out.

And I go last.

CHAPTER TWENTY-SIX

Something, nothing, something again.

I don't think any of us are so dead to the wonder and the vastness of it all that we don't feel fear every time through. The last time each life that eyes close, the final drops of blood, the finale of hearts and lungs and neurons giving out. There's a terror to it, each iteration. Maybe not always the same terror, but always in the same acreage.

What if, this time, this is it? What if there's no Between, and no local afterlife besides? Not that we've ever verified any local afterlives existing, but what if anyway?

Or, sometimes, the inverse. What if it's all real, and it's all going to happen again? What if I never get to rest?

I'm mostly split from life to life. Mark leans fear of death, but he's still young. Ellin and Jules are fear of forever, but I think it's a temporary thing for them, a flash of anxiety every time that gets pushed away as they approach their next project. I don't know what Molly is, but Six is, unsurprisingly, firmly on team fear of death. Ceaseless existence has never bothered him, even as his mind grew and his capacity for morose poetry expanded with it.

[Welcome back to the Between, intercessor. 1,222,050 heartbeats remain. Prepare yourself.]

Well. There's a point of evidence for endless cycle, I suppose. Though it's not like I'd ever know if it went the other way.

And so few heartbeats. Fewer than last time, but more than I've had to suffer under in the past. That's what I get for dying early, I suppose. I've been spoiled by the treasure trove earned from brainwashing an entire world.

Finding myself lying in the smooth sheets of my perfectly made sunken bed, staring up at the pipe chandelier that is the one souvenir I keep in my room and not in Bastion's, I take stock.

Scars? Gone. Limbs? All there, which is a nice change. Different skin, different eyes, both feeding me different sensations than I'm used to. But I've done this before, and I adapt fast, especially as I focus on the feelings.

I'm a different color than I got used to over the last thirty-three years. I think I prefer myself as I am now. Warm organic copper, instead of the kind of inoffensively pale green.

Dying one second and whole the next. At least, subjectively, if we ignore the feeling that I've been waiting in the empty nothing for a very, very long time. The remade and fake body is a comfortable shell to come back to. I keep checking parts of it. Fingertips? Sensing properly. Tongue? No longer pierced. I might pine for that for a little bit. Tail? Oh, I've *missed* this tail. Scales and diamond plates are a reminder that I'm back . . .

Home.

Back home.

I'm dead, and I'm home.

I sit up in my bed, wrapping slender arms around my knees as I settle my face against my limbs.

I'm trying to figure out when I started thinking that way. Was it last life? Checking yourself for mental alterations is hard, but I've got experience with it, and I want to make sure I'm safe before walking into Bastion's.

This life was almost a refreshing diversion. No depression, no suicidality, no dysmorphia, not living long enough to bring back memory decay. But here I sit, curling up on myself, trying to figure out why the word *home* resonates so powerfully with me now.

I am, admittedly, a little paranoid. After my conversation with Jules last time, and getting a sharp reminder of just how easy it is to start the slide into optimizer philosophy, I've been worried about every little change to myself. To the point that I know it influenced decisions in my last life, in several ways. Maybe I could have lived longer, if I weren't so focused on it. Been so directly concerned with regulating my own thoughts and behavior.

And now that little burst of relief at feeling like I could relax my guard in the Between is gone, as I wonder why I am suddenly *glad* to be back. Or maybe I'm just lying to myself, feigning ignorance when I already know damn well what the issue is.

I twist, using my single existing arm to prop myself up out of the bed and start to rise, before I realize why the maneuver feels awkward. Doing it again with both arms, I stand, kick the sheets away, and accept the truth of it.

I'm thinking of Bastion's as home because it is. Because I don't belong anywhere else, and I never will again. I can fake it, I can blend in, I can even enjoy being alive. But at the end of all those moments of putting up a facade, I'll still be back here, listening for Ellin's footsteps, arguing with Mark, learning from Six, being mercilessly roasted by Jules, laughing with Molly. And others too, I'm sure, as change is inevitable.

With that existential crisis quickly wrapped up, I extract myself from the remainder of the sheets wrapped around my feet and open a door. The only door my room has that isn't just dropping farther into the Between.

I step through, close it behind me with a light clack of the latch, and find Bastion's to be as welcoming as ever.

How welcoming it is can sometimes be an open question. Today, it is as welcoming as finding Mark behind the bar, cooking something that smells like peppers, and Ellin and Molly hanging off the side of the metal stairs up to the library so that they can reach a chancer that has wandered in.

"Luri!" Mark greets me cheerfully, flipping the knife he's using as a spatula into the air and letting it drop effortlessly into one of the loops of his dragon-feather toga. His thick muscles get shown off as he spreads his arms to greet me. "Put that away before—"

"Wow he really does tell that joke *every time*, doesn't he?" Molly's high-pitched voice calls down from where she's scrambling to reposition as the chancer floats slightly away from the stairs and closer to the library's railing. "Mark, you have decades, *centuries*, to come up with better comedy! You can do it! We all believe in you!" Her encouraging words are cut with a bark of exertion as the industrial pylons she calls legs shoot her upward at a vicious angle, letting her grab the edge of the library's flooring and reach out with her other claw for the floating . . . thing.

Ellin, deprived of her catch, just huffs and arches her arms over her head as she takes the stairs. The horned warrior could probably match Molly's athleticism, but she holds back, probably so she doesn't flatten the much smaller kobold. "Oy, oy! Hey, Luri! I'll be right down to greet ya proper!" she yells.

I nod at them, offering a tired smile as the dissonance between living and dead starts to catch up to me. I don't feel more tired than normal, but I also don't feel mentally ready. I grab a barstool, the black leather sticking to my newly made skin as I settle onto the seat and watch Mark cook.

"Drive it this way!" I hear Molly yell at Ellin from behind me.

"*You* push it *this* way!" Ellin snaps back, though there's a playful undercurrent to her voice.

Mark and I make eye contact and both bite our lips as we hold back laughter. There's something ever so slightly magical about the moment, hearing our friends going through a self-imposed and somewhat silly trial just over my shoulder. "So, taking a bit before talking again?" Mark asks me quietly.

I nod. Conflicting desires play inside my chest as I do. I *want* to speak now. I want to say it's a silly old habit that I only keep for the sake of being stubborn. I want to just let myself change. Let myself become a new Luri, who talks to my friends when I get here and not after some arbitrary deadline. But that's not the only thing I want, and I also still do yearn for the experience of seeing long-lost companions eventually walk through those doors, and am holding to my promise that my first words will be for *them*.

I don't know how long one person can keep a promise. Saying I'll do it to the end of the Between and beyond seems a little presumptuous, given how fragile I know my own ego can be. But it's at least worth an attempt; all it costs me is a little time, and time is the one thing that I seem to have an endless supply of.

"Alright." Mark nods and pulls a familiar old goblet out from under the counter, filling it with a pour from a shining glass bottle that he produces with a flourish before sliding my personal cup over to me. "No hurry. I'm here for at least a subjective octob." I cock an eyebrow at him, and Mark sighs. "Week," he corrects. "You ever get a world where society insists on being *quirky*?"

I don't have the heart to tell him that his home world was the weird one. So I just offer a peaceful grin, trying to keep the exhaustion out of my eyes, and then spin on my stool to watch Ellin and Molly have a go at accessing the chancer.

Chancers are—I *think*—between constructs like vendors or servicers. They show up from time to time, though it can be a score of lives between them, and while I *really* don't want to do the mental labor of applying statistical models to my peaceful Bastion's half existence, I know they're the rarest.

The one that's here now looks like a curling spiral of gemstones that glitter with light cast from directions that don't exist. Arms of the writhing glinting galaxy curl outward across several axes before intersecting each other and making something like a ball with attitude. It makes the kind of noise that metal makes when it's being cut apart with high-pressure water, which is sort of an aggressive squeaking, except modulated in a song that's *almost* pleasant. And it floats.

This one specifically is floating in the open space over the tables, just close enough to the library's wooden railing that Molly and Ellin *think* they can grab it and access its menu. And maybe they can too. Chancer menus are far, *far* simpler than vendors' or servicers'. Usually they just ask what you want to wager and what odds you're willing to accept.

As for why this particular one is playing tag with my friends, I couldn't say. It's not like it's possible to offend the Between's constructs.

I pause midway through a sip of the mixed wine Mark has poured for me. I must be tired if I'm having thoughts about how something isn't possible. The things the Between sends through its endless fractured spaces haven't ever reacted to us, but that doesn't mean they can't be offended. So maybe Ellin was particularly rude to this one.

What I can know is why they're after it.

We come back to the Between changed from our lives, most of the time. Or we come back tired, or triumphant, or maybe a little fucked up. But every time we come back, the Between shoves all these rewards into our metaphorical hands. Traits, perks, boons, auras, abilities, masteries . . . I'm forgetting at least one here, and it's on the tip of my mind, and it's irritating to not know. It's not important.

What is is that we quickly end up as hoarders. Different people handle it differently, but in *our* little family, there's a habit of treating our stuff collectively. Now, I'm not ever going to ask Ellin to borrow her ability that gives her some kind of fiat-backed edge whenever she's having a bowel movement. Because even after all these lives, I still have *some* standards. But if I did ask, she'd lend it to me. We swap resistances and small perks constantly when we need to fill little holes in our blueprints, and personally, I think it's fine. Often times we're shoring up protections against things that worry us, or trying to avoid repeating the same failure twice, pretty far from optimizer territory.

What we *don't* do though is throw stuff away. We hand out some of the stuff we find to new people, we trade with guests, we sell piles of redundant and useless aura layers to the more lively merchants. Not the ones the Between makes, I mean the ones that always seem to have more marks than sense. But we never throw anything out. Partly because throwing things out is an ordeal that requires us to take it somewhere far away in the Between and dump it and hope the metaitem doesn't find its way back to us like they *tend* to do. But also partly because it's just hard to let go sometimes.

When a chancer arrives, it gives us a strange opportunity. To clear out the cobwebs, sweep out the silt, and empty the inventory of things that we've never *actually* needed to help us remember. But not just to throw it out. Instead, it's a gamble. It might go away, but it also might change, become something new, a part of a story that doesn't need to come from any living world, but from right here, from us as we *really are* and not as we end up stuck when we're alive.

Gathering up those old metathings, the perks from lives long gone and the aura layers we never found space for, dusting them off, and putting them into the great wheel of fate to see if something comes of them? It's a game and a ritual all at once.

It's a signal that we're willing to move on. We're still here, still alive, still growing.

And also, now maybe we'll be able to find the proper Jump ability when Luri asks to borrow it for a life. But you can't find it, can you, Jules? Because you've unlocked more than fifty different abilities that start with *jeweler* or *jungle*, and you only ever alphabetized your inventory once, and then you gave Molly the tool you used for it, and then you *lost* an entire upgrade.

"Luri, are you muttering to your wine?" Mark's voice makes me jolt as I watch Ellin winding up to throw Molly like a torpedo in an arc across the widest side of the chancer. "Are you okay?"

I want to tell him that of course I'm not because I'm saving my first words for someone who might be coming. But I'm tired, and distracted, and there's a good chance that I am talking to myself again. It was a really bad habit that I thought I broke lifetimes ago. But maybe it's resurfaced. Resurrected along with me.

The funny thing is, no matter how old I get, I still feel young. Incompletely mature. I still feel like me. I'm just Luri; that's all. I don't have special wisdom just for being around this long. All I have is a bunch of weird tricks and the knowledge of how to build a submarine. And also I've had the time to learn how to be a little more emotionally open. That's all.

At no point has the Between given me a reward that would help me turn off bad habits that I don't like. Which is actually kind of frustrating because, at some point, every one of us has accidentally picked up a gambling or scarring or social media compulsion that we needed to spend time cutting out again. And a perk would have really helped there.

Mark has Addiction Resistance VII, I know, which probably opens up a lot of fun opportunities for drug experimentation. Jules has Overcoming Is Liberation, which is a pseudoquest that *rewards* him for breaking addictions, but doesn't do anything about habits or compulsions, and doesn't actually do anything *about* addictions either. I've got . . .

Nothing, actually. Because I loaned Mark mine and then forgot about it.

That's less important than everything else I've been thinking. Also, if there *is* a chancer here, maybe I should shake the exhaustion out of my unreal skull and find a handful of stuff in my own inventory to wager on it. Do a little clearing of my own.

"Hello, Luri. Hello, Mark." Six's calming and placid tone would make me jolt if I were alive, potentially spilling the half-full goblet I'm still holding in twisted fingers. But I'm not, so I don't have the same kind of fear reflex. Or at least, that's what I tell myself.

"Hey, Six!" Mark pokes something on the heat flat behind the bar with his improvised spatula. "Welcome back! How—"

He is interrupted by a heavy, meaty whump as Molly collides with the rough and sandy wood, narrowly avoiding clipping the edge of a table and ruining our limited attempts at interior design. The little kobold slides about ten feet, her fur and scales hopefully keeping her from too much pain.

A single claw pops up from her crumpled form, fingers splayed in a *V*. "I'm okay!" she yells into the floorboards.

". . . How're you doing this death?" Mark turns back to Six like nothing has happened as Molly pulls herself to her feet and makes a dash for the wall, using shelves and hooks and lamps as handholds to reach the library again in seconds while Ellin is still doubled over with breathless laughter. "Feeling alright? Want to try testing how durable you are?" He points his knife up at the duo who are reevaluating how to get to the chancer. It looks like Ellin is planning another throw.

"I believe I am marginally too tired for that. Thank you, Mark," Six says as he stops next to me, leaning in to wrap dull gray flesh around my upper body in a hug that is far more compassionate and warm than anyone meeting him for the first time would think he's capable of. "You seem tired too," Six says quietly.

I pat his arm and lean into the hug. Just letting myself feel loved for a moment, as a treat.

My last life wasn't bad, but it wasn't this. It wasn't comforting. Maybe I should be embarrassed that all it takes is a few seconds of contact and a few understanding words to make me feel like I'm melting, but if that *is* what I should be, it will have to wait until later.

Six pulls back and looks at what Mark is doing. "Ah, we have food again," he says before pulling up the inventory the Between has for us and looking for something. "I have a gift to add."

"You checked your bells already?" Mark asks with an easy smile on his stupidly handsome face. "You're always more efficient than me."

"No, though yes, I am. Thank you," Six answers as he procures a small cloth sack. "Last life I spent a number of marks of labor and life to add to my personal room a supply of topnuts. It refreshes on each death, and I have brought them back to share. Luri and Ellin said they missed snacks."

I *did* miss snacks. Living in a place like Bastion's, a place that is *obviously* a bar of *some* kind, feels wrong without snacks.

Six offers me the open mouth of the bag, and I snag one of the . . . Did he call them *topnuts*? I pop the emulation of a roasted morsel into my mouth and enjoy the dark, savory flavor as I hold back my desire to make a joke.

"Topnuts?" Mark says with raised eyebrows.

"Mark, please." Six stops him and then gestures a flat hand toward me. "Let Luri make the joke once their allotted time is up."

Mark bites at a smile as he meets my eyes. "Oh, yeah, that makes a lot more sense," he says, not knowing that Six is banking on my poor memory for jokes. The golem probably thinks that he's consigned this to the graveyard of humor, but the real joke is on him because Ellin and Molly are here. "So, we're just waiting on Jules now, huh?" Mark says. "And . . . I guess anyone else? Maybe the kid will drop by. Or that elf."

"I do like the elf." Six nods.

"How?" Mark snorts a laugh. "She never talks. How can you like . . . Oh, yeah, okay. That checks out." He shakes his head at Six's stare. "Well. Want a drink while we wait for—"

There is a blur of motion and another heavy thud, this time accompanied by a chair skidding across the floor and a table tipping sideways, spilling the tiny potted fern to the floor with a scattering of dirt that quickly returns to the void.

"I'm okay!" Ellin groans unconvincingly.

"What are these two doing?" Six asks. "And yes, I will take one of what Luri has." I point up at the chancer, Six following with pale eyes. He shakes his head and makes a waving gesture at Mark as he stands up and goes to help Ellin find her feet. "Perhaps hold on the drink, Mark. I will be back."

"Six! Hey!" Ellin exclaims woozily as she gets to her feet and throws a quick hug around the golem. "We're working on a thing!"

"Yes, I see," Six says, following Ellin to the metal steps pinned to the wall. "Would you like some help?" He scoops up the fern as they pass and settles it back in its place on the table.

The chancer continues to rotate its galaxy of gems, spiral limbs floating without purpose or concern, just out of reach.

I like this chancer. It feels like it's being sassy. The Between is a lot of things, at a lot of times, but it's never really felt *fun* to me. We make our own fun; we make our own home and our own family and our own love. But while the Between provides *things*, it doesn't ever even dip a finger on the scales of meaning or joy.

Maybe the things that I think are constructs, like the chancers, aren't. Or maybe they're one of the ways the Between has to express a little bit of levity. Or maybe I'm reading too far into how it's hovering just out of Ellin's reach, and how Six is trying to wedge the metal post of a coffee table into the railing so they have a platform to leap from.

"That's going to end badly," Mark comments before he blinks and frowns. "Or . . . No, I guess it's not." He whispers, "Is it? Nothing ends badly here."

In the corner of my vision, the unignorable count of my heartbeats hits a number that I was half waiting for, half dreading. I sigh and look at Mark with a long-familiar sadness in my eyes. "It never does, no," I say. "Nothing *ends* here. It just keeps going."

He tries to smile at me, but it barely comes out at all. "Oh, hey," Mark murmurs at me.

"Hey," I say, looking around the walls of Bastion's. "I . . . I don't think they're coming." I speak the words. The old ritual, the old hurt. Bleeding out the sorrow to try to let myself let go.

It almost works.

Mark sets a hand on the bar, and I lean back to reach a little behind myself and meet it. "Do you think they ever will?" he asks. "Really. Honestly. Do you actually . . . Are you still hoping?"

It hurts to think about. Hurts to even consider. There are tears beading in my eyes by the time I answer him. "I think . . . I think I'm still hoping, yeah. Still holding on to that want. But I don't think . . ."

There is a crunch as something gray and heavy drops from the library and lands on the green felt surface of our big table. Then it rolls sideways and makes another bone-grinding slam as it hits the floor.

Mark and I both blink. Any kind of morose emotional vulnerability banished in an instant.

"Uh . . ." we both say at the same time, looking at the lump on the floor.

Six extends an arm upward, fingers reaching for something to grab onto. Then slumps backward.

"Should we . . . help?" Mark asks, whatever he's cooking starting to hiss and sizzle on the bar's heat flat.

"I live," Six groans with more emotion than I've ever heard from him before.

"He's fine," I tell Mark. I spin on my stool, feeling the cool air of Bastion's on my skin, feeling the warm laughter from upstairs. My goblet slides across the bar as I give it a light nudge. "Can I get another? I feel like it'll go well with the show."

Mark looks at me blankly for a few heartbeats. Then he smiles, laughs, and nods as he looks at where Ellin is coming down the stairs to help Six up so they can all try again. "Coming right up," he says. "And Luri? I missed you."

"Thanks." I smile as I duck my head. "I missed you too."

CHAPTER TWENTY-SEVEN

D o you ever worry that you'll come back, and the Between will have rearranged stuff on the shelves, and, esk, nothing is *gone* exactly, but something is still *missing*, and you can never get it back because what was stolen was the organic and deeply personal evolution of the state of things, and there's no way to ever have it again because you'll always be chasing something that was lost instead of just enjoying the way things are going?"

The thought spills from me like a thunder fall of chaotic noise, speech with only the barest layer of thinking between the words and the feelings that drive them. I'm teetering back in my chair, the thin black metal frame supporting my weight with the help of my tail hanging out of the back slot. In a real world, it would have collapsed by now, but the universal resistance the Between grants means I can smoothly rotate on one chair leg as I push and twist with my tail to hold myself precariously reclined.

Across from me, Mark looks up from where he is slowly creating a pile of food-related metaitems on the table as he goes through his inventory. So young, and already so cluttered. Though that's also perhaps our collective faults. After a certain point, random rewards don't feel like things that are meaningful to hold on to, and the new guy became a willing receptacle for bonuses and extras. And now Mark can't remember which of Cook, Chef, Gilded Barista, or Sampler he had available. So far his pile includes none of those but *does* have Dice-Round-Vegetable Mastery III, which I quite honestly think is the most important if he's going to try to be a kitchen apostle next life.

While I get distracted by the shimmering stack of intangible physical objects, Mark is looking at me like I've made use of the Between's personal editor to give myself a second head again. "You," he accuses, pointing at me with a weirdly spiky iteration of Cleaver Skills. "Have the weirdest possible fears."

"Do not!" I protest, feeling for a tiny moment like I am a child again. A real child, crossing their arms and frumping at their parent and defensively denying everything. "It's reasonable around here!"

"You can just put the bookshelf back," Mark pointed out. "And if you don't *know* how to put it back, then it didn't really matter, and however you do it this time will be its own story because some kind of power that transcends death itself decided to mess with your sorting system." He looked over at the shelves and the handful of accrued texts. "Of course I say system with a bit of irony."

I think Mark has missed my point entirely. Of course there's no actual system; that's not the thing. But we, all of us, put those books there. Picked them up and messed with them, flipped through flawlessly worn paper, read them, fended off boredom with them, put them back in the wrong spots. The way the mismatched shelves look now is the result of chaos that cannot be replicated without lying.

"It'd be something lost," I say in a voice so quiet I'm not sure if I'm trying to hold the words back so that the demons of the Between won't hear them and try to realize my fear.

Mark goes back to arranging aura layers into a pattern he finds acceptable enough, though he's not ignoring me, and he certainly heard me with his elegant little ears. "I'm not saying nothing would be lost," he says as he tries to use his somewhat less elegant fingers to trace the shapes of his auras in the air and plan out a new shell in his mind. I think he's only half paying attention to me, but that's still more than I'd ever ask from someone working on their build; I don't believe in optimization, but I still believe in making things work and trying stuff out. "What I mean is . . ." He pauses as he hits a dead end and stows one of the apparently unsatisfying aura layers back in his inventory. "I'm saying that every time you remake something, you'll be making something new and special. Because the scars from last time will change your approach."

I watch him for a few hundred heartbeats. The silent reminder of my finite time with my real family ticking away in my vision as he toys with the idea of either being a master chef or just not having to order takeout so often. Takeout in some worlds just isn't a thing. I've had to reinvent it three times, but it never took off enough before I died to make it easier for me to order in. That is where a bunch of my business and finance perks come from, as well as one for evading the authorities, which I maintain doesn't count, but the Between doesn't like arguing.

Something about what Mark said worries at stray threads of ideas. I keep watching him, trying to remember something that feels like ancient history. Which is to say: something in my life. Every part of everything feels like ancient history to me. *Yesterday* is sometimes just as far across the chasm of the past as a century ago, though every now and then, every yesterday catches up to me at once and I feel the weight of all that time. Never in the Between though. Here, I only ever feel alive.

Midway through getting distracted staring at Mark's broad shoulders and arms that could suplex a sunline bear, I get distracted instead watching Jules arrive through the archway that leads to our little courtyard, and then seeing Molly tackle him from the side in a way that I know he could have defended against. I know because Ellin tries the same maneuver from his flank, hopping the bar in a smooth slide to throw herself at the mass of tentacles and red eyes and getting promptly pinned down before she can slam into her target. I barely get a "Hello, Luri!" to go with Mark's "And Maaaaar—" before Jules is dragged back into the hall he emerged from to be reunited with his love here in the Between.

"Hi, Jules!" I call back. "Have fun!"

Mark turns to watch the spectacle before shaking his head and turning back to his work. But his motions are stiffer, his smile sadder, and the living energy he brings into every death is gone.

So I ask a question I've asked before: "What was their name?"

"Hmm?" Mark doesn't look up, which is how I know I've hit on something.

"Whoever changed you this life. What was their name?" I repeat.

Mark sighs and drops the metaitem he's holding. For a few heartbeats, I think he might not answer at all. He turns in his seat, watching over his shoulder as Ellin piles reward after reward from her notifications on the bar, digging for something that she wants to show off to Six. I sit with him, still balancing on my tail and one chair leg, twisting back and forth like I'm impatient about getting to the endless expanse of time ahead of me.

He does look back eventually because he's Mark, and I know him very well. "Ahri," he says.

"Ahri. That sounds pleasant." A good name. Simple, clean, but with a lot of potential meaning. I've known enough Ahris in my lives that I can't track the number anymore, but I don't think I've hated any of them. "What were they like?"

"Kind. Quiet. We were students together. I was trying to get into veterinary medicine, but biology worked just differently enough there that I needed a refresher. And also some credentials." Mark doesn't smile as he talks, instead just watching me carefully. "Then the invasion started. And one day Ahri didn't come home. Siege missile took out his train."

"Oh . . ." I stop playing with my chair, bringing myself down to sit properly and focus on Mark. "I . . ."

But Mark keeps going. "After Ahri, it was Phada. He was less quiet, but just as kind. You'd probably call him fiery if you wanted to be flattering at the moment. The university was still trying to operate back then, and he was always looking for ways to help. He was arrested for agitation, and I never saw him again." Mark takes a deep breath. "It was longer before the next one. Her name was Remmy, and she wasn't kind or quiet, and by that point the university tunnels were resistance bunkers and there weren't many of us left. After she died, it was Corta, and they were quiet, and just . . . empty. We were all empty by then." Mark runs a finger around the lightbug centerpiece of the table as he talks, not adding heartbeats to it but just slowly tracing his skin across the glass jar. "You know what the worst part is?" he asks.

"I know what the worst part for me would be," I tell him honestly. "But not for you. What?"

"I . . . I know that I'll forget them," Mark tells me. "The names are like wounds, Luri. I'm bleeding out little bits of love and compassion from each of them. I'm sitting here fucking around with Chef abilities, but I don't feel like making food for anyone in my next life. I feel like getting a cowl and a knife and becoming the Crow."

I tap my fingertips on the table. "I don't get that reference. Is that like the Green Knight, or like *the Green Knight*?"

The question draws a long blink from Mark. "What's the difference?"

"I realize now as I say it that they come across the same. Weird coincidence. Uh . . . A spooky figure that might not be a person and operates on some form of alternate morality but also has powers, versus some kind of fallen noble that goes around murdering for vengeance."

"Oh. The second one." Mark sighs and rubs at his neck. "This doesn't matter. You see what I'm saying. Stop . . . Stop making it a game? Please?"

I nod, my face serious. I wasn't trying to play around, really. But I can reassure Mark of that later. "So you're worried about when you'll forget?" I ask softly.

"*No*," Mark says with a hard bite to his words that I don't hear from him often. "I'm *looking forward to it*. And it feels so painfully guilty to do. I know I'll forget. I know the wounds will turn to scars, just like they always do, but

I'll be different. What am I going to *learn* from this life? Do you ever think about that when you come back here? We get showered in prizes like we hit the big benny, but what do we *learn?*"

His voice has been getting louder slowly as he talks, until Mark is nearly yelling the last word. Six and Ellin looked over our way at the sound, and I saw Ellin make a motion like she was asking if she should come join us. I shrug, and she swipes at her horns in agitation before deciding to sweep her pile of lucre off the bar and make her way between the mismatched chairs of Bastion's to our table.

"I don't know," I'm saying to Mark as Ellin arrives and settles onto his shoulders without so much as moving him an inch, wordlessly trying to comfort the man. "Sometimes I feel like the only thing I learn from a life is how much people can disappoint me." The words feel like a poison on my tongue, stinging and harming their way into the world. The kind of thing I try to never speak, just in case saying it makes it real. "Sometimes I learn how bad things can get. Sometimes I learn how bad *I* can get."

"Kinda hard to think of you as a villain, heh?" Ellin says from over Mark's head.

"I mind controlled a world," I say.

Ellin nods. "Yeah, and I love you for it. All the power of a *world* and you decided to try to make people feel good about themselves and stop stabbing each other!" She flicks her eyes up. "I think. That was a couple centuries ago, sub."

Mark pushes her back, but Ellin just circles to drag a chair over. Plush padded purple leather that's eternally cracked and exposing foam that will never go bad. "My point . . ." Mark trails off, as he realizes he doesn't have a point.

So I tell him that. "You don't have a point. You don't need a point." My words are as kind as I can make them, even through the hard truth. "You're hurting because you've been hurt. There's no version of me that would tell you to ignore that. But you will heal. And . . . And I believe you'll still be a Mark I love at the end of it. Scars and all."

"Bah," Ellin adds diplomatically. "I'll love you through the scars. Scars are what make you a fighter."

"I hate fighting," Mark says with the voice that *I* use when I know I've got a stack of notifications from the Between piled up that are all going to give me accolades for the beasts and people and curses and elementals and *everything* I've killed.

"Every good fighter hates fighting," Ellin tells him bluntly, and Mark looks over at her like he isn't sure what to make of that, coming from the woman who seems to get stabbed in every life she lives. "Oy, hey, I don't like fighting," Ellin defends herself from the unspoken accusation. "I just won't let anyone own me. You live enough lives, you get good at spotting the sources of injustice. And we can kill those. Maybe we *should* kill those."

I fidget in my seat before standing, flicking my tail behind myself as I do. "It's in the label the Between gives us." I offer. "*Intercessor.* What are we supposed to be doing if not interceding?" I laugh at my own words because if I took my own advice I'd probably live a lot differently.

Mark is similarly unconvinced. "I just feel lost," he whispers to the two of us. "They're gone, and I'm not, and how is that *fair?*"

"Nothing about this is fair." Ellin shrugs, the motion of her shoulders so sharp it's like she's trying to cut the air for daring to be too close to her. "What're you gonna do about it?"

I stop pacing and look at her, while Mark keeps his eyes locked on the tabletop. He seems more deep in thought than shocked though. Me, I'm just not used to the question. It's the one question I tend to avoid here in my infinite endless ongoing string of lifetimes.

"Maybe I should just get comfortable interceding." Mark's voice is halfway between defeated and determined. "Maybe I shouldn't let it happen again. I mean, what do we have to lose? It's not like dying hurts *me.*"

"Oh, ashes, that's a fuckin' lie." Ellin laughs. "Dying hurts me every time!"

"Well, you get stabbed every time," Mark tells her, a line of a smile starting to re-form on his lips.

Ellin reaches over and places a long finger on those same lips. "You should try it sometime. Live a little!" she instructs the man we love.

With a roll of his eyes, Mark starts collecting his project auras off the table, making to stand himself. "All we do is live," he huffs.

"Then you don't have a choice! May as well lean into it!" I mouth the words along with Ellin's boisterous declaration. I don't know if she knows she's repeating words spoken here before. It's been so long, I don't even know if the memory is correct anymore. Lifetimes and years and days wearing away my precision when it comes to what happened between us and what happened in my dreams.

I feel like I'm feeling too much. I feel like I need a drink. And just as I say as much out loud, Six arrives at the table with a tray balanced with mathematical precision on his palm. Tall glasses of a bubble-filled pale-pink liquid are placed before us.

"Typically," Six explains, "this would be served in a curved horn. Though the tradition of it being a literal horn ended hundreds of years before I was born to that world, so I would prefer to use shaped glass. But we do not have malleable glass, so I choose to present this to you incorrectly." As I've always known him to speak, Six's voice is mostly monotone, as flat and gray as his body is. And *yet*, it takes no real effort to feel the passion for the art of inebriation.

Ellin holds hers up and looks through the bottom of the glass. "How do I drink it?" she asks, a similar sort of respect for the cultural motivators of alcohol.

"Slowly, in sips," Six says. "The people of the world were especially susceptible to the secondary substance—a form of honey—used in the fermentation. So it was a form of social drink that was often used for longer group gatherings and conversations. A small sip, after each addition to the conversation. Or rather, that is what the noble-presented image was. In reality, cheaper versions were imbibed regularly by the younger generations during bonding gatherings."

I love Six so much, and I smile into my glass as I take a small sip, halfway between respect for how things have been and how things are. No one else would turn an explanation of a drink that bursts across my tongue like a glittering lemon into a history lesson and an exploration of changing values. Well, no one but Jules. And sometimes Mark. And occasionally Ellin or Molls or *me* really if I have a good story to tell.

"So this is your own creation?" Mark asks, smiling as he takes his own, much more noble, sip. After properly adding his weight to propelling the conversation.

"It is, in fact, not," Six says, and we all give him mock-shocked looks as he settles into a chair along with us, the table becoming less lonely. Mark and I raise eyebrows. Ellin curls her horns slightly in toward themselves, which I didn't know she could do but looks decidedly strange. "A lifetime is of course enough time to master brewing," Six tells us. "But it was not what I wished to do. And while much carries over, every world is different." We nod; we've all been there. You can't even trust that you won't have to relearn how to breathe in a given life. "So I simply paid someone who was more adept than I to use my unorthodox method to create a batch. Barrels are *not* what is desired for a true batch, but they agreed, so long as I swore an oath to never blame them."

"Huh," Ellin says, downing a third of her cup. "This is . . . *weird*." She looks up over our heads and reels slightly. "Ahshoy. Kinda dizzy."

"That happens when you drink more than a sip, yes," Six says with a tiny sip of his own and a hum of mild appreciation. "A good flavor. My compliments to the brewer."

In all likelihood, the brewer is long dead by now. Maybe off to their own afterlife, maybe just now getting their own odd reward for the compliment somewhere in the distant halls and planes of the Between. Maybe we'll never know, but I hate the word never, and so I choose to imagine that one day they'll visit and meet Six and the two of them can complain about how the rest of us uncultured fools are drinking in the wrong pattern.

In time, before we've hammered away too many heartbeats, Jules and Molly come and join us, looking slightly more exhausted than when last I saw them. Six adds two glasses to our table and refills the four already there, and we all simply sit together under the slowly clicking turboprop engine, sandy floor under our feet. Or tentacles. Or whatever Molly has. Or . . .

"Ellin, do you have feet or, like, talons?" I ask as the first thing said in minutes, which gets a few smiles and sputter of laughter from Mark. That last part matters a lot to me; Mark isn't going to be okay, in the same way none of us are going to be okay. We're all going to get hurt over and over until we eventually break, but that doesn't mean we can't laugh at distractions in the meantime.

"*Feet*, you little gremlin." Ellin scowls at me. "So hey, since we're here. And talking." Her angled eyes flick across the group as she speaks, like she's working herself up to say something. "I've got a little story."

"Ooh! Ellin life stories!" Molly clacks her claws across themselves in her form of applause.

Ellin laughs, setting her cup on the table still half full and sliding it away from herself with one long finger. "Oy, uh . . . No," she says almost casually. "Not from my life."

"Not . . ." I catch on first, before the others say anything. "From the last go-around here. When you went out exploring." My voice carries through the false summer afternoon air of the bar. "You found something?"

"I found something." Ellin swipes a hand over her horns. "I found something weird. One of those things we kind of assumed we'd find after a life or two, but never showed up, you know?" She looks like she's waiting for us to interrupt her, but none of us do. Jules rolls his cup between two tentacles, Molly lays her long jaw flat on the table surface to look up at Ellin, Mark and I just wait patiently. Six looks like he's waiting to say something before drinking again, shackled to tradition. I won't be bullied by a culture though, so I take a small drink and enjoy the pop of the odd beverage on my tongue. "Alright, well." Ellin sucks in fake air to fake lungs. "I found a map."

Molly and I raise our hands at the same time, eager students ready to prove ourselves. Six overrides us by actually talking. "We've found many maps," he points out, and then literally points to the wall under the library. "We have a

heat map of the chargebeast spawns of Corrirriar right there." The pronuncia-
tion of the continent's name is the closest Six *ever* gets to stuttering. It's adorable on the gray golem.

"Oy, I'm telling the story! I get to be dramatic!" Ellin's anxiety shatters
as her natural state of righteous indignation blasts through. "Fine! I'll spell it
out! I found a map that showed the world I was gonna reincarnate into!" The
woman I love folds her arms across her chest, and I realize this is the closest I'll
probably ever see her to *pouting*. "I was building up to it, you ass."

Mark reacts first. "Okay, that's . . . really cool. Right?" he asks us all. "I
think that's cool. Did you get a door to it or something?"

"Nah, I didn't have any marks on me. I gave them all to some kid." Ellin
shakes her head and then sits back down as the lingering dizziness from her
drink flattens her. "Woooof. Okay. More of that please." She reaches back for
her cup and pauses before sipping. "I have no idea how to get back to it. I just
know . . . it can happen."

"We could know where we're going," Molly says slowly. "So we could prepare. Know what to pack for the trip."

Jules curls his mobility tentacles up underneath himself, tightly wound
springs of black leathery flesh pulling together into spirals like knots. "There is
something we never speak." He hums slowly. "Because it is the one thing too
painful to continually be denied." His triangular eyes spread out on his face,
looking to each of us around the table. "But we now know this can be true.
We know that we can influence our future lives through Mark's coins . . ." His
near-constant motion stills as he tightens in on himself in a tense ball. "What
we thought was impossible may not be. We could . . . maybe . . . find a way
to go . . . *together*."

The word spoken is like a curse of the worst kind. A tiny errant spark of
hope that we've all long since stopped nurturing. And I see the others frown or
wince or turn away as they remember *why* we stopped talking about it.

I would have too, once upon a time.

I don't know when I started changing. Or maybe that's stupid to say.
Maybe I never stopped changing. Maybe I never will, and that's what it means
to be alive. We die so fucking much that I think we sometimes forget that
we're alive.

So my voice startles them a little. "That sounds like it'd be a lot of fun,"
I say, sipping the pink fizzy honey thing that Six brought back to floor us
all with. "Probably not something we'll have ready for a while, but I can see
it." The casual tone, the easy acceptance, it catches my friends off guard. My
family turn to look at me like I've done the extra-head thing again, and I smile

over the rim of the inappropriately shaped cup. "What? You don't think it'd be neat? We could run a tavern together or something! We've got the experience! We can grow old and get sick of each other together, and then come back and laugh about it." I'm looking down into the still-trapped bubbles in my glass as I speak. "It doesn't have to be something we bank on. But yeah. Jules is right, you know? We know it can be done. And you all know me. I don't like the word never."

Mark quietly stands up, and I worry for a moment he's about to run away. But then he shifts to behind my chair and leans forward to wrap a hug around my bare shoulders. "Alright," he says after a while of nearly crushing me. He doesn't say anything else, just stands back up and breathes deeply before walking off to take some time to himself.

"Anyone else gonna be dramatic?" Molly asks, and Jules uncurls just enough to bop her on the top of her furred head. "What?!" she demands. "I'm not saying it like it's a bad thing! *I* was gonna be dramatic!"

I can't help it. I start laughing. And then it picks up, with even Six joining us in a geometrically perfect chuckle. From where he's leaning on the black stone of the bar, Mark laughs too. And for a moment, Bastion's is filled with the sound of people who are either accepting a different version of their lives than they expected to have happen, or people having manic breakdowns. Depending on your perspective. Maybe a bit of both.

Then there is the sound of a door closing, and someone new steps in. Not totally new; it's a familiar face: Shavoy, the kid who isn't a kid any longer, but is still younger by millennia than all of us, freezes in worry as he takes in the ongoing sounds that are starting to become the kind of gasping laughs you get when the joke only gets funnier the more you react to it.

"Did I come at a bad time?" he asks during a pause.

It's the funniest thing anyone has ever said to me. I think it is for the others as well. We laugh until we cry, before we're even *close* to able to greet our new newly old young friend.

CHAPTER TWENTY-EIGHT

There's an odd feeling when it comes to making new friends in the Between. Though realistically, there's an odd feeling with making new friends while we're alive too. I'm thousands of subjective years old. I've had dozens of childhoods, hundreds of parents. The histories of unknown civilizations float in the part of the mind reserved for loosely keeping hold on things learned in forward school and then never used. It's a bit hard to make a "friend my age" when I'm alive on a world and not feel like I'm being weird. I've seen things no one else could have, and likely never will, much as I hate the word. I've walked on enough streets of alien cities to pave whole worlds. It's really, really hard to meet someone as a peer.

In the Between, all those things are still true, but everyone else has not only done the same thing, they've also gotten slightly used to it. Not *bored*—we do our best to not get bored. And while I certainly feel tired, worn, weary, exhausted, drained, numb, empty, helpless, breaking, broken, and listless from time to time, I don't think this endless life has ever made me bored. Even when I've been at my lowest points, wishing I could just end, or even worse, I've never really felt like boredom was the cause.

Out here, wherever here isn't, we've all lived and died at least a few times. We're experienced mortalitists. There's a connection that forms pretty quickly, enough to cross over a span of a *lot* of lived days.

It's not a contest. You might be relative to a baby in true age compared to me, but it doesn't really work that way. We grow to a certain point, and then we keep growing, but it becomes a matter of detail. Little changes, almost *tiny* changes. Not huge leaps that make us unrecognizable to others.

I know all of this. It's not just something I know, it's something that's personal to me. Everyone who walks into Bastion's and peacefully sits down to have a drink and share a story is a potential friend, a potential wandering khara in search of a roost.

But I'm still trying not to burst out into giggles at the novice enthusiasm that Shavoy tells his story with.

"And there was this big mural there! Like, across the whole wall! I'd never seen anything quite like it. The guide that . . . *my* . . . family was with said something about how the paint for it was the reason for the city's trade position. The . . . *My* sister kept clamoring to go back and watch it every day we were there. And the whole city was like that! Color everywhere. *Everything.* I thought . . ." He trails off in his recollection of a simple family vacation. "I . . . I had thought . . ."

And all of a sudden, the rest of us around the young immortal watch something we all have to get used to. An entire life catching up. The weight of time suddenly making itself known. Like carrying a backpack and not realizing how many rocks you stuffed in it until you are oh so tired. Behind the bar, Mark and I stop polishing the glasses to the true clean state that the Between doesn't ever get them to and share a look that we've built up over moments between lifetimes together.

"You had thought you'd seen it all," Jules says in an almost nostalgic buzz. One tentacle wraps around Shavoy's shoulders gently, and the young man leans into the touch. "You had thought that you were past being surprised."

"I did." Shavoy suddenly sounds very old. "I know my first time was cut short. But I lived a *whole life.* I thought I'd been well traveled, thought I'd tried it all. And it took just three hauka of a new life to show me something I'd never seen."

"Okay, I don't wanna be *that* jerk," Molly starts, about to be that jerk. "But can you convert that to years?"

Shavoy looks down at the kobold who's flopped on her belly on the bar in front of Jules. "What's a year?"

That gets me to laugh. "Years are the most common timekeeping macrochunk," I tell him as I pour him a glass of water from our infinite spout. "The most common cycle chunk is a day, followed by a jump, and both of them are *about* a hundred thousand heartbeats. A year is three to four hundred of those."

The boy stares at me, and I see in his whiskers and amber eyes some of the true childish wonder mixed with fear that sparkled there when he first came to us. "Girl, are you telling me I have to do *math* to have this conversation?"

Five people reach into their storage and in unison pull out Intelligence or Basic Calculation metaitems and toss them onto the bar in front of Shavoy.

"It is easy to forget that most people have inadequate math skills," Six says instead of actually *helping*.

I stick my tongue out at him, flicking the forked appendage as I scrunch up my face and he gives the closest thing to a smug smile that Six ever gives back. "Don't listen to him," I order before correcting to, "Alright, don't listen to him in this case. Six likes math. But the Between offers a lot of work-arounds. I like this one!" I tap a Basic Calculation skill splinter.

By the time Shavoy has been taught how to implant a skill splinter, and then how to back it with an inbound characteristic like Intelligence, the group has turned to idle chatter. He informs us that a hauka is about three years, so he was nine years old when his conception of himself was turned upside down, which sounds about right to me. That's when I tend to get that feeling in most of my lives too.

Molly is telling Jules about how she had to be a fish last life, and he's pet-ting her back lightly while Mark tries to figure out how to politely shove her carcass off the bar. Ellin is flipping through her notifications looking for the one that'll bring back a tiny plant. Apparently her Harvester talent actually is weird enough that it brings back a *small* version of whatever plant she uses it on. I find this hilarious and imagine if my own ability to bring back one random book did the same thing. Just the smallest possible little tomes. Finger-length textbooks. Text you'd need to get Jules to read to you with his razor-sharp eyes.

I'm giggling when another form sits down on a stool in front of me, and I look up, my own dull-amethyst eyes meeting the living green of an elf who's been here few enough times that I can still count.

"Hello," I say with a smile, glad to see our old new friend again. If Shavoy is young enough to have still not cleared a few key moments in our immortal existences, then the elf is . . . Well, she also probably hasn't. But her first life was a *long* one. She's too old, not used to adapting to life after life, not born for it like someone who started as a human or orc would. It'll take her some time.

But then she surprises me. Meeting my eyes and slowly letting a smile creep in. "Hello," she whispers, a voice like the wind through the branches on a dry winter day. "Are you real?"

I have a lot of thoughts about that question, but I choose to simplify for the moment. "Yep," I answer as I duck under the counter, banking on her having developed object permanence by now, and try to find one of those jars of herbal lemonade we had a few lives ago. I know there's at least one, and I find the last one behind the bottle of suspicious poison. "Here! If you still like it." The others shift without needing to be asked, opening up a little space. Even Shavoy, though Mark does offer the new kid a quick explanation for why they're putting an extra barstool between our conversation.

We try not to spook people who might be too fragile.

"Oh," the elf says as she looks down at the drink, ears like lances pointing upward as she tilts her head. She reaches out a scarred arm, only pausing briefly to consider the pattern of marks on her skin before she wraps it around the bottle. "Am *I* real?" she asks with a waver.

"Also yes," I say. "Are you having an easier time thinking since we last met?" I speak quietly but firmly.

"I am. I almost feel . . . No, I don't know. But I am." It's the longest sentence she's ever said to me directly.

I nod and pour myself a cup of something that smells lethally alcoholic from a small clay urn. "You died. A long time ago, most likely. And then you were reborn, and died again, and again. At least a few times."

"Dreams . . ." she whispers.

"Not dreams," I correct. "They would seem that way to you, and not remembering them is no sin. Your first life was *long*, compared to most mortal lifetimes, wasn't it?"

"We . . . The people of the . . . the . . . I can't remember. Why can't I remember? We lived for an epoch. Each of us expiring only when our tethered species extincted."

"You can't remember because you just lived several lives not meant to contain the knowledge of an immortal. Your head is going to feel fuzzy, you'll find thinking to be too fast, like you're on a runaway sled, and you won't know things that you feel in your heart should be obvious," I tell her as compassionately as I can. "You're going to lose a lot of the details. It's painful, but there's no way around it. Lives as long as yours are *rare*, and you'll spend more and more time pressed into whatever you are reborn as. It should get easier now that you're waking up though."

She holds the jar of lemonade like a talisman. "Why?" she asks.

"We don't know." Would that I knew.

"When does it stop?"

"We don't know." If only. The intrusive thought stabs into my mind.

"Did I do something wrong?" she says, and her willowy voice cracks. Shattering into a sob as she asks the question that too many people have asked me over the endless years.

"No," I possibly lie, reaching out to wrap my own hand around hers. She almost flinches back from the contact, but lets me settle my skin to hers; she is cool and rough, like the bark of an ancient tree, and her pale complexion is a contrast against my own bronze coloration. "This isn't a punishment or a reward. It's not for a reason. It is neither natural nor unnatural. It simply is. It's just the Between. It's just how we live now."

And something in that sentence reaches her, and her eyes meet mine again, and she nods as if she understands. And maybe she does; a life of tens of thousands of years tied to an ecosystem, she must have a lot of experience with things that just are.

Her gaze stays far away. Not unfocused, not unaware, but like she is looking into next week from a hundred miles away. But when she does eventually speak, it's like she's broken through something that was holding her back. "I could be the elf of the Between," she states.

It's as good a life goal as anything else. If anything, it seems like she's accomplished something that I'm still working on. Which doesn't make me jealous at all.

"Heeeeeey." Mark's word ends in an abrupt spike in his voice that coincides with him finishing his slide up against my naked flank. A warm hand engulfs my shoulder, and I reflexively lean back into him before realizing that might not be something he'd welcome after his outpouring about his last life. But if it bothers him, he doesn't comment on it, instead just smiling toothily at our new elf guest. "We're moving over to the big table. Gonna play random-notification story time with Shavoy, try to teach by example. Want to come join us?"

I do. And after making a passionate attempt to explain to our new guest what it is about storytelling that resonates in me, the elf agrees to join us. I *think* I didn't have to explain anything, and I might have sapped some of the magic from it by trying. But either way, she settles in at the table next to me, claiming the chair of living wood and stone that we always avoid because it's a little too alive sometimes.

"Cups!" Molly demands as soon as Mark and I are sitting, getting exasperated groans from both of us as we push back out of the chairs we've been left in unison. "Hey, this is only my second or third time back, and we've only been here for ten thousand heartbeats or something! I wanna do the thing, and the thing requires our cups!"

"I *know*. I just didn't want to stand up," I complain. As designated bartender for this time around, it's my job. And Mark helps because he's Mark. I could have made Molly do it, but she's curled up on the sand pillows half buried under Jules's tentacles, and she looks too comfortable to disturb.

An old goblet for me. A kiln-fired clay mug with a steel straw for Molly. A coconut shell with a much more loopy and less metal straw for Mark. Etched ceremonial basin for Six. Glass stein for Jules. And of course, a frosted blue dinner glass for Ellin.

I love how Ellin's special cup is one that was almost certainly mass-produced.

"Do I get a cup?" Shavoy asks, his whiskers flicking as he looks around the table.

"Of course, of course, but it's a *boring* cup." Jules's buzzing laugh draws a smile from the young immortal, even as I am adding a perfectly boring thick glass tumbler to his spot at the table and filling it with whatever is in the bottle Mark gave me. "For each of us, our personal vessel is something utterly meaningless."

"Really?"

"No." Jules annihilates the poor question that walked into his obvious trap. "They are hardly artifacts of deep memory, but they are all mementos. Sometimes not even our own. Nothing special, and yet . . ."

I finally make it back to my seat, cool metal rapidly warmed by bare skin as I pour my own glass. "It's also just something silly we do," I say, sipping from my goblet like I'm a prince of decadence. Something I haven't been for a long, long time. "But that is neither here or where! It's story time! Ellin, go!"

Ellin shoots to her feet, the white wrappings around her arms trailing like an afterimage as she snaps upright and flicks open her list of waiting demands for attention from the Between. Running fingers over the display with her eyes closed like a musician, she stabs outward and selects something before cracking one eye and then reading whatever she's just hit.

"Oh!" she says, and then her shoulders droop slightly and she cocks her head to the side. "Oh. Hoy. How's am I supposed to . . ." I recognize the expression of someone in this game of ours who's just gotten a trickle of marks of labor for having spent too much time weeding rows of crops. "Alright, fine." Ellin huffs. "Spent apparently too much of that life as an apprentice to an apothecary. Which the Between calls being a junior pharmacist, and isn't that weird?"

"No?" Mark raises his hand like he's in a particularly badly designed school. "That's what that is. That's like whenever you do enough bricklaying and it calls you a mason. The Between is lazy."

Shavoy's head snaps around the table, his long whiskers bobbing in the air. "Are we allowed to say that?" he whispers.

"The Between doesn't give a shit," Ellin rapidly informs him. "Ah, whatever. A short tale of my menial labor." She thinks for a second, scratching at one of her horns while she muses. "One time a ged robbed us at blade point, and my master wouldn't let me stab 'em, and she just handed over a bunch of doses. And then only told me later that the only thing she gave up were laxatives and a little of our coin. We never saw that ged again, so I guess it worked."

"Ellin." Jules slowly runs a tentacle down the part of his core where his glowing eye slits are. "Why do *all* of your stories involve a certain scatological humor?"

"'Cause I'm hilarious," Ellin answers.

"All of them?" Shavoy whispers in my direction.

I nod knowingly. "Almost all of them. Ellin has a dedication to her horrible, wretched craft."

"Hey!" My friend and love tries to glare at me through a smile that lights up her face, matching at least that part of my own expression as she looks my way and sees me watching her. "Whatever. That's my story. Six, you go next. Your lives are more fun."

The golem stands as Ellin drops back down, both of them drinking in unison, setting their glasses to the table at the same moment before Six flicks his own display from the Between and pins something that I'm certain isn't actually random with a finger. "Ah, good," he says as he reads. "My last life was an Information Age society by the time of my death, nonstandard human, with a fairly basic warring-nations geopolitical landscape." He folds one hand over the other as he begins talking like a professor giving a lecture. I think I've mentioned it before, but I love Six's history lessons. "For a time, I worked as a teacher at a well-regarded academy—"

"I knew it," I mutter.

"Luri, please." Six doesn't exactly smile at me, but I can feel the faint amusement he puts off sometimes. "My tenure as a teacher was rather long, to the point that many students began to form legends around me. Conspiracies and shadowy rumors as to my true nature, often in direct relation to when I handed down poor assessments. There was one student I remember, a truly exemplary young lady who would have made a fine journalist, who went to great lengths to verify or disprove the claims about myself. She once outfitted my office with a number of geometric ritual symbols while I was on vacation, to test if any of them would have an effect. Ambitious, really it was."

Mark and I raise our hands at the same time, and Six points at me with all the calm gravitas I'm sure he learned in his time as a teacher. "Sorry, hi, Luri here, for the Between newssheet. What did you say the unfounded rumors about you were?"

"I did not," Six says, closing in on something like being smug, "use the word unfounded." He turns back to the table. "I was an exceptional history teacher, especially as the academy survived for long centuries and I became the only living expert of the history that was being taught. Of course, a select few knew of my nature, but it became something of a game for me to recommend the students who *truly* learned of who I was to the journalism program."

"I like this story," the elf next to me whispers. She is curled with her knees up against her chest, one hand holding the cup we gave her balanced on a single finger, her eyes fixed on Six.

Ellin just huffs. "Damn it, Six got to be a *vampire*, and I got to be a doctor. That's not fair!"

A buzzing laugh from Jules cuts in. "Ellin, darling, none of this is fair. Weren't you listening to Luri earlier?"

Her resigned no is like a shot to my heart.

"Hey!" I protest.

Six stops our antics. "Perhaps now that we have a pair of examples, Shavoy, would like to try?" He gestures to the new kid. Only a couple hundred years old, Shavoy is a baby compared to the rest of us.

Shavoy nods and stands awkwardly, looking for all the world like someone the teacher just called on to give a speech in front of the class. I raise a glass to him, while Molly offers what I'm sure she thinks are reassuring words. "Yeah! Show off what you've got!"

"Dear, you're not helping." Jules wraps a tentacle around her, pulling her back to the sand pillows.

Molly looks confused. "Helping?" Her muzzle pulls back in a poorly contained grin.

Something about it draws a chuckle from Shavoy, and for a tiny moment, I can see him as the old man that he grew up to be across two lives. "Well, I may as well take my turn before I have to head out, right? Okay. Like this, yes?" He taps something in the air with a claw and then flicks his hand up and down before landing it on another glowing line of words. "And then a story about . . ."

A banner of dull red-and-blue cloth lands on the table. Well, the middle of it does; the other twenty feet of the narrow strip of dyed and woven cloth flops across Jules and Molly on one side, and thuds into the sandy wooden floor on the other. Ellin, Mark, and I all set our various drinking apparatuses back in unison from where we'd yoinked them into the air as the memento spawned.

Shavoy stares at it like it's a ghost. "What . . ." he starts to say before picking up his simple cup and slamming back the whole drink. I consider telling him that it won't help; it never does when a memory follows you home. "This is . . ."

The others give him some appropriate silence. Even Molly as she claws her way out from under her new blanket. I shoot him a comforting smile. "This happens sometimes," I tell the new kid. "Do you want to tell us about it?"

". . . When we were in the city of blossoms. That place I was talking about earlier. My little sister wanted to see one of the murals up close." He's still staring at the fabric, running a hand across it and getting his dewclaws snagged in the material. Slowly, Shavoy draws a line around the woven image of a hawk in gold thread. "I went along. To keep her safe, I figured. There were so many little things I felt . . . I felt too *old* to do. Does that make sense?"

"You'll get over that soon enough," Ellin tells him, for once without a trace of sarcasm in her voice.

"I don't see how." Shavoy's whiskers twitch. "But it meant I was on the ground when she went climbing the off-limits ladders and carved steps. And it meant I got to see when she fell." I wince, prepared to hear a tragedy, but he's still smiling. "Is part of being old being paranoid? Because I had already made a plan for what I'd do when she slipped. I ripped a declaration in cloth out from the wall, and it didn't work perfectly, and she got tangled in it on the way down. It wasn't like in the movies from a whole lifetime ago. But tangled up wasn't hitting the stone, and my sister lived." He pulls a part of the banner up in a bundle and holds it close. "This one. This banner. Or is it? How *could* it be?" There are tears in the edges of his amber eyes.

"We never know," Mark mutters. "If it's a copy, or an echo, or the actual thing. We . . . There *might* be a way, someday. But for now, we don't know."

"Do you need a moment?" Ellin asks, looking away like she doesn't want someone's early earnest sorrow to be a show. "We can give you some space."

"No, no." Shavoy takes a deep breath, smelling the fragrance of the cloth as he slides part of it across our table and into a pile on the floor. "I'm . . . I am good. I am. Somehow, I think, this makes it real, doesn't it? Life was more than just a dream. There was someone else there who needed me, and she got to live her whole life after this moment because of what I did. I think that means it mattered."

Jules offers Shavoy an orbit of triangular eyes. "No matter what happens, our lives always matter to someone. Even if only ourselves. Remember that you are someone too; it can be easy to forget, especially as early in your journey as you are."

Shavoy laughs, a wet sound that's almost a happy sob, before he shakes his head and starts rolling up the banner of cloth. No one tells him that he can just store it in his inventory because this makes it more real. It also makes us all have to move our glasses around to avoid having them slapped off the table by the *very* long tapestry. "Well, that's my story. Who wants to go next?" He gets the words out around the smile and the tears. "The new . . . Oh."

I look next to me, at the least comfortable chair in Bastion's, to see that the elf has gone on ahead of us. Her cup sits perched on the arm of the chair like the living wood is cradling it. "She'll be back," I say with confidence. "How about me, then?" The others nod, and I stand up and stretch, maybe showing off my form a little bit to an audience that long ago stopped being shocked by me. "Okay. Last life *sucked*, so I'm sure this will be hilarious."

"Oh, don't say that, Luri!" Molly calls at me from her bed under her lover.

Ellin nods vigorously as I swipe at my notifications and try not to peek. "Yeah! Your lives are always great! Remember that time you blew up a tree and got those weird sap tattoos from it?" I don't have the energy at the moment to tell her that the event she is thinking of was sixteen lives ago and was Mark. Mark looks like he's considering it though.

He'll have to wait. I've made my selection.

[You have survived ten years with a missing primary limb: +20 perk cysts, +20 marks of labor. Perk—Amputation Compensation—is Unlocked. Ability granted—Monodexterity.]

"Okay . . ." I start slowly, trying to compose this in my head before I say it out loud in a way that won't make Ellin make fun of me, or Jules and Six give me pitying looks that are *like* making fun of me, or just ruin Shavoy's opinion of me as someone who knows what they're doing. "So." The word feels like it has a note of finality to it.

"I am already so into this story," Molly announces. I'm not worried about *Molly* judging me. Molly is going to think it's hilarious.

I nod her direction and make my start. "Before I get into this, has everyone lived a life where you had to watch a workplace-safety video for some kind of industrial equipment?"

Mark buries his head in his hands. "For fuck's sake, Luri," he grumbles.

The words set us off, and the whole table falls into laughter before I can get any further. Warm and alive and companionable. And for a moment, *nothing* gets into Bastion's that isn't the feeling of a growing family and our love for each other and the strange stories of our lives.

And then I actually have to explain how I lost my arm to a machine that was like if a wood chipper had a personal vendetta against limbs. But that can wait. No cost in heartbeats is too high to feel this way, together.

CHAPTER TWENTY-NINE

I dream of an old life when I was a deep-sea diver.

I don't remember how long ago it was, and I don't think most of the lessons of dipping into the oceans of liquid noctogen on a distant moon would be relevant to most of my activities. Even if they were, the skills are old and rusted, and I remember selling the expertise-style skill slivers for them a long time ago. But that doesn't matter.

What matters is I remember the feeling. I remember finding something unique down there on the midnight ocean floor. I remember having to run the calculations on if the shift in pressure and lumens would allow it to survive if retrieved to the surface. I remember tagging certain sites to be left as undisturbed, only to be visited by the brave and the foolish, and I remember retrieving certain things.

Pulling what might have once been a piece of unwanted junk up to the home ship. Carefully ascending with an object in my thickly gloved hands, digits encased in layers and layers of protection. Laying the object back out on a prepared and padded spot, gently and reverently, no matter that it was likely nothing. Examining, cleaning, gently turning and mapping every inch of it, studying, preparing it for display in a planetside museum.

And then the moment, sometimes whole turns later, when it would be unveiled. Often as part of a collection of similar artifacts. And something *truly* magical would happen.

An old bowl, a pitted navigation instrument, a line of preserved sailcloth, a broken storage cask, a handful of coins so smoothed down their origin is lost forever.

Junk.

And when the cloths come up and the exhibit is displayed and the knowledge and study and labor we've put in is out there, something happens. And a small child presses up to the security barrier and peers at a piece of a ship that was lost at sea before *our* society was dreaming of *fire*, and the junk is no longer junk, and instead a cherished treasure. An ancient relic cursed and blessed in equal parts with the spell to cause a deep and painful longing for something so distant it is almost utterly forgotten.

I wake up, lying in a woven hammock that is oddly comfortable. Normally the ropes pull on my skin, and we have no blankets here for some reason. But this time I feel safe and warm to go along with the pure rest that comes from sleeping in the Between.

I look down and see that I am lying on Ellin. She's still asleep, and stays that way as I roll off of her, the pale-green cloth wraps she wears providing just enough of an anchor point on my bare skin that I can get away without having to peel our bodies apart.

The dream that's really more of a memory starts to fade as I plant my feet and tail on the thin layer of omnipresent sand that coats the wooden boards of Bastion's floor. But the feeling lingers in my beating heart and sparking blood. Because Bastion's is absolutely full of the mundane turned mystical, and every single piece of it has a story behind it.

Overhead, the turboprop engine that we use as a fan turns, and I remember Jules talking about the final run of his warcraft during what might have been the last days of a world under siege. In the center of our good table, dim lightbugs flap luminescent wings, a reminder from Molly of the life she spent chasing them with someone she loved, however briefly. The jar they're in hides a tiny succulent in a tinier pot, something that Ellin brought back from a world where she spent a year subsisting on just the goo inside the flat and waxy leaves. A flicker of neon from over the bar makes me screw up my face in annoyance because someone has set the stupid anatomically correct drake lung aglow, but even *that* is a record of a life lived as a monster butcher and a happy time learning the secret places to get drunk in a city on the cusp of greatness.

Upstairs are a dozen books, including my favorite, which is different than it was a thousand years ago. Each of them comes from a world past, a life lived, places seen. And now every time I add to them, I know I don't diminish them but instead shelve another part of another life in there with the beloved moments. Even the horrid ones I would never want to leave behind.

The walls are adorned with portraits and landscapes, framed photographs and aluminum or bone crafts, and one towering colorful cloth banner that I'm not sure how my fool friends got up there without access to a ladder. All of them are hung in different ways: pinned to the wood with Ellin's refreshing Box of Nails earned from a life of toil as a blacksmith where she hardly needed to stab anyone at *all*, much to her disappointment; held up on shelves that came with Bastion's; attached to anchor points given as a reward by the Between; or just hanging by their own string or hooks from *other* trophies and loved items. The holes from the nails are temporary; the Between will heal them when the spikes come out. Lots of our displays may also be temporary; we've already taken down Molly's druid meditation loop because it was hypnotizing our guests, and while her life spent learning how to turn into a peacock was almost certainly a highlight for her, that doesn't mean we want strangers falling into trances in our main hall.

It's in the library now, where it can hypnotize fewer people but on purpose. A perfect compromise.

And some things aren't from us but *are* part of our lives. The hallway that leads to—or, rather, *is*—a summer evening and a garden of roses, blank slots in the rough adobe wall that go nowhere yet, wrought iron lanterns unlit under a dusky sky, that hallway didn't come from any of us. It was from a passing traveler and lover of art. To *him*, it might have been a memory of something painful or beautiful. For *us*, it's a reminder of that time a boisterous orc shared a drink at our bar and got into a lengthy debate about aesthetics with Jules before leaving with a prideful belly laugh. And both memories are real, and both are valid, and here sits the treasure to display the echo of them. You can sit in one of the wrought iron chairs and sip at our dwindling supply of lemonade and muse on the history, if you choose. Or you could simply enjoy the dusk and make a new memory.

I am in a museum of us, surrounded by treasures.

"Morning Luri." Mark breaks me out of my rite, the sculpted demigod of a man giving me a quiet smile from behind the black stone counter of the bar that we tethered half the hammock to. "You slept pretty well."

"Mmmyyyamhph," I reply, a mumble turning into a yawn as I stretch all five of my limbs out. "Yes," I settle on, after I feel more like I'm in my own body. Mark just laughs at me as I steal a barstool and spin a single loop in it. "It's so weird that it works, but . . ." I shrug.

He nods, a smile that's only a tiny bit sad touching his lips. "It's refreshing. All the old memories are there, all the hurts are still real, but it's just a little bit further away." He looks away from me, rubbing at the back of his arm.

Without hesitating, I reach out and clasp my own fingers around his larger hand, giving him a reassuring squeeze. Reassuring of what, I have no idea. That it'll all be alright? I haven't believed that for a long time. Or maybe it's simply become background noise. But I want to reassure him of *something*. "Thanks," Mark whispers, reassured to the extent of my ability.

I leave my hand there as I look around Bastion's for a livelier form of treasure. "Where's everyone else?" I ask.

"Jules and Molly are having tea out in the garden." Mark points at the archway snug between a pair of shelves that leads to the attached hallway. "I think they're actually having tea too and not making love. Six is upstairs reading. Shavoy, well, you said goodbye before you took a nap." Mark sighs. "That kid . . . I hope he'll be okay. I remember what it was like, striking out like that at first."

"Not knowing what's next, not knowing where you're going or if you'll make it, yeah. I don't miss that so much." I laugh with my friend. "But then, sometimes I do? We were never bored when we were young, were we?"

"We're never bored *now*," Mark says. "And sometimes it's a nightmare. Why can't we just have quiet lives?"

"The Between doesn't call us retirees, Mark," I remind him. "And I know you see the same thing whenever you open your eyes here after dying."

Mark nods. "Intercessor," he murmurs with closed eyes.

"Can't intercede in a quiet life." I shrug. "Maybe. Maybe that's just wistful thinking. Maybe no lives are ever quiet, really. Ours or anyone else's. But you're right. I hope Shavoy's okay out there. Living is hard sometimes." My friend silently turns away from me, and I can feel the pang of hurt coming from his soul as he remembers his last run-through. "Sometimes more than others," I mutter. "Sorry. Didn't mean to . . ."

A sweep of a hand and clipped words meet me. "It's okay." Mark cuts me off. "It'll be okay. *I'll* be okay. I have . . . I have a long time to learn to be okay, right? The time's gonna pass anyway, so I might as well work on it." He takes a deep breath and forces a smile. "Oh, you want a drink?"

"I just woke up." I roll my glittering eyes at him. "So, yes, but water please." Mark makes a show of doing a fancy bartending routine, but all in service of pouring from our infinite water source into my fancy goblet before sliding it across the bar to come to a perfect stop in front of me. "You're adorable. I love you so much," I whisper.

"Hmm?" Mark looks back at me from where he's turned and is sorting clean cups.

I just wave at him, twisting a smirk at his puppy dog eyes as I sip my water and let the refreshing peace of perfect sleep from the Between wash over me.

We should really get some beds in here. Bastion's is perfect as it is, and I don't want to lean too far toward an optimizer mindset, but maybe we could find a couple of rooms we could attach to the newly formed slots in the hallway and find a couple of bed objects to add to them. That doesn't seem over the line.

The biggest problem with trying to not be an optimizer is that I *want things*. And it's hard to try to get them without being a victim of the psychological tricks the Between uses to make you want things. But even knowing that, I still want to sleep on pillows that aren't part of Ellin.

There are a few hundred heartbeats of quiet spent between Mark and me, broken only by Ellin's snores and the light flavor of conversation from out in the garden hallway. He breaks the silence first. "Toward the end there, of my last life, I ended up in charge of a lot of what was left of our resistance." I stay silent, letting him speak. The words are personal, and probably painful, so I trust Mark is sharing them for a reason that he'll elucidate. "And every day, you know what thought I couldn't escape? That I was going to earn one of the stupid coins for it. That being in charge of a bunch of students with stolen rifles and homemade bombs was going to be *rewarded*." He doesn't meet my eyes or look in my direction, instead laser focused on gently placing individual cups in rows along our thick glass bar shelves. "I couldn't not think it. Every day, we'd do our thing, hanging on and trying to fight back, and at *some* point, I'd think . . . the Between thinks this is worth something."

He goes quiet. And I ask a question. "But was it worth it to you?"

"Absolutely," he says. "It was worth it to all of us, I think. Though the others didn't have this waiting. Didn't have a reward lurking on the limbs." He turns and faces me, a steady neutral mask plastered on his face. "But I couldn't get rid of the thought. And I feel like it makes me a bad person. I feel like . . . You know, you and Jules and Six, you three talk about optimizers a lot like they're some kind of fucking monsters, you know? You *barely* make choices about your perks. And I don't think I got it until this life. Not really."

"It hurts, doesn't it?" I ask, swirling the water in my goblet and staring at the clear and cool liquid. "Because it feels intrusive. But also, you know that reward will be so nice."

"Exactly," Mark says. "I've been holding off on my notifications. Because . . . I don't know. Because I'm afraid I'll enjoy it. And I get it now. I get *you* a bit more now." He takes a deep breath. "But I don't want to give up the pseudoquest because it might be a step toward what we *really* want. That thing we aren't talking about. A motion in the direction of waking up together, for a whole lifetime." Mark pours himself a splash of amber liquid in a short crystal cup and leans on the bar across from me. "How do you do it?"

"With the books?" I ask, and Mark nods. "I . . . I think . . ." I sigh and empty my goblet before offering it to Mark to refill with whatever he's drinking. He does so, and I sip at the fiery substance, fortifying myself to speak plainly. "I think that there's a place between optimizer and ignorant," I tell him. "For me, it's probably easier than you. But I was going to read anyway, and this just lets me pluck something wonderful back to share with you all. So here's what I'm gonna ask you. Would you have done it without the quest? Led them, fought with them, died for them? Would you have gone through it all again, without any reward at all?"

"Yes," Mark snaps off his answer. "Because they needed me."

"Then open your notifications without guilt," I tell him flatly, flicking my tail back and forth as it sticks off the stool behind me. "Because you *earned* it. Not by the measure of the Between, but by the measure of Luri. Thinking about the truth of things doesn't make you a bad person, Mark. It never will. But if you're going to confront the truth, you need to face the good parts too, not just the bad. *You would have done it anyway.* So I'm telling you, now, that it's okay. It's okay to acknowledge what's going to happen as a result of your own personal ethics guiding you."

Mark and I clink glasses, and drain our drinks, and then with a gasp at the burn he meets my eyes and decides to emotionally devastate me. "So, you feel okay when you read your notifications?" he asks me.

"Okay, *rude.*" I sputter a laugh, coughing as some of the burning alcohol gets into my false lungs, which just seems unkind of the Between to even allow. "And that's different!"

"You just said you'd be reading anyway. What else would you be doing if you weren't? Do you live your lives that way?" Mark challenges me. And suddenly, the words I put together on a whim to make him feel better come back to me, an outside perspective suddenly striking at the fear and anxiety I've been holding on to for seventy-three lifetimes. He refills my goblet, pausing to brush his knuckles against my hand. "You should feel peace too," Mark whispers to me. "If I'm allowed to do it, so are you."

My emotions stumble into themselves, piling up on the edge of my tongue. It's a thing I've told the others, sometimes more than once. But I don't actually remember anyone saying it to *me.* And . . . Is it that simple? No. It isn't. *But.*

Thousands of years of life and what I needed was to hear a friend tell me that it would be okay? How has it never happened before? I've been reassured, comforted, held, touched, and loved by these people, over and over, across lifetimes and centuries. Always meeting back at Bastion's to recover ourselves, find ourselves, center ourselves before yet another life. But never have these words been said to *me*.

"It's weird that I can still be surprised." I chuckle as Mark refills for us, emptying the bottle and setting it to the side to be reused for something else before the Between can eat it. "Okay. Okay! Together, then." He raises an eyebrow at me, his stupid-perfect muscle structure making the expression look both easy and irritatingly hot. "Open the notifications. And don't feel bad about it."

I think if anyone asked that of me, I'd have made a joke, laughed it off, and then gone off to distract myself for a few thousand heartbeats until I forgot about it. But this is Mark. This is someone I do really love, and also, he's practically a baby compared to me. And I can't let that challenge just slip by.

So I raise my goblet while he raises his cup, and we lock arms and drink, and I flick open a notification that I somehow *know* is the one I'm looking for.

[You have memorized 5,000 words of local literature: +2 perk cysts, +2 aura drops. Aura Layer—Scroll Harvester—has triggered. Souvenir granted—*Devotional of Cal-Cohal.*]

The actual literal scroll thumps onto the counter alongside a cascade of clinks from the pile of coins Mark dispenses. I can't remember what their official name is, and it's not the important thing right now. I'm thinking of how I had to learn to read during that life: sneaking into shrines, stealing scraps of notebooks from merchants, barely having anything worth reading at all from my perspective. Memorization is actually somewhat harder than people imagine. We just don't commit whole chapters of things to perfect memory, and five thousand words takes a while to add up. But I remember the moment when, with only one arm and having not eaten for a week, I had forced open the upstairs window of a condemned library and found myself a shelter that would last me months as I tore through the surviving volumes and scrolls. The cold weather and hateful city kept outside as I huddled there, pulling scraps of joy out of old pages.

My last life was shit for a while. But even there, I found something to treasure. And I've brought a piece of it back with me.

Mark and I look down at the bar together, slapping our drinking vessels to the surface with a united thunk. Then we meet each other's eyes and smile.

We also wake up Ellin, who tumbles out of the hammock with a barbarian yawp. "What's wrong?!" she demands, springing to her feet and sliding into a fighter's stance. "Who do I punch?!"

"You're in the Between, love," I tell her, as Mark falls into a fit of laughter across from me, the pile of emotional wealth forgotten between us.

"Oy, hey, I could still pay the marks to punch someone here!" Ellin protests, though she's already dropping her guard. "Sorry, sorry. I had a weird dream."

From upstairs, there is a creak of wood as a heavy gray form leans on the railing. How the railing can creak when we all know damn well it's impervious is a curiosity for later, as Six pokes his smooth head over to look down at the three of us. "Is everything alright?" he asks. "I heard Ellin yelling."

"We're fine!" I call back up. "Actually, I'm . . . I'm pretty good."

Six meets my cheerful smiling look, and his own expression, impervious as anything else in the Between, shifts ever so slightly. A softening of the eyes as he sees something in me that I think he always knew was there. I know how he feels; I've seen something deep in him that maybe he doesn't know about either. Maybe that's why we're friends. We keep looking for ways to draw those secret parts out. "That is good, Luri," he says simply.

"Hey!" Molly's sharp voice cuts off anything else he might be about to say. "Y'all alive in here?"

She is carried in by Jules, who roils across the floor with his jet-black tentacles. "I believe what my mate means is to ask if there is something wrong. As we are all, as it turns out, *quite* dead."

"Yeah, that." Molly nods vigorously from where she's tucked against Jules's flank.

Ellin throws her hands in the air. "You yell one thing about punching people, and everyone comes running," she complains.

The five of us share a circular look of amusement around her. "Yes, Ellin," Jules says slowly. "That is rather how it works. If only so that the rest of us could see the spectacle of you trying to fight something in the Between." He deposits Molly on a barstool next to me, the little kobold scrambling her claws to find a comfortable position as Jules settles himself against the counter next to her, his triangular eyes alight with amusement.

I join in the laughter, the sensation of warmth pushing through me, and not just from the alarmingly potent drink Mark and I have been sharing. There's no real point denying it; this is my home, and my family. Bastion's has become my natural environment, and the truth is . . . it was always going to be. I always would have done this, whether there was a reward waiting or not.

My eyes flicker to the side to check my heartbeats. A few subjective days. Plenty of time to spend with the people I love.

"Hey, since you're all here," I say, spinning around to lean my back against the edge of the black stone surface of the bar. "Would anyone like to play a game? I've got a few days, and I want to lose at Leaves and Branches at least once before I go."

"Mmh. Yes! I could go for a good complete failure right now." Ellin perks up. "I have a few things I wanna do before I go explore the Between, but I have subjective weeks left."

Our resident kobold speaks up as she spins on her barstool. "I've got two days left, but I'm pretty happy to hang out." Molly's tongue lolls out of her mouth as she tilts her head. "Is that a new one?" she asks. "I don't remember that one!"

"Impossible, my dear. I'm sure you've been here since we acquired it," Jules says. "But then . . . maybe not? Oh, and it's days for myself as well. The clock runs ever downward." He gives a buzzing sigh.

"Guess Molly gets to be the lucky one today." Mark cracks his neck like he's preparing for the utter trouncing that Six is going to give us. "Two days. Plenty of time to regret this decision."

"I would be interested," Six says from upstairs, already holding the eternally faded cardboard box that contains the pieces. I didn't even see him move; it's like he exploited the sliver of time between blinks to snag the game. "If you would have me."

"Six." I shake my head, holding back laughter. "Get your featureless gray butt down here and show Molly how to lose at board games."

"Yes, Luri," Six says, affecting an even more bland voice than normal as he struts toward the metal steps down from the library. "I will be certain to obey this directive to the best of my ability."

Mark starts stacking our special cups on the bar for me to carry over to the green-felt table. "Welp," he says, shaking his head. "At least it'll be over quickly."

A few days left. Days can sometimes be so long, and sometimes be nothing at all. And I don't know what these will be, but going into them here, now, with my friends around me, they feel special. Like they're the first days I feel actually light for the first time in lifetimes.

Not that every burden and responsibility is left behind, not that I'm foolish enough to think that abandoning myself and attempting to start over with a blank slate and a charred landscape of the self is a good idea. But something simpler. Something less pure and messier and perhaps a little wiser.

They feel like I've started to be better.

After all this time, I can still grow. I can still learn. And as I get into a brief race with Ellin for the comfiest chair that ends with the tall and powerful woman sitting across my lap and stirring the love in my heart something fierce, as I start to explain to Molly the rules of a board game that was made for a species with either different limbs or different philosophical principles of motion, as I look on in horror at the mixed drink Mark places in a pitcher on the table next to the jar of lightbugs, I think that maybe I've been doing that this whole time.

Even if I didn't think of it that way, there was really no escaping it. I was always going to change because I was going to do it anyway, and the Between didn't need to pressure me with rewards to make it happen. That was just who I was, and will be. The kind of person Luri is. Not forever and always because those words are dumb, but here and now.

And here and now, for the first time in a long time, it doesn't hurt as much anymore.

CHAPTER THIRTY

'm going to miss you all," I tell them. It doesn't really communicate anything new; of course I'm going to miss them, and of course they know. They're the only people who understand me. No one in the world is going to really *get* what it's like, to live this long, to hurt this much, to see this far. They might try, and they'll glimpse a portion of the whole, and they'll nod and comfort me and weep, or maybe try to put me in a box and study me, for all the good that would do. But they wouldn't be my friends, who *know*. "So much," I add, adding nothing.

But I say it anyway. Because I want them to know. Not just to sort of know, but to *know*, to feel it in their hearts when I say the words and the sound reso-nates off what they already suspect I feel and it turns to liquid truth in their souls. I want to pour every scrap of myself into these people who have become and been my family between life after life, and to have them wake up on their next worlds with the pure knowledge that no matter what happens, no matter how long it is or what pain is between the gap, that I will see them again and love them the same as when we said goodbye.

We've had good days together. Just a couple, running out the clock on these unliving lives, though still not enough to wear each other to annoyance. After hundreds or thousands of years, it gets harder and harder to actually be irate with the people you love, even as it becomes ever easier to sigh deeply in exasperation at them.

I read an old favorite book in the hallway that looks out over the roses in the dusk-touched garden while Ellin played around with aura permutations for her next attempted rebellion in a living world, and the two of us talked about how we had both come to like the feeling of our bones not quite fitting while growing up in human bodies. Molly and I had raced to throw a collection of marks at Six when one of the vendors showed up so he could buy a coffee maker and only learned afterward that the coffee maker is essentially a fancy paperweight without roasted and ground coffee *beans*, which of course we don't have. Mark and I spent a thousand heartbeats in an unmoving hug, the both of us drawing warmth and comfort from each other as we tried to patch over lifetimes of lost friends and healing scars. And I cheered with the others when Jules precisely guessed how many times Six had disguised himself as a low-ranking noble in order to infiltrate a crime ring that operated out of a sewer.

Good times, shared with good people. Time I'll take with me to my next world, and that will buoy me through the life that I don't think I'll feel that connected to anyway. But I'm going to try. We've all made the promise, again; we are going to *try*.

Try for what, I don't know. I don't think any of us do. Maybe it's the wrong way to say it. Maybe it would be better to say we're all going to take it seriously. Commit to the game of living, and do it without feeling like we should overthink it.

"You know what I hate?" Ellin asks as we all cluster around the bar for one last drink together as she smiles sadly at my comment.

Mark, expertly showing off at pouring from three different sources of wildly different drinks in sequence and juggling bottles and a teapot while doing it, answers without hesitation: "Slave empires. Judging by how many different traits and perks you have for murdering their leadership."

Jules and Molly separate from a passionate kiss that I don't fully understand the mechanics of given that neither of them really has baseline human lips. "It's not murder if they're acceptable military targets!" Molly reminds us with a gasp of air that her false lungs still burn for.

"I was going to simplify it to unjust authority, but also my dear is correct as well," Jules adds, his triangular red eyes shifting to upturned points.

"Not stabbing things," Six suggests with a monotone quip, not looking up from where he sits with one hand holding open the religious text I brought back, perusing the words idly.

I decide to add my own joke to the pile, and then falter with my mouth open. ". . . Six stole mine. Sorry, Ellin." I wrap my tail around one of her legs, trying to tickle her through the wraps on her foot.

"That's fine. I know you still love me." Ellin's toothy smile strikes my heart through the fog of anxiety about leaving soon, and I find myself smiling back without thinking about it.

Mark starts sliding us our drinks, and we all take a moment to appreciate the last of Six's home brew, or a burning draw of rice wine, or in Jules's case, the calm sip of hot tea. "So?" he asks after taking an appreciative sip of his own amber liquor.

"So what?" Ellin asks, breaking away from staring into my eyes to instead fix the same kind of loving gaze on Mark.

"So what do you hate? Or do we keep guessing?"

"Oy!" She slaps the counter. "I forgot! You all made me forget! Buncha gremlins, all of you!" And then Ellin does something I don't see much from her, and sighs, settling back with a relaxed slump to her shoulders. "It doesn't matter much though, does it? Ach, eh. Maybe I should stop worrying about what I hate. Especially here. What am I supposed to hate here that I can actually do something about? Everything I could change is stuff I love. Like you. Not that you all count as stuff, exactly."

Mark and Six both tip their heads in different little motions of agreement. Molly gives a canid grin, her long tongue lolling out of her mouth as she smiles at Ellin's turn toward her own more cheerful assault on life.

And then I speak up. "You know what I hate?" I say, and Molly and Jules shatter into fits of giggles and buzzing laughter. Mark just presses a fist to his mouth, while Six gives me an actual honest grin and Ellin bursts out in a belly laugh that turns to her swearing at me while the others get caught up in the tide of humor and their laughing becomes less steady and more gasping.

"What do you hate, Luri?" Six says, one gray finger wiping at the corners of his uncompromised eyes as the others try to catch their breath and recover.

"I . . ." I stop myself as I realize I've actually thought of something. "I hate that I'm not going to wake up tomorrow and see you all again," I say.

The words we're not supposed to say. Because it's not fair, and it's stupid, and we can't do anything about it. Life comes for us all, eventually. The Between cannot be denied, no matter how we try. The best we could hope for is to have a moment of clarity and then never show up again, moving on to . . . what, something else? Something greater? Or just nothing?

I don't want *nothing*. What I *want* is my family. But even now, I've wasted our precious last heartbeats together on complaining about something we can't ever fight.

"I hate that we have a coffee maker that doesn't make coffee," Mark says, coming to my rescue. "You know how badly I wanted coffee?"

"I could take it with me as an equipable," Six offers. "And fill the barrels with coffee for you."

"That is . . . an utterly wretched idea. That would *not* do what you think it would do." Jules's voice is a humming wince so sour that it vibrates my heart in my chest. "Six, you are a sworn companion to me; I have known you for years that stretch across eras and eons, and we have taught each other so much that we qualify for the librarian's oath a dozen times over. Have you, in all your lives, *never* had coffee and I am only just now learning this?"

". . . It smells unpleasant," Six says, drinking his rice wine that smells like cleaning fluid waiting for an excuse to catch fire.

Ellin's hand grabs onto the base of my tail as she reels in shock. "Oh. Oh! Everyone with the plant pseudo, slot that shit *now*! We need to bring back a coffee kelp for Six to experience!"

". . . *Kelp*?" Jules's tentacles fold against the top of his main stalk with a pressure that would crush most people. "What *are* all of you?!" he demands.

Molly turns on her stool next to him, stopping herself with well-placed taps of her long-clawed feet and wrapping her legs around Jules's form. "Hey, I love you *so* much. I feel like it's time I stopped keeping this secret from you . . ."

"No."

"I pretty much only get blended espresso drinks that're mostly sugar."

"*No.*"

"Like, I know they're bad for me, but I kinda use them as a socially acceptable excuse to eat whipped cream and pudding orbs and sprinkles? On the worlds that have the kind of economy that let me get away with it, obviously."

Jules looks like his world is collapsing around him. "Luri. Luri, precious Luri. Please. Tell me not you too."

There's a temptation to tell Jules that I'm allergic to coffee and see how he processes that, or if I have actually found a way to deal psychic damage to someone in the Between. But I opt for honesty and kindness. "I like the frozen coffee-concentrate stuff so I can make nactan ices," I say.

"I've died, and this is my punishment," Jules whines.

Ellin snorts at him. "Oh, you big baby. Only half of that is true." She thinks for a second and then adds, "Though it is true over and over again, so as a percentage, that sentence is *mostly* correct. Also *you* bring back a coffee . . . vine? Is it a vine?"

Jules gives an utterly defeated buzz. "Tree."

"Tree! If you're so into it! Read Luri's book about trees and get the tree buff and then show us how it's done!" Ellin challenges him. "I bet you I can find a better coffee thing than you can. Come on. I'll ante up two random perks. Let's do this, Jules." She offers a hand to shake on the bet.

"I'm going to miss you all," Jules says instead of accepting or denying the wager. "So much."

"We're all going to miss each other," Mark comments. Not maliciously, or like he's annoyed. He's just saying the thing that we all know. "We're . . . irreplaceable to each other. At least you all are to me. *Everyone* is irreplaceable though, aren't they? We're just the only ones who don't wear out under scrutiny from the universe."

Molly raises a claw. "I wear out!" she states with chipper glee. "Ask Jules!"

"Do not ask me about that," Jules countermands with a pointed tentacle at each of us.

"I'm serious though." Mark smiles as he reaches a long arm across to refill Jules's tea before pouring himself a cup and forgoing any of the eight traditional ceremonies we've shared with each other. "I'm going to miss all of you. But we'll miss the people we leave behind in thirty, fifty, a hundred years just the same, won't we? We'll come back here and find each other waiting all over again, but we'll never get that with the ones on the other side."

Six sets his cup down, a small thunk on the black stone of the bar, the reflection of overhead neon off the polished surface briefly interrupted by the obstacle he adds to it. "We've all always known," he says. "And when next we are here, I will tell you the stories of those lost, Luri will take a small vow of silence in their honor, and you will openly speak the emotions that we all roil in and be better for the sharing."

"And I'll keep everyone at spearpoint, and Jules will drown himself in art or something!" Ellin helpfully adds. "While we're alive, I mean. And, and . . . Molly, how do *you* cope with it?"

"I love people," Molly says with sharpened honesty, scratching her claw along the fur of her flank. "And all that love is real, but I know it won't be forever. I'm like Luri, you know? Never and forever aren't real words. Being temporary doesn't mean it isn't real, and knowing that doesn't mean it doesn't hurt, but I refuse to give up!" Her muzzle forms a beaming grin while her eyes show her ancient age.

"You know what I'm going to miss?" I say, twisting the cup I'm holding and watching the liquid inside stay level. The others look to me, and I take a deep breath. "A bed."

Several voices chime at once with varying levels of confusion. "What?"

"When I come back." I tell them, tilting a hand in the air by my head. "Because we *will* be back, right? I'm gonna miss a bed. I've got one in my

Between room, but I don't ever stay there. But when I'm alive, I usually get a bed maybe . . . two-thirds of the time? I'll miss that!"

Ellin catches what I'm doing and leans against me, pulling my tail up to hold in her lap. "I'm gonna miss being hungry," she states.

"*Really.*" Mark looks at her with a majestically cocked eyebrow. "Hunger you'll miss?"

"I mean, it's convenient here, sure. But have you ever gotten a stick of roast meat from a street vendor in the dead of night when you're *super* drunk?" Ellin settles her elbow on my shoulder and shakes her head, lost in a wistful dream. "*Nothing* tastes like food when you're starving."

Jules shifts his bulk, tentacles pulling him back into place between the barstools. "I was prepared to say that I will miss the feeling of missing here," he offers. "But that is perhaps slightly too recursive, and epochs of life experience have not prepared me to want to sort through that many layers of conversation. So instead, I am going to tell you, Luri, that we *did* purchase a closet from the vendor. We could put a small bed or perhaps a cot in it and *have* a bed here for you."

"But what would I miss!" I throw my arms in the air, dislodging Ellin as I do so. "You're undermining my entire point about how there's something worth living for!"

"Yes, yes, it's very poetic, but *also* you are significantly less grumpy when you have had a nap in the Between, and I simply wish to make that experience available to you." Jules puts an aristocratic air on the humming sniff he offers.

Molly, beautiful as she is, tries to gnaw on one of Jules's tentacles for me. I don't even have to ask, which is the measure of true friendship.

"I do not believe I will miss anything," Six says, watching Jules try to fling Molly off him and ending with her arcing straight up in the air. Briefly. "Living is often interesting and provides opportunities to learn," he says as Jules frantically catches his lover in a writhing embrace, "but when I think about things I will miss, all I truly think is that nowhere is as accepting as here."

Mark nods with pursed lips. "Nowhere out there is as safe as here, really," he says.

"Nowhere out there," Ellin adds as she turns to look between me and Mark, "is as happy for me as here with you."

"Nowhere out there lets me be myself," Jules grudgingly admits. "Not like this."

Molly hugs him, her struggles dropping in an instant as she senses his need for comfort. "Nowhere out there has you."

I don't have anything to add, except to say the one thing that all of them have spoken *parts* of. "Nowhere out there is home." I raise my glass in a toast, and everyone around me mimics the motion. "So we will simply have to come back."

We drink whatever we're drinking, glasses hitting the bar in sequence. Overhead, the turboprop engine fan turns with its slow clicks, and the neon sign buzzes. Around us, a collection of evidence that we once lived adorns walls and shelves. And while none of us *want* to leave, we've had time together to say what we really wanted to this time.

That we want to be here. And that we won't give up. Not yet.

It's the *true* unspoken thing. That it would be perhaps too easy to give in to despair, and live listlessly, and simply not care. To stop and falter and fall and never bother getting back up. To watch heartbeat counts get lower and lower, until life and death perhaps become a blur of flickering nothing and our minds think no thoughts at all. To accept oblivion through apathy.

We have many things we don't say too often, or perhaps hold ourselves back from, even now. Vulnerability is a stubbornly learned process when so many lives and worlds harden us. But there is one thing we *never* say. Never think, if we can help it.

That we could give up.

But we say the antithesis, without any reservations. That we want to be here, we want to love and be loved, we want to live and die and shine brightly doing it. Sometimes I think about stepping off that edge. But not today. I will again, I'm sure. But it may not be for a very, very long time, with my family here to call me back.

Molly and Jules go first. They're both low on heartbeats and have already timed it down to the moment by feeding extras into the tree Jules brought back a few lives ago. It sits up in the library, in a season now that looks like a volcanic eruption and with leaves that glow with veins of magma.

The two of them are embracing when their time runs out, and the rest of us press in around them to offer a final hug and last-minute whispered goodbyes that will never ever feel like enough. Molly laughs, and Jules sends a shivering vibration through everyone as his own anxiety takes over against the pressure of what comfort we can offer, and one of them starts to say there's not enough *time*, and then . . .

There's four people left.

Six leaves next, his own clock running down. He's more stoic about it, but that doesn't make it hurt less. He gives Ellin and Mark and me individual hugs in turn, and I revel in the touch of his cool gray flesh against my bare skin as he offers the last bit of companionship that I'll see from him for who even knows how long.

He says he needs to add the text I brought back to the library shelves and waves almost casually as he ascends the metal steps on the far side of Bastion's to meddle with our loosely organized board games and books and the occasional tiny plant that we keep moving around for our own amusement. He doesn't come back down.

"So," Ellin says to Mark and me. "It's just the three of us now. Wanna fool around before we're out of here?"

"Ellin, I've never actually loved anyone like you before, or anyone as much as I think I do you," Mark states as he goes behind the bar and calmly finishes putting a few bottles and urns and jars back on the glass shelves in front of the mirrored wall. "I love people when I'm alive. I love everyone here. I mean, I love *Luri* too. Hi, Luri. I love you, in case you didn't know. But you, I love you in a way that I find impossible to describe." He turns and locks eyes with the grinning horned woman as he steps up to her, one strong arm wrapping around her as he runs a finger down her chest with an uncommonly seductive smile on his face. "You also have the *worst fucking timing—*"

And Mark is gone too.

Ellin's grin turns brittle, grief showing through the slowly fading facade of teeth and sly humor. I set a hand on her shoulder, and she turns to me with a wet sniff as she pulls back tears. "So!" Ellin is almost crying as she forces out laughing words. "It's just the two of us . . . !"

I burst into giggles, wrapping my arms around her torso as we both slowly start to cry, the reality of our goodbye sinking in. Even if it's temporary, it's still happening, and we can't ever roll back the clock.

"I don't think we'd enjoy it much," I tell her sadly. "Not now. Besides, we don't even have a bed!"

"We've got . . . some grass? Out in the garden?" Ellin suggests before shaking her head and snorting. "Nah, I know what you mean."

"I'll bring back a bed for next time. I'll form an emotional attachment to some big plush canopy thing with a ton of pillows and the softest blankets," I tell her, maneuvering in our hug to kiss her neck softly.

Ellin snorts again. "Oh? How are you gonna make yourself love a bed?"

"Easy! It'll be a reminder of bringing it back to you!" I smile against her rough skin, feeling her shake as she either laughs or tries not to cry into me. My voice softens, and I hold her closer. "It'll be okay, you know," I say. "I'll see you again, and I won't stop loving you. I promise."

"Yeah, yeah." Ellin pulls away, but I see the secret relief in her eyes as she wipes one of her arm wrappings against her face. "How . . . much longer do you have?" she asks me.

"Not long," I say. "A few hours, if I want. Why?" I see her face screw up with a guilty expression, and before she can shake her head and tell me that it's nothing, I cut her off. "Don't wanna watch me go?" I ask. And Ellin nods, slumping back into a barstool and trying not to look me in the eye. "That's okay," I tell her softly. "Ellin. Hey. Look at me." The gentlest touch forces her to do so with leverage that has nothing to do with physical force. "I'm heading out anyway. And I don't mind a little time alone with Bastion's. Say goodbye, properly, and then go out and have an adventure in the Between. And when we're both back, you can tell me what you find, okay?"

I can almost see the thoughts clicking through Ellin's mind as she looks at me with a mix of relief and apologetic guilt and love. Then she lunges her body forward, still sitting on the stool, and catches me in the powerful gravity of a kiss that goes on for long enough that I feel my heart start racing and I become *certain* I've just lost an hour to the electricity of that one act of affection.

An hour I wouldn't give up for anything in this world or the next.

"Gonna miss you a lot," Ellin says.

"And I'll miss you." I smile up at her as she stands and lets me go, stepping back but lingering without making moves to leave. "Find someone really awful and stab them in my honor," I tell her. "Then imagine me doing *this*." I shake my head slowly, a disapproving look on my pursed lips. "It'll be like we're together for a little bit."

Ellin bursts out a startled laugh. "Alright! Well, *you* go break into a library and imagine me poking around and knocking stuff over while I nod approvingly and it'll be like *I'm* there with *you*!" She bites her lip as her eyes narrow. "Hey, yeah, wait, why do you *break into* a library in almost every life? That's weird, right?"

"I'll see what I can do." I grin back. "Goodbye, Ellin. For now!" And then we kiss one last time before Ellin squares her shoulders and steps through a door that vanishes behind and around her, consumed by the Between as she heads off to explore the endless and chaotic expanse of this broken nonlife.

And then I'm alone, with my thoughts and an open bar and a couple of hours of false life left.

I stand there, exposed to the Between, and just breathe. Alone, but not really. The lingering presence of everyone I care about in the universe is still here. Mementos and souvenirs, memories and marks, stories and scars. I'm by myself, but I'm not alone or lonely.

Every time I make it back here, I start the experience with silence. Saving my first words for people I don't truly expect to see. And I'll add to the list of people I keep quiet for this next life too, in all likelihood. But I'm not afraid this time.

I'm going out into life like I'm stepping out to head to work. A quick jaunt to the corner store to pick up milk and nuts and a book and twenty thousand days of memories. Just a short little excursion, really, not something to write home about. Except I *will* write home about it, when I come back and share stories with everyone.

I wander the space, running my hand across the rough stone of the hallway and its cool wrought iron lanterns. Feeling the small holes in the metal steps poke into my feet as I ascend to the library. Smelling the mix of sand and alcohol and old paper as the whole place warms my unreal blood.

Old friends and new. Mark and Ellin, loves I'm still learning how to love as more than just a fling. Six and Jules, teachers and students all of us to each of us. Molly, a compact package of joyous chaos. Shavoy and the lady elf who still hasn't named herself, new to us but not new to themselves and growing old before our eyes. And others too. Small friends who stop by sometimes, who add flavor and color to life. And those missing, who have either gone on ahead or left us for their own reasons.

It's life. That's all it is. Life that doesn't end, but life all the same. Even dead in the Between, I don't really stop living. And I think, finally, I have become *okay* with that.

This whole time there has been a thought in my mind that I refuse to give voice to because the only words that would properly express it would be a horrified scream that never ended. The thought is simple, and abyssal, and so layered with the strata of lifetimes that I don't know if I recognize it anymore.

Sometimes, I think, I want it all to end.

I want this to stop. I want my life to truly come to a close. I want oblivion, or even just a different after that mortals are meant for, or *something*. I want to *die*. I want a finality that will never come.

But it will never come, so I bottle up the screams and hold them close and never *ever* will I share them with the others.

Yet now, here, at the end of another series of soft moments and compassionate meetings . . . the screams are silent. The back of my mind has nothing but cobwebs and an empty bel nest, with no desperate self-destructive longing to be found.

For the first time in lifetimes that stretch so far back I cannot see my own horizon, I want to keep going.

And into that quiet moment of self-acceptance and optimism, the Between intrudes, and as the Between ruins my calm it *chooses me*, and I see the future. The shape of things to be, laid out in the geometry of the cosmos. For a brief, terrible moment, I know a fragment of the truth, not just with my thoughts but with my entire being, and with something beyond that too that I could never hope to explain but in this instant can see the vectors of as well. A tiny piece of a celestial machine that is both beyond everything I have ever been and yet somehow *broken*.

A clarified moment. The other way out of the Between, aside from running out of heartbeats. The way that doesn't have a return. The way that, *apparently*, you have to be selected for, in your most vulnerable moment.

It doesn't feel fair. I finally want to be here, and that yearning has brought me to knowing myself so strongly it is taking me away. But I don't know how to stop thinking what I am thinking now, and I am locked onto the singular thought of the conceptual shape of eons and my place within the pattern, and I know the terrible truth that my next step forward will be my last one here. Forever.

And then the sound of a door shakes me, and I look down from where I'm leaning on the library's railing, a simple noise distracting me from the picture of all reality. Lifetimes of reflex causing me to curiously shift my thoughts to wonder what's just happened, who's just arrived. An almost automatic mental shift to putting up a small social shell, preparing for a conversation with someone new.

And just like that, I can no longer see the true nature of things.

The Between loses interest in me. If I had *wanted* forever to end, I would scream. But . . .

But I'm learning that there might be some parts of never and forever that I love. Some people to share them with that I cherish more than I would carry a yen for an ending.

I look away from the next infinity and back to Bastion's in all its personal and lovely worn glory.

A boy steps into sight, looking around with an exhausted stance. A white cloak covers most of his body and face, but I can see a familiar fox muzzle sticking out. He's missing a dozen little pieces of gear, along with his swords and his right arm. And when he looks up at me, I see the most important change of all: eyes that are his own.

"Tenebral! Hi!" I call down with a confident smile. The moment is gone, my understanding no longer properly aligned with constructed truth and my brain on its own now too mortal to re-create it even intentionally. "Thank you!" I feel compelled to add as the clarified moment slips further and further from me.

Maybe next time. Maybe later. Maybe *never*. I might get there eventually, but I've never been in less of a hurry in my unlife before. I still don't all the way know who Luri is, but I've avoided being an optimizer so far; a few extra years not strategizing for enlightenment should be easy.

The fox samurai stares up at me with the kind of deep shame and terror that only comes from *knowing* you are going to be rejected. "I have . . . learned." He gets the words out painfully. "I return . . . seeking wisdom."

"I'd give it away for free if I had it! Sounds like you've got a good story to tell," I say, settling forward just enough that I don't scrape my breasts on the wood of the railing like I've stupidly done before. I know he won't know exactly what I mean, but that's part of the fun. I need to keep up my air of mystery for the new kids, especially if I'm going to be seeing more of them. "And I'd love to hear it, but I gotta go. Hey, keep the lights on for us, would you? Just don't deplete anything behind the bar. Oh, and don't mess with the weird bottle of mystery poison! I keep forgetting to do something with that! And if anyone comes in being a jerk, you have permission to kick them out!" I try to think of what else to tell my conscripted bartender. "You look like you're on the right track!" I yell down. "Just remember, there are no clean endings, and life just keeps going, and that's okay!"

"I only just *got* here!" the fox samurai yips back at me. "I do not know how to run a bar! I don't even know what I am doing, or half of what you are saying!"

And I have a thousand things I could try to say. A hundred insights I have picked up from my friends, an equal number of stories that each tell us something about ourselves and each other. I could tell him I look forward to seeing him again and learning who he really is. I could tell him I hope he will be a good friend until the end of time itself. I could tell him any of the myriad secrets to being happy I have learned, used, mastered, and then sold off because it was more important to replenish Bastion's stockpile of bar snacks at the time. I could try to fit in one last little moment of connection and truth and comfort so I could close out this loop with something that felt like a real *ending*. I could tell him that I didn't really want to go, and that I'm going to owe him for every life I have, forever.

But I'm out of time. And real endings are a luxury for other dead people.

So I just smile, and wave, and trust this fumbling newcomer to take care of my home for a little bit. My last moments dead aren't particularly peaceful and quiet as I'd intended, nor are they suitably dramatic, or personally meaningful. It's just like that sometimes. *Most* times, I guess.

I go next.

But I'll be back before I know it.

ABOUT THE AUTHOR

Argus is the author of Sublife Crisis, Kitty Cat Kill Sat, and the Daily Grind series. They started writing sci-fi short stories a decade ago and have spent the majority of the time since trying to capture within narrative the feeling of not knowing what is happening while simultaneously overexplaining what is happening. Argus lives in the Pacific Northwest, where they studied and worked a number of unconnected jobs before becoming an author. They didn't know if this biography should be in first- or third-person so, as with any uncertainty in their life, have decided to turn that fact into a joke.

RESPAWN YOUR CURIOSITY

follow us on our socials

podiumentertainment.com

@podiumentertainment

/podiumentertainment

@podium_ent

@podiumentertainment